PRAISE FOR JUDITH MOFFETT AND TIME, LIKE AN EVER-ROLLING STREAM

By Judith Moffett
Published by Ballantine Books:

PENNTERRA*

THE RAGGED WORLD

TIME, LIKE AN EVER-ROLLING STREAM

*Forthcoming

TIME, LIKE AN EVER-ROLLING STREAM

A Sequel to THE RAGGED WORLD

Judith Moffett

A Del Rey Book

BALLANTINE BOOKS • NEW YORK

A Del Rey Book
Published by Ballantine Books

Library of Congress Catalog Card Number: 92-22153

ISBN 0-345-38275-7

This edition published by arrangement with St. Martin's Press, Inc.

Manufactured in the United States of America

First Ballantine Books Edition: August 1993

Pam's dedication: For Ronna, who was there the whole time

Liam's: For Edward

in several editions of *The Book of ...* ... available from *The English Sunday School Institute, Princeton*.

... account of how to ... ... from *The*

Acknowledgments

The popular old hymns "Peace! Be Still!" and "There Is Power in the Blood," along with "Blessed Assurance," can be found in several editions of *The Broadman Hymnal*, available from The Baptist Sunday School Board of Nashville, Tennessee.

The description of how to milk a goat is adapted from *The Homesteader's Handbook to Raising Small Livestock* by Jerome D. Belanger (Emmaus, Pennsylvania: Rodale Press, 1974).

The description of swarming bees is drawn from *Keeping Bees* by John Vivian (Williamson Publishing, 1986).

I am grateful to Val Gonzales of the Franklin Institute's Fels Planetarium, Philadelphia, for the information that the moon will be gibbous on May 11, 2014, and in the last quarter on May 21 of the same year.

Lori Ferguson provided newspaper accounts of the 1974 tornado that devastated Hanover College, using the college library files as well as personal materials.

Alvin Johnson, Emeritus Professor of Music at the University of Pennsylvania, checked Liam's setting of Pam's poem "Stars" for gross errors of notation and composition. Liam has broken the rules in one measure, but he was warned.

I wish to thank Chief Engineer Dennis Shenk of the *Delta Queen*, for answering my host of questions about navigating a steamboat on the Ohio River.

Special thanks to Marshall Hampton and Steve Fought, and the other students in Mrs. Regina Keller's spring 1990 BC Calculus class at Strath Haven High School, Wallingford, Pennsylvania, for instructing me in the ways of math prodigies.

Very special thanks go to my editor, Gordon Van Gelder, whose fertile imagination and very hard work have helped make this a better book.

All the characters in this work are products of my imagination, save two. Hannah and Orrin Hubbell are modeled upon real people named Anna and Harlan Hubbard, who died in 1986 and 1988, both well up in their eighties. In presenting Orrin and Hannah I have tried to be as faithful to the models as possible, apart from taking the one small liberty of attributing to Hannah Hubbell the journals that Anna Hubbard never kept, but which so many of us wish she had. To the interested reader I recommend *Payne Hollow: Life on the Fringe of Society*, by Harlan Hubbard (New York: Eakins Press, 1974), and *Harlan Hubbard: Life and Work*, by Wendell Berry (Lexington: University Press of Kentucky, 1990).

Prologue

From the November 2026 issue of *Time*:

. . . Liam O'Hara, 28, the mathematical wizard chiefly responsible for the discovery (see cover), was all of twelve years old in 2010, when the Peach Bottom Nuclear Facility meltdown ousted his family from Main Line Philadelphia. Relocated to Maryland, young Liam attended the College Park Friends School. Three years later, phenomenal aptitude and achievement scores brought him to the attention of the Hefn Humphrey, then recruiting budding math geniuses for the first class of Apprentices at the brand-new Bureau of Temporal Physics, headquartered in Washington. (The BTP has since been moved to Santa Barbara, where the Hefn sleep response to cold weather is not a problem.)

The first pricklings of the ideas which were to eventuate in the Hot Spot formulas came the following spring. . . .

If proved "in the field," as most experts expect them to be, the O'Hara Equations are certain to give an enormous boost to the force of the Gaian Mission, whose youthful Missionaries have been at work among us for the past couple of years. Carefully selected, intensively educated by pre-Takeover environmentalist veterans (drawn from the top ranks of such well-credentialed groups as Greenpeace and The Nature Conservancy), rigorously trained in research of the human past at the BTP, the Missionaries have been rapidly changing the way many people think and feel about Planet Earth.

Asked to comment on the discoveries, the top Gaians had plenty to say. "We know that all ground is holy ground—in itself, and potentially for people who know how to live upon it appropriately," says the "gafr" of the San Francisco Mission, Beatrice Trace. "If the O'Hara Equations prove that some ground is 'holy' whether anyone lives appropriately on it or not, the implications are just terribly exciting. Because what happens when you put the two things together—when a Hot Spot *has* been the dwelling place of people who have 'lived into' that ground for many years in a deeply interdependent way? Think about it!'' Adds Tran Van Ky of the Saigon Mission: ''Dy-no-mite!''

Reactions among other Gaian leaders are more cautious. ''This is an exciting development, but it's important not to let the sexiness and glamour of the 'holy places' idea make us lose sight of the homelier truth that *all* ground is holy ground,'' advises Michael Kamante, Chief Steward of the Kikuyu Mission. . . .

''We're going to do the calculations for a few obvious potential Hot Spot sites first, check them out,'' O'Hara explains. ''Lourdes. Stonehenge and Avebury. Delphi. Nazca. Rennes-le-Château. That place in Mexico, I forget its name, where the Virgin has been seen so many times, and another place or two I know about.''

His reference to the Nazca desert, in Peru, is a reminder that there is another group every bit as excited as the Gaians by the discovery of the O'Hara Equations. This is the remnant of a once-numerous association of amateur archeologists, chiefly British, who call themselves ''ley hunters.'' *Leys* are straight lines drawn on the landscape, on which important features such as churches, castles, stone circles, burial grounds, and natural features are precisely aligned. Of prehistoric origin, they are nevertheless found worldwide; the Nazca lines are perhaps the most famous.

Half a century ago, ley lines briefly appeared in the popular press, as a host of credulous people came forward to claim that certain leys had been seen by psychics to glow with magnetic force, that they were dowsable, that they were part of a global network of power. Inevitably, serious investigation suffered as leys became linked in the public mind with crackpot theories and ''New Age'' spiritualism.

O'Hara himself is generous about all this. ''I've learned a lot about leys since the story of the Equations broke. Some of it sounds pretty mumbo-jumbo, but not all. Maybe some of those New Age types really could see a glow. Many leys radiate out from a central point, usually a hill or a mountain, with a tradition of being a holy place. Lots of aligned churches in England are built on the former sites of pagan temples. Those sites are *old*—and *nobody* knows what the leys were there for—nobody! Now we have a tool we can use to find out if primitive peoples, people with a relationship to the landscape we can't even imagine, may have been sensitive to forces most modern humans can't sense at all."

He looks happy, as well he might. "There may be thousands upon thousands of nodes where the beelines of electromagnetic power intersect—we're using 'beelines' for that and 'leys' for the lines on the ground. Now, not counting my chickens or anything yet, but *if* these equations work out, so we know for sure where some of the Hot Spots are, and *if* they coincide with the sites of ancient holy places, it'll be great news, the greatest."

Why? The answer reveals O'Hara's Gaian sympathies. "Well, I don't want to go too far out on a limb, but if it turns out to be true that prehistoric people could tune in to the Earth's magnetic currents directly, then I'm betting we can learn to do it too. We've got the time transceivers, they'll help. And who knows what that might lead to, in the way of connecting up to the Earth again?"

But if ordinary people could sense the nodes and lines, what further use would the Equations be? Wouldn't the mathematicians' noses be put out of joint? O'Hara smiles a wide, charming smile. "Finding out how to live here still has to be everybody's top priority," he says with obvious sincerity. "No, the really great thing would be if all this math should become completely unnecessary."

21 December 2026
Hurt Hollow, Kentucky

Dear Mathematical Wizard,

Sorry I've been out of touch for so long, and especially sorry never to have answered your letter from last summer, which was interesting and amusing and cheered me up at a bad time.

I want to thank you for hanging on throughout my long silence, and for checking in with my mother every so often. Your messages are always faithfully passed on. She was terribly *excited to find you and Humphrey and Bea on the cover of* Time, *by the way; she bought two copies, one to send me and one to keep for herself. (Shouldn't they have invited a ley hunter to be in the picture too?) I'm fully expecting to find that cover picture, matted and framed, hanging on the wall of the living room when Humphrey and I go there for Christmas dinner. Mom continues to think of you as the brass ring on the merry-go-round, that I'm*

3

too bonehead stupid and stubborn to grab. "You never had one ounce of sense about that boy, and he's always been so crazy about you! He'd have married you ten years ago if you'd a let him," etc. etc.

I haven't had the heart—or maybe the energy—to tell her different, but one of these days she's going to pick up a copy of People *magazine and get the shock of her life.*

Actually, that's not true. I am about to give her the shock of her life. Sometime after the holidays are over I'm going to talk to her about Dad; and once that blow has fallen I doubt that even a shot of you emerging from the baths with a beautiful youth on each arm would have much impact. (Even if you make the cover again.)

I have sometimes pointed out that she's proceeding from obsolete assumptions, that there's almost no incentive anymore for young people to rush into matrimony. She argues back that even in her day people didn't usually get married just to start a family, or just to get a break on their income tax, or from fear of getting AIDS, or so the wife could get in on the husband's health benefits. She says they did it because it was a way for young people to make a public commitment to each other. The implication being that even with no assurance that the Baby Ban will ever be lifted and no legal advantages whatsoever to entice them, serious and decent-minded young people would want to get married anyway.

I'm afraid of letting her irritate me to the point where I find myself asking just what the Sam Hill was so hot about her marriage that she should feel qualified to take this pious tone with me, so when we get that far I change the subject.

They managed to get the story pretty accurate, didn't they? Humphrey sent me an advance copy of the report for Science, *as I expect you know. You can imagine how fascinated I was to read about*

22 December 2026
Hurt Hollow

The scene: latest in an even stream of quiet evenings before the fire. Solitude, lamplight, my chair dragged close to the logs and flames, here at the end of another long, *ferociously* satisfying day of plain hard work. The work: chiefly cutting wood, but also feeding and medicating hives, putting cold frames to bed, milking Floria, making cottage cheese. The other does have been dry for a month and Floria's not far behind them now,

4

but I'm glad she lasted this long. Humphrey would be disappointed not to get his cottage cheese. And I've been saving a surprise Christmas present for him too: a hard cheese with a nice rind, painted with beeswax and aged in the springhouse since early fall, before finishing the novel swept all before it and I had no time or energy to undertake extra projects, making cheeses and such.

I'd let a lot of things slide—including, obviously, keeping this journal current; impossible to manipulate words one way all day and another way all evening, impossible at least for me—while writing my way down the difficult home stretch of the novel, and had gotten way behind in the seasonal chores. The woodpile, even with this mild autumn we've been having, was down to practically nothing. So I've been cutting wood for three or four hours every day. And I butchered my first goat, something I probably shouldn't have tried without help—it was hard, bloody, unpleasant work, one chore I never helped Jesse do, so I had to proceed, in a manner of speaking, with a book in one hand and a gun or butcher knife or saw in the other.

My chosen victim, the male kid, had been destined for this end from birth, of course, but I truly hated to kill him—kept seeing visions of him as a youngster, bouncing around, butting Gloria's udder, bopbopbop!—but I need meat for the winter and the Hollow doesn't need another buck yet, Moria's good for a couple more years anyway, and those who are not prepared to accept the terms of the homesteading life should clear out and make way for others who are. There would be no shortage of takers, after this discovery of Liam's, if he turns out to be right (which I've no doubt he will) and if the Hollow turns out to be a Hot Spot (and how could either of us doubt that?).

Anyway, it's done: thirty-one quarts of canned goatmeat down cellar, and a tough, stiff, black-and-white hide stretched on the wall of the studio. Also fried liver for supper several days in a row, with onions and potatoes. After Christmas I'm going to read up on tanning leather and see what might be made out of goathide—moccasins, maybe? Book covers (next year's Christmas presents)? I saved the hooves (and horns) with some vague notion of boiling them to make glue, another project undertaken, so far as I know, by neither Orrin nor Jesse and another case of book-in-one-hand, etc., but why not? Next year's Christmas presents for selected friends: small, attractively packaged pots of goatsfoot glue . . . why not? Everybody needs glue.

Last night after supper I started the letter to Liam. I didn't get too far with it. Very difficult to know how to put my request. I sat and thought for a long time between sentences, till I began to feel exhausted. Yet tonight I pick up this book and the words tumble out with no effort at all.

After the long year of solitude, talking to myself has obviously become all too easy.

Tomorrow I'll try again. It should go better, now the pump's been primed.

F

My name is Pam Pruitt.
I don't like to do it.
I've never been partial to effin'.
Eff man or eff woman?
Eff intersexed human??
I'd sooner be effed by a Hefn.

If all is proceeding according to plan, Humphrey is in Cincinnati tonight. He was flown from Santa Barbara to Washington nine days ago, intending to meet with assorted government officials and spend untold hours with the Hefn Directors at Thingvellir, after a hurried visit in College Park with Carrie and Terry. Humphrey does hate those sessions at Thingvellir. I picture them all gathered together in the round room, fifteen or twenty of them, sitting on proper Hefn chairs drawn into two concentric circles, eyes opaque and beards waggling, bald spots showing here and there in the pelts of those who've been on duty the longest, from the anti-hibernation drugs. Occasionally one of them forgets and simulates a human facial expression. . . . H. won't have enjoyed himself one bit, even though they all kowtow to him now and listen to everything he tells them—this time, I'd guess, that something needs to be done soon about the Baby Ban.

The last time I was over at Mom's, she was harping away on The Little Granddaughter theme again. ''You were always such a roughneck! Oh, I'd just love to have a cute little girl to fuss over and play with, etc.'' I told her grumpily that I'd never thought much about having a kid anyway, but *if* the Ban's lifted and *if* they let us choose the sex, then I might have one, but it would definitely be a boy. She was hurt, as if I'd said this out of pure contrariness, but I meant it. She'd get more satisfaction out of Liam's sister Brett, who's turned into exactly the sort of sour-tempered childless woman I'd have predicted . . . though if the Ban's lifted soon she's still got plenty of time to have at least one baby, which I'm sure is all anybody's going to be allowed at best. I'm also sure Humphrey would prefer for the Gaians to create enough voluntary restraint in enough people so the Hefn didn't have to manage the situation at all, but there isn't going to be enough time. Either there'll be a Hefn-monitored transitional period, or a lot of geriatrics are going to be raising a lot of test-tube babies. Assuming the Mission succeeds at all, on the necessary scale, and humanity doesn't just follow the dinosaur into oblivion.

Anyway, after the meetings Humphrey was to take the train as far as Cincinnati. If nothing's happened to screw up the plan, he should board the steamboat tomorrow morning and be here by 1:30 P.M. or thereabouts on the 24th.

This afternoon, after cutting and hauling my day's stint of wood off the hillside, I took a hatchet and scouted around until I found a little cedar, about four feet tall and growing too close to an enormous sugar maple to be likely to get much bigger. It's standing out in the workshop now in a bucket of water, waiting for Humphrey and Christmas Eve. How happy I was to see Hannah's little sack of clip-on candle holders when it turned up last spring, when I was moving in; and how carefully I've kept track of it ever since, against this very need. Humphrey will love dipping candles and stringing popcorn for the tree—he's invariably delighted by that sort of thing—and I'm looking forward to reliving the Christmases I did all that with Jesse, when I was back home for the holidays at fifteen and sixteen and seventeen, and had managed to give my parents the slip for an evening.

At some point while he's here I'm going to try, one more time, to make Humphrey understand why I left—had to leave—the BTP. Up to now, every time I've tried to talk to him about it—Dad's accident, my panic attacks and subsequent (probably consequent) loss of intuition, the discoveries I started to make with the emergency therapist in California, all that—he just gets wistful and blank. Maybe the Hefn don't have breakdowns; only what would you call the Mutiny then? Elphi didn't take up his life as a hob in Yorkshire by choice. Humphrey talks about ''the rebellious Hefn'' as if they were a fascinating variant on the

7

basic pattern represented by himself; then he'll allude to difficulties caused by his own obsession with bonding, which from the way he's always talked about it is clearly disapproved of by the Gafr.

I suppose it would be no different for them than for us: a spectrum of normal, abnormal, non-functional. Humphrey's abnormal; Elphi/Belfrey and the others were non-functional in Hefn terms when they mutinied. Maybe if I drew the analogy like that it would get through to him, finally.

As a matter of fact I think Humphrey may experience my leaving the BTP as a violation of *our* bond. I *have* become an analog of a rebellious Hefn—alien in a way not covered by the fact of our being technically aliens to one another. And I would like to be able to make him understand that it's nothing to do with him and me. That the curve of my life would have had to break off at some point no matter what, and be reorganized, and that this necessity could have been forecast from the time I was nine at the oldest, which was before the Hefn even came back. But I don't know if he'll believe me.

The psychological screening they did for the BTP Apprentices was designed specifically to tag and eliminate people who were unlikely to go the distance; but how are you supposed to get a useful answer if you don't know the right question to ask?

23 December

You can imagine how fascinated I was to read it, the elegance of the calculations and the relevance to me, my life in the here and now.

You might have wondered what I've been doing down here, apart from keeping the place going. Well, I've been writing a novel. That's what the box of pages underneath this letter is: the novel. Not poetry. Not fiction either, not exactly: a novelization of things that really happened. What things? he asks himself. Ho-ho. I bet it's about that spring in the Hollow when we were kids.

Indeed. What else would it be about? Nothing else that important ever happened to me; but my reasons for writing a novel at all are kind of complicated.

You know, of course, that this is not even the first novel I ever wrote in Hurt Hollow. Remember how you were always pestering me to let you read the first one? And I never would (and I never will, either!); but I'll tell you this much: that early effort now strikes me as uncannily like the book in this box. All the same themes and obsessions are already present, and most of the same characters, or versions of them, at their same ages, with the exception (as I've had you point out in Chapter 14) of the Liam-character. Yet the first is pure wish-fulfillment fantasy, while this second—

—is my one-shot all-out effort to recall—and, 'more to the point, to re-feel—everything that happened as it appeared to me then, *during that crucial week in May 2014. It's all been viewed through a lens which is small, personal, tightly focused upon my fourteen-year-old self; I've tried my damnedest to reinvoke my own exact experience of that time, unelaborated by anything I've learned or understood since.*

What made me undertake such a project? There were a couple of things.

After I lost my intuition and couldn't set coordinates any more, and slunk off home with my tail between my legs to teach math at Scofield, I continued to go through various stages of hell. I probably didn't let on to you how really bad it got. The therapist I saw a couple of times in Santa Barbara thought I should start seeing somebody when I got back here, and gave me the names of some people in Louisville, but it would have cost a bundle and I didn't feel up to all the traveling back and forth, and I guess maybe the real truth is that I just didn't want to do that right then.

But I was in such terrible shape that I felt like I had to do something. *So I read a lot of psych books, and lights started to flash on; and one day I was suddenly struck by a funny notion: that by becoming a sort of time transceiver myself, I could make contact with my own past and recover the memories and feelings that were so hard to get at because they'd been repressed so deeply and so long. It was a powerful metaphor for what I needed to do; I got very excited about it.*

Besides that, I'd always kind of assumed that one day I would write a personal account of that time, putting what happened on the Delta Queen, *and here in the Hollow, into the big picture. You can imagine the kind of thing. The book would describe in vivid detail the post-Directive and post-Broadcast resistance movements—people scrambling to change their means of production faster than was strictly possible, and fuller of rage the harder they scrambled and the hungrier they got—Gafr fed up and teetering on the very brink of deciding we could never be made sensible and tractable by any deterrent they could devise— ready to leave for a hundred time-dilated years and return (if*

9

they did return) to a planet sterilized of people—and so on and so on. Then with the context established I was going to show how you and I and Humphrey, and the flapping of a butterfly's wings in Peking, turned it all around.

I figured I could write the public book and the therapeutic personal one all at once, and kill two birds with one nonfictional stone; because the one placetime I knew to start looking for answers to questions I'd never before asked out loud was Hurt Hollow in May 2014, where the historical narrative (ley) line and the personal one had intersected.

Makes sense, right?

Well, I tried. Many, many false starts later I finally admitted that before I'd be up to making a balanced assessment of what had happened to the human family on a global scale, I was first—and not simultaneously—going to have to work out the meaning and resonance of those global-scale events for and within my own family, my own life. I'd understood by then that trying to write the history of that placetime, even a personalized history, was actually quite an effective way of evading the answers I needed. And once I knew that much, I also knew that my account would have to be cast in the form of a story.

This was all happening right before Jesse died. I'd been coming down here to the Hollow every few days to take care of things anyway all the time he was sick, so when he died and left the place to me—The Place Where Time Stands Still, as the tour guides used to tell their charges—the next steps seemed natural. I quit my teaching job, took myself to the site where the events I needed to make contact with had occurred, locked the gate behind me, and focused the fixed lens of memory upon May 2014. I was able to set the coordinates precisely.

23 December 2031

Snow! Whoopee! When I got up this morning the light coming through the big window felt so diffuse and strange I couldn't imagine what could be going on, till I looked out and saw white everywhere, all the way down to the obsidian expanse of the river. Only an inch and a half, but the temperature stayed down around 25° all day so it's all still out there, and when I got through milking, about an hour ago, and came out into the dark, big furry flakes had started sifting down again. The creek has a skin of ice on it, and there's a rime of ice along the riverbank.

I don't suppose it'll stay below freezing for long, it never does, but what a treat—and so well-timed! I haven't seen a snowfall since January 2019—in Louisville, back here for Granny's funeral—and that was just a flurry, enough to powder everybody's coats and hats at the cemetery and give the dead zoysia grass the look of a blond-haired person going gray. Seven years ago next month. The morning of Dad's funeral, almost four years to the day after Granny's, was so freakishly mild nobody was even *wearing* a coat, which made the occasion feel even more surreal than it did already.

Hurt Hollow hasn't had a white Christmas in twenty years; I looked it up. Though five will get you ten that over at Scofield, where they're presumably enjoying the same weather I am here, Mom's on the phone with somebody right this minute, complaining about how you used to be able to heat a house by turning a dial, and how the snowplow used to come through and clear the roads so you could ride around in a car in weather like this all warm and comfy, before the Hefn came. She thinks the greenhouse winters a great improvement, like retiring to a milder climate without having to leave home—but I'll defer to the season and not go on being snarky about Mom.

Humphrey would *love* a sleigh ride. We'll have to go over to Scofield for Christmas dinner anyway. I should be able to fix it up, if the cold weather hangs on another couple of days.

I wish I could learn to forecast the weather, not just better but at all! I had no idea it was going to snow. Jesse always knew what to expect. Of course, if I end up living here as long as Jesse did . . .

Weather be damned; how about learning to forecast my life?

I wrote some more on Liam's letter last night. It went better, though I still haven't worked my way round to explaining why I'm sending the novel to *him*.

Leafing through it this evening, trying to anticipate Liam's reactions to various things, I caught myself feeling chagrined about the constricted viewpoint of that wretched young girl, my point-of-view character. It's hard to tell, from her perspective, what an atmosphere of crisis people were having to live in at that time. I picture Liam shaking his head and musing, in a condescending way, that he hadn't realized, back then, the extent to which Pam couldn't see past the end of her own self-absorbed fourteen-year-old nose.

I wouldn't blame him if he did. By 2014 Liam O'Hara, future public figure, was nowhere near as sunk into himself as I still was. His problems—the meltdown, Jeff's death—were traumatic, not chronic like mine. By 2014 he'd pretty much come through, and was able to look around and take an interest. Or so I surmise. And I couldn't. And of course as an Apprentice, a member of a privileged elite, it wasn't too hard for a kid as quietly desperate as I was then to remain oblivious to the desperations of outsiders. Not my fault; but I do regret it—and also am nervous that Liam will hold it against me or the book, when he reads the book, if he does read it.

Supposing there'd been no Jesse and no Hurt Hollow, might I have been equally oblivious as a teenager to the fate of the Earth? Because I wasn't at all. It's worth asking. I grew up, after all, in a world without Missionaries, Gaian ones at least; but I think my arboreal childhood and natural sympathies—and even, strange to say, my identification with Dad, which has otherwise been the source of so much anguish—would have inclined me to care more about the Earth in any case than about its teeming human population. Just like the You-Know-Who. So I probably would have thrown in my lot with the You-Know-Who if I'd never gone to Washington or Santa Barbara, never known Humphrey or Jesse, or needed them as alternatives to Dad.

Certainly I had a lot of faith that the Hefn would do what the people had refused to—that they would fix things—that when they got through doing whatever they were doing here, the world would be a better place.

Now, I think I probably trusted them mostly because they *weren't* people.

Having said all that, it still seems odd that I didn't wonder more about what they were, in fact, doing. What (for instance) was the importance of the BTP? What were they training Apprentices to operate the time transceivers *for*? To what end? I never asked. If the Pam of the story strikes me now, at 26, as having been regrettably blank about people's problems, she also strikes me as being dangerously trusting about the fate of the world (and her own self?) in Hefn hands. Whatever occasional doubts she feels, like after the *Delta Queen* incident, get pushed conveniently out of consciousness, along with all the other stuff in her life too confusing or painful to confront.

I dunno. Call it intuition. I felt more at home in an institution run by aliens than I'd ever felt in my own family or school or society, and made my choice accordingly. And every morning since last March, shifting into Post-Pubescent Pam gear, I watched the lens of Reality spin down to one small circle with myself at the center, and felt "the real world" draw away, become an underwater backdrop of incomprehensible sounds and blurry images, from which my personal lens-field of that time felt wholly and hopelessly disconnected.

From James Merrill's Ouija-board book:

> And the outside-world crayon-book life we led,
> White or white-trimmed canary clapboard homes
> Set in the rustling shade of monochromes . . .
> The Sound's quick sapphire that each day recurs
> Aflock with pouter-pigeon spinnakers
> —This outside world, our fictive darkness more
> And more belittles to a safety door
> Left open onto light. Too small, too far
> To help. The blind bright spot of where we are.

Funny (sad too) how Pam-of-the-novel is always trying to see what's *there*, in "the outside world," and constantly failing because of what's *there* in her own messed-up head. To save her life, she cannot see out of the blind bright spot of where she is. Working on the book, I often felt just abysmally sad and sorry for that poor, awful kid, so sorry and sad I cried buckets through some parts, as if it were all about somebody else. She blunders around so pitifully, myopic, deaf and faintly preposterous, bumping into all the furniture (painfully). How could anybody love such a freak? Then I consider what she was able to do in spite of everything and feel love for her myself. Very confusing. She was both so awful and so brave. I do love her sometimes but it's hard to like her much.

It's exactly her sort of myopia that explains why Missionaries all have to be such straight-arrow types, unlike what you might expect in the way of a person with a Vocation—why they couldn't be self-selected but had to be screened from the general population like the other Apprentices and the Engineers, only at an even younger age—why volunteers weren't taken (and still aren't, despite the now-complete disappearance of an age-appropriate general public to screen).

A reminder of this aspect of the present-time world situation arrived today in the form of a Christmas card from Colin Yost, the bright kid who used to bike over from Madison to take my calculus course, that last term I taught at Scofield. He'd scribbled a page of news: graduated early, decided to skip college, going into his father's hardware business as an accountant, living in Indianapolis. He'd been a Steward since the first months of the

13

mission, but had picked his Ground only after looking around very carefully for almost a year. He enclosed a picture of last summer's garden (very pretty) and signed the card "Yours for Gaia, Colin T. Yost, One of the Youngest People Alive."

I was much more aware of the aging, vanishing children while living in California, and then at the college, than I tend to be since I came to the Hollow, but Colin's card made me sit up. At the time he was taking calc with me, Colin was a nominal high-school junior, except the class structure had pretty much broken down. There were only about eighty kids left at Madison High, all sophomores, juniors, and seniors, all taking whatever sub-jects they liked, meeting at teachers' homes for small classes, etc. Colin must have been 15 that year—born in 2008, five years before the Broadcast. He really is one of the youngest people in the world.

It would appear, judging from the card, that in his case the Missionaries did their work well.

I want to record here my great pleasure in the hard physical labor I'm doing after these many months of brainwork, also in the steady, visible accomplishment, the progress toward (rather belated) preparedness for winter. No wonder whole generations of thinkers found such value and virtue in the doing of these simple life-sustaining tasks, no wonder the Missionaries have derived the idea again and again from their searchings of the human past. Liam's Equations don't change any of that; all they do is confirm and amplify something I already knew—or at least "knew"—to be true, and I'm far from the only one. I think Liam's right: as more and more converts are made and more and more people "live into" their particular places over time, I think our ability to sniff out these Hot Spots will grow and grow, from the vague perception the Hollow tourists used to feel to a clear and undeniable certainty, like a smell or a sound. So that Liam's Equations and what people experience directly will *converge*, like the minds of Darwin and Wallace, at the same nodal nexuses, all over the world.

(I've not been troubled at all by insomnia or restlessness, by the way, since I switched to full-time homesteading a week ago. Earlier, at certain phases of the book-writing, sleeping at night became almost impossible; I survived on long naps after lunch, a terrible waste of the short daylight but the only time I ever seemed to feel *sleepy*.)

And no wonder the Gaians have targeted our brief, transitional, pastoral/agricultural era as the one we most need to stay in contact with. I believe them when they tell us that even if there were any way for us as a viable species to be hunters and gatherers again, which there certainly will never be, such a life *for humans* has less to recommend it. And what is small-scale herding and diversified planting, with a little hunting and foraging thrown in, but homesteading—the most wholesome way people have ever devised for living upon the Earth, the happiest balance between nature and culture, the best way to use natural resources without using them up.

(Answer: Native American and other tribal life, sometimes. Amish farming, virtually always. Maybe the kind of intensive agriculture they practice in China. Those are just the ones I know about, there are probably more.)

I would have made a great Missionary if I'd been born a little later. Would they have taken me, I wonder? Much less likely that I'd have had to leave the mission field because of having had a breakdown—less likely, I mean, that the traits that make a person a good Missionary would have been lost, as my mathematical intuition was lost; though I'll never know.

I'm a hophead. If I hadn't been an Apprentice *then*, there would be no Missionaries *now*.

I must be as famished for journal-keeping as I am for physical work, judging by the length of this entry and the previous one. Last night, writing hypnotically for hours, I got to bed much later than usual and so woke up later, to be awed and then dazzled by the snow.

Today's mail brought an assortment of cards besides the one from Colin—including quite a few for Jesse, a surprising number of people apparently not having heard of his death—and also a letter from the gafr of the Chicago Mission, who wants me to call her to discuss the possibility of setting up Hurt Hollow as a shrine. Not right away, of course—after I leave, or die, or whatever the hell it is I do to vacate the place. She says everyone at the Mission fully expects that the Hollow will turn out to be a Hot Spot, and that there's a tremendous amount of interest now because they all know it was here that Liam's mind first started to play with these ideas. She says they could offer a fair price.

My first reaction was to be indignant. Humphrey knew what he was doing when he closed Hurt Hollow permanently to the public. A Mission gafr, of all people, ought to see the risk of

15

acting like a Hot Spot is holier than any other parcel of ground, even if that's not the impression the *Time* article gives.

My second reaction was less cantankerous. If the Hollow's a Hot Spot it *is* a special one. Some kind of museum-type arrangement might eventually be fixed up; though I'll be damned if I'll let them call it a *shrine*. That's exactly the wrong word, even if I understand why they thought of using it.

I've run out of time and energy to finish Liam's letter tonight. Tomorrow then, without fail.

Just stepped outside to check on the snow. Perfectly windless, perfectly still. "Softly, softly, slow and white, the sky is falling through the night . . ."—thick enough so I can't see the lights from the ridge, let alone over in Indiana. Two inches and getting deeper. The tracks I made, coming and going through the day, are muffled, nearly erased. If not a white Christmas, we're almost sure to have a white Christmas Eve.

I had an impulse to go down and clear the snow out of the johnboat, but the thought of sullying the newly whitened page of the bluff and riverbank stopped me. Stay put now. Tomorrow I can see to the boats, make sure there'll be no problem getting over to the landing to collect Humphrey—but what harm can a little snow do? It's only the unusualness that makes me fuss.

Remember to shell some corn for the birds tomorrow.

The snow ticks at the window. The fire flutters and ticks in the fireplace under the copper hood: how many years of winter evenings in this house? The clock ticks on the wall. From the river, not a sound.

Time, like an ever-rolling stream . . .

Christmas Eve 2026

Everything's as ready as I can make it, house cleaned, four days of meals planned and partly prepared. The snow's sagging and settling as the temperature rises—it's above freezing now, 35° the last time I looked, around ten o'clock—but we had a total of four inches so I think the Hollow should be able to keep its Christmas-card appearance long enough to blandish Humphrey, if the boat's more or less on time.

I cleared the snow out of the johnboat before it could get slushy. Everything's shipshape.

Coming back up the hill, I stopped by the grave markers: Hannah's and Orrin's shared stone shaped like a small runestone, with its elf's cap of snow; beside it, the blank snow covering Jesse's metal plaque.

16

In my album are maybe a dozen pictures of the house—*my house*—taken from the especially advantageous angle of that site. One picture that somebody gave me, of Hannah and Orrin sitting close together on the hillside, looking shy, the glazed gable of the house sailing behind and above them like a prow through the bare trees and blue sky. One big one Jesse took of Orrin on a cloudly autumn day, standing beside the stone marker he'd made for Hannah and himself, both their names engraved already though only Hannah's ashes were buried there as yet. A nice one Dad took of Jesse and me together—same view of the house, same runestone now marking both graves—when I was fifteen or sixteen. And one of me there, alone, shot by Ralph on the pale-blue March day I moved in—standing where Orrin had stood, looking not at the grave markers, stone and bronze, but beyond them, up at the house, just as Orrin had done.

Each of these pictures was taken at a different season, the weather, presence or absence of foliage, and colors of the ground are different in each; but the house on the bluff sails on exactly the same, through the changeable blue or gray or marbled sky—its gable window flashing the same statement, summer or winter, rain or shine.

All of that is why the Gaians want the Hollow for a shrine— if Liam's right, or maybe even if he's wrong.

I called Mom and told her we wouldn't be coming over to church tonight *or* tomorrow. She took it pretty well—said the forecast was calling for fog(!) and she can tell people the weather kept us home. And an hour later, sure enough, a thin mist is rising off the river and the melting snow on the bluffs. I'm telling myself not to start fretting yet. It could stay thin. It could clear up in no time.

If Liam were coming, he and I would have our own private Festival of Carols while we decorated the tree. Not much to hope for from Humphrey in that direction.

Liam . . .

Arrrrgh.

But it's got to be done so *quit stalling*.

Christmas Eve
This will be the third and final installment of this letter.
I wanted to add that my false starts on the book did serve one useful purpose: of giving me a new sympathy for how angry and desperate people felt back then, with their social and economic underpinnings all dismantled and the future a big scary blank.

17

I used to believe it bloody well served them right, since they should have cared about the World's future before the the Hefn came to make them act as if they did, instead of greedily building up their own private worlds and families at the larger world's expense. Now I think that while all that might be true, saying it was their own fault just doesn't get us very far. When the trauma of the lost future started to wear off, most people weren't able to feel anything but rage and fear. Then the rage increased relative to the fear as the new state of things took hold, and the Klan capitalized on that, and we were off and running.

Well. One day that other account will get written.

Humphrey should be here soon, unless the fog gets worse and they have to tie up someplace (remember they called that "choking a stump" on the Delta Queen?) I invited him to come for Christmas, as I'm sure he will have told you. I knew you weren't going to be free, but I did think of asking you too. A few days of Hurt-Hollow-style homesteading and you'd be knocked right off your big-guy-city-slicker high horse, no offense, and happy and relaxed again; it would do you good.

Imagine if you will the following Work (entitled Evening Routine) in four dimensions and five or more senses:

Dusk. The heavily swaddled human being comes in from the cold, into the thick smell of soup or porridge from the hob, and the full kettle steaming on the cookstove—lights the lamps—hangs its coat and hat on their pegs and its wet, dirty work clothes on theirs—pours hot water into a wash basin, adding spring water from the bucket with a dipper—stands on a towel to wash itself arm by arm and leg by leg and everything in between—rubs dry with another towel—pulls on clean, dry socks and pants and shirt and sweater—pours out the water and hangs both towels up to dry—settles down to the soup or porridge of the evening, and a good book or a magazine—and, eventually, sleep.

Something to think about for the future, eh?

And speaking of the future . . . I'm having a lot of trouble making myself ask you this.

I guess the best way is just to come out with it. I'm sending you this manuscript because I need your help.

I already explained about deciding to write the novel in order to get answers to some hard questions. As an experiment in making contact with the past it worked wonderfully well. I saw, more and more plainly as I proceeded, how Jesse and Humphrey were both substitutes for Dad, each being like him in certain ways but also crucially unlike. I saw, or thought I did, that you were wise to Dad from when you first met him. I understood my physical self-hatred and my terror of growing up in the light of the clear and detailed vision of Dad that took shape through the process of writing the book. It was a tremendously therapeutic exercise, very upsetting, very enlightening, ultimately very cathartic, just as I'd hoped when I set out.

But the book's finished now. It's been finished for a long enough while that I honestly feel I've understood everything important about what was happening in my family during the time I was growing a woman's body; and I've finally had to acknowledge, with a lot of disappointment, that that must not be all, because the anxiety and dread aren't gone. There must be something else, and I don't know what. I don't know where I'm missing the boat—I don't know what it is I'm not seeing.

So I'm writing now to ask a big favor. I'd like you to please read this manuscript and see if you can—well—sense where the ley lines cross. Calculate the location of the invisible nodes, the ones I haven't been able to find. Or rather, haven't been able to see; because this story feels complete to me. Whatever the mystery is, I haven't left it out. I simply can't see it for looking, and I thought—hoped—that maybe you could.

I know the Hot Spot stuff will be taking up all your time for a while, and I hate like the dickens to bother you, but there's nobody else to ask. You're the only other person who was there the whole time, involved in it all up to the eyeballs, as much as I was. The only one who can speak with corrective authority about this version of what happened, where I got things right and where I overlooked or twisted them. My only Ground-level witness, and therefore the only living human being whose opinion counts.

There's another reason, a more embarrassing one. For months now, the whole time I was working on the novel—the whole time I wasn't keeping in touch!—I've been dreaming about you. All sorts of dreams, vivid and often intense. I'm in most of them too. We're both always about twelve years old, doing all sorts of things that kids do, only in the dreams I'm never myself, I'm always Jeff.

I don't have to be a psychiatrist to understand that these dreams suggest I would do well to look more closely at our relationship; but I have looked at it and I just don't find anything useful.

However, I can see that my novel resolves all the relationships put into it, except mine-with-Dad, and ours; and that does make me think there's an answer there someplace, if I could only see the nose in front of my face.

So if you could possibly do this for me, I'll appreciate it more than I can say.

I'd better sign off now, and mount a lookout for Humphrey's boat. Are you coming out soon to do a Hot Spot check on Hurt Hollow? Let me know. In the meantime, Merry Christmas and Happy 2027, and please give my love to Carrie and everybody the next time you talk to them.

P.S. I've put some blank pages with specific questions on them between some of the chapters. Please answer those if you can, but don't feel like I'm trying to direct your responses. You should say anything you like.

THANK GOD THAT'S DONE!

The fog's getting thicker; Humphrey will be late. Too bad.

I've been paging through last month's *Time*, with the picture on the front of Liam looking like the cat that swallowed the canary. Months since I looked at the paper or a news show. I don't seem to have missed much. The Gaians have opened missions in Lima and Athens. The gafr of the New Mexico Mission is a 52-year-old Navajo medicine man who was picked to be trained with the kids. Klanspeople tried to firebomb the Baton Rouge Mission but the fire was brought under control by vigilantes. Famines in India and China, massive death tolls. London flooded. World population now at seven billion, expected to drop to six billion by 2034. World temperature up half a degree. All this is predictable stuff. Hot Spots are the big news, but I knew about them.

I brooded quite a while over the "Twenty-Five Years Ago in America" photo, an appalling shot of Central Park right after an "AIDS Ain't Licked Yet" rally. The Lowenfels vaccine had been discovered earlier that year, 2001, and the gay community—a lot of whose members were already HIV positive—was scared it was just going to be abandoned, so they held a lot of big demonstrations like this one: speeches, posters, slogans. And trash—unbelievable heaps and pools of trash. Abandoned placards all over the ground, newspapers blowing, the grass *covered* with small "throw-away" items, many of them obviously made of plastic—cups, spoons, big bags, little bags, clear bags, colored bags, wrappers, all sorts of nameless plastic stuff. How could they do that? Gather to support a cause so worthy, and then behave like pigs and wastrels, like criminals, right there on the holiest ground in all of Manhattan? Was it because they might be dying that they didn't care? Would I?

I don't think it was because they were dying. Everybody lived like pigs then. If they held that rally now, Gaians would be there in large numbers humaning recycling bins for everything, picking up after the diehard slobs, handing out returnable leaflets, making it easy for people to behave respectfully toward the park and impossible for them to throw stuff around without thinking about what they were doing.

A picture worth a thousand words of *saying* how much things have changed since the Directive spawned the Gaians.

Because of *me*. (Incredible thought.)

There's a review of what sounds like an interesting book, *Doppler Effect*, by a Yale sociobiologist (retired), Gilly Tatum. His thesis: We know the BTP was established to train the Apprentices to use the transceivers, so we could locate the place in history where humanity crossed the magic line where nature and culture were in balance. The idea was to get us back to that place and keep us there. But it's *natural* for all terrestrial life forms, us included, to exploit and multiply and strive for an easier, more comfortable life, out-competing other troups or packs or tribes along the way if necessary. Like other species, we're programmed to behave according to the principles of natural selection. The ironic upshot is that in order to live in balance with nature, humanity must cease to be *part* of nature! He concludes that the history of life on earth is tragic, that the dice of evolution here were loaded and that life contained the seeds of its own ultimate destruction from the very beginning. When the Gafr intervened, the whole biosphere, with us at the helm, was plunging toward self-annihilation. He quotes part of a Lyle Van Outer poem:

> . . . our DNA impels us to survive
> by being avaricious letches, fleecing
> competitors and founding dynasties,
> same as it ever did; now, overnight,
> we're meant to stop competing, stop increasing,
> just *override* these headstrong helices
> three billion years went into getting right!

Van Outer's point was that it was inhuman to have to make those choices. Then the Gafr came and the choice was taken out of our hands, with almost fatal results. Now the Gaians are taking their turn. I should see if the library has this book, the next time I'm on campus on a non-holiday. Also look for *Sexchange*: *The Ultimate Conversion Experience*, by some off-the-wall Gaian who turned into a woman, more fool him, or her.

Too twitchy to sit longer and it's like porridge outside. Maybe I'll split some kindling.

(Midnight.) He finally made it, he's here. The boat was tied up for hours in the fog. So instead of having the whole afternoon to get used to being together again, and a leisurely evening in which to trim the tree, it was after seven by the time I saw the packet rounding the bend, running lights glittering, and shoved off to meet it. We were both starving when we got back here; my plan of photographing Humphrey by the grave markers— Snowscape With Hefn, a notable addition to the collection—had to be scuttled. But we were lucky at that. The fog might not have lifted for days.

There was a weird moment as he was climbing down from the landing into the johnboat, twinkling and chirruping, and I saw the black case of a time terminal in his hairy hand. Déjà vu doesn't quite cover what I felt; it was more like *Oh. Of course*. Of course he would bring a transceiver, taking advantage of this chance to finish what we started here so many years ago. I also felt a little pang at my lost gift for operating a *real* transceiver. But I owe my being here to that loss. It didn't hurt much or last long.

After supper I melted a tin of beeswax, old comb and cappings hoarded up for this, and we dipped candles and popped corn, and made popcorn strings for the little cedar. Humphrey enjoyed the candle-dipping so much I asked him if this reminded him of some custom from his own past, his home world. I knew it was bad manners to ask; but instead of reprimanding me or not replying he simply said "Yes."

He's taking his Sleepynot while away from balmy California and is wide awake. He crept out about half an hour ago, thinking me asleep (fat chance), and is probably now either poking around in the goat stable or noshing on cottage cheese in the springhouse. Remembering the pictures in my beat-up old copy of Jenny Shepherd's *Tomten* translation that Carrie gave me years ago, he said how delightful it would be to play tomten/hob for the snow-swaddled Hollow. The first instance I ever knew of a Hefn charmed by make-believe, but Humphrey is of course not your typical Hefn, as I was observing a couple of days ago in these pages. I wouldn't be a bit surprised to find him out there, making sure the goats are all tucked up snug.

I'm sizzling with complicated feelings, better than Sleepynot any day for keeping a body wide awake.

After Humphrey went out I got out all the presents and arranged them under the tree (snuffed and dark now, but we kept a whole set of candles in reserve for tomorrow): a jar of comb honey, a blackberry pie, and for his abacus a rabbit-skin cover/pouch, which I've dubbed a "rabbicus." And the cheese. And, to take back to Liam, the T-shirt embroidered with the fractal butterfly in yellow, orange, and mauve, my physical therapy through the worst of the novel-writing—and the carbon copy of the novel itself in its box, with the letter on top, wrapped up in hand-stenciled Christmas paper.

I must try not to be mad or crushed if Liam fails, partly or wholly, to try to do what I've asked. (But if he doesn't it will be, let's face it, the ultimate rejection. No matter what the reason.)

Hmm. If I feel like that . . . I could still take the package back from under the tree. Not even Humphrey knows I've been writing a book.

I've got the rest of the night to make up my mind.

TIME, LIKE
AN EVER-ROLLING
STREAM

1

A WOMAN
[WHICH WAS] DISEASED
WITH AN ISSUE OF BLOOD

Matthew 9:20

"Humphrey says, we're leaving in five minutes and are you coming?"

Pam had been staring dully out the window at the dullish day. She looked around. There in the open doorway of her room stood the cutest boy she had ever known in her life—blond and broad-shouldered and dressed just right, in jeans and a pink sweatshirt with BTP in purple calligraphy woven into the fabric. The pink clashed outrageously with his bristly wheatstraw-colored hair.

Pam swallowed and shook her head. "Nope. Tell him I don't feel like it, but thanks anyway."

At once the pink ducked away and disappeared. She could hear the boy, John Chalmers, pounding down the stairs, yelling "That's what I *toooooold* him you'd say!"

After a little Pam walked over and closed the door, then crossed to the bed and lay down carefully on her side on top of the spread. She had cramps and felt wretched, but probably wouldn't have gone to the National Gallery with the others even if she'd felt okay. Saturdays were almost her only chance to write, or just be by herself for a while.

Though, as it happened, she didn't especially want to be by herself today.

All eight of the other Apprentices at the Bureau of Temporal Physics were boys. Pam was the only girl. She had occasionally wondered whether, if her parents had known that in advance, they would have let her begin the process which had ended with accepting the Hefn's invitation to live at the Bureau and be educated by them in math and science, even though it was such a tremendous honor and such a great opportunity, and the Apprentices were international minicelebrities.

27

Even people who hated and resented the Hefn—and there were plenty of those—were interested in and curious about the BTP, and especially in the Apprentices. At the time of their selection they'd been featured in magazine articles and TV interviews, and Pam, as the only girl Apprentice, had—in the beginning—come in for a lot of special media attention. Somewhat to her own surprise, she had enjoyed the fuss; but the truth was, the interviewers and photographers hadn't been given much to work with. Pam wasn't pretty; her fine brown hair hung straight halfway to her shoulders, and her nose was too big. Nor did she have the kind of "personable" quality that comes across effectively on camera. In her own school, back in Madison, Indiana, she had never been one of the popular ones. There was an oddness about her, a chronic tension.

From the journalistic point of view, the most interesting thing about Pam was that she was a girl math prodigy; they were pretty rare. (She wrote poems and stories, too, but that was a private business, not for media consumption.) Rareness aside, though, there was nothing much about being a girl math prodigy—or a boy math prodigy, for that matter—which necessarily made good copy.

The two Apprentices who kept the television people happiest were the lightning calculators, Will Stumpf and Roger Dworkin—especially Will, who could also juggle six bowling pins or balls or beanbags at a time. Calculating (and juggling) had always been good show biz—better prior to the computer era, of course, but quite effective even now. Pam had read a book about it. The knack of doing what Will and Roger did often showed up when the people concerned were very young children, barely able to count, sometimes too young to have learned to write numbers or even read them. In bygone times, it was not unusual for such children to be carted around by their parents, much as the little Mozart had been, to give demonstrations of their ability to extract cube roots and factors and work out in their heads, say, the number of seconds in seventy years, seventeen days, and twelve hours (as Will had done on *The Today Show*: 2,210,500,800, calculated in a minute and a half). The parents would charge admission. One girl in India, Shakuntala Devi, was so tiny that her father used to stand her on a table to do their show. A century or so before that, a little boy called Zerah Colburn had been dragged by an avaricious father on a transatlantic tour that started when Zerah was only six and lasted for

28

years. Pam had shuddered when she read this, nauseated by the desperate helplessness of such a child in such a position.

Pam herself was no mental calculator; when she wanted to multiply five digits by five digits, or raise nineteen to the eighth power, she used a mechanical calculator like anybody else (except Roger and Will). It was a handicap only on TV for an Apprentice not to be a lightning calculator, since the Hefn regarded the ability to manipulate numbers mentally in the light of a parlor trick. There were computers for that sort of calculating. What the Hefn had sought in their Apprentices—the most important of several essential qualities—was extremely highly developed mathematical *intuition*.

Historically, some calculators had been intuitives and some had not. Pam had learned that while certain of the famous lightning calculators had been mathematical geniuses, like Karl Friedrich Gauss in the nineteenth century and John von Neumann in the twentieth, there were also a fair number of *idiots savants* on record who were able to do that parlor-trick sort of calculating. The Hefn valued understanding, and chose accordingly.

And they chose Pam, whose brain had been dazzled with numbers since she was four years old.

Being glad about that—and she *was* glad, no doubt about it—didn't mean there weren't difficulties. Besides being the only Apprentice who ever got cramps, Pam also seemed to be the only one who didn't terrifically enjoy living in Washington, D.C. The boys all claimed to be crazy about Washington, and were always demonstrating this by dashing off together to the Smithsonian or the National Whatever. They were all city kids, maybe that had something to do with it. Apprentices had been recruited from all over the country—the math exams and psych tests had been given to every eighth- and ninth-grader in America in May of 2013—and all the other kids came from places like Chicago and Los Angeles and Houston. Madison, Indiana, was just a town on the Ohio River, a few miles from the small Fundamentalist liberal arts college where Pam's father was head librarian and her mother worked as a secretary in the president's office.

All her life, Pam had lived with her parents on the Scofield College campus; she'd walked the mile to Scofield's elementary school, Southwestern, and had ridden the school bus the five miles to Madison High School, along with the other faculty kids. Compared to the schools the eight other Apprentices had gone to, Madison High was a joke. Had Pam not been tutored from the age of seven by one of the math professors at the college, she'd never in a million years have made the cut.

But she *had* made it. Seventy-three finalists had been flown to Washington to be interviewed; nine of these had been chosen, and when the dust had settled, Pam, at fourteen, was one of the nine.

The Hefn hadn't been coy about the fact that they were concerned exclusively with developing mathematical talent for the purpose of running the Bureau. They were not at all interested in opening a reform school for hyperactive cut-ups or young people with "undesirable" personal or social habits like taking drugs. Neither of these traits proved to be common among mathematically gifted young people, who if anything tended more, as a group, toward the nerd-with-a-slide-rule stereotype; but those exceptional cases that did appear—usually among bright, talented kids from lower-income families—had been swiftly weeded out. The Hefn were not an Equal Opportunity Employer, they had no interest in Affirmative Action. They had no social conscience either, absolutely none.

Nor, perhaps more surprisingly, had they accepted any allround geniuses—kids possessing other, i.e. non-math, intellectual or artistic gifts of a very high caliber, gifts that would demand to be nourished. During her research phase Pam had read a book called *Ex Prodigy*, the autobiography of Norbert Wiener, a famous mathematician and the inventor of cybernetics. It was obvious that Wiener would *not* have been chosen by the Hefn, for all his brilliance; he had been too good at too many things besides math. It was equally obvious that Richard Feynman would have failed the psychological tests; *he'd* been too much of a wiseacre and practical joker. Phillip Barrish, at Cornell, was, in addition to being a star-quality mathematician, currently regarded by music critics as one of the most promising young classical composers in America. *He* would probably have been cut for being too artistic.

There *was* one Apprentice who played the piano all the time, but the Hefn must not have thought his talent as a performer big enough to pose a problem.

The aliens were aware of Pam's verbal aptitude scores, and had seen some of her poetry, but evidently they hadn't rated it highly enough to view art as an obstacle in her case either; or else they had simply failed to understand the essential difference between the way the developing human brain handles numbers and the way it handles words.

Norbert Wiener's book could have clarified that issue, if any of the Hefn, particularly Humphrey, had cared to read it. Wiener had been admitted to Tufts at the age of eleven. On the same page of *Ex Prodigy* where he writes, "I was already beyond the normal freshman work in mathematics," he also says, "I had not yet reached the proper stage of social maturity for my English courses." Obscurely comforted, Pam had underlined both these sentences in her copy of the book. All her poetry was so strongly metrical anyway, maybe it looked more numerical than verbal from the Hefn's point of view (whatever that was).

How she had survived the battery of psychological tests was more of a mystery; but, here again, the Hefn had standards and purposes of their own. Pam was quiet, serious, cooperative. She had never played a practical joke in her life, nor was she very likely to; and she was virtually proof against peer pressure (if not indifferent to peer opinion). Her deviations from the norms were not of a sort that would interfere either with her training or with the community life of the Bureau, and were in any case undetectable to the Hefn, who were unaware, or unconcerned, that a person with Pam's profile probably wasn't going to *contribute* much to community life either.

Because the Hefn wanted to keep language and cultural complications to a minimum, and because the Bureau had been set up in Washington, all the Apprentices were Americans. The complication ensuing upon their putting one awkward, humorless, small-town girl into an intensive group-living situation with eight city boys had not been taken into account.

The Hefn were like that. They would think of many important considerations, and then overlook a few others completely.

Pam didn't think about it either, usually. She was used to boys. She'd been terribly glad about being chosen, glad of the distinction and glad in another way to get away from her parents and the people who had known her all her life; home life had become difficult during that last year in Scofield. But being stuck in Washington, D.C., on weekends was a genuine hardship for Pam, a heavy price to pay. Washington was immense. She missed the country; the Scofield College campus took in several hundred acres of wooded bluff above the Ohio River, where since early childhood Pam had spent most of her Saturdays and summers ranging and playing, and there was another bit of river bluff over in Kentucky that she cared about even more.

She missed her mother, too, but they talked on the phone a

lot and it was definitely easier for the two of them to be living apart right now. Not this one day, but in general.

A second "class" of Apprentices was to be recruited in May, from among the current crop of eighth- and ninth-graders. Pam hoped there would be at least one decent girl in the new group, and at least *one* person from a place that was not a megalopolis. Being fussed over and interviewed on TV was fun; having cramps all by yourself, with nobody to cosset you or sympathize, wasn't. Right now, this minute, she would happily have traded being a celebrity for the company of one other person who knew how it felt to feel as horrible as this.

She thought about calling home, or maybe calling up her friend Betsy, who got horrible cramps too. There was a phone right in her room; but the thought was cold comfort. What *would* be comforting would be if there was somebody *there*, to bring her a hot drink in a mug and rub her back. Pam had known her period was due; her breasts—humiliatingly huge in the first place—had been swollen and tender for a week. She'd made sure of being adequately equipped with pads and pills. So that was all right. Except the pills never worked fast enough, and she could still feel a distant griping as her insides clenched and released, deep within the bloatedness below.

A different girl, alone and miserable, might have cried. Pam wasn't even aware that she felt like crying. A *boy* wouldn't cry, and since the age of eight, when her breasts had first begun to make little points under her T-shirts, Pam had viewed herself—though only intermittently conscious of this—as a boy in disguise. (An increasingly poor disguise, admittedly, as time went by.) Though she was required to do girl *chores*, her parents having definite ideas about whose job it was to scrub the kitchen floor and that kind of thing, she had trained herself to resist all girlish weakness. At home, it was Pam who staunchly emptied mousetraps and carried spiders—captured between a drinking glass and a piece of cardboard—outside to be released. Determined to be tough, she cut her fingers with jackknives and abraded her elbows and knees. She had helped build a tree house and a soapbox racer. She could swing the rope swing higher than anybody.

Then, at twelve, puberty had arrived, ruining everything.

Pam rolled over—carefully, but something hot and nasty slipped out anyway, and again her belly griped. Whimpering wretchedly, she pulled her knees up, doubling over herself, and hugged a pillow hard against her abdomen.

The Hefn Humphrey, who was the Apprentices' teacher as well as General Director of the BTP, was for some reason deeply curious about relationships between human beings. Pam, the only girl he regularly saw, was of interest to Humphrey *as* a girl; but like Ted Koppel and the other journalists he had found himself delving in stony ground.

Humphrey understood, of course, that there was a difference of gender between Pam and the other Apprentices. He was aware—the boys weren't shy about it—that most of them were being driven wild by hormones. Humphrey wanted to know if this was also true of Pam. She assured him energetically that it was not.

"Are you sexually attracted to male adolescents? To any of the other Apprentices, for instance?" he had asked her politely.

"Yuck!" said Pam. "Not really," she corrected herself; Humphrey's good opinion mattered to her. A picture of John Chalmers floated through her mind, dazzling smile and wheat-straw hair, but nothing happened in her body at all.

"Might that be because you don't as yet know these boys very well?" Pam shook her head. "Perhaps however you've got a boyfriend back home?"

"Unh-unh. Sorry."

It went on like that, Pam wanting to please but unable to pretend; and after a while Humphrey had sighed, or done whatever it was the Hefn did to make their gestures and expressions seem like human ones. "Tell me, Pam Pruitt, would you say that you are a *typical* adolescent female of your species?"

And Pam had said emphatically, "Nope, I sure as heck am not!"

Humphrey mimed surprise. "Whyever do you say it like that?"

"Because girls are idiots. Most girls," she amended, thinking of Betsy, who spent *her* Saturdays schooling her horse, Wickiup, to compete in show jumping, and kept her saddle in her room. Betsy and her brother had been the only black kids in either of their classes, all the way through grade school. You could hardly call Betsy "typical" either, given her circumstances. "Typical girls are idiots, let's put it that way," said Pam.

Humphrey had sat back in his chair, one of the Hefn chairs built to fit creatures with short, strangely jointed legs, for whom sitting in a chair wasn't much more natural than it would be for a sheep. "Do you simply mean that by comparison with your-self, most girls are deficient mathematically?"

"Well, that too of course. But not just that."

"Not just that?" Humphrey peered at her with his flat, unreadable eyes. "But I may take it that when you say 'idiots' you are not literally suggesting that girls are mentally deficient, compared to boys?"

"Oh, I guess you may," said Pam grudgingly, "but most of them don't seem to mind *acting* like dopes. Personally, I like boys a lot better. At least I used to," she added in gloomier tones, thinking of Charlie and Steve.

"You like them, but are not sexually attracted to them?"

"Right. I like them as friends."

"Which is different from boyfriends, yes?"

"Yes. A friend can be any sex, it doesn't matter."

Humphrey appeared to ponder this, his odd, hairy, double-thumbed hands twitching on the arms of his chair. "And these boys who are not boyfriends, are *they* sexually attracted to *you*?"

"No," said Pam shortly, understanding that the Hefn had no idea how tactless this question was.

Humphrey studied her with a peculiar expression; Pam wondered which human expression it was supposed to suggest. "I wish one of the rebellious Hefn had survived to talk with you," he said finally. "They grew to dislike behaving the way Hefn were supposed to behave. They would have enjoyed meeting a similarly disposed human; but they could also have told you that being different from the group is a costly business."

"Nobody needs to tell me that," she had replied. "I found *that* out when I was still a little kid." But she was grateful to Humphrey, not himself one of the rebellious Hefn, for having understood about this.

Pam was just barely able to remember having felt excited about the idea of growing up. She couldn't at all remember not wanting to be a boy. Her clear memories went back to age five, by which age she had been fully alive to the second of these wishes. The conscious dread of growing up had struck later, at ten or so, and she was ashamed of it, but events had confirmed the rightness of this dread: the realities of puberty had proved, quite simply, devastating.

To Pam, being a girl had always meant being infuriated by gender-specific restrictions, by her mother's insistent nagging: "Sit with your legs together, keep your clothes clean, this isn't ladylike, that's too dangerous, you're getting too old to be climbing trees all the time." It also meant that peeing in the woods was an indignity at best and an awkward, freezing inconve-

34

nience at worst, compared to how the boys did it when they had to go; she envied them terribly. But being a *post-pubescent* girl had turned out to be a nightmare, far, far worse than she ever could have imagined. Her eighth-grade year had been the worst year of her life. It wasn't just her bulging, bleeding body that had betrayed her; Charlie and Steve, who had been her best friends since second grade, suddenly started moping around after wimps like Carole Cosby, who was beautiful and sleek but too dumb to endure, and Elaine Coulter, who giggled and shrieked like a banshee and wore long, extravagant earrings—jawbreaker-size lumps of translucent pink quartz in nets of string, or shoulder-length mops of colored paper streamers—in her pierced ears.

At first Pam couldn't believe it. "How can you *stand* those drips?" she demanded of Charlie. "Last year you said Carole Cosby was going to end up in an institution for the criminally stupid, and now you and Steve are both fooling around with her and Elaine for an hour after school every *day*. You all sound exactly like *Goofy*—Ayuk, ayuk, ayuk!" she imitated bitterly.

"Ah, they're not so bad," Charlie said. "Listen, you oughta grow up, you know it? We're gonna be in high school next year, for Pete's sake. You can't hang around out here in the *woods* for the rest of your life, swinging on the end of a rope."

"Why can't I?" Pam said dangerously. "*You* are! Why shouldn't I?"

She had practically dared him to say it because she didn't think he would stoop that low, but she was wrong. "Because you're a girl, that's why!" Charlie rounded on her. He sounded angry, but also uncomfortable. "You act like you don't even know you're a girl! Look at you! It's about time you started thinking about how you *look*!"

First her body, then her oldest friend. Pam was so outraged she could hardly see. "*I don't want to think about how I fucking look!*" she screamed, and stomped away, crashing blindly through the blurry woods—not that she was crying—with a too-clear picture still vividly in mind of Charlie's red, embarrassed face—embarrassed *for* her in some way. She ground her teeth and vowed never to speak to him again, never, never, never. He had said the worst thing anybody could have said, *both* things really, that her own mother was constantly saying or hinting at: *You're a girl. You have to grow up now.*

Why the thought of growing up should be so terrifying to Pam, and not terrifying at all (as far as Pam could see) to Carole

Cosby, was a question she had never thought to ask herself. The idea of turning into a woman filled her with so much horror, and the image of sleek, self-satisfied Carole Cosby filled her with so much loathing, that the truth about both seemed, to her, self-evident. That no one else seemed to perceive this screamingly obvious truth was her life's most maddening mystery; that her parents failed to perceive it was her life's deepest danger, for their power to make her act the part they wanted her to play, that of Normal Teen-Age Girl, was very much greater than hers to resist them.

And then, in the very nick of time, the Hefn had miraculously come—Pam thought of it literally as a God-sent miracle—and lifted her out of Scofield and Madison, out of Indiana and the Midwest, away from her parents and the people who had known her all her life, and set her down in Washington transformed, a globally recognized prodigy, a famous person.

Famous, but still female. Some of the time the recognition, and even more than that the deep satisfaction of the work in math, made her relatively content; but on the first day of a period nothing seemed to matter beside the mess and pain—not math, not poetry, not being on *Nightline*. When it was worst, not even Humphrey really mattered, and there was only one other being on Earth that she loved as much as she loved him.

A lot of people despised the Hefn. Pam's parents did, for instance—like virtually everybody else connected with the college—though when push came to shove they hadn't been able to resist the lure of having their gifted ugly duckling turned into a glamorous Somebody who got interviewed on network TV, and educated for free.

But there were perfectly legitimate reasons for hating the Hefn, Pam appreciated that. They had taken over the world and clamped down on it, setting up rules about what people could and couldn't do that meant just about everybody was less comfortable now than before. Daily life was governed now by a million new restrictions, all of them aimed at the same goal—saving the world. The Hefn were what a lot of people used to say the world needed: benevolent dictators. But their benevolence was directed toward the planet itself, not the people living on it; the Hefn didn't care what became of people, whether they starved or froze or broiled or got sick from drinking contaminated water or killed off one another in huge numbers (so long as they didn't use nuclear weapons to do it with). Almost the only concern the aliens had with people was that there not be any more added to their numbers for a good long time.

And the weird and terrifying thing was, they could make that happen. They *had*. Last June, nearly three years after their arrival and right after Pam had found out she would be coming to the Bureau of Temporal Physics as an Apprentice, the Hefn had engineered a mass hypnosis by means of a telecast from the United Nations Building, translated simultaneously by UN translators and carried by satellite all over the world. Saturation advance publicity had ensured that hardly anybody, anywhere, had missed the show.

The Hefn speaker had announced that every human being in reach of his voice, every single one, would be from that moment onward unable to conceive, or to father, a child.

Since that evening when humanity had been sterilized en masse, hundreds of thousands of babies had been born to women already pregnant at the time of the Broadcast. A few thousand babies had also been conceived, since the Broadcast hadn't actually been heard by every single human being in the world. But, in principle, there were going to be no more babies till the aliens said there were, a fact that had evoked a degree of hatred for them far broader and more profound than all the hatred of their restricting rules. The Catholic Church joined forces with religious fundamentalists worldwide—quite a few Scofield College faculty members had gotten into that act—to challenge the Hefn and, through them, their bosses the Gafr, over the issue of global infertility; but this had been without effect.

Pam had watched the Broadcast with her parents. She was therefore sterile herself, so all this appalling behavior on the part of her reproductive system was even more ironically pointless now than it would have been before the Hefn came. The prospect of maybe never having any babies of her own she didn't particularly mind; but the prospect of a world where no children were at all filled her with bleakness. Childhood, androgynous childhood, before periods and breasts, before friends changed into idiots and traitors, glowed in Pam's memory like firelight in a warm wooden room. Lost forever, yet forever sacred. A world without *childhood*—that would be a desolate world.

The Hefn hadn't said there would *never* be any more babies born to humanity. They never gave a straight answer, but there were reasons to believe that this measure was as temporary as it was extreme. Pam preferred to suppose, when she couldn't simply ignore the question, that by the time she might get interested in having babies herself (if that ever happened) the Ban would surely have been lifted.

The pills finally worked. Suddenly there was a late-afternoon quality to the light, and the sound of knocking filled the room.

Groggily Pam got up—wrinkling her face at the hot flood that descended as she stood on her feet—and went to open the door. "Oh," she said, "hi. I didn't think anybody else was here."

"I'm the only one," said the person in the doorway. "I've been to the National Gallery about seventeen times. I stayed behind to play the piano. But I'm going home for dinner tonight, and I suddenly thought, maybe you'd like to come home with me."

Surprised, Pam stood with her hand on the door handle, trying to think if she wanted to go. Her caller leaned against the jamb in his sock feet and stuck his hands in the pockets of his jeans. Liam O'Hara was his name—the pianist whose playing had not been viewed as an obstacle to selection as an Apprentice. He was also the only "local kid" in the bunch, and had known Humphrey longer than the others. Pam was a little jealous of him, on account of his closeness to Humphrey, but apart from that had no opinion of him at all.

To stall, she asked him where he lived exactly.

"In College Park, Maryland, right by the University of Maryland. It's about a forty-five-minute ride on the Metro, but the College Park Station's only half a block from the house."

Pam detected in herself a faint stirring of interest, maybe because her cramps were gone. "Did your mother say it was okay?"

"I haven't asked her yet, I only had the idea about a minute ago, but I know it'll be fine with her. She's always after me to bring people home, she'll be pleased. How about it?"

"Well—okay," said Pam, making up her mind. "Thanks," she added.

"Great." Liam stood up straight again. Without shoes his brown eyes were exactly on a level with Pam's, who was five feet five. "Could you be ready to go in half an hour?" She nodded. "Okay, great, I'll meet you at the Mall door."

He started to pad away. Pam called in sudden anxiety, "Hey, wait a second."

Liam spun around. "What?"

"Well—I was just wondering—how come you're asking me? I mean, this isn't a date or anything, is it?"

Liam considered, tilting back his head in order to regard her from under lowered lids. His brown hair, cut straight across his forehead, was eyebrow length. In a detached voice he said finally, "Oh, I'd say it went something like: We're the only ones here tonight, Pam'll have to have dinner by herself, that's pretty dreary, maybe she'd like to come home with me."

Pam smiled for the first time, an embarrassed grin. "That's all I wanted to know. Sorry if I'm being ungracious."

"I mean, I wouldn't take it *personally* or anything if I were you."

"Okay, okay, I *said* I was sorry."

"As a matter of fact," said Liam, "I've never had a date with a girl in my life. My record's completely unblemished."

Too embarrassed to speak, Pam looked at the floor. The moment stretched out, while she stood hanging awkwardly half in and half out of the doorway.

Abruptly Liam spun around again and walked away, stiff-legged in his stretched-out white socks on the slippery floor. "Half an hour at the Mall door," he said loudly over his shoulder. "I'll call my mom."

Okay, sure, I'm game. No big deal.

#Christ, what a chapter title! If you were trying to publish this, somebody would make you change that.

#I saw Chalmers in DC at Xmas and got a shock. Fat, seedy, most of his hair gone. Drinking, I think. You'd be shocked too. Sic transit gloria cuteness.

#—Jesus, Pam, I had no idea you were this miserable back then! You seemed sulky at times as I recall—before we went to Hurt Hollow I mean, not so much after—but to think you were in this much pain makes me feel terrible. I wasn't all *that* wretched myself by this time—what are we talking about, fall 2012?— though I was very self-absorbed and certainly had my ups and downs; but nothing at all like this. Poor you.

#I can't say I actually remember coming to your room and in- viting you to dinner that day, but the way you picture me rings true: bangs, socks, irony and all. Irony was my handiest de- fense, and I think I was pretty effectively defended that year.

2

WHO HATH MEASURED THE WATERS IN THE HOLLOW OF HIS HAND?

Isaiah 40:12

The summer she turned fourteen, the summer before coming to Washington, Pam had written a novel.

This work, called *Pinny's Secret Hefn* at first, and then just *Pinny's Hefn*, had been composed in longhand, in blue ink, on 164 sheets of paper with three holes punched down the left side, so they would fit into an ancient, ratty looseleaf binder that had belonged to her father. Writing it had taken the whole summer; she had started in June and finished only a week before leaving for the Bureau. Some of the book had been written in her tent during rest hours at camp, some in her room, and some on the screened side porch of the house when nobody else was home; but most of it had come slowly into being in a place which was also the principal setting of her story.

Five miles downriver from Scofield College, over on the Kentucky side, was a place where the valley of a small creek broke the steep shoreline and the creek itself emptied into the Ohio River. This sharp notch in the river bluff bore the supremely inappropriate name of Hurt Hollow.

The Hollow had once been part of a plantation belonging to a slave-owning family of a different name; who Hurt had been, and when he had lived, no one now remembered or cared. During the steamboating era a road wound down the bluff to the river, where a landing had been built: Hurt's Landing. Steamboats plying up and down the Ohio would call there to take on produce and livestock bound for market, or to offload mail and goods from the cities.

Then, with the demise of the steamboats and, later, the small stern-wheeled packets powered by gasoline, things changed. The two small farms established in the Hollow were given up, the road was not maintained, and the 1937 flood scoured the valley

41

bare. For a time—half a century, perhaps—Hurt Hollow subsided again into obscurity.

But now this unassuming spot had become famous, far more famous than the college whose water tower could just be seen by a person standing on the dock at Hurt Hollow on a very clear day. Fifty years before Pam was born, a remarkable middle-aged couple had settled at the Hollow. They built a small house, functional and beautiful, dug a well, put in a garden, added goats and bees, added outbuildings, and homesteaded the spot for the rest of their very long lives.

Their name was Hubbell: Orrin and Hannah Hubbell. The magical simplicity and grace of the life Orrin and Hannah made together at Hurt Hollow had touched and affected nearly everyone who came to see them there; and many thousands did come. Orrin published three books during his lifetime, books which moved people from every part of the world to seek him out—a considerable challenge, given the vague, meandering nature of the country roads dividing the flat farmland above the river—and to see for themselves the experiment in living he had described and illustrated so appealingly in pigments and in print.

Unlike Scott Nearing, with whom he shared many traits and interests, Orrin Hubbell had been a pure visionary, a man totally unfitted by mind or temperament for academic or political discipline, or for following an ordinary sort of career in the world at large. A painter, chiefly of landscapes, for twenty years he had worked in desperate, soul-grinding solitude before, by a stroke of uncanny good fortune, he and Hannah had met and married. And it was to be a good many years after that before his pictures would begin to be valued in the art world, though the smallest Hubbell woodblock print sold at Sotheby's now for a cool one million dollars.

Orrin made many paintings of the towns and farms and woods of the Kentucky countryside, but his great subject was the Ohio River in all its weathers and seasons. He and Hannah had spent five of their first eight years of married life adrift upon the Ohio, riding from Brent, Kentucky, all the way down to the Mississippi bayou country in the shantyboat designed and built by Orrin himself. Boats appeared in many of Orrin's river paintings: sternwheelers remembered from his youth, barges, tugs, all the varieties of commercial river traffic (but never the powered pleasure boats that seemed to increase in number and aggravation, weekend by weekend, as Orrin and Hannah began to age).

The seemingly miraculous coincidence which had brought the

couple together against such odds—for Orrin had long believed that no woman would ever accept the sort of life he knew himself compelled to lead—came into play again shortly after Hannah's death in 1986. A young building contractor from Louisville, who had known about the Hubbells for years but never managed to meet them, came down to the Hollow with a mutual friend one fall day to do some repair work on the termite-damaged thirty-year-old wooden buildings. This was Jesse Kellum. After that first visit he came again and again, bringing his wife, his skills as a carpenter and builder, his youth and strength, and a profound, almost worshipful respect for the life Orrin and Hannah had created in the Hollow.

Time passed. Gradually, unofficially, the young couple assumed more and more practical responsibility for Orrin's well-being. Having no children made this more possible, not that it was ever exactly easy. Marion, a registered nurse, worked flexible hours at the Madison Hospital, and Jesse was able to make an arrangement with his boss in Louisville, another great admirer of Orrin Hubbell's. Eventually, one or the other of them was walking down the trail into Hurt Hollow every day. Together, with patience and tact, they watched over Orrin during the last few years of his life—no easy task or commitment, for he remained fiercely independent to the end, and long-suffering Marion in particular had occasionally to put up with a good deal of peevishness, born of the proud old man's frustration. But they bore gracefully with this treatment, sustained by a deep and abiding shared conviction that caring for Orrin Hubbell in his last days was the most important work either of them could possibly find to do.

That the Kellums stood perhaps to profit materially from the arrangement, or be suspected by others of trying to worm their way into the childless old man's debt and affections, and thence into his will, occurred to them—they could hardly have failed to wonder what would become of the Hollow when Orrin died—but the possibility of inheriting Orrin's house and land had not the least bearing on their reasons for wishing to make the sacrifices involved in undertaking his care. They were worldly enough to expect their motives to be misconstrued. They chose not to let it worry them.

So when Orrin, on his deathbed, called in a lawyer and willed the Hollow—sixty-one acres of wooded river bluff and creek bottom, the house and its contents, the studio, the goat shed (crumbling; the goats had been given up some years before), the unfinished guest house, the tools, wheelbarrow, johnboat, canoe, and the damaged but still magnificent view of the river—to Jesse and Marion Kellum, they were not astonished, but neither was this something they'd been counting on. Orrin, for his part, had never breathed a word about what he intended to do with his property until the day he made the legal arrangements. It would have been entirely in character for him to feel that any offer of compensation would insult them. There's no way to put a price on what Jesse and Marion had done for Orrin; he knew that and so did they.

There's no way, as far as that goes, to put a price on such a place as Hurt Hollow, and the Kellums were very happy indeed when things turned out as they did.

Jesse and Marion got the land and "improvements," two magnificent oil paintings, and several hundred drawings. Scofield College got some of the other art. Most of it, thousands of paintings in oil, acrylics, watercolor, charcoal, and pastels, and a number of woodblock prints, went to the University of Kentucky, where Orrin's papers were archived. A month after Orrin's death Jesse and Marion rented their house in Louisville, moved permanently down into Hurt Hollow, and took up the Hubbells' "experiment in living" where Orrin had left it off. They dwelt there happily and productively together, increasingly in the public eye, until Marion's death in 1999. Since then, Jesse had carried on alone.

Orrin and Hannah had died a long time before Pam was born. They were a legend, like Abraham Lincoln, whose birthplace in Kentucky she had visited on school trips practically every year. But she had known Jesse Kellum all her life, and had loved him for years with a desperate, wordless love. She also loved Hurt Hollow—which was in a way the same thing as loving Jesse (and, for that matter, the same as loving Orrin and Hannah, something Pam knew without knowing she knew it). From the college it was quite an easy six-mile bike ride to the landing across from the Hollow, and her power canoe, once inflated, could cross the half-mile of swiftly flowing muddy water to the opposite shore in twelve minutes flat. Pam spent a great deal of her final "Indiana" summer in Kentucky.

And it was there at the house in Hurt Hollow, within reach of Jesse's mostly silent yet dependably benevolent presence, the SAT Math score of 800 and "Pass" on three psychological tests under her belt, a place in the Bureau of Temporal Physics offered and accepted, the years-long alliance with Charlie and Steve

44

dissolved forever, her reproductive capacity suspended, that Pam sat on the patio and wrote most of her novel—on a clipboard, in longhand, because in that holy place the NotePad felt wrong. Someone had had to type Orrin Hubbell's own books for the copy editor. Each had originally been written down before dawn and after dusk, by golden lanternlight, in brown pokeweek ink, in Orrin's blocky cursive script. It was a tradition Pam was happy to respect.

Her story centered on three characters: a girl (modeled on herself), a grandfatherly man named Joshua (modeled on Jesse), and a Hefn called Comfrey, who had been sent to Hurt Hollow by the boss aliens, the Gafr, as an Observer. Hefn Observers *had* now been placed with the Old Order Amish and a number of Native American tribal councils, as well as at the Rodale Research Center in Pennsylvania and at certain locations in Sweden and Switzerland and Japan—wherever, in the judgment of the Gafr, human beings had inherited or figured out a way to live partly or wholly in balance with their environment. By that definition Hurt Hollow deserved a Hefn, and Comfrey had been assigned.

But to forestall criticism that the Hollow was much too little to have a whole Hefn Observer to itself—there were, after all, only forty of them worldwide—Comfrey had been instructed to conceal his presence from the steady stream of visitors to the place, lest uneconomical deployment of resources should cost the aliens support among their human friends. (This was a weakness in Pam's plot; her premise was true enough, but the Hefn were about as indifferent as possible to human opinion about what they did. But it was necessary to the story for Comfrey to be a secret.)

Joshua didn't tell even his trusted Pinny about Comfrey. But night after night the man and the alien worked together on a splendid scheme for saving the world. During the day Comfrey hid out in the root cellar of one of the vanished farms, or wandered about on the wooded hills, working on refinements to the plan.

Then one morning the girl, called Pinny (for Pinocchio, because of her very large nose), who spent a lot of her time at the Hollow, met Comfrey coming to the creek for water—and managed to win his trust and become his friend. The whole first half of the book, in fact, was about the beginnings and growth of the improbable, but mutually rewarding, three-way friendship between Comfrey, Pinny, and Joshua.

In Pam's novel, just as in real life, lots of visitors crossed the river or walked down the gravel road to see Hurt Hollow. There was a daily ferry in high season, one on weekends throughout the year. Afternoons between two and four o'clock, from the first of April to the first of November, the Hollow was often packed with strangers.

But every evening, when the dock and hilltop gates had been fastened, the Hefn would slip up to the house. Man, girl, and alien spent many a happy summer evening together; and when winter came, with early darkness and ice lining both shores of the river, they would light the kerosene lanterns and draw their low chairs close to the fireplace with the copper hood—hand-beaten by Orrin Hubbell sixty years before—and the dry old paneling would give back the warm glow of the fire. (Out of indifference, Pinny's parents let her stay overnight at the Hollow as often as she liked, something Pam's own parents would almost never let her do, partly for fear she would be a bother to Jesse, partly out of Pam's mother's belief that it wouldn't "look right," unless a friend came with her.)

Naturally Joshua and Comfrey let Pinny in on the secret scheme. Pam left the details vague, but made it clear that Pinny turned out to be a big help to Joshua and Comfrey while they were working out their plan for saving the world.

Later, when the intense cold made Comfrey sleepy, he chose to stay and hibernate in the root cellar—by then he was that reluctant to leave Hurt Hollow and Pinny and Joshua.

By then, plenty of other things had happened too. For example, one night in August Comfrey had fallen out of the johnboat. In the world of Pam's novel—and maybe in the real world too, nobody knew—Hefn were unable to swim. It was Pinny herself, demonstrating great presence of mind, as well as great strength and knowledge of life-saving holds, who had dived in naked and supple as an otter and towed Comfrey to the dock through the inky, moon-burnished water. It was Pinny, while Joshua was still desperately rowing back toward shore from the middle of the river, who stretched Comfrey out on his back on the dock and gave him mouth-to-mouth resuscitation while water streamed out of his beard and pelt. It was Pam-alias-Pinny who saved his life—and heard him say he would be grateful to her as long as he lived (and a Hefn lifetime is a long, long lifetime).

Another day, when the bare November woods provided poor cover, Comfrey had almost been stumbled over by a family of snoopy tourists. It was a very close call. Pinny had adroitly distracted the visitors while the Hefn slipped into hiding.

When not busy rescuing Comfrey, Pinny passed her time at Hurt Hollow in the role of Apprentice to Joshua. She dug, planted, and weeded the garden; helped pickle, dry, and can the harvest; tended the trot lines and the hives; smoked fish; milked goats; cut and split firewood; and replaced a section of termite-weakened floor in the studio; all with equal competence and energy. Pinny was at least three or four times as muscular as Pam, and knew ten times as much about homesteading (though Pam herself had actually learned quite a lot about it). There was a trade-off, however. She wasn't a poet, and she wasn't the most mathematically gifted eighth-grader in the state of Indiana.

So she wasn't Pam, not truly. Nobody, incidentally, had ever called Pam "Pinocchio" to her face or teased her about her big nose. The cruel nickname was a projection of what she imagined people were saying behind her back; but there was another reason, and a more despairing pain, behind this naming of her doppelgänger after the wooden puppet who had wanted to be a real boy.

Riding out to College Park on the Metro, Liam and Pam talked about math.

"The earliest I can remember is when I was about three or four," Pam said in response to a question of Liam's. "Did you know I grew up on a college campus? Well, one of the math profs used to come over to our house, and he noticed that I was always counting things—the number of peas on my plate, the number of each different color of thumbtack on the bulletin board in the kitchen, the number of photoelectric cells on the car, the number of buttons on people's clothes . . . if there was a lot of the same kind of thing around, I counted it. Marbles in the fishbowl, bricks around the fireplace . . . I remember just *relishing* the names of numbers. I loved to say them; I learned the names of the numbers from one to one thousand in Latin, French, German, Spanish, Russian, and Hindi! I thought they were just delicious, like fudge, or ripe peaches or something—nine was always my favorite, I remember thinking of it as brown, and I remember four and seven felt like they were related, like green and blue. I drove my mother nuts with all that counting in different languages, so she tells me. She made me stop doing it out loud.

"So anyway, this math professor, Doug, got interested and

47

started watching me, and he was the one who realized at some point that I wasn't *counting* things that were arranged in regular patterns anymore, I was getting a total by multiplying. And of course this was long before we were supposed to be learning the times tables in school. So he asked me some question to try to figure out what was going on in my head, and then he told my parents he thought I was gifted and wanted to tutor me. So they said okay and he did, every Saturday morning, starting when I was seven. We went through arithmetic, algebra I and II, geometry, pre-calc, trig, and calculus, and we were just starting linear algebra when the Hefn came. Oh, and I took high-school physics in summer school, the summer after the sixth grade,'' she ended in a rush. "What about you?"

"I was kind of a late bloomer compared to you, I guess. I went to a good school, a Quaker school in Philadelphia, through the sixth grade, and math was always easy for me, but my teachers weren't knocked off their feet or anything. I wasn't even always the best in the class. Then we moved to Washington after the meltdown, and I started to school down here, and all of a sudden I could do all these things with numbers that I'd never been able to do before."

"Meltdown? Oh!" Pam said in alarm, "You lived in *Philadelphia*! Sorry, I hadn't really taken that in. Gosh, that must have been terrible." She broke off awkwardly, uncertain what to say to someone who had lived through a disaster and lost his home and everything he owned, like a displaced person in a war. She vaguely remembered when the power plant at Peach Bottom, on the Maryland-Pennsylvania border, had had the meltdown four years back, in 2010, right before the Hefn had returned. But westerly winds had spread the radioactivity the other way from Indiana, and Pam had only been ten years old at the time, and a long way from the danger.

Liam did nothing immediate to relieve her discomfort. He looked out of the train window, though there was nothing to see, and was silent. The muscles of his jaw bunched and tightened, and he swallowed once. Pam felt terrible.

But after a minute he shifted back toward Pam and cleared his throat. "Do you know much about prodigies?"

Seizing this gambit with relief, Pam said, "Not a whole lot. I read about Norbert Wiener, and a book about that poor guy William James Sidis, and some other stuff."

"Yeah. Well, there's a theory that everybody's mind goes through a major development, or reorganization, around the age of twelve. That's probably what happened to me, and it seems to be the case that prodigies in math are late bloomers generally, compared to chess and music and, well, human computers like Stumpf and Dworkin—they could calculate as very small kids, the intuitive ability didn't appear till later. Incipient math prodigies hardly ever get spotted before they're ten or so. You're the exception there.''

''Wiener and Sidis were too, then, because I know for sure that Billy Sidis was doing differential calculus when he was younger than that, and so was Gauss, and so was Kurt Lueders.''

''I know, and Pascal and Leibniz and John von Neumann,'' said Liam, ''but those guys were all-around geniuses, not specialists like us.''

''True.''

Liam stretched in his seat and laughed. ''The only sign of future greatness anybody in my family remembers about *me* now is, well, they tell me I was uncommonly *neat* as a little kid. I'd organize everything. Toy cars for example: I'd arrange them on the shelves in descending order of size within groups of the same color. They all thought my left brain was just fantastically hyperdeveloped, and they used to tease me about it because the rest of my family is a bunch of slobs.'' He grinned as he said this. ''You should have seen my sisters' rooms when they were in high school. I never understood how they could abide all that clutter, and my mom's at least as bad as them. My dad's cousin, who's a *very* tidy person, used to take me home with her every week or so and let me go through this unvarying set of routines— lock all the doors, have doughnuts and tea using the same cup and plate, draw a picture while playing a certain tape and watching ''Sesame Street,'' and so on. Anyway, *now* they think—I mean the psychologists do—that an orderly nature may be associated with mathematical ability in some cases.''

''Not in mine,'' said Pam ruefully. ''Though I'm not a true slob either,'' she added in justice to herself, thinking of the house at Hurt Hollow, as economically appointed as the cabin of a ship, and how easily and naturally she had always fitted into those extremely close quarters. ''There's one other thing that showed up very early in me. I've got this phenomenal memory for metrical poetry. Not a photographic memory, I don't visualize the pages or the screen, but an auditory one. Like, I memorized 'The Rime of the Ancient Mariner' last year in two or three readings, the whole thing, without even realizing it, and I was even quicker as a pre-schooler. But it has to be metrical, it doesn't work with free verse, or ordinary prose.''

"Carrie's going to like you, then," Liam said with a grin. He had a nice grin, a little crooked, one side of his upper lip rising higher than the other and showing some gum. His face from cheekbones to chin made a sharp V. "Carrie's my dad's cousin, the one I told you about, the one who used to take me home with her to let me obsess. She lives with us now; she'll be there tonight.''

"Why will she like me?''

"She teaches English at the University of Maryland," Liam said, "and before she lived with us, she and her husband were both English professors at the University of Pennsylvania. They're always quoting poetry, mostly at each other because the rest of us are illiterates by comparison.''

"The other thing I can quote besides poetry," Pam told him, "is the Bible. The King James Version. The prose is very rhythmical. But I have to sweat a little to get Bible verses to stick in my head.''

"So why try?''

"Well because," said Pam, "we're Baptists in my family. The college in Indiana where my father's head librarian, Scofield College, is affiliated with the Southern Baptist Convention, even though we're a little bit on the wrong side of the Mason-Dixon Line. Baptist kids all have to memorize a lot of Bible verses, it's one of the main things they do. They bribe us with Bible bookmarks and Wordless Books and pictures and certificates. Ask me to show you my collection of Bible bookmarks sometime.''

Evidently it was Liam's turn to feel alarmed. "Not Southern Baptist as in Brother Gus Griner! Please! Say it isn't so!''

Pam shook her head vigorously, laughing at him. "Gladly! 'It isn't so.' Gus Griner's a Grand Dragon or whatever they call it in the Louisiana Ku Klux Klan! You must have heard him ranting on TV about the Hefn. He's got this big mansion in New Orleans and a full-time staff of servants because of all the money people send him; he just *steals* it! He's a crook! He's a *maniac*! We have nothing whatsoever to do with Brother Gus Griner.''

"I'm relieved to hear it," Liam said, *sounding* relieved.

"No, I mean Southern Baptist more as in Billy Graham, if you know who he was.''

"I've heard the name, I think, but . . .''

"Or wait, there's another televangelist called Tom Grey, who's pretty much on the same wave-length as us, but you might not have ever seen him preach. He's nowhere near as notorious as Brother Gus, but *I* really think he's good. Or, hey, I know: Jimmy Carter. Like that. I *go* to the church Jimmy Carter used to go to in Washington and it's a whole lot like home, only bigger.''

"So," Liam said warily after a moment, "do *you* believe all that?"

"All what?"

"Well, you said like Jimmy Carter. Wasn't he the one that made the expression 'born-again Christian' a household word?'' Pam nodded. "So do you believe in being born again?''

"You sound like you're hoping and praying I'll say no," Pam said, "but I pretty much do. And excuse me for saying so, but I doubt if you know what being born again means.''

"Just tell me if it's true that Baptists don't believe in evolution.''

"Some do, some don't," said Pam. "*I* do. I'm not a strict Fundamentalist, I know Adam and Eve and the Flood and all that are myths. But I believe in Jesus, and I do believe in being born again. Are you sorry you asked me to dinner?''

"No, no, I guess I'm just a little taken aback." Liam grinned apologetically. "I don't think I ever knew a Baptist before, and you have to admit that the idea of a born-again math prodigy working for the Hefn is a little mind-boggling, in the light of Gus Griner and types like that. You've got a serious public relations problem in that guy, by the way.''

"You're telling me.''

"How does your church square the Hefn with the Bible, anyway?''

Pam smiled. "Actually, there's no consensus yet. It's only been four years, we're still working on it. But there's Ezekiel's wheel in the middle of a wheel—''

"Way up in the middle of the air?''

"That's the one. Well, *there's* precedent if you want to look at it like that; and we've got a bunch of people reconsidering the Book of Revelations in the light of the Hefn and Gafr being here. Did you ever read Revelations? It's the last book of the New Testament.'' Liam shook his head. "The whole thing front to back is symbolic so there's lots of scope for interpretation. But I don't much care what they finally decide," said Pam, "I believe in being born again because I had a conversion experience. It happened to me. I was born again—dumb phrase, but that's what Jesus is supposed to have called it.''

51

Liam's brown eyes brightened with interest. "You really had a conversion experience? What was it like?"

"I don't think I can explain it to you very well here on the Metro," Pam said dryly, "though there's precedent for that too. The apostle Philip preached the gospel to a eunuch while driving along in the eunuch's chariot." Liam's face twitched, but Pam barreled right ahead: "I'll tell you about it some other time though if you want."

"Okay. One of these days I'll remind you." Liam looked out the window as Pam felt the train slowing. "Whoops, here we are. This is our stop." He stood up, and Pam got ready to stand too, with a sudden sinking of the heart. Self-consciousness, which had vanished during the talk about math and religion, flowed back into her at the immediate prospect of meeting a group of adult strangers; despite her mother's best efforts Pam was pretty short on the social graces. As she pulled herself up by the pole, a sudden unnerving outflow of hotness and wetness, invisible of course to Liam, set the muscles of her face in planes of tension.

An escalator ride delivered them onto the sidewalk. Up in the world it was dim twilight, the wet pavement deepening the chill of the air, though the rain had stopped. "Half a block and there we are," said Liam, and led the way, graceful in his bulky down-filled cotton jacket, along the sidewalk. "Actually, I just thought of something else in connection with what we were talking about before. When I was four or five, Carrie took me and—and another kid into an Ed Psych class at Penn. The teacher, who was a friend of hers, needed some live models to demonstrate the development of spatial perception. Carrie always tells this story. The psych teacher had a small glass that was full of water, and she poured it into a bigger glass, so the water only filled it about halfway, and asked us which was more. We were supposed to say the full glass was more, but I said they were the same. Then she took a piece of Play-Doh that was shaped like a sphere and rolled it out thin, like a sausage, and asked us which was bigger, and I said *they* were the same. It screwed up the whole point of having us come in."

Now too nervous to follow closely, Pam still had caught the drift of this and did her best to respond. "So they found out you had a hypertrophic spatial sense. What did the other kid say?"

Liam ducked his head. "Oh, he just said what I said. He knew I'd be right about stuff like that."

"But did he really think—" Pam started to ask, but Liam

interrupted: "This is it. Right through here." He turned smartly through a gap in a decades-old privet hedge, massive and thick as the green wall of a fortress, and up the walk of a large frame house, three stories tall, painted white, with a white railed porch wrapped around two sides. The house was set in what appeared to be at least an acre of lawn, and in the dim light managed to look both ramshackled and elegant, with all its porch lamps burning and all its curtained downstairs windows aglow.

Bleeding furtively, heart thumping, Pam followed Liam up the steps to the door.

#Think of an Orrin Hubbell *anything* fetching only *one* million bucks! I enjoyed the simplicity and clarity of this Hurt Hollow history a lot, and really liked how completely you screen out any hint of all that was to come. It gives the description a peculiar fin-de-siècle feeling.

#I read through the synopsis of *Pinny's Hefn* with a big smirk on my face, till I got to the end. You did have a time, didn't you? I solemnly swear that I never once thought about your nose being big, and was quite surprised when you had the operation— like, what for?

#I do remember that train ride and the subject of the meltdown coming up, and being smacked with a wave of grief about Jeff. And I can remember thinking "*Uh*-oh," when you told me you were a Baptist. Did we actually say all those things to each other, or did you just reinvent the dialogue from whole cloth? It does sound pretty much in the right key, but I sure couldn't swear whether either of us did or didn't use those exact words.

I wouldn't think anybody could possibly remember the details of a thirteen-year-old conversation, except you say my face twitched when you made that remark about "eunuch," and if you *had* made one then my face probably *would* have twitched. Right around that time I'd started to get really worried about myself because all the other guys were so perpetually randy, and I never had any sexy impulses at all, unless you count wet dreams. And it was my body that was having those, not "me." "Eunuch" would have struck me as all too painfully apt.

3

HOUSE DIVIDED
Matthew 12:25

By the time dinner was over and everyone had moved from the table to the sitting room with their cups of coffee or tea, Pam was beginning to get the different people sorted out. Liam's parents, Phoebe and Mark, seemed like updated characters out of black-and-white televisionland. Phoebe was Harriet, Mark was Ozzie. "Housewife" and "Businessman." They were nice, especially Phoebe, but less interesting than Mark's cousin Carrie and her husband Matt, who shared the house with Liam's family; and most interesting of all was the other guest: Terry Carpenter, the famous senator from Pennsylvania, who chaired the Senate Committee on Alien Affairs. He had worked with Humphrey to set up the BTP, and something about his manner with Liam suggested to Pam that he had also had something to do with Liam's being made an Apprentice. So that might mean he was also connected in some way to the mysterious special relationship between Humphrey and Liam—which made him a figure of fascination in Pam's eyes.

Though dying to know more about the Carpenter-Humphrey-Liam connection, Pam couldn't think of a way to bring the subject up without sounding nosy or rude; she had been brought up to speak when spoken to in the company of adults. These particular adults had been very friendly and pleasant, asking where she came from and about her family, and how she liked living at the Bureau, but none of them had exactly invited personal questions. She sat balancing her teacup in her lap, staring so fixedly at Senator Carpenter that he felt her gaze upon him and glanced in her direction during a lull in the conversation. Embarrassed, Pam blushed and looked away, biting her lip.

Liam had been talking learnedly about the time transceivers. "It takes the higher math to operate them," he was saying. "See, the machinery can be built and maintained by engineers, they don't need us for that, but to *use* them the coordinates have to be set mentally, by brain waves. Eventually, we—the Apprentices—we'll be able to link up directly to the transceivers, when we've learned enough math and acquired enough mental control to set the shimmer patterns and field and place the numbers. That's why the Hefn screened for visual intuitives: any mathematician could grasp it intellectually, but you have to *see* it and *feel* it, *and* your mind has to comprehend it too. It's hard! It might be another couple of years before any of us will be ready to set shimmer coordinates, depending on how something we're doing that involves a thing called J-sets works out.''

" 'Shimmer coordinates'? 'J-sets'?'' Terry's voice made it clear that he didn't expect to understand the answer.

"J for Julia, but it's probably too complicated to explain. It has to do with fractals, and Chaos theory. I could loan you a book about it.''

"No, no,'' said Terry hastily, waving his hands, ''thanks all the same but I'm afraid it would take more than a book.''

"So'm I.'' The two grinned fondly at one another.

" 'Link up directly,' '' Phoebe mused dubiously. ''I don't much care for the sound of *that*.''

"Presumably they don't intend to implant a socket in your brain, and plug the time transceiver into the socket, like in all those B-grade sci-fi movies I used to go to when I was a kid!'' Matt smiled and shook his handsome head; to Pam he looked exactly like somebody type-cast in Hollywood as a professor, even to the tweed jacket with leather elbow patches. His beautiful silver hair and toothbrush mustache were the finishing touches. *Not one* of the professors at Scofield College went around looking that elegant.

Liam laughed, relaxed and clearly enjoying himself, there at the center of his family's regard. ''No, no, no, this is a much more subtle interface—no Frankenstein surgery or cyberpunk stuff. 'Transcendental' is what Humphrey calls it.''

"What's cyberpunk?'' Pam asked, and almost at once regretted breaking her silence. Everyone in the room, including Liam, became motionless for a couple of pulsebeats. Nobody looked at Pam; nobody looked at anybody else. In mounting alarm Pam put her cup and saucer down on the end table and gripped the arms of her chair. What was it—what had she said?

Then Carrie crossed her legs and smiled, answering so naturally that Pam wasn't sure she hadn't imagined the momentary tension. "Cyberpunk was a kind of science fiction that was popular for a while about twenty-five years ago. Have you ever read or seen any science fiction?"

"I saw *Star Wars*."

Carrie nodded. "Well then, you can see how it would have taken all the joy out of inventing Wookies and such when the Hefn turned up, big as life."

"And twice as ugly," Phoebe muttered aside to Matt.

Matt perked up. "I saw an article a couple of weeks ago by a famous sci-fi author who was making exactly that point. She said a devastating crisis of morale had swept through the field. The writers are all confused, they don't know what to do. She said they were sure to get back on their feet eventually, because they're such inventive people, but right now they're all still immobilized and demoralized by the overwhelming reality of the Hefn. Or words to that effect."

Liam's father stirred in his chair. "Why don't they write about the Gafr? Nobody knows anything about *them*."

Carrie rolled her eyes. "*Anyway,* Pam, cyberpunk posited an ultra-urban near-future—the present, now!—that would be dominated by computer networking and drug-related crime. Very fast-paced, lots of excitement, lots of action. Lots of hackers plugging programs into their brains, or *becoming* programs by being engraved on microchips. It was quite a craze for a while. It would have a wildly outmoded feel to it now, and not just the idea of computer hackers running the world, instead of the Hefn—think how computers themselves have changed since the Directive."

"Science fiction was never supposed to be predictive," Terry Carpenter said quietly. "Life overtook it, ninety-nine percent of the time."

He smiled—sadly, Pam thought—at no one in particular. She cast about for something to say. "A little part in our home computer died not long after the Directive and my father couldn't get a replacement part anywhere, everybody was sold out and they weren't making any more by then. We had to get a whole other computer, much bigger and bulkier. And every so often now you notice the old ones around campus, like in the library, disappearing and new ones sprouting up. The old ones are being cannibalized for spare parts now, but sooner or later I guess they'll all be gone."

"Most towns have a hospital for non-working pre-Hefn computers," Terry said. "Lots of moribund ones come in, a few go back out with organ transplants, and when the donors have donated everything useful they've got, off they're carted to the recycler. Eventually, as you say, the species will be extinct.''

Mark stirred again and addressed Pam. "What have you got out there in Indiana—IBM?''

"I don't really know. I think it's IBM compatible.''

"Macintosh is doing more and more with fiber-reinforced bioplastics,'' Mark informed her. "Your NotePad—you've got a NotePad, haven't you?—is probably made from cellulose produced by bacterial metabolic action.''

"Mine is,'' Liam put in. "Mine's cornstarch, basically.''

"No, I've got one, but mine's made of recycled petroplastics. There's a place in Louisville that makes them out of the plastic they dig out of landfills. It's an ugly color but the bioplastic ones cost a mint out there.''

Pam's insides chose that moment to release a perfect deluge of fluid. Terrified of bleeding through her clothes, she stood up abruptly and addressed Phoebe: "Could you tell me where the bathroom is, please?''

Carrie stood too. "Come on, I'll show you. It's just through here.''

Pam followed the woman out of the room, snatching up her backpack from the floor in passing and praying there was no wet red spot on her pants or the sofa cushion. The bathroom opened off the family room next to the living room where they were all sitting; Carrie pushed open the door and snapped the light on—and then, surprisingly, laid her hand on Pam's stiff arm. "Honey, you didn't say anything wrong before. The reason we all acted so funny is, Terry had a son called Jeff, who was Liam's best friend from the time they were both babies. Jeff died in the Peach Bottom disaster several years ago. He was a great science fiction reader. The only reason the rest of us know what cyberpunk is, is that Jeff used to talk about it. See? Your question made us all remember how he used to go on about it, all excited. He really admired the cyberpunk writers, old-fashioned though they were.'' She sighed. "We miss Jeff a lot, he was a marvelous boy. But you had no way of knowing and you mustn't feel bad, all right?''

"But I *do*!'' Pam said, aghast at what she had done. "I feel terrible! I'm so sorry I upset you all—I—''

Carrie gave Pam's arm a little squeeze and withdrew her hand. "Everybody understands that,'' she said kindly. "But life goes on. Don't stay in here too long, now; there're some questions I've been saving up to ask you."

Thoroughly flustered and upset, Pam put out her icy hand and pulled the door shut. She put her backpack down on the floor, unfastened and pulled down her pants and underpants, and then hooked her thumbs over the elastic of her sanitary belt and pulled that down too. The pad stuck to her crotch. As it came loose the smell assailed her and she thought, as always, that there couldn't be a worse smell in the world.

Pam sat on the toilet and inspected the situation. The pad was soaked, saturated. Blood had overflowed its sides and stained her underwear.

Grimly she set about undoing the tabs attached to each end of the elastic belt from their toothed metal hooks. Nobody, nobody in the world, used belts and pads like this anymore; you couldn't even buy them in the store, you had to order them out of a medical supplies catalog. Everybody else used pads you could stick directly onto the fabric of your underwear crotch, or tampons that went up inside of you where you didn't have to see or smell or even feel them.

Pam used tampons too, but she came from a long line of heavy bleeders and right from the start her periods, for the first two days, had been too much for them; even a "super" tampon lasted about ten minutes when matters were proceeding in the faucet-like way they were right now. And regular underpants weren't tight enough, they let the stick-on pads move around too much. It was bad enough during the day, when she could sort of monitor what was going on. Nights were impossible, the mess went all over everywhere. So she wore the elastic belt and the pads with tabs.

The doctors said there was nothing wrong with her. Some girls bleed a lot and some don't. Some girls wear a D-cup in the eighth grade and some are still in training bras they don't actually even need. People are different. All this is perfectly normal.

There were two thin parallel lines stenciled in blood on the inside of her jeans, but at least she hadn't bled through. Pam scrubbed at the lines with toilet paper, to dry them. She rolled the soiled pad up tightly, cocooned it in more toilet paper, and stowed it in her pack. She got out a fresh pad, threaded the tabs through the little buckles and knotted them. She used reams of toilet paper and a moistened wipe to clean herself up. Finally she stood and, layer by layer, put herself back together.

While she'd been sitting there the water in the toilet had turned a deep pink and accumulated a floating mass of wadded paper. Pam's stomach turned. She flushed the mess away and looked around in vain for some air freshener.

Throughout the grim process of coping with her body's loathsomeness, part of her mind had also been agonizing over her unwitting faux pas. Hindsight told her that the "other kid" Liam had referred to must have been his dead friend—and that that awkward moment over the meltdown, on the train, had been about a loss more dire even than the loss of his home. No person important to Pam had ever died; she couldn't imagine what the experience of such a death could possibly be like. How was she going to go out and face them all, after re-opening that terrible wound with her blunder?

But finally it began to seem more embarrassing to stay in the bathroom any longer than to go back and join the others. And when, eyes on the carpet, Pam had slunk back to her seat and gradually settled down enough to be able to take the conversation in again, she realized they were talking about Humphrey—the one subject absorbing enough to divert her at once.

"He did go back up to the ship and take a kind of hibernation *nap* for a few weeks last summer, remember," Senator Carpenter was saying, "but he's been on the drugs again since around Thanksgiving and they're starting to affect him. He feels uneasy, and his pelt's starting to fall out in patches. It looks to me like the Bureau's going to have to adjust to the realities of Hefn physiology. You kids might have to take your vacation from November to April, and work all summer—either that, or the Gafr will have to put one of us in charge during the cold weather."

"They'd never do that," Liam opined a little smugly. "Not yet anyway. Later on, when one of *us* could take over, they'd probably agree to *that*—but I know they wouldn't let anybody else run the Bureau. They would never believe they could trust any human unless it was a human trained by Humphrey. No offense, Terry."

"Can you possibly be suggesting that *I* haven't been trained by Humphrey?" Terry had been holding a needlepointed cushion in his lap; he now pitched this hard at Liam, who caught it, laughing. "I don't claim to have acquired any transcendental skills, but do you seriously think anybody could spend as much time working with Humphrey as I have, and remain unchanged?"

"I didn't say changed, I said trained!" said Liam. "I know

Humphrey's had a big effect on you, but the Gafr still wouldn't let you run the Bureau—''

"*I* don't want to run the Bureau! Good God, what an idea!''

"—because, for one thing, you don't know any math!''

"We haven't seen old Humphrey out here in quite a while,'' Matt put in, interrupting this exchange. "Isn't it time we had him out to dinner again? We could bake him another blackberry cobbler, Phoebe.''

"We could if we had any blackberries left. That jar I opened a couple of weeks ago was the last one.''

"How many pints did we put up, anyway, fifteen? Twenty?''

"Twelve, I think.''

"That's all? I could have sworn it was more than that. No wonder we ran out. This year let's see if we can't can enough to last us all winter,'' Carrie suggested.

"I'm sure I can't imagine what you mean by 'we,' '' said Phoebe.

"Well,'' said Carrie, "I did pick a couple of washtubs full of the things, even if it was you and Matt who did all the slaving over the hot stove.''

"His beard was stained purple all around his mouth, remember?'' Matt put in, grinning with what certainly looked to Pam, whose attention was riveted on the conversation, like affection.

Phoebe grinned back, then looked put out. "Remember when you could just walk into a supermarket any time of year and get all the frozen blackberries you wanted? You can tell Humphrey from me, Terry, that he'll get blackberry cobbler in March when the Gafr withdraw the Directive, and not before.''

"Oh, no, not the good-old-days lament!'' Liam wailed. "Don't let her get started!'' He glanced over at Pam. "Mom likes Humphrey a whole lot, but she doesn't like anything else *at all* about the Hefn takeover.''

"We're a house divided against itself,'' Carrie explained. "Matt and Phoebe disapprove of the Directive. Mark and I think that on balance it's probably a good thing.''

Pam cleared her throat. "Looks like you're standing pretty solid, all the same.''

Liam butted in. "Standing on what? What's that supposed to mean?''

" 'And if a house be divided against itself, that house cannot stand,' '' Pam quoted. "Mark 3:25. The passage Lincoln used about the Secession.'' She looked down and blushed furiously.

Liam's face lit up with wicked glee. "I forgot to tell you guys:

Pam's a Baptist. They memorize the Bible a lot, so she says. That college in Indiana she comes from is a Baptist college.''

For a moment every adult in the room sat looking at Pam as if he or she were thinking *My God! How is this possible?* Pam felt like a specimen in a laboratory tray, a fetal pig or something. She blushed harder. Carrie, recovering first, said kindly, ''That reminds me, there's something I was meaning to ask you, Pam. What do *you* think of Humphrey? We're very fond of him in this family, and that includes Phoebe and Matt, but I'm curious to know how he seems to somebody who knows him only through the Bureau, and chiefly as a teacher.''

At the center of everyone's attention, Pam's wits deserted her. ''I—well—he's a very good teacher,'' she began. ''He knows math, he really *knows* it. I never knew anybody who could talk about it as well as he does. And what he's teaching us is hard, like Liam said before; it's hard to put into words, but Humphrey can do it somehow. It's like poetry, really, the way he explains math and the way he talks about the principles behind the time transceiver. Even though his English is a little weird, otherwise.''

In his rocking chair across the room, Terry chuckled. ''A little weird indeed. Eccentric, I calls it. Tell me, Pam,'' he said, using her name for the first time, ''what do you think of Humphrey as a, well, a *person*? He's not a person, obviously, but you understand what I mean.''

They were all watching her, waiting for her to answer. Pam felt a stab of panic. Unwilling to express what she really felt to this roomful of kindly strangers, she dropped her gaze again and said, ''Oh, he's—easy to get along with. And he's very, um, nice to us.''

After a moment's silence Liam's father stood up. ''More coffee, anyone? Tea?''

''Good thing Washington's a port,'' Pam blurted desperately, gaze still on the carpet, ''my mother says we haven't had affordable coffee or tea out in Indiana for nearly a year.''

Walking back to the Metro station in the dark, Pam couldn't prevent herself from asking Liam, ''Why is everybody in your family so fond of Humphrey?''

Liam took eleven steps before replying. ''It's a long story,'' he said finally. ''Maybe I'll tell you sometime, but not tonight, okay?''

''Okay,'' she said stiffly, embarrassed by the gentle rebuff.

"And maybe if I do," he added, "you'll tell me what you *really* think about him."

She smiled sideways at Liam, mollified. "As a person, you mean."

"Right. As a person."

"Well," Pam said, considering, "okay . . . if you decide to tell me your long story, maybe I'll decide to tell you mine."

"And you promised to tell about your conversion experience too, don't forget."

"I know. I won't. I don't mind talking about that. In the right circumstances."

Humphrey was not a person; it was sentimental of Terry to call him one, though to do so also captured a kind of truth. The Hefn, hairy dwarves with short, oddly jointed legs, were humanoid physically but mentally quite alien (though far less alien, it was generally believed, than their overlords, the Gafr, who commanded their ship). The Hefn had first visited Earth, undetected by humans, in the year 1623. At that time some members of the crew had started a rebellion, and Earth had been a convenient place to maroon them. One group of mutineers had been put off in England—these included Elphi and the other Yorkshire "hobs"—and another in Sweden. The intention had been to teach them a lesson, not to strand them permanently; but mechanical difficulties and time dilation had combined to delay the ship's return for nearly four centuries—a long time even for the extremely long-lived Hefn.

In 2006 the ship had finally reappeared in the solar system. A Hefn delegation landed, searched for several months, and finally succeeded in locating traces of the Yorkshire group (and also in nearly precipitating an international crisis). Then they had just gone away, apparently determined to have no further contact with humanity at all—which suited most of humanity very well indeed.

But then, following a shift of power aboard the ship, the aliens returned—four years after their departure, and immediately following the meltdown at the Peach Bottom Nuclear Facility. They parked the ship on the moon, and the Gafr faction now in command announced—through their Hefn worshipers/slaves, for no human had ever seen a Gafr—their intention of saving the fouled nest of Earth from its own hatchlings, using whatever means might prove necessary.

Without fuss or difficulty, the Hefn then took control of the world.

For most people the effect of the Hefn presence on Earth was indirect and slight, at least in the beginning. Terry Carpenter was one of the very few who dealt directly and frequently with the aliens from the outset. For him, and for the people close to him, their being around made a big difference.

Just as the existence of the Bureau and almost daily contact with Humphrey made a tremendous difference to the nine BTP Apprentices—above all, for different personal reasons, to Liam and to Pam.

Because of this, and other things, it seemed in retrospect almost inevitable that Liam and Pam would form an alliance, a relationship that resembled, but was not quite, a friendship. The two of them *connected*—not powerfully, but in a way that neither had managed to do with any of the other Apprentices. Both were loners; the others had rather quickly divided into two groups of three (Roger, Raghu, John) and four (Will, Nguyen, Marshall, Ellis).

Mathematically speaking, each of the nine young people had been light-years ahead of everybody he knew at home. Ellis De Marco, from Baltimore, had attended one of the summer math courses offered by the Center for the Advancement of Academically Talented Youth—the CTY—at Johns Hopkins University. There, for the first time in his life, he had met other boys and girls almost as bright and talented as himself. Some of the CTY students reacted with dismay to the discovery that dozens of kids their own age were as good at math as they; others were jubilant at the sudden wealth of peers. Ellis had been one of the latter. From the beginning the Bureau had felt to him like a very small, very exclusive CTY.

Ellis's enthusiasm and energy were the centrifugal force at the center of one group; handsome John Chalmers was the focus of the other. Whereas Ellis was a dynamo, uniting his gang with the electric charge of his personality, John was a social smoothie—affable, blond, cultivated. His parents were divorced. Both New York lawyers, they had been extremely well-to-do before the Hefn came and were still managing well enough under the Directive. John had had every educational and cultural advantage imaginable, but the true secret of his success was a style compounded of personal attractiveness and natural charm. He was a living refutation of the stereotype of mathematician as nerd.

Neither group suited or attracted the two outsiders, though both found the members of Ellis's gang more sympathetic than the members of John's. To Pam's Indiana-bred sensibilities, John seemed effete. She was sharply aware of his good looks and good build, but admired these in the purely abstract spirit in which she admired her friend Betsy's handsome gelding, Wickiup, or the trim, efficient lines of her own battery-powered canoe.

Pam and Liam were allies, not really friends, certainly not sweethearts. In the bond that formed between them there was not the least hint of romance. From earliest childhood Pam's best friends had been Charlie and Steve; she was used to having boys for comrades. Charlie and Steve had metamorphosed into girl-crazy aliens; very well, but they were the changed ones, not she. If Liam had teased or flirted with Pam—treated her in a way that emphasized, or even recognized, the fact that she was a person of opposite gender to himself, a sexual potentiality—there would have been no alliance; Pam would not have tolerated such behavior for a minute.

That he never took this tack despite all the time they spent together seemed to her perfectly natural and right. When Raghu Kanal asked one day if she and ''her boyfriend'' were planning to spend the spring break together, Pam stared at him blankly and asked in honest bewilderment what the Sam Hill he was talking about.

The question forced her to consider that other people besides her mother might view the association in this—to her—lurid and offensive light. It made her hopping mad. What business was it of Raghu's, or anybody's? Still, the important thing was, Liam himself knew the score. As long as the two of them were in agreement, there was no danger to Pam. As long as they agreed, in fact, knowing Liam and his family amounted to a great big plus in the general picture of Pam's life in Washington, D.C.

#I won't comment further on the travails of girlhood, except to say again that I simply had no idea you felt so bad about it all. I'm positive Margy and Brett never had this much trouble. What you mainly heard about from them was PMS.

#"That he never took this tack despite all the time they spent together seemed to her perfectly natural and right." And to me too; but it wasn't right and it certainly wasn't natural. What a sad pair we were!

It disturbs me to read this and I'm sure writing it must have been disturbing for you. Jeff's death had deep-sixed my capacity for sexual response. Your father's carryings-on had obviously had the same effect on yours. Between us there must have been enough repressed, unconscious sexual tension to re-start Peach Bottom, and we never suspected a thing.

4

AND ENTERED INTO A SHIP

—John 6:17

Fifty years earlier, a Scofield College student setting out to visit Hurt Hollow could get there in one of two ways.

Either way required a car (or great determination).

From the campus she could drive five miles in the wrong direction, cross the Ohio River by the bridge at Madison, turn right after her steep ascent of the bluff on the Kentucky side, tack the car between flat cornfields for several miles—until finally, at the point where a gravel road angled away from the paved one, she would spot the giant mailbox, dominating a row of ordinary-sized ones, with ORRIN HUBBELL painted on the side.

She could pull the car off by the mailboxes and park it, and start walking (after checking to see whether there was any mail in the box for Orrin and Hannah; if there was, she would carry it along). At the end of the short gravel "road"—really a lane that dead-ended in a barnyard—the gullied track of the old, ruined road to Hurt's Landing began. The student could tramp through the woods, following this track or (usually) picking a way just off the edge of it, since the road carried runoff in wet weather and could be very muddy. After ten or fifteen minutes she could begin watching eagerly for the moment when a footpath would suddenly burst from the left side of the road and plunge straight down the steep hill. This was the path to Hurt Hollow, the shortcut that would bring a walker more quickly to the house and the river. An intrepid student would surely take the shortcut instead of the stony, muddy "road" eroded halfway back to plain hillside.

The footpath led steeply downhill for a mile, more or less, till it reached bottom land and crossed a level meadow where the chimney of a burnt-out farmhouse still stood. Our student would follow on to the creek; there she would cross from the low, near bank to the much higher far one by a footbridge canted up at an angle so steep that Orrin had nailed laths across it to keep muddy boots from slipping, giving the bridge almost the appearance of a ladder with a handrail. This was the creek, never called Hurt's Creek—nor by any other name, for that matter—whose flowing action had over the millennia created Hurt Hollow.

The student would cross—or rather, scale—the bridge, and ascend the path where it continued steeply up along the creek on the far bank. In only another minute the path would flatten out, leading a walker horizontally across the wooded hillside. Soon this walker would see a small gate, and beyond that a cluster of buildings, and beyond that the trees incompletely screening the wide Ohio; and she would have arrived.

The other way to come, back then, was by water. Orrin had hung a dinner bell on the Indiana side of the river for visitors to ring—a long-distance doorbell. Instead of heading up the river toward Madison, our student could drive, or cycle or hike, along the river road to the landing across from Hurt Hollow and ring the bell. Occasionally this didn't work. If Orrin and Hannah were playing duets, he on the violin and she on her Steinway grand piano, their music might drown out the clanging of the bell. But what usually happened was that the sound of an answering bell would carry faintly over the water, and after a while—ten minutes or so—a visitor would be able to make out the tiny figure of Orrin coming down to launch the johnboat, and see boat and rower very slowly grow larger and nearer, and finally Orrin would bring the boat in with a flourish against the dock—and the student would climb in to be ferried across to Kentucky.

At Hurt Hollow the Ohio River is almost half a mile wide—a long way for an old man with no pins in his oars to row twice in a day, or maybe more than twice on a particularly sociable day. There are powerful currents in mid-river and, not infrequently, stiff winds. Nevertheless, for a long time—until he was nearly seventy—Orrin had resisted the outboard motors that well-intentioned friends tried to press upon him. Eventually, however, he made this one grudging concession to the machine age and allowed somebody to give him one; and still later, after an exhibition of his paintings had sold particularly well, he had actually bought a new one for himself.

But even with the motor mounted on the johnboat, the fetching and returning of visitors was at times demanding, intrusive work. Homesteading is a labor-intensive way of life, and Orrin was an old man, and an artist as well as a homesteader. A right-thinking student—one who, moreover, very much wanted not to wear out her welcome—would nearly always walk in to Hurt Hollow, thereby sparing Orrin the effort and time it would cost him to come get her and, later on, take her back. She could always have a ride in the johnboat anyway; once there, she could go along with Orrin to see if there were any catfish on the trotline. He would let her row.

But just once in a great while, for a particular treat, even a right-thinking student might drive down to the landing and ring the bell.

Fifty years ago the land around the Hollow had reverted to second-growth wilderness. The Kentucky shore at that point rose so abruptly from the water's edge that the river road from Milton, across the bridge from Madison, forged inland well before it reached the Hubbells; extending it further west would not have repaid the effort and expense of cutting a roadbed into the hillside. The house and other buildings at Hurt Hollow, all sited higher up the bluff than the high-water mark of the 1937 flood, stood open to the river and the view. Directly across in Indiana a modest vacation trailer park had been established—a small disagreeable smudge in the riverscape—but the shoreline on both sides lay otherwise unmarred.

It was not until 1980 or thereabouts that the tranquillity of the Indiana shore had been seriously menaced. Around that time, not far downriver from the trailer park, construction on a nuclear power plant had begun. The near-meltdown at Three Mile Island was all that saved Orrin and Hannah from having the Marble Hill power plant for a neighbor. In the aftermath of that accident, the facility under construction on the Ohio River was abandoned.

In the Hurt Hollow of fifty years past, with that close call still pretty far up in the future, homesteading as a way of living had made beautiful, harmonious sense. Pam's family owned a copy of a TV documentary film made of the Hubbells back in those vanished days, when Orrin's ongoing "experiment in living" had been at its most successful. Pam had seen the film dozens of times, maybe hundreds. Even with the camera's intrusive presence, you could tell that these were people going through the deeply familiar routines of their daily lives: living without modern conveniences, by choice, in a manner that made joy of the constant labor; living with elegance and grace in a handmade house so plain and perfect it was impossible to imagine why everybody didn't yearn to live in one just like it. It was obvious what special people the Hubbells were. The film showed Hannah canning tomatoes on the wood-burning cookstove, her least movement somehow conveying a deep reverence for what she was doing—stoking the fire or ladling tomatoes or wiping the rims with a rag before sealing the jars. How could canning tomatoes be like prayer? Pam had not figured this out, nor had she ever discussed it with anybody—not even Jesse—but she knew about prayer and she knew that what Hannah was doing was it, the genuine thing.

Not that Hannah had been a *saintly* person. Jesse had described to Pam how she used to complain just like anybody else would have, when Orrin would climb up from the garden, with the temperature in the nineties, bringing still another bushel basket full of dead-ripe tomatoes that if not processed would go bad in a day. Orrin was the gardener; the putting by was Hannah's part of the work, and she did it with prideful skill, seldom letting Orrin help; but that sweating for ten or twelve hours over a sizzling cookstove, during what was often, even then, the tropical swelter of August and September in the Ohio River Valley, was very hard on Hannah in her old age, and pride didn't prevent her from saying so, though not to just anyone.

She was a person whose friends, by definition, did nothing disagreeable—who viewed their doings in a benign, encouraging, charitable light that passed no judgments. Orrin was blunter and saltier, much more inclined to cheerfully call a spade a spade. Yet by nature Hannah was more of a worrier than Orrin, more conservative, more *particularly* critical, or at least more vocal in her criticism. When a woman in a bikini appeared on Hannah's terrace one Sunday afternoon, showing exceptional tastelessness even for the weekend boating crowd—when an old acquaintance, recently separated from his wife, brought a new live-in girlfriend down to meet the Hubbells—when ceaseless streams of visitors seriously interfered with Orrin's deadline for a book's illustrations—Hannah would remark upon these events, at least to trusted friends, with disapproval or distress. What Orrin thought was not recorded.

The camera crew had followed Orrin through his usual day's routine: inspecting the trotline, smoking river catfish in a drum, cutting wood, hoeing, bringing a couple of ripe watermelons up from the garden to serve to the crew when they got through filming. Like Hannah's, his measured, deliberate movements marked him in Pam's eyes as a holy person. For the camera Orrin's hands, knobby and huge, gripped the carving knife that sliced the melons, dipped the rag in the pan of water to wash the nannies' udders, pumped up and down in the rhythmic spondees of milking, held the violin and bow while he and Hannah (on the Steinway) played Bach, and turned the pages of *Candide*, which they were reading aloud to each other in French. While Orrin read, in his high voice, the camera played over the built-in bookcases stuffed with volumes: *Walden*, *Two Years Before the Mast*, *The Canterbury Tales*, *Paradise Lost*, *The Complete Shakespeare*, *Huckleberry Finn*, *Great Expectations*, the poems of Rilke and Robinson Jeffers, *Kon-Tiki*. Orrin had not permitted the crew to film him painting, but let himself be persuaded to drag some finished pictures out of storage and stand them around the floor of the studio, and they filmed those. The soles of his beautifully shaped bare feet on the floorboards of the studio were tough as goathide.

They were very beautiful people, both of them—tall and lean, with white hair and fresh complexions. Pam—normally no noticer, let alone connoisseur, of skin tones—thought Hannah the most wonderfully colored white person, and possibly human being, she had ever seen in her life.

She was in love with them both, though both had been dead for a dozen years when she was born. So it was a very lucky thing that Jesse Kellum resembled Orrin Hubbell more closely than most sons resemble their fathers, that the Hollow had passed from Orrin and Hannah to Jesse and Marion, and most of all that Jesse didn't mind having Pam around, as long as she kept out of his way and was more of a help than a nuisance.

Pam's mother, Frances Pruitt, was the one who had suggested inviting Liam home with Pam to Indiana for the spring break. The break was going to be a long one, four weeks, because after this year the Apprentices' school calendar was being changed. Humphrey was apparently the only Hefn aboard the ship suitable at present to be a teacher for the BTP Apprentices. The decision had been made to train a Hefn understudy for him; he'd been awake for two years, except for a short nap nearly a year before, and would have to sleep when the cold weather came again.

The nine Apprentices, who'd been hard at work since the previous September, were to have a fairly long vacation now, and then work on through the summer, right up to Thanksgiving—at which time Humphrey would go back up to the moon, where the Gafr ship was parked, to hibernate, and the Bureau would close down. It would reopen in January if Humphrey's understudy was ready to take over; if he wasn't, it would be decided at that time what should be done with the Apprentices till their teacher woke up.

So they were all to be given four whole weeks of freedom, while every other kid their age in America was in school. Most of them, it turned out, planned to divide the free time between their fathers and their mothers, since every single one of the nine Apprentices except for Pam and Liam came from broken homes. Terry Carpenter had wondered whether it wouldn't be a good idea to organize a group trip, some kind of supervised excursion they could all take together, but nobody had wanted that. "We see each other all the time, who wants to go hiking in the Smokies with the same old faces?" said Marshall Hong, and the rest agreed. "Anyway, it's too much like a touring company: 'Hurry, hurry, hurry, step right up and see the amazing BTP Apprentices, for only five hundred dollars they will do your entire income tax return for you in their heads'—none for me, thanks."

And then Ellis's gang got busy and planned a trip anyway, just the four of them, for the second two weeks of the vacation. They were going to Walt Disney World, where the "Hefn Home World" attraction had just opened. Ellis's father and stepmother were going with them; they and Ellis would board the train in Atlanta and hook up with the other boys, who would already be aboard.

No sooner did they get wind of this than John's gang devised a counterplan. They settled on a week in New York City, where both John's parents lived, and another week "camping" in the Catskills at his father's vacation lodge.

That left Pam and Liam, as it usually did.

Each of their mothers, for her own reasons, was pleased about the alliance between the two. Both misunderstood its nature; Frances Pruitt was miles off the mark, Phoebe O'Hara was closer but with a judgment weakened by wishful thinking.

But when Frances conceived, and Phoebe energetically promoted, the idea that Pam would go back home for most of the break and that Liam would come with her, the kids fell in readily enough with the scheme. Without discussing it, each understood that the two mothers were trying to push the relationship where it had no wish to go; but each also had a clear enough sense of the other by this time to feel confident that, pressure or no pressure, no awkward developments would occur on either side.

Liam, who had never been west of Pittsburgh, didn't object to seeing a little more of the country. Pam herself figured she had nothing better to do than demonstrate to a great lout of fifteen that the Middle West actually existed. Better than that, she would take Liam down and show him Hurt Hollow, and introduce him to Jesse. Nothing she had seen in Washington was half as wonderful. They could paddle the big canoe down from Scofield Beach, instead of taking the little power canoe, or the steam packet and ferry. The more Pam thought about this plan, the better she liked it.

They traveled by train as far as Pittsburgh, where they were to board a steam packet for the trip down the river to Scofield Beach, below Madison, Indiana. There Pam's parents would meet them.

The trip would be long, three hundred miles by rail and another six hundred by water, but interesting and fun, and a new experience for Pam as well as for Liam. The Hefn had flown Pam out to Washington for the interview a year before. For several years now, air travel had been restricted to those purposes the Hefn considered essential. Candidate interviews they had deemed essential; vacations for Apprentices were another matter. No Gafr was going to approve the consumption of jet fuel to send a few kids to Indiana and a few more to Orlando and New York City.

However, in the three years since the Directive had gone into effect, surface transportation all over the world had expanded and improved so much the older people could scarcely believe how traveling had been transformed.

Improved, that is, in frequency and reliability of service. You could get just about anywhere, quite affordably, by public transport. Not improved, though, if you meant creature comforts. The Hefn didn't hold with those. They heated the trams, buses, boats, and trains, and cooled them moderately; all the rest of the available energy went into moving them along.

The electric train Pam and Liam took to Pittsburgh had been retrofitted to operate on power packs which were exchanged along the route, like mounts along the route of the Pony Express, as the juice in each was exhausted. Electricity to recharge the packs was generated by a variety of means, depending on what you had to work with at a given location—dependable sunshine or fast-flowing streams or whatever; diversity was a byword with the Hefn. In the part of the Midwest that had been prairie the energy source was mostly wind; along the coasts they were finally really getting someplace with wave power. It all worked. The design of the power packs was constantly being tinkered with, in an attempt to increase storage capacity and charging efficiency. By former standards the trains were slow—their top speed hovered around sixty—but their net consumption of energy was almost zero.

Had time been a factor, the kids could have taken a different train six hundred miles to Cincinnati and transferred there to the steamboat for the final ninety-mile leg of the journey. That would have meant an overnight aboard the train. Each of them would have been assigned a tiny private cubicle with a pull-out sink and toilet and a chair that converted into a narrow berth. You brought your own towel and sheet sleeping bag, which had a pillow pocket sewn into one end; the train provided the pillow and blankets and a little flake of soap. Nothing more luxurious was available to anybody at any price. The richest person had to provide his own linens, just as the poorest did, and take them home and launder them after the trip. And there was no food service anymore, though dining cars were provided for people to sit in while they ate what they had brought with them or bought from vendors selling "travelers' fare" on the station platforms along the way. Many passengers used the dining cars just to sit in and talk while they watched the countryside glide by.

That would have been fun, but Pam and Liam—especially Liam—had ridden on a lot of trains. Pam had been to Louisville and Cincinnati by packet, but those were both day trips from Madison. They consulted together and agreed, with Humphrey's approval, to forgo the experience of a night in a train cubicle in order to have three nights on the steamboat.

People had never stopped traveling by train, of course. Rail systems and rolling stock already existed; more were needed, but the only real challenge had been to work out a "sustainable" way of making them operate, and that technology had actually existed for a long time. All that had been lacking was sufficient incentive to develop them, and the Directive had supplied the lack.

But river boats had gone the way of ocean liners. Except for a few working museum pieces, like the *Delta Queen* and the *Belle of Louisville*, kept afloat for nostalgic reasons (and to provide the wealthy with an unusual vacation), paddle-wheel-driven steamboats had vanished from the rivers of America—been turned into trendy restaurants, or wrecked and sunk, or scrapped. They were slow, ungainly vessels compared to every other sort of public transport; but the Hefn were fanatics on the principles of conservation and diversity. Rather than build more railroads where none were now, they wanted to move people on the rivers, which were already there. Freight, once the bread and butter of the steamboat lines, could still be moved more cheaply by barge and towboat and would continue to be moved that way, but people were another matter. The Hefn wanted river and coastal travel to exist as competitive options for passengers. To that end, steamboats were being built again.

The boatwrights and engineers were prepared to reinvent the boats from scratch, inside and out, but they had encountered unexpectedly strong public feeling about the way a steamboat— at least those built to ply the inland waterways—ought to look. The engineers were welcome to experiment with engine design; interiors could be plain enough to content the strictest Gafr; but people had seen the classic musical *Showboat*, and the extravagant remake of *Huckleberry Finn* released early in 2010, the hundredth anniversary of Mark Twain's death. They had ridden the replica steamboats at Disneyland and Walt Disney World. If the boats were slow, they said, let them be fun. However spartan the accommodations within, let them look like floating palaces from the shore.

"Floating palaces" is how steamboats had been referred to in their heyday, the period when Mark Twain, a licensed pilot, had taken boats all up and down the Mississippi River system, the one he had written about in *Life on the Mississippi*. The builders had read his description of how a Western Rivers steamboat used to look and gazed at each other with a wild surmise. These boats were to be the Greyhound buses of the rivers, stopping at every landing, taking on wood, letting people on and off. The lavish interiors of Mark Twain's day—gilded filigree-work, pink-and-white flowered carpets, intricate crystal chandeliers, skylights, upholstered armchairs in the lounges, a porcelain knob and an oil painting on every stateroom door—were out; both Hefn guidelines and common sense precluded them. Interior fittings would be cramped, simple, easily cleaned, and tolerably comfortable, but luxury was an abomination that stank in the nostrils of the Hefn.

But the exterior, which could be shared by everybody aboard

and anyone on shore who happened to see the boat go by, was something else.

In Pittsburgh Liam and Pam stood on the wharf with their duffies and shouted in delight. Instead of one of the recently constructed packets, their boat was to be the venerable *Delta Queen*, eighty-eight years old and in her fourth incarnation (after Sacramento River night boat, U.S. Navy ferry, and pleasure boat on the Ohio and Mississippi) as flagship of the new Father of Waters Passenger Line. Flagship or not, she took her turn in the scheduled trips and charged the same for a ticket as any of the nine others in the fleet. It was pure luck that Liam and Pam had been booked aboard her; you couldn't request the *Delta Queen*, you took your chances like anybody else, even if you were rich as Croesus. The Apprentices had simply come up lucky.

They thought it was lucky. The new boats might look a little more like authentic Mississippi River steamboats, with the pilot house perched amidships instead of forward, but the *Delta Queen* was one of a kind. In every other detail—tall twin stacks feathered at the tips, gilded antlers over the pilot house, gleaming white paint, gingerbread trim, single red paddle wheel astern, even the steam calliope—the entire line had been modeled after her. The few sidewheelers, built last and only now being added to the line, were to sport the same circus-like decor.

All the new boats burned wood to make steam. The *Delta Queen*, built to run on crude oil, had had to have her boilers redesigned and her original short single chimney replaced by two taller ones (for a better draft). The panels that had enclosed the main deck were now removed and the space between decks left open, so that fuel could conveniently be carried aboard and stacked near the boilers. The beds in her first-class staterooms had also been removed and the rooms fitted with multiple bunks, to serve as small dormitories; but the oak paneling in the lounges, and even the teak handrails and mahogany grand staircase trimmed in brass, were left in place, the Hefn acknowledging that stripping the boat of her tropical woods, logged many decades before, would not bring back the rainforest destroyed to supply them. So there was something a little rakish and corrupt about the beautiful old boat. She seemed like a stylish dowager, allowed to go on wearing her leopard-skin coat because everyone understands that taking it away from her now would not restore life to the leopard.

Pam and Liam scurried up the broad gangplank, showed their

tickets, and dragged their duffles up two flights of narrow metal stairs to their stateroom on the top deck. "Stateroom" seemed a grandiose name for a tiny cubicle with bare lower and upper berths and a row of pegs to hang things on; but they also had their own bathroom, private baths being another nicety, not found aboard the new packets, which the Hefn had allowed the *Delta Queen* to keep.

Pam wanted the upper berth; Liam had no objection. That settled, Pam threw her bag on her bed and, not stopping to unpack, went out with Liam to visit the engine room on the main deck.

In Mark Twain's day, steamboats had been almost as dangerous as they were romantic. Twain had written harrowingly of disasters involving exploding boilers and death by scalding, or by inhaling steam. His own younger brother had died of burns when a steamboat blew up, and he narrowly missed the same fate himself. But technology to make the boilers virtually fail-safe existed now. A wooden boat might still catch fire, or strike a snag and sink, but neither of these unusual events was likely to result in loss of life, since the boat would never be more than a few minutes from shore while afloat, and since the odds against sinking in a hurry were very high. The boats were all equipped with buoyancy devices built into their hulls, in the space where the *Delta Queen* had once carried her liquid fuel, and these would keep her afloat even with a very serious puncture for at least an hour—plenty of time to get everybody into the lifeboats.

Discomfort and inconvenience were still possible. Exposure was possible. Death was also possible, but not much more likely than being struck down by a falling tree limb. A whiff of recklessness no longer played any part in the glamour of cruising down the river.

By the end of the great steamboat era, around 1870, both packets and towboats had switched from wood to coal, but coal—like oil—was proscribed by the Directive. The Hefn did allow wood to be burned, but the regulations called for boilers of exemplary efficiency, and for catalytic scrubbers in the stacks.

Wood was piled all over the main deck of the boat. When the kids arrived to watch, workers were bringing more of it aboard, carrying it on their shoulders up the stage from an enormous heap of seasoned hardwood on the wharf. Pam had stood at the landing in Madison and watched the steamboats take on wood. From her trips to Louisville and Cincinnati she knew that almost every time the *Delta Queen* called at the various landings between Pittsburgh and Scofield Beach to let passengers on and off, it would also take on more fuel from the mountainous stacks waiting at all but the most insignificant ports of call. And she knew from school, and from TV, that all over the country people were now scrupulously managing existing woodlots and steadily planting hardwoods bioengineered to grow rapidly, so that the ''renewable'' part of using wood as a renewable resource would be a fact and not just an idea.

''Tote dat barge,'' said a man watching the line of woodcarriers climb the stage, dump their loads, and go back for more. ''Lif' dat bale.'' He said this to nobody in particular, in a soft, ironic voice, and then, becoming aware of Pam, turned toward her. ''Just talkin' to myself,'' he told her in a friendly way, and when she smiled back, ''This scene's just like something out of the antebellum South. *People* hadn't done this kind of work for a long time, before the Hefn came—not in this country, anyhow. This is what you call slave labor.''

''How would a job like this get done, if people didn't do it?''

The man leaned his forearms on the railing and watched the moving line of men. ''By conveyor belt, probably. You reckon it's a coincidence, most of these fellows bein' black?'' He was about Pam's father's age, late thirties, and wore a dark blue business suit and a straw hat with a narrow brim. He threw her a sideways glance. ''You're probably too young to remember what things were like before.''

Pam leaned beside him at the railing, feeling shy. ''I don't remember too much, but my parents go on about it all the time.''

The man nodded. Liam, who had been talking to the chief engineer, silently came up and leaned beside Pam. Straw Hat gave him a nod; then a startled look came into his face as he took in the two of them standing side by side. ''He-e-e-y, don't I recognize you kids from somewhere? Haven't I seen you on TV or something?''

They had been afraid this might happen. Being famous was fun only when you wanted to be in the limelight; when you didn't want to be it was a bother. That nobody had appeared to recognize them on the train had given them a false sense of getting away with traveling in public; but of course the atmosphere aboard the steamboat was bound to be more relaxed, people were bound to look around more and notice more. The Apprentices grinned sheepishly at each other and Liam opened his mouth to confess; but just then a stir of interest among the other passengers on deck drew the attention of all three toward the wharf.

A Hefn was coming aboard the *Delta Queen*, trudging on his short hairy legs up the wide landing stage toward the tickettaker. Accompanying him was a small, official-looking group of humans. The people all around Pam and Liam murmured excitedly, some looking curious and some angry. Behind them an elderly woman said, in a deeply offended voice, "You don't mean to say that thing's taken passage on this boat!" Her middle-aged companion replied, "If it has, I'm getting off right now, Mother, and so are you!"

"That's Jeffrey," Liam said.

Pam stared, hard, down at the Hefn's face swathed in long gray hair that blended into a long gray beard, but she could tell only that he wasn't Humphrey. No wonder that to the general public all the Hefn looked alike. "There's a *Hefn* called Jeffrey? An Observer?" Liam nodded. "Which one is he?"

"Water quality control, I'm pretty sure."

As the little group passed beneath them and disappeared, many of those who had observed the boarding crowded through the doors into the main lounge, aware that the Hefn and his party would have to come up the stairs and pass through the lounge to reach the staterooms.

"Have you ever met him?" Pam asked quietly. Liam shook his head. "You didn't *know* he'd be aboard, did you?" Another headshake. Pam jerked *her* head toward the lounge. "How about going in? Maybe we can find out what he's doing here."

Before Liam could reply, the man they had been speaking with before startled them by saying "You kids take my advice and keep as far away from that monstrosity as you can get!" His pleasant face had become red and furious, his voice so choked it was hard to understand him.

Pam stared, not knowing what to say. Liam touched her arm—"Come on"—and they backed away together along the deck toward the lounge door.

They had just reached it when the door swung inward and the Hefn stepped through. The two young people stopped abruptly; the Hefn, shorter even than Pam, halted too and looked up into their faces with no attempt to conterfeit surprise. "Hello, Pamela Pruitt. Hello, William O'Hara," he said in a gravelly voice. "I call this a pleasant coincidence."

Despite his words the alien's manner bespoke pleasure no more than it showed surprise. Stuck in the doorway behind this odd figure, the three men and one woman in his party peered over one another's shoulders as if trying to discover what obstruction the Hefn had regarded as important enough to leave them thus awkwardly situated. Pam could feel herself blushing and grinning, so deeply gratified by the cool greeting that she was too flustered to reply. *I'm exactly like some stupid puppy dog*, she raged inwardly, *just let a Hefn be a little bit nice to me, any old Hefn, and I go all to pieces with pride and joy*.

For Liam the situation was much less complicated. He smiled with complete friendliness. "Was it really a coincidence? When I saw you come aboard I thought maybe Humphrey had somehow set this up."

"No, not so. My trip is I think you would call it spur of the moment? Yes? My friends from the Water Bureau here," he said, moving away finally to let them through the door, "agreed that the time was ripe for inspecting the state of factory effluents along the Ohio, Mississippi, and Missouri Rivers, and also possibly the Cumberland and the Tennessee . . . and perhaps we will fit in the Kentucky River, if conditions are favorable. We considered commandeering a whole steamboat for ourselves, but I frankly saw no need. This is only a semi-official inspection. Justin, here," indicating one of his companions, "can drop his specimen bottles overboard as we cruise past the outflow pipes, and Karen and Carlos can analyze the water quite easily in a very small working space, using our portable lab. So here we are."

"Then you're Jeffrey," said Liam. "I thought you must be."

"You thought correctly. Allow me to introduce my assistants: Justin Smith . . . Karen Sorvig . . . Carlos Cooke . . . and Stanley Watanabe. My friends, here are two young Apprentices from my colleague Humphrey's special project, his little brainstorm might we say? The Bureau of Temporal Physics. Yes. Taking a brief vacation from their training."

The Apprentices and the Water Bureau people all shook hands. Pam was passionately interested to meet some adults, other than Liam's family and Terry Carpenter, who were on intimate terms with a Hefn. These four didn't seem especially friendly, unfortunately; but actually she was far more interested in the Hefn himself, who talked in Humphrey's style but somehow broadcast a quite different personality—more of a taskmaster, even less of a sense of humor, and disdainful beneath the courteous surface. She watched after him a bit yearningly as he led his party along the cabin deck to find the quarters they were to share.

Then she turned back to Liam, but he was looking past her. Following his gaze, she met the hard, accusing glare of the man who had quoted "Ol' Man River." He had been standing there the whole time, evidently; he realized now why they had looked familiar—and he didn't approve. "Let's go, Pam," Liam urged.

The man leaned back stiffly against the railing and crossed his arms. "It's the collaborators who won't be forgiven," he said in the same low, furious voice as before.

#Well, I'm certainly fascinated by all this. Like viewing a set of souvenir videos labeled *Hurt Hollow 1964* and *Delta Queen 2014*. Over and over your chapter keeps telling me: You Are Then and There—and because I *was*, my own feebler memories of those times are rekindled till it's hard to sleep for thinking about them. This traveling in time seems to be a cat that can be skinned in quite a variety of ways, no?

Brain awhirl with fresh images of Hurt Hollow, I'm off to Melbourne tomorrow—conference on Hot Spots, we're to be taken to a piece of Aboriginal holy ground in the Outback, all full of Songlines!—and I can't wait to find out if it's going to feel anything at all like being at the Hollow. And I can't *wait* to get back there again; but this is, no lie, the next best thing. I'm really, really glad you asked me to read this book.

Many bumhead suggestions of Hot Spot sites in Europe coming in to the Bureau since the piece in *Time*, most of them to do with leys. The serious ley hunters must have been driven to gibbering despair by all the crazies trying to make common cause with them. One great thing about numbers—either they are or they aren't. Either some beelines coincide with leys and some Hot Spots with ray centers or they don't. End of discussion. No arguments. (Just between us, *boy* do I hope at least some of the leys do match the beelines!) The equations are valid and important either way, but so much more useful and meaningful to us now if there's resonance between mathematically designated Holy Ground and humanity's traditional *sense* of holy places—lost, but why not regainable?

Do you catch yourself wondering what the local Indians used to think of Hurt Hollow? I do.

5

WHICH HAVE EYES, AND SEE NOT

—Jeremiah 5:21

Just before seven P.M., two crew members in tight white uniforms sprinted down the landing stage and across the wharf. The steamboat was tied up by cables to two giant cleats at opposite ends of the slip; the crewmen unfastened these and ran showily back up the stage, the cables were winched aboard, and the stage was hoisted by its derrick so that the boat was no longer connected to the shore. At precisely seven P.M., calliope playing furiously, flags flying, bell ringing, whistle tooting, the *Delta Queen* backed into the river, "straightened out," swung her stage forward on its boom and raised it to a rakish angle, like a broad bowsprit, reversed her great red paddle wheel, and began to move ponderously downstream. At that moment the low sun gleamed out from behind a bank of clouds; instantly the whole brown face of the river was a mirror on which the boat's vivid reflection was borne along. Her gilt and brass flashed out and her white surfaces shifted from merely bright to dazzling.

Like nearly everyone else aboard, Pam and Liam were on deck to watch and wave to the people on shore who had come down to see the departure, and those on the bridges they passed under. There was no doubt everybody enjoyed watching the steamboats go by. And the *Delta Queen* was special; people knew about the sturdy antique and cheered as she steamed beneath or past them. For fifteen minutes after casting off, the calliope piped out steamboating tunes like "Cruising Down the River," "Steamboat A-Comin'," "Dixie," "Beautiful Ohio," "The Boatman Song," and "The Glendy Burk." All this spectacle cost nothing and produced an innocent, anachronistic sort of pleasure for everyone. It was exactly the kind of thing the Hefn liked to encourage.

Waving and smiling at the people on shore, Pam looked around for Jeffrey and his colleagues, but they were either on the larboard side of the boat or tucked up in their stateroom doing whatever they had to do to set up the water-quality experiments. She didn't see the man in the straw hat either. The old lady and her daughter hadn't gotten off after all, but stood together waving and laughing at the railing of the cabin deck—one deck down from Pam and Liam, whose stateroom was on the sun deck where all the tiniest cabins were. Near the two women, one of the cables that had secured the boat lay in a coil three feet across, dripping water onto the foredeck.

As Pittsburgh fell behind, the calliope player stopped playing and the passengers began to drift toward the Texas lounge and the refectory. In the now-failing light, the *Delta Queen* chugged beneath the last bridge in the city and headed down the channel. For a little while longer Pam and Liam lingered on the sun deck below the pilot house, watching the bluffs of the river lose their civilized character and become wilder, the dense trees shaggy and rumpled-looking with new foliage still lush and full, as yet neither tattered by insects nor dusty with greenhouse drought. The date was May 11. A week earlier the leaves had still been growing and patchy, and it would have been possible to spot the scattered houses built on the bluffs. Now, except where a light gleamed out from a window, they were invisible.

"It's almost dark. Let's go get some dinner," said Liam. "We can come back later."

Pam looked up. Above her head was the pilot house, blocky and dark against the evening sky. There was no light and no one to be seen up there. At night, of course, it would be impossible to see *out* if there were a light inside; but even by day you could never catch a glimpse of the pilots on watch. They stood too far back from the window to be visible, even to people standing on the sun deck, just below them. It looked like nobody was steering; but the boat moved deliberately onward in its course, and the kids went below secure in the sense that somebody, invisible but capable, was in charge of their passage.

In Mark Twain's time, a river pilot had to memorize not only the towns, but the location and shape of every snag, rock, bar, shoal, island, point, reef, bend, sunken wreck, pile of lumber, and dead one-limbed cottonwood tree in twelve hundred miles of river, going both directions—and then memorize them all over again on every trip up or down the constantly changing Mississippi. It was a prodigious feat, one that set the pilots above even the captains as aristocracy of the river.

But even by the time of Twain's death, this was no longer true. Electricity had lighted the banks and equipped steamboats with floodlights, so the pilots no longer had to be able to take a boat through a pitch-black night on memory alone. The channel was charted and buoyed, so that even in a fog the pilot's memory had the charts to help it. Later came revetment of the banks with rocks, concrete, and blacktop, mile markers, depth sounders (replacing the lead lines), locks to control water depth, and radar.

Whatever security the pilots gained with each of these improvements, they lost glory and glamour to that same degree. A god does not need radar or floodlights in order to steer in the dark.

But then as now, to get a first-class pilot's license for any particular stretch of river it was necessary to be able to draw the shape of the river on graph paper, putting in the buoys, pipelines, cable crossings, "dikes," revetments, bridges (with the height, name, and width between piers), tributary streams, shapes and names of the mile markers ("Smoke Bend Light," "Punkin Pizette"), names of the bends, bridges, dams, towns . . . no minor feat, if less impressive than the early pilots who navigated, not just by memory, but by intuition and ESP. For radar and depth sounders are but aids to navigation, and they can fail. They were never a substitute for personal knowledge of the river—or, put another way, a substitute for a personal bond between the river and the pilot.

There were plenty of eager applicants for this newly recreated profession, especially from the towns along the rivers. More than one of Pam's acquaintances at school in Scofield and Madison talked about wanting to become steamboat pilots, boys and girls both—just as they had (not the girls, of course) when Mark Twain was a boy in Hannibal, Missouri.

Pam woke in her upper berth the next morning to find the light seeping through slits in the louvered shutters covering the stateroom window. She had worn her watch to bed; it was 7:13 A.M. Wriggling out of her sheet sleeping bag, she eased herself down the ladder as quietly as she could, carrying her clothes. Liam was still sound asleep facing the wall, a lumpish blanket-covered shape in the dark space between the bunks. Pam changed out of

85

her rumpled pajamas in the bathroom, took up her field glasses, a book, and her computer NotePad, and let herself carefully out the door.

The refectory was nearly empty. Pam carried her breakfast tray to a table by a window, so she could look up occasionally from *The Wind in the Willows* to scan the passing scene. She was peering through the field glasses at a towboat built like a lopsided four-decker wedding cake, with *Ann Miller* painted on it, pushing a string of loaded barges upstream against the current, when a voice said, "Mind if I join you?"

A woman in a white lab coat—Karen Somebody, the one traveling with the Hefn Jeffrey—was standing by the table holding a tray. "Oh, sure," said Pam, not altogether pleased, for she had been enjoying herself. The woman set her bowl of oatmeal, a pitcher of milk, and a shiny yellow apple on the table one at a time, added her tray to a nearby stack, and sat down on the opposite bench.

Pam spooned up some of her own oatmeal, ducking her head, unsure how to talk to this person. But the woman seemed much friendlier than she had the day before. She smiled at Pam. "Where's your chum? Still sleeping?"

"Um-hm."

"So's the rest of my group—not Jeffrey, of course, but he always brings his own food. I left him enjoying a bag of *raw* oats in the stateroom." She gave Pam a smile that said *You, a fellow insider, know how the Hefn are,* and this time Pam smiled back. "My name's Karen Sorvig, by the way—I know Jeffrey introduced us yesterday, but you probably didn't catch all our names."

"I remembered the Karen part."

"You're heading home to visit your family, am I right?" Pam nodded. "And you're from where, exactly?"

"Scofield, Indiana. My father's head librarian at a college there. It's right on the river—not the town, but the college. You can see the cupolas on a few of the buildings from the water if you look hard."

"Fifteen miles or so this side of Marble Hill?" Pam nodded. "I remember Scofield. Actually, there's a factory in Madison we'll be checking up on tomorrow. I probably shouldn't tell you which one . . . but there's only one factory in town that puts water back in the river, so you can probably guess."

Pam was mortified to realize she had no idea what Karen was talking about. Was there a factory right on the river? That Japanese company, that made computer components—where was that? She gave an embarrassed laugh. "I don't guess I can. I never thought much about factories when I lived there."

Karen chuckled tolerantly. "Oh, kids have better things to do." She had been stirring molasses and raisins into her oatmeal while chatting with Pam; now she poured on some milk and began to eat. "If they can provide fresh milk, why can't they provide eggs, do you suppose? They must keep chickens as well as cows along the upper river here. Oatmeal was never one of my very favorite things in the world, other than in the form of cookies."

"Yeah, mine either. I'd rather have muffins or biscuits or something, even toast. I don't know why they haven't got any, unless it's just that baking's more bother."

"Humph. Even if nobody was selling baked goods at any of the landings this morning—which I very much doubt—they certainly ought to have had anything you can think of in Wheeling—we could have stocked up before we left Pittsburgh."

Despite the line of conversation, Karen was eating steadily. Realizing the woman was probably in a hurry to get finished and get to work, Pam screwed up her courage and said, "Excuse me if everybody asks you this, but what's it like, working with Jeffrey?"

Karen glanced up at Pam from beneath her eyebrows. "How d'you mean?"

"Well," said Pam, feeling awkward. "I'm very, very interested in the Hefn, but the only Hefn I know is Humphrey, so I was just wondering if . . ." She hesitated, not sure exactly what it was she wanted Karen to tell her.

"If all the Hefn are the same, you mean? Or if I *like* associating with Jeffrey?" Pam nodded, though neither question was precisely on target. "Let me ask you one," Karen countered. "What do you think about the Hefn presence on Earth?"

This was one question every Apprentice had to be prepared to answer. "Well, this might sound like a cop-out," Pam said readily, "but I don't feel like I can judge that. I've thought about it a lot, but I'm too close to it and getting too much benefit from it to be objective now. I'll have to decide about it someday, but as long as I'm an Apprentice I've decided to suspend judgment."

Karen nodded, accepting this. "Well, let me explain my own position. I'm known publicly as a Hefn-lover—I've already been called one this morning on my way to breakfast, as a matter of fact—and in the sense that foulmouthed bonehead meant it, it's true. I really believe the takeover, Directive and Broadcast and all, is best for the world. I wouldn't work for the Water Quality Bureau if I didn't believe that.'' She pushed her empty bowl away and bit into her apple, crunching thoughtfully for a moment. ''I support Jeffrey and am proud to be part of his staff, and proud of the work we do. We have an excellent working relationship; but if you asked me whether I find him good company, or am fond of him personally, I'd have to say—not really. At the personal level, I'm afraid he leaves me pretty cold.'' Seeing Pam's disappointed face, Karen said, ''I take it your feelings toward Humphrey are different.'' She took another bite of her apple.

Pam said, ''Um-hm. We all like him. Well, some more than others, but I don't think any of us would say he left us cold.''

''Maybe Humphrey has more personality than Jeffrey. If 'personality' is the word. 'More Hefnality,' would it be? Or maybe it's just me. One of my colleagues on this expedition, Justin Smith, gets much more pleasure than I do out of just hanging out with old Jeffrey.''

''Does *Jeffrey* enjoy that?''

Karen rolled her eyes. ''Who knows what Jeffrey enjoys? I doubt he enjoys the companionship of humans though. You know how he acted with you and your friend yesterday? Pleasant but chilly? You may have thought that was because he views the BTP as a madcap scheme of Humphrey's—he does, you know, like most of the other Observers—but he wasn't giving you two a special cold-shouldering. He treats us exactly the same way. It's just that Justin doesn't mind. Or maybe notice,'' she added thoughtfully. ''But why not ask him yourself? If you can separate him from his lab equipment long enough.''

''Well,'' Pam said, ''I guess I might do that, if you think he wouldn't mind.'' She hesitated before blurting, ''I guess I hadn't realized the other Hefn don't think much of the BTP.''

''Sorry to be the one to tell you,'' Karen said.

''Why don't they?''

She shook her head. ''Beats me. I don't know enough about what Humphrey expects to accomplish. Do you?''

Pam was mildly shocked to realize that she had no idea what, if anything, Humphrey expected to *accomplish* by training humans to operate the time transceivers.

After breakfast, belongings clutched in one arm, Pam climbed the steep metal stairs to the Texas Deck. Chairs and tables of cast iron, painted white, lined the deck on both sides of the boat; she found an empty one and sat down, piling the field glasses and NotePad and *The Wind in the Willows* on the table in front of her. The morning was hot and close, but Pam, in loose genie pants and tentlike T-shirt, and canvas shoes (which she removed), was mostly indifferent to the stifling effect of the water-laden air. This was the same tawny river that flowed past Hurt Hollow; she was going home. In just a few more days she would see Jesse again.

The kids had spent yesterday evening on deck, watching the lopsided gibbous moon, reflected in the black water, making a tapering, burnished track astern of them, the light shattered by the big wheel and winking in the boat's wake. There had been a breeze then. They hadn't talked much. The river had exerted its powerful effect on Pam, who'd spent most of the evening making up a poem in her head and watching the chimney swifts flutter and dart above the surface of the water.

Liam had seemed absorbed in his own thoughts. But their silence was comfortable and they both smiled often.

Now Pam set her NotePad in her lap, opened the cover, and typed out the poem she had composed:

Follow the River

I'll follow the river as far as I may
And never shall wonder why—
I'll follow as far as the farthest star
Where the water flows into the sky—
I'll follow the river wherever it goes
As it pushes down to the sea,
And the riffles and eddies that form as it flows
Will tell their secrets to me.

I'll know the ink-black river of night
When the moon, like a jewel rare,
And a million stars, in a shower of light,
All shine reflected there.
I'll know the river of power by day
When the shores go sliding by
And the shining blue of the water blends
With the polished blue of the sky.

O follow, come follow! the river sighs,
And I'll follow, bend after bend,

Till the valley flattens before my eyes
And I meet the sea at the end;
And there, where the river and ocean mix
In a swirl of spray and foam,
I'll turn at last on the way I've passed
And follow the river home.

The river is Life Itself that flows,
Each person a single drop;
And whither it goes the river knows,
And where it will have to stop.
The river's been here for many a year
And water goes by each day,
But every single drop in the world
Shall travel but once this way.

Pam read this over when she finished typing, mostly pleased but also a little dissatisfied. She liked the sound of the poem quite a lot—she could always make a poem sound musical, that was what she did best and enjoyed most about writing one—but apart from the music, something seemed to be lacking. What?

Slowly she read it through again, frowning with concentration.

Yes, definitely pleasing; but what *was* it then about the poem that made it feel so thin? A third reading, and then a fourth, failed to reveal the problem. Metrically there was certainly nothing wrong, nor was there anything wrong with the poem's musical embellishments. She named them over lovingly to herself: parallelism, alliteration, repetition, internal rhyme . . .

Then she had a kind of glimmering. The truth was, the lines had such a nice, swinging rhythm, it was hard to pay attention to the *words*. All the feeling—and therefore much of the meaning—was in the music. As a matter of fact, Pam realized she'd written ''Follow the River'' with only the tiniest part of her mind focused on meaning; she'd chosen particular words much less for their sense than for their sound—because they made the lines sound prettier. No wonder the poem didn't seem to mean much, in the ordinary sense of ''mean.''

Had Pam been writing about some other subject she probably would not have noticed the thinness—she never had before, though quick reflection told her that a lot of her poems shared this same imbalance between sound and sense. But the Ohio

River happened to be a subject she did have powerful feelings about, all tangled up as they were with her feelings about Jesse Kellum and Hurt Hollow. And the new poem struck her as only faintly touched by this power; even here, paddling along on board the *Delta Queen*, surrounded after long separation by the slapping, swirling, broad, mud-brown reality of the Ohio sliding between its rumpled blue-green bluffs, the poem she had written only *pretended* to be about the actual river.

What it was *really* about—she saw this now—was a certain poetic form, much loved of Kipling (who used it for "The Ballad of East and West" and "Tomlinson" and God only knew how many other poems), described as either tetrameter/trimeter or heptameter verse, in four- or eight-line stanzas, generally iambic but with grace-note dactyls and anapests plentifully thrown in, rhyming *abab* or *abcb*, and with a generous mixture of internal rhymes.

In other words, the poem was really about itself.

Resentment followed enlightenment; Pam sat back stiffly, making an exasperated noise through her nose. So her poems got "A" on music and "C" on meaning. Was that really so terrible? Was she obliged to feel bad about it? Could *that*—infuriating possibility—be why the Hefn had considered her writing no obstacle to their accepting her as an Apprentice?

Liam had come up onto the Texas Deck while she brooded and fumed, and now he ambled over and flopped down beside her, jarring the table. "Hi."

Jerked from her reverie, Pam stared at him blankly. "Hi. Did you get any breakfast?"

"Naaah. They're closed. I don't care, it's practically lunchtime anyway." He yawned, looked dubiously at Pam's NotePad. "What's that for? Not still diddling around with that stuff on Hubbard trees, I hope. We're supposed to be on vacation."

Pam didn't answer immediately. She scowled at Liam, making up her mind. Finally she said, "I've been fooling around with a poem."

"Yeah? What's it about?"

How naturally people asked: What's it about? Why did they never say: What form is this one in? You wouldn't ask a composer what his music was *about*, would you? Even if it was a song, with words; the words would just be there to carry the melody, they were never as important *It's about itself*, she felt like saying; but what she actually said was, "The river."

"Oh yeah?" As he spoke Liam yawned again, stretching himself into an X in his chair. "So how's it going? Any good?"

Pam glared very hard at Liam. Had he shown the slightest spark of genuine curiosity about the poem, or asked to see it, she would certainly have refused; but he looked so slack and sleepy and *uninvolved*, sitting there at the table in his sunglasses, that instead she abruptly told him, "You can read it if you want."

Liam took the open NotePad out of her hand and activated the screen. At once Pam's stomach clenched up; she almost snatched the poem back—but hung a bit too long between self-protection and desire. Before she could bring herself to act, the four stanzas had already scrolled through.

Finished, Liam looked up at Pam. "Hunh!" He blanked the screen and closed the cover, set the NotePad on the table, pulled off his dark glasses, folded his arms behind his head, and began to recite with gusto:

"The Colonel's son to the Fort has won, they bid him stay to
    eat—
Who rides at the tail of a Border thief, he sits not long at his
    meat.
He's up and away from Fort Bukloh as fast as he can fly,
Till he was aware of his father's mare in the gut of the Tongue
    of Jagai,
Till he was aware—"

If Liam had turned without warning into a magician in a spangled robe, with a long white beard like Gandalf's, Pam could not have been more shocked. For the seventeen seconds it took him to get that far, she sat rigid and speechless with astonishment. Then, clutching her hair with both hands, "Yes, yes, *yes*!" she screamed. "That's *it*! That's *right*! *That's right! Where—how—how did you know?*"

Along the decks of the *Delta Queen* people turned and craned to identify the cause of the commotion. It was Liam's turn to be astonished. "Hey, take it easy! Simmer down! Everybody's looking."

Pam ducked her head and flushed deeply; she loathed being at the center of attention. She sat stiffly and waited. After a minute, when people had stopped staring and gone on about their business, she pleaded again, more quietly, "How—did—you—*know*?"

"Carrie, that's how." Liam leaned back and gazed out over

the railing, toward where the shore was slipping leftward. "My cousin Carrie used to read poetry to us all the time when we were little—Kipling, Tennyson, stuff like that. Story poems. Jeff was the one that really loved them and kept asking for them, but we heard 'The Ballad of East and West' so many times we both memorized the whole thing. I forgot about that, that time we were talking about memorizing poetry. On the Metro, remember?"

Pam nodded; she remembered very well.

"I mean I'd literally forgotten. The memory was gone." Still gazing off toward shore, Liam said quietly, "I know Carrie told you about Jeff."

Pam nodded again. "Just a little." Shock had left her queasy; she wrapped her arms around her stomach and squeezed. "What do you mean, the memory was gone?"

Liam didn't answer right away. Finally he said, "Remember you asked me that night why my family thinks so much of Humphrey? Well, part of the answer is, he saved my life last year—but I don't want to talk about that right now. The other part is that he wiped my memories of Jeff. I was having a lot of trouble accepting Jeff's death, to put it mildly, and Humphrey offered to wipe just those memories, and then sort of leak them back to me a little at a time, in bearable doses, till I got the whole thing back and remembered all about it. I've been working with a counselor too. Julie. Humphrey retrieves something, then I talk it over with her. I've got quite a lot of it back now, but that night we're talking about, I still hadn't retrieved learning 'The Ballad of East and West.' But sometime between then and now I must've."

Everyone knew the Hefn could erase and retrieve memories; that was one means they had used to seize control of the world. Whatever it was that gave them memory control was the same power that had enabled them to sterilize the world's people through a television broadcast. When they set coordinates on the time transceivers they also drew upon this power. Pam accepted Liam's story at once; it seemed a lesser wonder than what had just happened to her—the thrilling, scary, electrifying shock of realizing this boy she thought she knew had correctly identified the musical pattern of her poem.

Liam picked up the NotePad and read "Follow the River" again. "I like it," he said, sounding pleasantly surprised. "It would make a good song. I don't know about that 'whither,' but on the whole—I might do a musical setting of it. Would that be okay with you?''

''That would be great,'' said Pam—of course! Liam was not only mathematical but musical, that explained why he had connected so quickly with the meter—''except I don't think it's really finished. There's something wrong with it still.''

''I don't think there's anything *wrong* with it, unless you just mean that it's not, you know, really about the river.''

Again Pam's stomach tensed defensively; she had only just succeeded in rejecting this idea. ''How do you mean?''

''I just mean it's not really about *this* river *as* a river. It's not, is it? Instead of mud and scum and floating sticks we get 'The river is Life Itself that flows . . .' *River*'s a metaphor, it stands for something else, right?''

Pam snapped, ''So what's wrong with that? What's wrong with making it a metaphor? Hey, what the Sam Hill makes *you* such an expert? Just because you can *quote* something!''

Liam gave her back the computer and put his sunglasses back on. ''You're the one that said there was something wrong with it, not me,'' he protested. ''I think it's fine the way it is, I was just trying to figure out why *you* thought there was something wrong.''

He was hurt! Pam looked with alarm at his stiff shoulders and straight mouth and mumbled, ''All right, okay. Sorry. I shouldn't have said that. Actually . . . I guess you're probably right. I was thinking before you came up that all the feeling's in the sound—which is probably just another way of saying what *you* just said. I guess I was just embarrassed.''

Liam grinned, at ease again. ''I know. It *is* embarrassing to be criticized. I get furious if people act like they don't think my music's completely perfect.''

''Do you do much composing?''

''Not a lot. More just recently. Mostly though I just fool around, playing. I like Scott Joplin a lot.''

The screen was still activated. Pam glanced briefly at the poem again and wrinkled her nose, forgetting to be self-conscious Pinny. ''This is definitely not completely perfect. You know what I think? I think without realizing it I've usually been imitating other *poems*, instead of focusing on the real thing, the thing in the world, that I'm supposed to be writing about. Other poems about rivers, or other poems in a certain kind of formal pattern—like 'The Ballad of East and West.' '' She flipped the cover up, depressed the scroll button and frowned down at the screen. "I wonder why I *do* that."

"You mean, like a computer artist generating a fractal forgery, instead of copying a real landscape directly?"

"Well . . . more like a painter copying a picture of a landscape. Only he's got his easel all set up on deck here and *he really thinks* he's painting the real river. He doesn't realize there's a picture of one in his head and he can't see past it to what's really there. You know something," she said. "I think that just about *always* happens when I try to write a poem. Like here: I didn't know it, but I couldn't even *see* the river that's right in front of my nose, because Kipling and Frost were getting in the way."

"Where's Frost?" Liam took the poem out of her lap and scanned it yet again.

"In the last stanza. The river as metaphor, like you said. A lot of Frost's poems wind up with a philosophical summary."

"Oh," said Liam. "Well, I still like it. Except maybe . . ."

Pam prompted him. "Maybe what?"

He looked up. "You won't get mad?"

Pam grimaced. "No, I promise. Not this time."

"Well," said Liam, "I mean—how old are you anyway? Fourteen? Well, don't you think the subject of Life Itself is maybe a little much for a fourteen-year-old to take on? Even a fourteen-year-old math prodigy, and everybody knows how superior *they* are." Pam grinned; Liam grinned back. "And besides that, when you get right down to it, I don't know that this is a very *original* observation. Kind of 'You only live once.' Pretty ho-hum, really, don't you think? You promised not to get mad."

Pam hunkered forward, very serious now. "I'm not mad. I'm not a bit mad. I just realized something. I'm not even *interested* in the river as a metaphor for life! I just thought I was *supposed* to write that way for some stupid reason; I thought—I just *assumed*—but you know what? What I'm really *interested* in is, one, the form, and two, the mud and scum and—what else did you say?—sticks, floating sticks!"

It felt like a momentous discovery. Her hands wrung together, her voice shook. "Maybe I should read less. My mother's always telling me I should."

"Well, you *could* try reading different things for a while, and work at being more observant. As a matter of fact," Liam said, sounding pleased with himself, "I've got a recommendation for you. Richard Wilbur. Late twentieth century. Carrie's crazy about him. Perfect form, *plus* lots of sticks and mud.''

"Thanks, but maybe I better not read *anything* till I get better at seeing what's really *there*, and writing it down. I mean, Kipling has mud too.''

"Mud, blood, carrion—'' Liam pulled his sunglasses off again, folded his arms behind his head, and began:

"They have ridden the low moon out of the sky, their hoofs drum up the dawn,
The dun he went like a wounded bull, but the mare like a new-roused fawn.''

Swept up by ecstasy as if by wings of light, Pam joined in. Voices rising, ignoring the turning heads, they chanted the galloping couplets in unison:

"The dun he fell at a water-course—in a woeful heap fell he,
And Kamal has turned the red mare back, and pulled the rider free.
He has knocked the pistol out of his hand—small room was there to strive,
' 'Twas only by favour of mine,' quoth he, 'ye rode so long alive:
'There was not a rock for twenty mile, there was not a clump of tree,
'But covered a man of my own men with his rifle cocked on his knee.
'If I had raised my bridle-hand, as I have held it low,
'The little jackals that flee so fast were feasting all in a row.
'If I had bowed my head on my breast, as I have held it high,
'The kite that whistles above us now were gorged till she could not fly—' ''

Liam: In 2014, did you know the BTP was "Humphrey's little brainstorm"; and did you have any idea what he was trying for?

Yes and no. I was aware that there wasn't much support for the BTP among the other Hefn. I guess I assumed Humphrey cared about people more than the others did (his bonding thing) and was teaching us how to contact the past as a gift. I *didn't* realize he had any larger purpose in mind, and didn't wonder about it any more than you, being almost as inwardly focused as you were back then for reasons of my own. I do have a vague recollection that the other guys speculated about it sometimes, especially Raghu. I think Raghu actually asked Humphrey about it once, but he can't have been told the truth.

#The parenthetical aside that "of course" girls didn't aspire to be steamboat pilots in Mark Twain's day sent me back to your cover letter. You feel there's something you're not seeing about yourself in this story—okay, but I'm not sure I'm completely clear about what it is you think you *do* see. The novel makes a big point of how nightmarish adolescence was for you as a girl, but it looks to me like you'd been thinking boys had it much, much better than girls long before that.

A question to ponder: Exactly when did your father start with the funny business? And are you sure that's all he did?

#Weird to have understood this only now. Before today I'd have sworn that when I started quoting the Kipling poem on the boat, it was *your* button that got keyed. Yet unconsciously I must have felt some barrier in me go down too, because right after your screeching fit (which I *do* remember! Mama mía!), there I was, telling you about Jeff—the first person not a Hefn or a shrink I'd ever talked to about him. Isn't it obvious that the poem-quoting must have breached my isolation, just as surely as it had breached yours?

Something *I* hadn't seen about *my*self, till today, and quite unsettling.

#By the way, as a direct experience of holy ground the Outback was a bust. At least for me it was. I think the country and culture may just be too different—I don't have any feeling for deserts. Edward Monte from New Mexico thinks he got something but I have to say I personally was deaf as a post to the holiness of the place we were taken to. Doesn't prove a thing, of course. We're calculating away out here and should have some hard results pretty soon.

6

BUT THE LORD SENT OUT A GREAT WIND . . . SO THAT THE SHIP WAS LIKE TO BE BROKEN

—Jonah 1:4

The weather continued sunny, humid, and hot. Few passengers lingered on deck, except when evening brought a breeze and a little relief. Early in the afternoon of the third day the sky became heavily overcast, and the air so thick and sultry it was hard to breathe. The captain had posted a notice that the Apprentices and members of the Water Quality Bureau were invited to his quarters after lunch. Jeffrey sent regrets, but the others were all there—Karen left her lab coat behind for the occasion and had brushed her blond curls into a nimbus around her face—and afterwards they spent a pleasant quarter of an hour in the moderately conditioned air of the pilot house. Pam kept a covetous eye on Justin Smith, but he darted out ahead of the others to get ready to run a test on a plant they were approaching.

When she and Liam had thanked the pilot on watch and come out into the hot, humid day, the river water had changed color from tawny to olive drab; and as the afternoon wore on, the dark sky gradually took on a queasy yellowish cast. Passengers boarding at Patriot, Indiana, reported that a tornado watch had been posted until midnight.

The *Delta Queen* continued downstream, occasionally hitting eleven miles an hour when there was a long enough stretch between stops, pulling in at landings on both sides of the river and extending her landing stage like a broad tongue sideways to the shore to let people on and off, load fuel and provisions, load and unload mail.

Despite the heat, Pam and Liam stayed on deck and watched the action. Pam saw a crate of eggs come aboard at Rabbit Hash, Kentucky, and smiled to think of Karen's pleasure when she found them scrambled in the steam tray tomorrow morning. Once she caught a glimpse below of Justin with several stoppered bottles tied to strings, hurrying along the cabin deck. Jeffrey she saw not at all.

Below Cincinnati the bluffs widened until they were sometimes a mile or more apart, with the narrower river hugging first one bluff, then the other, showing how its channel had snaked and wandered during the millennia it had taken to grind through soil and sediments to its present level. Between the water and the distant bluffs lay the flat, rich bottomland, flooded nearly every spring, already plowed and sown, where row upon row of young corn would stand by the time they made the return trip upriver.

At every approach and every departure, from the larger towns to the humblest landing, the whistle blew a salute of one long hoot and two short ones, and the steam calliope player tootled through his repertoire. Pam began to be a little tired of "Beautiful Ohio," but some of the livelier tunes—like "Dixie"—might well have been composed specifically for the calliope.

The Apprentices were recognized by three little girls who hung near their table on the Texas Deck for a while, giggling and whispering, before the oldest came up to get their autographs. Probably there would have been more of that sort of thing, if the weather hadn't kept people indoors.

The three girls and their mother got off at Warsaw, Kentucky, where the boat was tied up an unusually long time before calling at Florence, directly across the river in Indiana. By the time the *Delta Queen* left Florence, the wind was turning up the pale undersides of the maple leaves and blowing up whitecaps on the water, and there was a continuous distant rumbling of thunder. At six-thirty, as Pam and Liam were finishing their dinner, a crew member came into the refectory to announce that the captain had just given the order to "choke a stump"—tie up to a tree—until the approaching thunderstorm had passed. This would not significantly delay their arrival the next morning in Madison, since they would soon have tied up for the night in any case, owing to the fact that boats were never put through the McAlpin Lock by night, even in fine weather. As an afterthought the crewman mentioned that the tornado watch had been changed to an alert, and that a small twister had been sighted on the ground between the Indiana towns of Friendship and Farmer's Retreat, about twenty miles away.

Pam and Liam had barely made it back to their stateroom

when the storm struck the boat with a tropical cloudburst of rain. The thunder which had accompanied them all afternoon, now nearer, now farther away, began crashing down a split second after each lightning bolt. Their one small window faced upstream at an angle; through it they could see the bolts forking down through curtains of rain to strike the far shore, and then there would be an immediate crackle-*WHAM!* of tremendous intensity, followed by another just as great, and another, and another. The racket was so deafening that conversation was impossible.

Pam was scared. She had grown up in Tornado Alley; every spring and early summer of her life had been made anxious, and dangerous, by the threat of tornadoes made more frequent and more deadly in a single generation by the global warming trend. Nearly every year a tornado would strike somewhere not all that far from Scofield: over in Kentucky, nearby in Ohio, all over Indiana clear up to Chicago, and on into Michigan. Pam had never actually lived through a tornado herself, but the college had been devastated by one forty years before, and The Tornado had become part of Scofield folklore. Pam had seen the photographs of smashed buildings and snapped-off trees, and read the eyewitness accounts, as long as she could remember. Every structure on the campus had been damaged. The legs of the water tower had bent like an erector set, its tank narrowly missing several faculty homes as it smashed to the ground and split open, crushing the maintenance building, its tons of water sucked up and carried away by the funnel cloud. The graceful cupola atop Donder Hall had been lifted off and flung into the Quadrangle. The circuit-rider weathervane on the auditorium was found a mile away, on the fifty-yard line of the football field.

Many people in Scofield and Madison, children at the time of the tornado, remembered vividly what they had been doing when it struck and what the experience had been like. Pam's sixth-grade English teacher, Mrs. Hopkins, had terrified three generations of schoolchildren with stories about being trapped all alone in the basement of her flattened house for six hours before rescue workers had freed her.

Of course, on the campus it was mainly stressed, first, that providentially not a single person had been seriously injured, let alone killed; and second, that the college community had responded to the challenge of wholesale destruction by bounding back with phenomenal determination and courage. Alumni contributed with both hands to the cleanup and reconstruction projects. The place had risen again from the rubble, better than ever.

During a lull in the downpour Pam tried to tell Liam something about the Scofield Tornado. They were sitting side by side in their raincoats on Liam's lower bunk, which was wider than Pam's upper one. She was describing what had happened to her own house (long before her family lived in it, of course) when a sudden clatter drowned her out.

"Wow," yelled Liam, jumping up and running to the window. "Is that hail?" He pulled the door open a crack, stooped over, and turned to show Pam a handful of ice balls half an inch in diameter. "Wow, if this stuff fell on you, you'd *know* it!"

His cheerfulness and excitement infuriated Pam. "This isn't the evening's planned entertainment, *peabrain*! Big hail is one of the things that usually comes with tornadoes!"

There was a pause. "Well," Liam said reasonably, "there isn't anything we can do about it anyway, so we might as well enjoy it as much as we can."

"Enjoy it!" *You couldn't do anything about Jeff getting killed either; did you try to enjoy that too?* The realization of how close she had come to saying this frightened Pam so badly it blanked out both her outrage and, for the moment, her terror of the storm.

"Tell you what," said Liam after a moment during which Pam stared into her lap, face burning. "I'll run down to the refectory and see if I can get us something to drink—a pitcher of cider or something."

"The refectory's closed."

"Well—the bar, then. The Texas Lounge. They've got stuff besides booze in there. I'll go see what I can find, okay?"

"Okay," said Pam faintly. When he had fastened up his slicker and dodged out the door, she got up, took off her own raincoat and hung it on a peg, and then went and splashed water on her face in the bathroom. In the little mirror above the basin she stared aghast at her flushed face. Even if Liam had been insensitive—though he was probably just covering up his own nervousness with bravado—to have said what she almost said would have been truly and permanently unforgivable. "What's wrong with me?" she asked her own scared-rabbit face. The impulse to say it had been totally unchristian. She was appalled at herself.

Then Liam burst back through the door and slammed it behind him, showering rainwater all over his bed. "Listen, there's trouble! I was in the Texas Lounge just now, waiting to ask the bartender for some cider. There are some guys in there, drinking and talking about the Hefn. They were talking pretty loud." His words tumbled out so fast Pam could barely follow. "One of 'em was saying he had a pretty good life before the Hefn came. He was a coal miner from West Virginia, doing pretty well, but then his wife left him because they couldn't have kids, and he lost his job because of the moratorium on coal, and the economy of the mining towns went bust, and he had to sell his house for almost nothing, and his whole life was ruined because of the Hefn. And another guy said, 'Man, you think you got it bad, my brother lost his business *and* ten years out of his memory for doing something the Hefn didn't like, and his wife up and left him because she thought the Hefn were right!" Another guy asked him what his brother did and this guy says it was something to do with agricultural chemicals—he was making stuff to kill some bug that eats corn and selling it to local farmers. He got caught. In the old days he'd have been fined or something for breaking the law, but the Hefn wiped his *mind.*"

The news wiped Pam's former train of thought out of her own mind. "Did they recognize *you*?"

"No, I started edging out of there once I got the drift of the conversation. But I was just outside the door when they started talking about Jeffrey."

"What'd they say?"

"The one who used to be a coal miner said there was one of the hairy little varmints on board this boat, and he'd sure like to teach him a lesson. And then another man started talking, and as soon as I heard his voice I realized he was the guy we talked to yesterday on deck."

"The one that said 'It's the collaborators who won't be forgiven'?"

"Yeah. Good thing he'd been sitting with his back to me. He didn't sound as drunk as the other three. He told them he knew which stateroom Jeffrey's staying in, and he'd be glad to show them."

"What?"

"Yeah. One of them said what about all those other people he's traveling with, and another one said besides, the Hefn can read minds, if we threw him over the railing they'd find out we did it. But the guy from yesterday said, 'Not if they think it's an accident.' Then they started talking in lower voices and I scrammed out of there. I think we should tell the captain.''

The violence of the storm had abated a little, but rain still fell in solid sheets as they struggled along the Hurricane Deck toward the end where the officers' quarters were. The two Apprentices were the only ones abroad in the weather. They found the captain's cabin with no difficulty—they had been there as guests that very afternoon—but no one answered their knock and they stood hunched in the downpour, trying to decide what to try next.

"Maybe we should warn Jeffrey himself," Pam shouted.

"I don't know which stateroom's his, do you?"

"No, but it's one of the big ones on the cabin deck, the Water Bureau people are all in together. We could just knock on doors till we find the right one.''

They hurried down two ladder-like flights of stairs and along the cabin deck to the door of the main lounge. They entered gasping out of the storm—and there was the captain, seated in an armchair in the center of a group of passengers who had drawn their chairs into a cluster around him. He was talking in a reassuring way, and the group was calm. "Should we tell him?" Pam asked Liam.

He hesitated. "Not the best circumstances. Let's see if we can find Jeffrey first. We can always come back here.''

The large multi-bedded staterooms had once been first-class quarters, with doors into a central lounge area that connected with the main lounge where the captain was holding court. Liam worked his way along one side of the row of staterooms and Pam along the other. It was disagreeable work. Some people were already in bed and unhappy about being dragged out. Some doors refused to open, even to repeated knocks; either nobody was in or they chose not to be disturbed. No one seemed to know which room was being occupied by the Water Bureau personnel. Pam disliked what she was doing so much that she was ready to go back and rudely disturb the captain when Liam flew across and grabbed her wrist. "They just went through the main lounge and out the door. Come on.''

They barged through the swinging doors into the forward cabin lounge and out onto the deck. It was still pouring, but the thunder and lightning were much farther away, and it felt as if the worst of the storm had passed.

Which way? Liam hesitated, then hurried aft. Pam grabbed his arm. "Let's split up and each of us go opposite directions around the deck—that way, if they're here, we can't miss them," she panted.

"Nothing doing. These aren't nice guys. We stay together."

Together, trying to be fast but stealthy, they circled the whole circumference of the cabin deck. Neither Jeffrey nor the men Liam had seen leaving the lounge were anywhere in sight. Neither was anyone else.

"Up or down?" Pam puffed when they arrived back at the doors to the lounge.

"Up, I guess." So up the slippery stairway they climbed, Liam in the lead. He poked his head cautiously up at the top, but the Texas Deck seemed deserted too, and followed by Pam he slipped aft along the row of staterooms toward the stern of the *Delta Queen*, keeping tight to the side of the boat.

And there in the stern, leaning against the railing, stood the small, obscure, solitary figure of the Hefn Jeffrey, wearing nothing but his own plastered and streaming gray pelt, gazing out across the river or perhaps down upon the motionless paddle wheel. He seemed to take no notice, standing there, of the rain that had sleeked him down and made him look so pathetic and small, at least from the rear. "Drowned rat" might have been a metaphor invented for the purpose of describing a wet Hefn.

He gave no sign of being aware of them. Liam hung back, uncertain; still less than the captain's sociability did Jeffrey's meditative isolation invite disturbance, and the men were still not in evidence.

Or were they? While the Apprentices hung fire, pressed up against the larboard side of the boat and sheltered from the rain by the floor of the hurricane deck above, there came a muffled scuffling and several bulky shapes lunged toward Jeffrey from the starboard side. There were stairs on that side too. If Pam and Liam had taken those, or begun their circuit of the deck by heading forward, they would have seen the men in time to raise the alarm; now they stared in panic for an instant before Liam took off, sprinting down the slippery deck and flinging himself down the stairs, obviously going for help.

The rain chose that moment to become heavy again. Between the darkness and the downpour it was impossible for Pam to see what the men were doing to Jeffrey. No voices, human or Hefn, carried above the pelting rain. She found herself running as fast as possible toward the other end of the boat; a picture of the bell had flashed into her mind, the bell hung in a frame right on the deck, that was rung by a rope every time the boat cast off. Was the bell on this deck or the one below? She couldn't remember and she couldn't see. *Help me, help me, Father,* she prayed, and flashed past the stairs—and as she went by the boat suddenly lurched, almost sending her headlong down them anyway. A moment later Pam had reached the bell and was dragging on the rope, making a clang, erratic but emphatic, that sounded peremptory even above the rainstorm.

Pam stopped ringing only when she saw the lights pouring through the doors. Then fast as she could, she raced back to the other end of the boat, dodging between people and pushing when things got crowded.

Between the crowding and the rain and darkness, it was impossible to tell what was going on, except that Jeffrey was all right. When several muscular members of the crew had collared the miscreants and taken them away, Jeffrey was left standing there by himself in a little circle of clear space, looking much as before. For ten minutes or so there was minor pandemonium, everyone asking what had happened and nobody able to say. Pam couldn't find Liam in the melee. Then the boat's public address system came on, along with the exterior lights that until then had been turned off, and the first mate made an announcement: The Hefn Jeffrey, alone on deck, had been assaulted by three men. The men were in custody and Jeffrey was fine. Everybody should go back to what they had been doing when the bell sounded; they would hear the whole story in the morning.

Pam couldn't find Liam in the throng. She glanced down at the paddle wheel, still now, its brightly painted paddles dark as blood in the gloom, and decided to do as the first mate suggested. The little stateroom was still empty when she got there, but she'd been waiting only a couple of minutes before Liam came in, so wound up with excitement he couldn't sit still. Pam, who had been feeling a letdown after the rescue attempt, got fired up again by Liam's electric tension and listened raptly to the story he told.

Disappointingly, Pam's bell-ringing hadn't roused the crew; the boat's lurching had done that. When Liam burst through the lounge door, the captain had been in the act of bursting through in the other direction, heading for the engine room. Liam had to grab him and shout above the thrumming of the rain to get him to abandon that goal and head instead for the stairs and the stern of the Texas Deck. As they ran, stateroom doors were opening and people were peering out to see what the commotion was about.

They had come up to the Texas while Pam was still ringing the bell, and were the first people to arrive on the scene. There they found Jeffrey standing calmly in the rain, his back now to the railing, commanding his assailants in a voice that carried perfectly above the racket. "They were pussycats. They stood there with their heads hanging, soaked to the skin, just like great big kids being scolded. One of them was holding a trench coat. When the crew members ran up and the captain told them to grab the three guys, and started marching them away, I heard one of them say to the mate who had his arm twisted behind his back, 'Let go of me, God damn you—what are you trying to do, prove you can break my arm off? That hairy little bastard is stronger than five of you musclebound jerks put together.' Or something like that.''

"Did you hear what Jeffrey said to them?''

"Not the words, except just as we got there he was saying''— Liam lowered his voice to a growl—'' 'Had there been many, many more of you, still you could not have harmed me.' ''

"So what actually happened? What was that lurch? I almost went down the stairs on my head!''

"I don't know. We'll probably have to wait till morning to find out, like everybody else.''

Too excited to sleep, they stayed up talking till after one A.M.; but finally Pam went into the bathroom to brush her teeth and put on her pajamas. When she came out, Liam had fallen asleep in his clothes. She killed the light and climbed into her bunk, still wide awake.

Then abruptly it was broad daylight, and Liam was gone. Outside the window the shoreline was flowing past again; they had cast off and were under power. Pam rolled out at once, dressed quickly, and rushed out, barely noticing in her haste that the storm had passed, leaving behind a bright cool day without the least hint of tornado threat.

Liam was sitting in the refectory at a table by the window, eating scrambled eggs and pancakes with apple-raisin compote. From him she learned the rest of the story:

While the men in the Texas Lounge were trying to think of a way of getting at Jeffrey, one of them sitting facing the door had seen him come into the cabin lounge, pass through it, and go out on deck. Though still without a plan, they immediately got up and followed. On deck, one of the men suggested that the other three go after Jeffrey, throw something over his head so he couldn't see or speak, and pitch him overboard. The object would be to make it look like he had accidentally fallen in and drowned.

In order to achieve this, the fourth man would himself go to the engine room while the others were stalking Jeffrey and figure out some way to make the paddle wheel turn for a second; this would drive the boat against the bank, an action which might very plausibly knock anyone standing at the railing overboard. He would give them ten minutes or so, then signal the others when he was about to start the wheel. The plan depended heavily on luck—Jeffrey's remaining on deck alone long enough to be caught, nobody else being around to see them, the fourth man's being able to bribe or distract the engineers on watch—but they were drunk enough to think it worth a try. All of them believed the hearsay story that the Hefn were unable to swim.

Events favored the plan. Not only did Jeffrey remain alone, he even positioned himself in the perfect place, in the stern of the Texas deck, directly above the wheel. Not another soul was on deck in the drenching downpour. In the engine room, the fourth man had been delighted to find only a single engineer on duty, seeing to it that the boilers stayed fired up enough to run the galley and the interior lights. He was bored, and quite willing to explain the machinery to his visitor. The interloper had showed much interest in the boilers and pestered the engineer with questions until he understood which lever closed the switch to start the paddle wheel; then he had keyed a signal on his pocket communicator and an instant later activated the wheel, which had begun to turn. Since the boat was tied up, that quarter-turn of power had driven them against the shore; that was the lurch they had all felt.

The men had intended to heave Jeffrey overboard onto the wheel, to be crushed or drowned. One of them was wearing a trench coat; he took it off, and at the signal they had all rushed Jeffrey and thrown the trench coat over his head. Then, as the boat plowed into the shore, they attempted to pitch him over the railing onto the blades of the paddle wheel; but they had not reckoned on his phenomenal strength. Even taken by surprise, Jeffrey had apparently been more than a match for the three of them, and of course, as soon as he had fought off the initial rush, he had had no problem swiftly taming them by means of the legendary Hefn "power of suggestion."

"So *we* didn't rescue him. We weren't really any help," Pam said, disappointed. What had thrilled her most about the events of the previous night was the odd sense of having acted out her fantasy, of saving Jeffrey's life as Pinny had saved Comfrey's, and all without conscious thought or planning.

"Nope, we didn't save him." Liam was quiet then, staring at his empty plate; and Pam, by a momentary grace of intuition, knew exactly what he was thinking: *I didn't help save this Jeffrey's life, any more than I helped save the other one's.*

Hefn "justice" was swift. The four men were put off at Markland, Indiana, where the boat went through the McAlpin lock just thirty-three miles above Scofield Beach. While yoked teams of oxen walked round and round the huge pulley that closed the gates behind them, allowing the lock to leak water until the level inside was as low as the level beyond, Liam and Pam watched the men be marched away and loaded into a paddy wagon that had driven out from Madison to meet the *Delta Queen.* Among them walked the man in the straw hat. Now that police cars, fire engines, and ambulances were almost the only vehicles still allowed to operate with internal combustion engines, a lot of people came on deck to watch the procession of uniformed officers and prisoners, some as interested in the car itself as in the arrest.

The lock was interesting too. Pam poked Liam: "Hey, see the big blind guy with short hair, helping the oxen turn the wheel?"

Liam stared, then looked at her like she was crazy. "What blind guy? What are you talking about?"

Pam sighed. "It was a joke. I meant Samson. You know, as in Samson and Delilah?"

"Samson and who?"

"Forget it."

The boat stopped at Ghent, Vevay, Carrollton, and Brooksburg, and everybody who got on wanted to know about the assault on Jeffrey; the boat buzzed with the story. They arrived in Madison at 1:17 P.M., and the *Delta Queen* dropped its landing stage onto the sand at Scofield Beach at 2:21. Pam's parents were both there at the foot of the stage to pick them up, with one of the college's solar taxis. As soon as Pam had stepped off, hugged her mother, pecked her father's cheek, and introduced Liam, her mother said animatedly—and somehow disapprovingly—"You've been having quite a trip, I hear!"

"You heard about it already?"

"There's not another thing on the news today."

Her father said, "They're making a big to-do about it because this is the first time anybody has actually assaulted a Hefn. They

109

want to be sure everybody knows what happened to the guys who did it.''

"What *happened*? You mean they've already sentenced them?'' Liam asked.

"Sentenced and passed sentence,'' Pam's father replied. "All their minds wiped to age three. They're showing them on TV, humiliating them in public. It's a very peculiar sight, very peculiar, to see four grown men talking and whimpering like little children—and a couple of those men have children of their own!''

Pam and Liam exchanged unhappy glances. Pam's mother said, "I don't approve of them trying to kill that Hefn, that Jeffrey, but I don't think it's right to shame those men like that either. Honey, are you real sure we're doing the right thing, letting you go off and work with creatures that would do that kind of a thing to people?''

"They're just doing what they said they'd do, Mom, it's not like those guys weren't warned. And they were drunk as four skunks, too,'' she added, knowing this would carry weight with her mother. But she was far from easy in her own mind, and from the look of him Liam wasn't thrilled about it either. She wished the whole thing hadn't happened.

Her father had tossed the luggage in the trunk and now turned to the others. "Pile in, and let's get on home. Plenty of time to talk about it later, Frances, these kids'll be around for quite a spell.''

Pam climbed into the back seat ahead of Liam, leaned back, and closed her eyes. She saw a picture: the dark night, the lashing storm, a rain-sleeked Jeffrey leaning small and solitary against the railing of the steamboat, unaware that three assailants were creeping up behind him. He hadn't heard or otherwise sensed them. He had fought off the attack because one Hefn was physically stronger than three men, and armed with mind control besides; but if there had been enough of them, instead of only three to one . . .

The newscasters that evening avoided this train of thought, but privately it was mentioned again and again. The lesson of the affair, ultimately lost on nobody, was that a stronger attack— by a dozen football players, say—might have had a very different outcome, and that a Hefn with a trenchcoat over his head, gagged and blinded, prevented from speaking or making eye contact, is no more masterful than a human being in a similar fix would be.

#*I* know what made you almost say that about Jeff: an impulse to put the barriers back up. Having one's isolation breached is thrilling but threatening; those walls are there for a reason. I understand perfectly.

#"Paddles dark as blood," eh? Very atmospheric.

So much has been written about the *Delta Queen* Incident, it was fun to read this kid's-eye, participant-observer view of it all. Exciting, too. Funnily enough I'd forgotten a lot of what it felt like. This brings it all back.

#You were right, that's exactly what I was thinking. I don't recall words, but I do clearly remember sitting there feeling sad and helpless because, like this one, the other Jeffrey had been beyond any saving by me.

It's taking more out of me than I expected to go back into these events and times. I keep being surprised to find how much of the emotional stuff I'd blocked out. But I did enjoy this chapter. In a sense, I guess you could say the whole story is foreshadowed right here.

7

TRAIN UP A CHILD
—Proverbs 22:6

The night before they were supposed to leave on their canoe trip, Pam and Liam watched the Hubbell film together. When it was over Liam said thoughtfully, "I think Humphrey should see this."

"What for?"

"Just a hunch. I think it would interest him a whole lot."

"A documentary made in 1977?" Pam was skeptical. "As you'll see tomorrow, things have changed since this was made. There's a locked chain-link fence around the whole property, sixty-one acres—Jesse had to have it put in because of vandalism, and I think because of the insurance company too. Orrin and Hannah never had trouble with vandals in thirty-five years, I doubt the thought of insurance ever crossed either of their minds. Hurt Hollow, the place, still looks pretty much like it did back then, but the area all around there has been completely built up—the Hollow is an oasis now in the middle of the suburban sprawl. Jesse lives inside the fence like a museum caretaker, or like he's in a fort." Pam sat up and said intensely, "This just isn't the answer to anything anymore—there aren't any Hurt Hollows left!"

"I didn't say there were, I just said Humphrey would be interested in this. What are you carrying on about?"

Pam wondered about that herself. In *Pinny's Hefn* she had, after all, arranged things so that the Hefn Comfrey had been assigned as a secret observer to Hurt Hollow. In the novel, she had fixed it so that Comfrey, with help from Joshua/Jesse and Pinny/Pam, had devised a way to save the world. Yet it made Pam uncomfortable to hear Liam suggest that Humphrey, a real Hefn, might be interested in Hurt Hollow. These two loves, effortlessly combined in fiction, suddenly seemed impossible to put together in real life; the very idea felt disagreeable. Humphrey was wonderful and desirable in one way, the Hollow in a completely different way. Pam didn't want the wonderfulness of either compromised; and right then it felt to her as if, by being juxtaposed, they might be.

Pinny's Hefn had been written from start to finish before Pam had gotten to know Humphrey "as a person" at all. During the selection process for the BTP she'd actually only met him for about five minutes. Humans had done most of the interviewing; Humphrey had only come in long enough to "interview" the candidates' brain waves.

No, the two wonders had to be kept separate. They shouldn't be muddled up with each other; that wasn't what Pam wanted at all.

The next day, a Saturday, Pam woke up to discover that her period had started.

She had known, of course, that this was imminent—all the signs had been there—but the cursed thing was so wildly irregular! For all the intricate mathematical calculations she knew how to make, Pam could never predict the day of her period's arrival; the sudden smear of blood in her pajamas or underpants still came as a semi-surprise.

Disappointment took the form of rage. Pam sat on the toilet and fumed with frustration and a sense of injustice. Now she would have to wait two days, till the stage of cramps and heavy flow was over, to see Jesse. Today's weather was close to perfect, but the short string of hot, bright days was due to break before Monday. She clomped down to breakfast in a horrible mood. When Liam greeted her cheerfully she snapped back, "We're not going."

"How come?"

"I'm sick, that's why not."

"You are? What's the matter?"

"I don't want to talk about it."

"Oh," he said. "Oh, I get it. Well, nuts. How come you didn't know that was going to happen? My sisters always do."

His quasi-accusing tone made Pam snarl, "Well, good for them. I *never* know, and I feel lousy, so don't give me a hard time."

Pam's mother came into the kitchen at that moment, a short, rather dumpy woman with a cloud of beautiful dark hair. "How many sandwiches can you eat, Liam? I'm going to start packing you kids a lunch.''

"We're not *going*," said Pam through clenched teeth. "I can't go today. We'll have to wait till Monday."

"You're not *going*? Why not?" And then, not waiting for a reply, *"Oh,"* Frances said, looking hard at her daughter and mingling surprise and comprehension in her tone. "Oh, no. Oh, isn't that too bad." She glanced uneasily at Liam, not quite sure what etiquette was appropriate to the occasion.

"He knows about it," Pam said glumly.

A little flustered, Frances remarked in a falsely bright voice, "Well, I guess I don't need to make you-all any sandwiches after all!"

"Should we let Jesse know we're not coming?" Liam wondered.

"We can't. He hasn't got a phone. That is, he's got one, but it only makes outgoing calls. The insurance company made him put one in, in case a goat butts one of the tourists or somebody drowns or something."

"He didn't want a phone at all, did he?" Frances put in, to let Liam know she knew something about the subject.

"Unh-unh."

"How come?" said Liam.

"It doesn't really fit in. He hasn't got electricity or plumbing either." Pam's voice became a little less crabby-sounding as she warmed to the subject of Jesse and Hurt Hollow. "He keeps the place pretty much like the Hubbells used to have it. It'll be easier to show you—"

"Liam, can I get you anything?" her mother interrupted. "We've got some apple coffee cake, granola, yogurt . . . let's see . . . I can make you some toast. Would you like a glass of milk?"

Eyeing Pam's furious face, Liam said, "Toast would be fine. I can get the milk. What were you saying about Jesse, Pam?"

"I was *saying*, we don't need to let him know we aren't coming, because he didn't know we *were* coming. You can never arrange anything with Jesse on short notice, you just show up." Blurry pain twisted at her insides, making her hold her stomach and her breath. "Mom, could you bring me something to take some pills with? I've got cramps."

Her mother opened the refrigerator door, took out a pitcher, and poured out a small glass of apple juice. Setting this down before her daughter she remarked sympathetically, "Honey, you

114

do turn the most bilious shade of green. Don't you want to go back to bed?"

"Maybe later." Pam tossed back the pills and downed the juice. "It's times like these I miss being able to have orange juice in the morning."

"Oh, I do too!" Frances cut two slices from a brown loaf and popped them in the toaster, talking all the while. "And do you know what your-all's misbegotten Hefn have done now? Called a moratorium on new refrigerators! I saw it in the paper this morning. When the ones already made have all worn out, a few years down the road, guess what they expect people to do?"

"Retrofit them as iceboxes," said Liam.

"Iceboxes!" Frances exclaimed. "Did you ever hear the like? And community deep-freeze units, no freezers in people's homes anymore either. Course, you two probably know all about what the Hefn have up their sleeves before anybody else does, talking to that Humphrey every day." The toast popped up; she put the slices on a plate and set it in front of Liam. "There's butter, right there. Now, what kind of jelly would you like? I can offer you strawberry, apricot, and I think there's a little grape."

Liam smiled up at her. "Thanks. Strawberry's fine, and have you got any peanut butter?"

Pam said irritably, "Mom, for Pete's sake. Refrigerators and freezers use CFCs. CFCs damage the ozone layer. You *know* we can't go on releasing CFCs into the atmosphere! That's why they made everybody stop making air conditioners."

"Liam, it was so hot here in this kitchen last summer I like to died," said Frances. "Does it get as hot back in Washington as it gets here?"

"Last summer we went over a hundred degrees I think it was seventeen days in a row," said Liam.

"We broke a hundred *nineteen* days in a row, in July—and the humidity! It was hot as Billy Blue Blazes, it was just like an oven. I used to sit in front of the fan and just pant. I wonder how long it'll be before those durn Hefn'll be telling us we can't have electric fans any more either?" Frances said animatedly, showing off for Liam.

Pam groaned to herself. It was no use trying to reason with her mother. Frances read the paper and watched the TV news, she knew the facts, she wasn't stupid; but her personal feelings were the basis of her opinions about *everything*. If she was hot, it was the Hefn's fault for taking away the means of keeping cool. In a hundred ways her life was now less comfortable than it used to be, and the Hefn were to blame. That wasn't all Frances knew about it, but it was all she cared.

Pam would have been even more embarrassed had she not heard Liam's own mother, Phoebe O'Hara, talk pretty much the same way more than once—Phoebe, who actually knew Humphrey and was fond of him.

She was impressed at how good Liam was being with *her* mother. Spreading peanut butter on his toast, he was saying pleasantly, "I don't really think there's much risk of that. Electricity can be made in a lot of non-polluting ways, and it doesn't take much power to run a fan. Have you seen any of those new water-cooled fans, that blow a current of air across a reservoir of water? If you sit in front of one of those, it's pretty pleasant." He finished mortaring on the peanut butter and began to spread jam on the other slice of bread.

"No, I don't think I've seen one. Myrna Molloy told me the Fraziers got one—Doug Frazier is Pam's old math tutor, Liam—you ought to stop by to see Doug and Katherine while you're home, honey—anyway, Myrna said it was a big old thing. She said they had quite a time mounting it in the window. The water tank has to sit on a table right underneath. I don't know if I want one or not. Course, Pam's father doesn't mind the heat, but it sure is hard on me. Honey, don't you want anything to eat? I could fix you some oatmeal."

Pam's stomach lurched. "Ugh, no thanks. I don't want anything right now. I might later on, after the pills work." She glared at Liam. "You finished?"

"Have some more toast if you like," Frances put in. She was chattering and interrupting, as Pam was aware, partly out of excitement and partly out of nervous discomfort. Frances loved the idea of her ugly-duckling daughter having this mannerly, presentable young man for a boyfriend, and was unbudgeable in her determination to view Liam in that light; but boyfriend or no it was hard for her to take in the idea of his knowing about Pam's period and its attendant miseries. Obviously the canceling of the canoe trip had required an explanation, but Frances would have preferred a genteel half-lie—"I've got an upset stomach"—to Pam's blunt, factual, "I have cramps."

"One more piece, if that's okay." Liam made a comical, apologetic face at the dirty look Pam gave him—*Pig-hog!*—behind Frances's back, acknowledging that he knew she was in a hurry to get out of her mother's presence.

Unable to wait, Pam scraped her chair back and got up. "I'll be out on the porch. I'm going to call Betsy and see if she wants to ride over later.''

It was taken for granted in the Pruitt household that everyone, family and guest alike, would be in church on Sunday morning. Pam might not be up to a canoe trip, she might decide to skip Sunday school, but she was up to going to church. Liam had brought nothing really suitable to wear, but 10:30 the next morning found him standing beside Pam in a shirt and tie borrowed from her father, sharing a hymnal.

They had walked with her parents the short distance from the campus into the small town of Scofield, where the church was. Pam herself was unrecognizable in a blue dress with a full skirt, and two-inch heels. ''Do you dress up like this for church in Washington?'' Liam had muttered as she clacked along beside him, and she muttered back, ''Not bloody likely.'' Graceful as a cat, hands shoved into his pants pockets, as silent in his gum-soled boat shoes as she was noisy in her high heels, Liam easily kept pace beside her. ''Well, you might have warned *me*. I haven't tied a tie in at least a year, but I do actually own a couple.'' His words were more accusing than his tone.

''I never thought about it. Believe me, packing a suitable church wardrobe was the last thing on my mind.'' Pam felt better. The first day of a period was always the sickest, though she was still bleeding in many hot secret plops as they walked. Impulsively she said, ''Listen, if you're still interested I could tell you about my conversion experience this afternoon.''

He turned his head to smile at her, and said in a gratifyingly lively way, ''Tautologically. Need you ask?''

''Let us stand and sing hymn number one hundred and twenty, 'Blessed Assurance,' '' the music director called out, and then began to quote the words above the stir of people standing and the rustling of pages: '' 'Blessed assurance, Jesus is mine! Oh, what a foretaste of glory divine . . .' '' The organist played a few introductory measures. Pam held her side of the hymnal to be polite, but in three stanzas she never once glanced down at the words of this old chestnut. Liam gamely sight-read the hymn; Pam sang it with energy and pleasure. She enjoyed singing in church. Her voice, though not very strong, was accurate and clear. On the other side of her, her mother's singing quavered against the gruff backdrop of her father, who stood and droned out the bass line with his feet planted stiffly apart. Frances, like her daughter, had been born into the Born-Agains; her husband hadn't.

The college choir director, Rodney Benson, who was also Youth and Music Director for Scofield Baptist Church, used great sweeps of his arms to conduct both the choir and the congregation at once. Pam noticed, and wondered at, Liam's rapt attention to the performance. When the hymn was over and they were seated again she nudged him and asked what was so fascinating. Without looking at her Liam whispered that Rodney's style of leading the singing was so different from the precise, intense style of the conductor of the Philadelphia Boys' Choir that Liam had found it hard to take his eyes off Rodney.

"Different how?"

"That other guy, Christopher Shanks, was totally focused. This guy's diffuse, he's all over the stage, trying to get everybody involved."

Prayers and announcements followed the singing. The minister welcomed Pam "and her young man" back from their important work in Washington, D.C., "carrying the witness to the invader."

"What's that supposed to mean?" Liam hissed when the congregation had stopped craning around to peer at them; and Pam hissed back, "The church officially disapproves of the Hefn, I told you that."

"But 'carrying the witness'?"

"The Christian witness." And when he still looked blank, "I'll explain later. Don't worry about it."

The hymn between the announcements and the sermon was one of Pam's favorites. She threw herself into the thrumming tom-tom rhythms with some of the same joy she had felt reciting "The Ballad of East and West." *Would: you be free: from your bur: -den of sin? There's power: in: the blood—power: in: the blood! . . .*

There Is Power in the Blood

L. E. J.

L. E. JONES

1. Would you be free from your bur-den of sin?
2. Would you be free from your pas-sion and pride?
3. Would you be whit-er, much whit-er than snow?
4. Would you do serv-ice for Je-sus, your King?

There's pow'r in the Blood,

pow'r in the Blood.

Would you o'er e-vil a vic-to-ry win?
Come for a cleans-ing to Cal-va-ry's tide.
Sin stains are lost in its life-giv-ing flow.
Would you live dai-ly His prais-es to sing?

There's

CHORUS

won-der-ful pow'r in the Blood. There is pow'r, pow'r, won-der-working

There is pow'r,

pow'r in the blood of the Lamb. There is pow'r, pow'r,

In the blood of the Lamb. There is pow'r,

won-der-work-ing pow'r In the pre-cious blood of the Lamb.

Liam sang this one with more relish, and when it was over murmured, "Hey, not bad!"

There was a guest preacher that Sunday, an evangelist Pam had never heard of, from Little Rock, Arkansas. When the sermon started, by lifelong habit Pam's attention shut down. She settled into an agreeable fantasy:

The Hefn Comfrey (now modeled closely on Humphrey) needed an important job done that only Pinny could do. Hurt Hollow was being watched by people hostile to the Hefn; someone had chopped a hole in the johnboat and Joshua had been unable to repair it; time was running out. Pinny would have to swim across the river at night, carrying the plans for the new social order—or should it be some invention? no, a non-material cargo would be best, she could carry most of that in her head—across to Indiana, and deliver them to the President of Scofield College (a kindly, grandfatherly man), who would see that they were sent safely to the Secretary General of the United Nations.

Everything depended on this dangerous night swim. Though there was a full moon, rain was forecast; the night should be dark enough, but the river would be roiled by rain and wind. "I wouldn't let you go if there were any other way," Comfrey told Pinny, sick with worry for her safety. "I don't know how I'd be able to stand it if anything happened to you. You and Joshua have taught me the meaning of human love. I want to stay with both of you forever."

Pinny stood straight and tall with pride. "And *you and Joshua* between you have taught *me* the meaning of human love. I promise I won't fail you, Comfrey. I'll get the plans to President Hackney, and I'll swim back here again the first night I can—the first night there's enough cloud cover."

Joshua came in, exhausted from his frantic last-ditch effort (unsuccessful) to patch the hole in the sabotaged boat. "Pinny, love, please be careful. It's a rough night to be on the river even if you could use the johnboat. There's a storm brewing. If you're to swim across, you should go now—there's not a moment to lose."

Pinny allowed Joshua to embrace her, then stripped—she was nearly as flat-chested and fully as muscular as a boy—and strapped the waterproof fanny pack containing documents essential to the plans around her waist. With a long, intensely meaningful look, first into Joshua's eyes, then into Comfrey's—by means of which everything they hadn't said became known

120

to all three of them—she blew out the candles and slipped through the door into the now-drumming rain.

Out in the chill dark, buffeted by the rising wind, she made her way sure-footedly down the steep, slippery path toward the dock and the vast, heaving, elemental thing, blacker even than the inky night, that lay beyond. At the edge of this vast blackness she looked around one last time at the house, at the candle now relit in the window and the two shadows moving on the walls; and then, sharply drawing the battering wind deep into her lungs—

"Holy Christmas, where does this guy get off?" Liam muttered, shoving Pam hard in the ribs. "Are you listening to this?"

The whole congregation seemed to be looking right at them again. The preacher from Little Rock was actually holding out his arm and pointing to the place in the balcony where they were sitting. "My brothers and sisters, I call it a crime!" he was shouting. "I call it a sin and a shame! You say to me, 'Brother Bemis, the corruption of a group of innocent children is not the worst crime these inhuman creatures have perpetrated upon us.' You all saw on the television what they did to those poor fellows on the *Delta Queen*—human beings, just like you and me—and it made you sick to your stomachs. You say, 'Those aliens have humiliated us, they've taken away our freedom, they've taken away our rights, they've taken away our progress, and worst of all they've taken away our babies!' You tell me, 'The loss of our rights as American citizens affects every man, woman, and child in the United States of America.' You say to me, 'Brother Bemis, the Hefn's interferin' in our God-given right to have a Christian family is a whole lot more important than the corruption of nine little children out in Washington, D.C.'

"But I would remind you all this morning of the words of our Lord and Savior Jesus Christ, when he said, 'Suffer the little children to come unto me, and forbid them not, for of such is the kingdom of heaven.' And I would remind you of the Book of Proverbs, chapter twenty-two, verse six, where we read: 'Train up a child in the way he should go: and when he is old, he will not depart from it.' And I want to say to you that if Jesus Christ was here today, he would go to the parents of those Apprentice children, and he would tell them, 'Protect your sons and daughters from corruption! Keep your sons and your daughters, that God gave you to raise up in good Christian homes, away from the evil of the alien invader!' "

He paused for breath. Pam wanted to sink through the floor.

She was aware of her mother beside her, stiff as a poker with embarrassment and fury.

"Now I know there are some among us here today, right-thinking Christian men and women, who would like to speak up right now and say, 'Brother Otie, God created the Hefn just like he created you and me.' Well, let me tell all you good people, if you said that you'd be right. You surely would be right. *Yes*, God created the whole universe. *Yes*, God created every living thing, whether it be in this world or any other; and yes, he also created the Hefn.

"But brothers and sisters, let me remind you of one thing. Let me remind you of one thing this morning if I may. *God created the Devil too!* The Hefn are a part of God's creation— just like Satan is a part of God's creation! And I believe just as surely as I'm standing here before you today, that the Hefn are part of God's plan—just like Satan is part of God's plan for human beings on this earth.

"And I would ask you to consider two questions, brothers and sisters. I would ask you to prayerfully consider two very, very important questions. The first question is this: *What are they here for?* Think about it, my good brothers and sisters in Christ. What are they here for? What message was God sending to you and me when he sent the Hefn down to earth?

"And the second question I want to lay on your hearts this morning is this: *What are God's people going to do about it?*"

"Don't judge us by *him*," Pam told Liam late that afternoon. "You saw how everybody acted—Mom and Dad both furious, Pastor Seidler apologizing all over the place, people coming up and saying it was an outrage . . . I can't imagine how the guy got invited to speak here. He must be a little cracked. He's a deep-south Southern Baptist, anyway; a lot of them are still pretty racist."

"Right, I get it. One Baptist's Hefn is another Baptist's gook."

"Oh, for Pete's sake," said Pam disgustedly.

"And Brother Otie Bemis is nothing but a bush-league Grand Dragon Brother Gus Griner."

Pam made a face. "You could be right about that, anyway."

They had walked around the drive surrounding the college buildings to the Point, where there was a stone bench, a mass of blooming redbud trees, and a long view down over the wooded bluff to the river. You could see Hurt Hollow from the Point— no details, but Pam had explained how to spot the general location, just beyond the big bend. It was a mild, sunny afternoon, but the swirls of high cirrus clouds boded ill for the next day, the revised date of the canoe trip.

"What I wonder is, how many other people feel like he does? Mom and Matt both 'disapprove of the Hefn' as you put it, but what *they* mean by that is just that they think we ought to be left alone to work out our own problems, even if we can't. There's something really disturbing about Otie Bemis, Pam, no joke. I wish I knew how many of him there are around the country."

"Around the *middle* of the country, I bet you mean. East-coast chauvinist. Believe me, as far as I know, Otie Bemis is unique. Are we going to talk about him all afternoon? I thought you wanted to hear about my conversion experience—or did Brother Otie put you off that subject for good?"

"No, no, no. I do want to hear about it. All right, I agree to suspend judgment on Baptists for now, but I'm calling Humphrey tonight all the same."

"What for?" Pam asked, instantly defensive. "You don't think Humphrey has to worry about Otie *Bemis*, do you? A crackpot preacher from Little Rock, Arkansas? What are you trying to do, make me look bad?"

Liam stared at her, mouth slightly open. "Come on. Tell me you didn't mean that. You didn't, did you?"

His surprise was so genuine that Pam felt ashamed. "I guess not. At least, not that you'd *try* to make me look bad. Sorry. But you could make me look bad without trying, you know." She took a deep breath and looked directly at Liam. "I'm jealous of you and Humphrey, that's the trouble."

"Oh." Liam looked away, considering. The idea that a person might be jealous of his special relationship with Humphrey appeared not to strike him as remarkable. After a moment he said, "Well, I *am* going to call him, but not just to tell him what happened at church. He asked me to check in. We've been gone almost a week." He smiled at Pam. "You can say hi too. Why not? He'll be glad to see you." (Pam made a sarcastic face: *Oh sure.*) "Okay, what about the conversion experience? How old were you when it happened?"

"I can't tell it like that." She paused to think. "Okay. When you grow up knowing about the idea of getting saved, it never *hits* you the way it hits other people when they hear about it for the first time. I always knew the Plan of Salvation, I can't re-member not knowing about it. We learned it in Sunday school. C, B, A: Confess, Believe, Ask. There's something called the

Age of Accountability, that differs from kid to kid. I was baptized when I was nine, but I probably shouldn't have been. I mean, I wanted to be, but nothing had really changed with me. Mom just brought the subject up one day while she was shampooing my hair . . . actually it was kind of weird. She said something like, 'If anybody at church asked you if you wanted to be baptized, and you said, "My mother and daddy don't want me to," that wouldn't be true. We don't mind.' A pretty roundabout way of going about it; but I went forward the next Sunday, and the Board of Deacons questioned me, and the next time Pastor Seidler baptized a bunch of people he baptized *me*."

" 'Went forward'?"

"Yeah, at the end of the service, while they're singing the invitation hymn. You just walk up the aisle, to let everybody know you want to be saved or join the church or whatever."

" 'Invitation hymn' as in inviting people to 'come forward'?"

"Right. We sang one this morning but nobody went forward."

"Put off by Brother Otie." Liam pondered this and shrugged. "What questions did they ask?"

"The deacons? Oh, like, why did I want to be baptized. I told them what had happened, about my mother washing my hair and what she'd said—which is ridiculous if you think about it—but the deacons all understood the same thing I'm trying to explain to you, that for a kid who grows up in the church there's no sudden realization that Jesus died for your sins. I mean, it's something you've heard since you were born, and anyway it's hard for a nine-year-old to understand what sin *or* dying means. So I think that part was just a formality. I *had* recently asked Mom how old she was when she got baptized—I was getting really interested in it. I did really want to be a full member of the church, that's true enough. But there wasn't any change in me—radical change, I mean, as opposed to gradual change—until last year. Whenever people say 'When were you saved,' I always say I was nine, but I always *think* of it as happening last year, on a retreat, almost exactly one year ago."

Liam looked mildly amazed. "People actually say that to each other? 'When were you saved?' "

"Mm-hm."

"How old *was* your mother?"

"She was eight. So anyway. This was an Easter vacation retreat for the middle-school and high-school youth groups, at a camp we go to. The last night of the retreat we had a big campfire and sang a lot of gospel songs, and then Rodney—he's the Youth and Music Director, I like him a lot, he's a really nice guy—he gave a talk, and then people were invited to come up one by one and put a stick on the fire and give a testimony."

"What's a testimony?"

"Just a personal statement. People say what they're thankful for, or—like—that from right now they're going to dedicate their lives to Christ. I remember we were all humming 'Only Believe.' "

In a different voice Liam said, "Want to know something? I just realized this. The only time Jeff and I ever sang anything *together* was on Scout campouts. Jeff was a singer, did Carrie tell you that?" Pam shook her head. "I mean he was really good—he was a soloist with the Philadelphia Boys' Choir, and I can barely carry a tune."

"You sounded all right this morning."

Liam shook his head. "Not really. Definitely not compared to Jeff. Plus he liked sacred music, which is what the choir mostly did, and I never really went for that—though I got so I liked it better over time." Liam shoved his hands into his pockets and kicked the ground under the bench. "I probably could have learned to like anything if Jeff sang it. He had a beautiful voice—like a flute. Anyway, I remember what it's like, singing around a campfire."

Liam stopped talking. They sat together quietly. Pam understood that for Liam, talking about Jeff was an experiment, a risk, and that the moment called for delicacy. Recognizing this made her tense up. She thanked her stars that at least the thing she had almost said on the boat had remained unspoken.

It appeared that up until now, Liam had reminisced about his lost friend only with Humphrey and his therapist, never with a friend. The thought made Pam realize that as far as she knew, Liam *had* no friends, not even a friend like Betsy, who was more of a comrade-in-arms (against the social expectations of peers and parents) than somebody she felt close to. It made her feel funny to realize it, but the closest thing Liam had to a friend was herself.

Except, of course, for Humphrey.

They were still sitting in silence, gazing off toward Hurt Hollow in the distance, when—speaking of lost friends—her own ex-friend Steve strolled around the curve of the drive and saw them there. He started, recovered, then visibly made a decision to cut across the lawn toward them. He was carrying a stack of books. "Hi, Spam. Saw you in church. Hi, I'm Steve Harper."

Liam got up, told Steve his name, and the boys shook hands. As they did this, Pam, who did not stand up, had several surprising thoughts in rapid succession:

Steve assumed that Liam was her boyfriend. There must be a general rumor around the college to that effect, probably put about by her mother.

She was glad Steve was wrong; but she was also glad he had jumped to the wrong conclusion.

She despised him for the new respect with which he was regarding her, but also craved it and was grateful to Liam for making it happen. And she despised herself, a little, for this craving.

"I'm going the long way round to the library, I've got a history project due tomorrow," Steve informed them amiably. "Hey, what about that Otie Bemis?" He laughed. "What a dildo-brain! I thought your dad was gonna go down there and break his nose."

"What was he doing here, anyway?" Pam asked, for something to say. Liam sat down again on the stone bench.

"He's going around to different churches and preaching against the Hefn," said Steve. "Bad luck he happened to turn up here this Sunday. Everybody was embarrassed. A lot of the people here wish the Hefn would go back where they came from, but they wouldn't tell your dad to his face that he had no business sending you to Washington—even if that was what they happened to think."

"Unh-hunh, and it *is* what they happen to think," Pam said with heavy irony.

Steve grinned. "Hey, what's it like, hanging out with aliens? I saw you guys on *Good Morning Americas*, and somebody brought a magazine to school that had an article about the Apprentices. Sounds like a lot of work to me."

"It is a lot of work. I like it, though."

Steve grinned again, a knowing leer. "Yeah, with the right company I guess you could have a pretty good time." He included Liam in this heavy humor, but Liam stared up at him with no expression at all and Steve started backing away. "Whoops! Three's a crowd! Nice meeting you. Good seeing you, Spam old sausage. How long you gonna be around?"

"Two weeks, about."

"Maybe you guys and Carole and me could get together later on."

"Carole *Cosby*?" said Pam in horror; and then, so as not to forfeit her newly acquired credit with Steve, "We're going to Hurt Hollow tomorrow, if it doesn't rain, and then—the rest of the time is pretty packed already. But tell her hi from me."

"Okay, I will." By this time Steve had backed all the way to the drive. "So long, if I don't see you again."

"So long."

"So long," Liam echoed, and then *sotto voce*, "Carole *Cosby*?"

"Miss 2013 Southern Indiana Middle School."

"Aha."

"Believe it or not," said Pam, trying to laugh, "I spent the first twelve years of my life as the inseparable companion of that jerk Steve, and another guy named Charlie Garner. In those woods right down there. We had a camp, with a tree house and a rope swing over the creek."

"Aha," said Liam again. There was a short silence. Liam cleared his throat. "I take it that was before he discovered Carole Cosby."

"She was there all the time. He used to hate her." Pam's mouth felt dry.

Liam watched her alertly. After a while he said, "So what happened? Did you go up and put a stick on the fire and give your whaddyacallit—your witness?"

"Testimony. As a matter of fact, I didn't," said Pam. "I just sat there humming 'Only Believe,' but somehow or other things just kind of—came together. I can't explain it, or even describe it very well, but like I knew I belonged right there, with those people, and the reason was that we all cared so much about the same thing."

"What thing?"

"God, I guess," said Pam.

"I don't know what you mean by 'God.' "

Pam bowed her head and thought hard. How had she felt that night by the fire? "God's the short answer. The long answer is, the Christian life. Living for Jesus. Living *like* Jesus, as much as you can. Not getting sidetracked by worldly values."

Liam squirmed a little. "Give me an example of a worldly value."

"Money."

"I notice they took up a collection."

127

Pam narrowed her eyes. "Are you serious about this or what? They have to run the church, get the choir robes cleaned, pay the minister, pay the electric bill—"

"Pay the water bill," said Liam; and then quickly, before Pam could get mad: "No, sorry, I *am* being facetious now. It's because this subject makes me kind of twitchy. I'm afraid I'm going to find out you're some kind of fanatic, so I keep trying to lighten the mood. Sorry. I *am* interested, no kidding."

"One more crack and that's *it*," said Pam. "You know perfectly well what I mean. My grandmother, my mother's mother, she was an ultra-Yuppie. Her first husband was a lawyer in Louisville, and Granny worked in an ad agency, and between them they just *raked* in the money from what I hear, but they weren't happy at all. Her husband drank, on top of everything else. Then one night Granny went to a tent meeting to hear a traveling revivalist—just for something to do, like it was a circus or something—and she got saved. And her whole life changed around. She quit her job, divorced the drunk, married my grandfather and had Mom—"

"And lived happily ever after? I'm really asking," Liam added hastily.

"Yeah, she did. Or rather, she still is living happily ever after, down in Louisville."

"What does your grandfather do?"

"He owned a Veggiburger franchise. He's dead now."

Liam processed this information. "Have you told me why you didn't put a stick on the fire?"

"I guess not. Oh, I don't know. I didn't know what to say, I guess. But the next day, at the service we had before we left, Pastor Seidler asked everybody who wanted to rededicate their lives to Christ to stand up, and I stood up."

"Okay, so tell me this. What's the practical effect of 'living like Jesus'—apart from not getting sidetracked into chasing after money, et cetera?"

"You try to be honest, not cheat, work hard, not say malicious things about people behind their backs, help people as much as you can—that kind of thing; and you do it all for—well, for the Lord I guess—God—though we usually say 'for Christ.' It's all the same thing. In prayer meeting people are always praying, like, 'Lord, help me to serve Thee, show me what Thou wouldst have me do, help me to live according to Thy will.' It feels good," she said. "It's not dreary, it's not like you're just giving stuff up and denying yourself any fun. You do it *for* the Lord, because you want to.''

Liam was looking at her incredulously. " 'Wouldst'? Did I hear you say 'wouldst'? I haven't heard anybody say 'wouldst' since I was at Germantown Friends School!''

His scandalized expression made Pam laugh. "We still use the King James Bible and pray in Elizabethan English. You should hear the three-year-olds do it! Just like speaking a dialect! Listen, I'm cold. Let's go back. It must be nearly dinnertime.''

Clouds had almost covered the sky, and the air was getting chilly. They got up and started walking back to the house. "So if I understand you,'' said Liam, "what you're calling a conversion experience was more or less a really intense moment of realizing, or, like, connecting with, some things you believed in already.''

"That's what it was for me,'' Pam said, "but for Granny it was like a ton of bricks fell on her.'' And she thought, but did not say, like the way I felt when you started quoting "The Ballad of East and West,'' aboard the *Delta Queen*.

Liam shoved his hands in his pockets and kicked a piece of gravel into the shrubbery. "Okay, that's you and your grandma. What about your parents?''

"Mom grew up in the church, like me. That's where Dad met her, when he was eighteen or nineteen.''

"He met her there—but he didn't grow up there?''

"No.''

"So did *he* have a ton-of-bricks conversion experience, like your grandmother?''

The question made Pam feel queasy. "I don't exactly know. He doesn't talk about stuff like that. He told me once he had one, that's all I know about it.''

"Just to play devil's advocate,'' said Liam, "strictly speaking, should you have said what you said about Carole Cosby?''

"Strictly speaking,'' Pam replied ruefully, "no. Though I didn't really *say* anything about her . . . but I did imply it, and that's just as bad.''

"Well before you reform completely—that guy Steve; what did you ever see in him, anyway, besides the obvious? Was he at the campfire that night?''

"Yeah, I guess he was . . . he used to be okay when we were kids,'' Pam began, and then broke off and glared at Liam. "What do you mean, 'see in him'? It wasn't like *that*! We just used to play together, I was never *jealous* of Carole Cosby!'' She stamped her foot. "You can take that smirk off your face right now! It's not funny!" To her horror, her voice broke a little as it rose; she could feel herself shaking. To have Liam insinuate about Steve what Steve—and Raghu Kanal—had insinuated about *him* felt like the end of the world.

Liam looked taken aback. "Okay, okay. I was just teasing, I didn't mean to get you upset. Jesus, you keep *surprising* me." They started walking again, Pam glaring furiously at the ground. After a moment Liam said cautiously, "What exactly is so terrible about me thinking you might have had a crush on a big good-looking guy like that?"

"Because I didn't," she answered in a muffled voice. They walked in awkward silence for a while. Liam was scowling. "Do you really think Steve's good-looking?" she asked after a while.

"Are you kidding? He's no John Chalmers, maybe, but he's still a very good-looking guy, and he's also about a foot taller than me."

"Is he taller than you?"

Liam's jaw dropped. "Are you *kidding*?" Suddenly he whooped and punched her in the arm. "Hey, where'd this wind blow up from? Come on, sourpuss, race you back to the house."

"I can't *run*, you lamebrain," Pam protested. "I did pretty well just to *walk* this far on the second day!"

"Boy, am I ever glad I'm not a girl," Liam said, but he said it in a friendly and sympathetic way.

"Then you're not as dumb as you look," said Pam, her tone—like his—rather gentler than her words.

130

Liam: Is this more or less how you remember it? I have extraordinarily complete memories of everything up to Scofield, but had to make up the breakfast scene and the rest. I know we watched the Hubbell video, and that Otie Bemis preached at church, and I remember running into Steve. And I'm sure my period started, delaying our departure. The rest is a blurry jumble. Was this when we talked about my conversion experience?

To think of you (or anyone) knowing about the Pinny's Hefn *"sequel" makes me squirm like an eel—but in for a, er, Pinny, in for a pound!*

I don't think the conversation with Steve happened like this, but it all seems true to the spirit if not the letter. Interesting that getting home makes you blank out. I too remember us as sparring a lot, sometimes playfully but sometimes for real—both of us conflicted between opening up and staying in our shells, I guess.

This was *probably* when we had the conversion-experience talk—either at Scofield or later in the Hollow. In any case I'm positive that by the time Humphrey and I had our heavy discussion about conversion, not long after, you'd already told me all this.

#You give Pinny your "big" nose but make her muscular and flat-chested. To me she comes across as being, not just a non-girl, but virtually a boy (a *very* sentimental one). I do see why my teasing you about Steve "felt like the end of the world," and I was certainly happy not to be a girl, just as you have me say. But I keep having this hunch that I *don't* see everything about why *you* didn't want to be one.

8

TWO YOUNG ROES
THAT ARE TWINS

—Song of Solomon 4:5

Despite the pessimistic forecast the fair weather held, though the temperature began to climb. Monday dawned sunny and warm. After breakfast Pam left her mother happily making sandwiches and went up to change into her bathing suit and an old pair of canvas gym shoes, and to pack some clothes and a few necessities like sun block and Tampaxes.

She hadn't thought to wonder whether her bathing suit still fit. What she saw now in the mirror was dismaying. Though otherwise all right, last year's suit had become hopelessly too small for this year's breasts. Pam tugged at the stretchy fabric and pushed at her own soft flesh, struggling to cram herself more adequately inside the top of the suit. It was like trying to cram a down sleeping bag into its stuff sack—except that eventually, if you kept at it, the sleeping bag would go in.

The fabric wouldn't stay stretched out. Her breasts would *go* in, but they wouldn't *stay* in. They'd gotten bigger since last summer, really quite a lot bigger, that was the truth and the trouble; moreover, at the moment they were sore and distended even further because of her period. After a while Pam stopped poking at herself and tried to think what she'd better do.

They'd planned to stop someplace for a swim on the way down to Hurt Hollow, it was supposed to get up into the upper eighties today. She could wear something else—shorts and a top—but any kind of regular top would have to have a bra underneath. The idea of swimming in her shirt and bra, then paddling a canoe for several miles with the tight, wet bra clasping her skin, was very disagreeable. She pictured herself coming out of the river, the shirt streaming water, clinging to her, skin-tight and semitransparent . . . no. The bathing suit would be less obscene than that. It would have to do. Anyway, there would be nobody

132

but Liam to see her, and he wouldn't care. Pam glared into the mirror one last time, shrugged, and pulled a loose T-shirt on over the indecency. The thing now was to *get going*. She stuck a handful of Tampaxes, a bottle of sun block, and a couple of old towels into a bookbag and bounded down the stairs.

Her father and Liam were attaching the canoe rack to the roof of a college car, reserved for the morning. She stood around, useless for the moment, while the two males, working together in a competent, muscular way—Liam, though short, had broad shoulders and well-developed arms—lifted the canoe onto the rack and tied it on: her father's canoe, an old aluminum veteran dented everywhere from its many encounters with rock-fraught rapids, but essentially indestructible, the one in which she had learned how to handle a canoe, how to make the neat J-strokes that would keep it moving in a straight line and the backpaddling strokes that would turn it around, and how to sidle up to a dock.

Pam's scrawny arms and shoulders, inherited from her mother, had once sufficed to carry her up poles and saplings, dangle her from ropes, and flash her wriggling from one end of the monkey bars to the other. But when her proportions had altered and her center of gravity had shifted downward, most of these former feats had become impossible. Where formerly she had climbed a pole by gripping the pole above her head as high as possible and pulling her body up, over and over, her clamped legs holding her in position while her arms reached up, now she found it necessary to hold her position with her arms and use her legs to *push* herself up the pole; those arms had simply become unequal to the weight of her adolescent pelvis and thighs.

She hadn't ever been able to lift one end of the old canoe above her head, as Liam was doing easily now, to settle it on the rack. But she could control the canoe in the water, her arms were strong enough to do all that was necessary and she made up in skill what she lacked in strength. The sooner they were waterborne, therefore, the better. "Let's go," she muttered under her breath. "Let's go, let's go, let's go."

Finally the canoe was secured, Frances had waved them off, and they were driving down the steep road from the campus to the beach, the bow of the canoe shading the windshield like a hawk's enormous beak. In no time after that the canoe lay tilted with half its length on the sand and half in the water; and Pam and Liam were tossing in their bags, life jackets, kneeling pads, lunches, canteen, and a book of Ohio River charts, and were ready to push off into the muddy shallows.

The beach was airless and the morning already hot. When Pam had crawled forward into the bow and settled her weight on her knees and her knees on the dense foam pad, and looked out ahead over the shining expanse of water, the sun and the sudden whiff of freedom were too much. *I'm back!* she exulted. *Everything's just the same as ever!* And with a reckless gesture she pulled the shirt over her head and threw it behind her into the bottom of the canoe with the other stuff. Then she took up a paddle and grinned back at Liam, who was steadying the canoe, and at her father. "All set! Cast off!"

Liam waded at once right into the water in his ratty shoes, shoving the canoe ahead of him. As he stepped neatly into the stern, "You're bursting out of your suit," Pam's father pleasantly remarked.

Both their heads snapped back toward shore. Shelby was staring at Pam's chest, a pleased smile on his face. "What?" she croaked.

In the same pleasant, interested voice, her father repeated his remark. He chuckled. There was no trace of embarrassment in his manner.

"It's last year's," Pam said. "When are you picking us up?"

"Noon tomorrow. Be on time; somebody's got the car signed out for one. I'll meet you at the landing at noon sharp. Say hi to Jesse for me."

"We will." They had been drifting slightly during this exchange; now Liam thrust his paddle in and deftly guided the canoe around a floating clump of sticks.

"Pam, I think you'd better put your shirt back on before you get to Hurt Hollow," her father called after them. He chuckled again. "I don't expect old Jesse's quite up to the sight of you in that bathing suit."

Pam hunched her bare shoulders a little and started paddling, putting her back into it. "Bye," Liam called back to Shelby. "See you tomorrow." To Pam he said nothing. If Shelby was not embarrassed, Liam and Pam were. Pulling hard, they widened the strip of water between them and the beach, and were soon far enough from shore to be caught and carried along by the current. A breeze sprang up. After a bit Pam glanced back to see if the car was gone. It was. She laid her paddle across the gunwales, twisted around to get her T-shirt, and put it on, not looking at Liam. A sick loathing filled her mind, beyond words, beyond coherent thought.

Boobs. A pair of pallid, wobbly blobs of flesh—part of herself,

134

yet separable. An affliction so recent that nostalgia for the freedom of the before-time often made her ache with loss; she tried to avoid thinking about it. A cancerous distortion of her body that once, not very long ago, had not been there at all. Worse, really, even than periods, which disrupted only about 17.14285 percent of her life, less than a fifth (though they came upon her so erratically it was hard to be really precise). But the boobs, they were there *all the time*, bulbously flopping within her large bra when she tried to run or make Wickiup trot, like she was some kind of nanny goat transformed into a person. Every morning of her life, when she woke up, there they still were. There they would always be.

All Pam's female relatives on both sides of her family were big-breasted; there'd never been much chance she was going to be flat, but it was not a doom she had dreaded in advance, or thought about at all, until the curse had actually befallen her, or begun to.

"Thy two breasts are like two young roes that are twins." Once, maybe, what Solomon wrote might have applied. At eleven Pam had been a nice size—for a sixteen-year-old of her general body build. At twelve her arms made skinny brackets on either side of her chest. At fourteen, when the breasts had finally stopped getting bigger, they were already much, much too big for proportionate beauty or comfort or hope that things would balance out later on. They were like two porky sows, two bags of blubber. She *despised* them.

Pam's hatred for her breasts was well-known within the family circle. When he first became aware of this it had bewildered her father, even angered him. "You must be plain crazy," he used to say. "That's what the boys *like*." She had fizzed like an aerosol bomb with frustration, thinking mutinously—but not saying—*Who gives a shit what the* boys *like? What about what I like? What about how I feel?* "They're just mammary glands!" he would say, taking another tack, trying as he often did to reduce something bodily and difficult to a technicality.

Neither of her parents took her own feelings about her breasts as a sign of a serious problem. Frances assumed that Pam would outgrow her attitude; it never occurred to her to view it either as reasonable or as worrying.

Indoors, or doing some few outdoor things—swimming, or cycling—Pam had learned to live with her protuberant chest— that is, it no longer made her movements so ungainly. Paddling a canoe, though, her breasts got in her way. She hadn't done much real canoeing since becoming so buxom. There were problems with balance and arm action. She bumped into herself. It was distressing and humiliating, and for the first ten minutes she suffered acutely; but Liam was a skillful canoeist, easily following the rhythm of her strokes though they had never tried to paddle together before. Gradually Pam settled down, looked around, forgot about her father and the difficulties of her body and let the realization surge again within her that at last she was really on her way to see Jesse and Hurt Hollow, after nine months in dirty, crowded, paved-over Washington, D.C.

The river as seen from the frail canoe, almost at eye level, was different from the same river seen from the deck of a steamboat: more powerful, more immense, more austere, more to be placated and catered to. The broad sweep of water, blue on the surface and brown in the ripples, filled the world; the tree-covered slopes ahead and on either hand, seen through haze, looked *dusted* with sunlight except where the gigantic shadows of clouds darkened them in passing. Logs and sodden planks floated on the current alongside the canoe. In the channel a towboat, the *Reliance*, was pushing seven laden barges downstream, probably bound for Louisville.

Pam looked with pleasure at her arms and hands as they lifted and pulled and pushed on the shaft of the paddle, the heel of the left hand flat against the grip, the right hand down near the blade, the arms themselves—their first awkwardness overcome—rotating, levering, pausing, rotating again, in a smooth and practiced rhythm which in its economy and efficacy, its sufficient strength, seemed beautiful to her. She watched with satisfaction—and then, abruptly, with a thrill of terror. Between one stroke and the next, a lens had swiveled down between Pam's eyes and everything they saw. She looked at her own arms and hands and saw they had nothing to do with her. She looked up, ahead at the river, knowing what she would see, knowing already that the world would have become unreal.

Last year this used to happen all the time. In Washington, never. She'd not thought about it for months, this sudden slight dizziness and then—everything drawing back, turning shiny and artificial, as if seen through the wrong end of a telescope, as if embedded in a gigantic cube of clear plastic. It had happened several times in school in Madison. Twice, right in the middle of history class, she had heard angels singing and thought instantly that the hidebound old-timers at church were right and the Rapture had come. You were supposed to be glad about the

Rapture; even in the midst of her terror Pam was surprised at how terrified she felt, heart thudding, breath short, the hand holding a pencil cold and clammy as ice. She had forgotten all about it, had never told anyone; now the memories sprang back to mind, as vivid and terrible as if the attacks had never stopped.

And then, just as suddenly as it began, the fit was over. Her arms and hands were her own, the paddle was real, the water it moved through was real. The whole world to the horizon was alive again; and Pam, weak with relief, turned to flash a grin back to Liam and point up at the bluff behind them. They were a quarter of a mile below Scofield Beach, and high above the river, sticking out of the trees at the very top, were the water tower and several white cupolas of the college buildings, all that could be seen of them from the water in summer.

They had decided before launching to stay close to the Indiana shore for the first couple of miles, because Pam knew about a gravel bar where they could stop for a break and a swim, and because they would need to hug one shore or the other all the way to Hurt Hollow in order to avoid the strong midstream headwind. For half an hour they paddled along in an intensely agreeable way, not talking, looking about them. The dissociation did not recur, and the tension of thinking it might gradually seeped out of Pam's muscles. Once Liam suggested switching sides— he had been paddling on the right, Pam on the left—and once Pam called his attention to a red-tailed hawk riding a thermal, but neither attempted regular conversation. A wagon and team went by on the little road at the far edge of the bottom land, under the bluff, and then a car. They passed the mouths of several small creeks, also a number of rowboats tied to jetties or ladders. There were no other canoes.

"How come there aren't any other canoes?"

"Not the best way to get around on a big river like this. If there's any wind and you're by yourself, you can't steer. Whereas a rowboat—"

"Oh. True."

"The Kentucky River's the kind where you want a canoe. But with two people this works okay."

They reached the gravel bar around eleven, beached the canoe, and crawled out. Liam was wearing cut-off shorts, not exactly quick-dry bathing dress, but the day was so hot it scarcely mattered. He stood knee-deep in the river and pulled his shirt over his head. Pam started to do the same, hesitated with her arms crossed and her hands gripping the bottom on either side, swallowed, looked away. Instantly Liam, the soul of sensitivity and tact, flipped his shirt into the canoe and flung himself into the water, stroking quickly and steadily straight away from shore. Hastily then Pam jerked her own shirt off, dropped it on the gravel, and flung herself after him. Safely submerged to the neck in the cloudy water she called, "Don't go out too far! The current's tricky!" Liam stopped, waved, started to swim lazily back.

The water was cold, but not so cold you couldn't get used to it. They splashed around for half an hour, admiring the world from river-level. Upstream in the direction they had come from, the Ohio—a crinkled, reflective surface where they floated and trod water—spread out smooth and blue, with almost a metallic burnish in the distance, and around and ahead of them the tree-rumpled bluffs were the many light greens of spring. A painting of Orrin's in the Scofield College library, a view of the river from the Point, was filled with these same beautiful tints of green and blue. Thinking of that, of how things fit together, Pam's heart once again bravely filled up with happiness.

After a while she splashed up onto the bar and rummaged in the bookbag for the towels. One she wrapped around herself, the other she tossed onto the warm stones for Liam. She got out the lunch bag and called, "Hey, want a sandwich?" Liam came willingly and they sat side by side on the kneeling pads, streaming water, arms around their knees, holding Frances's sandwiches in wrinkled, sunblock-slippery hands.

Pam quickly got too hot to want to stay swathed in the tent of the towel. Turning her back on Liam, she struggled back into her shirt. When she looked again he was staring downstream in a self-consciously casual way, watching a tree float by, the back of his wet head turned to her. Fury at her father, whose words as they were launching had drifted like a cloud's shadow across the whole of the morning, struck her like a fist, making her grimace, set her jaw and look down.

Change the subject. In a tight voice she said, "Tell me again what Humphrey said last night," though she remembered exactly what he had said.

Liam swallowed the last of his third sandwich and brushed the crumbs off his chest. Some stuck to his skin, snagged by the sunblock; he picked these off while he spoke. "He said, as I already told you twice, that the Hubbells and Hurt Hollow sounded fascinating, and could he borrow the video or could we copy it for him. I said, better yet, why not come and see for yourself? He said if I still thought he ought to after I'd been down there today, maybe he would another time, but there's a lot of rancor stirred up against the Hefn right now because of those guys on the *Delta Queen* and it would probably be a good idea for him to lie low for a while, and besides that the Apprentice interviews are coming up soon, and he has to get ready for that and be there. And he sent you his regards. If you're so interested, how come you didn't just talk to him yourself?"

Paralyzed by shyness when push had come to shove, Pam had declined to get on the phone with Humphrey. Liam knew this perfectly well. Pam told him, "You know why. Don't play dumb."

He smiled and punched her lightly in the arm. "Okay, I know why, but you're playing dumb too, a little, aren't you?"

Pam smiled sheepishly and slowly nodded, more pleased than embarrassed at having been seen through.

Liam punched her lightly again. "You'll get over that about Humphrey when you get to know him better."

"*If* I get to know him better." She scanned the river and stood up. "I think we probably ought to get going. We can cross over now, before that barge gets here, and follow the other shore. It's another three miles, or a little bit more; right here's where we are, just about exactly at Mile 562, see?" She showed him the map in the chart book.

"We'd both better put on some more sun block, we've been dragging these shirts off and on—" Abruptly he flushed to the roots of his hair. After all his tact and care, he'd mentioned the unmentionable.

This was getting stupid. *Change the subject.* Gritting her teeth, Pam doggedly met his eyes. "You're very good in a canoe. Who taught you to paddle like that?"

Liam squirted sun block into his palm and handed her the bottle. "I learned in Scouts." He dabbed the stuff on his cheeks and forehead and started to rub it around. "And then, Terry's family used to have a cabin on Lake Wallenpaupack in the Poconos, and Jeff and I just about lived in boats for part of every summer. They had a sailboat and a canoe. We used to take the canoe on the Delaware, but we paddled it around on the lake sometimes too, when it wasn't too windy. You're good yourself. Who taught you?"

"Dad did." She closed her eyes, took a deep breath. "Listen, Liam—this is dumb. I'm sorry, you don't know how sorry I am, that you heard him say—that thing he said. He *talks* like that, he always did. I don't know why. He says things all the time, words, like 'mucus' and 'defecate' and—and 'mammary glands'—I—it's so *mortifying*. He says them right in front of people. Sometimes he gives Mom fits, but he just keeps on doing it. One time—one time Betsy was over and he came in my bedroom, where we were sitting on the bed, and stood right in front of us, and—and he said, 'Girls, can you tell what kind of underwear I'm wearing?' "

"He *did*? Wow! Why, why'd he do that?"

"I don't *know* why! I don't *know* why he does stuff like that, and I don't know why he doesn't know he's not supposed to!" Pam looked away from Liam's scandalized face. "I just mumbled no. Then, after he left, I asked Betsy if *her* father would ever say something like that. She said, 'I think my father would be embarrassed to.' But why isn't *he*, why isn't he embarrassed? How come he doesn't know any better?" Abruptly she started to smear a palmful of the smelly sun block over her face and forearms.

"Wow." Liam sounded relieved, but at a loss. "It *did* seem weird that he would come out with it right in front of me. I can't imagine *my* dad saying that kind of thing to either of my sisters, I have to admit."

"Yeah, me neither. Or anybody's dad." She gave the sun block back to Liam. "Maybe I shouldn't have mentioned it, but I just didn't want us to go on tripping over the subject all the rest of the day."

"Well—thanks. I guess. Anyway, it's not your fault. Did you ever try asking him to quit saying stuff like that?" Pam shook her head no. "Maybe you should."

"Maybe," Pam said with no conviction at all, "but Mom's asked him about a million times not to blow his nose and then hold the handkerchief out and look at it, and he's never paid the slightest attention to her. He still always does that. He does what he pleases." She shook her head. "I don't think it would do any good."

"Well. I guess you would know." Liam chucked the sun block into the bottom of the canoe. He pitched in the bag of trash, and picked up his own situpon and Pam's.

Without moving Pam said, "He used to be really mean. When I was little. He spanked me all the time for nothing, and Mom couldn't make him stop that either—she told me they used to

140

fight about it. And he'd do these really cruel punishments . . . and then he quit. But this is almost worse.''

It was such a relief to get the embarrassment out in the open that in the first confiding flush Pam had an impulse to tell Liam another shaming anecdote; but she thought again. Better not. It had to do not only with her breasts but with her nose, which was actually another sensitive and unmentionable, or at least thus far unmentioned, subject between them. Enough revelations for one day. She resettled herself in the canoe; Liam braced his hands on the gunwales, shoved off the gravel bar, and stepped in. ''I'll take right.''

''Okay.'' Pam began paddling on her left side, and they both got down to work and started for the far shore, quartering from right to left across the current.

The thing she had almost told Liam had happened at Hurt Hollow the previous spring, exactly a year ago. Shelby Pruitt was a birder; Hurt Hollow was full of birds. Shelby and Jesse talked about birds and books, and that was pretty much the extent of their relationship; but her father liked to drop in on Jesse every so often. On this particular day they had all three been inside the house when Jesse heard a ripple of birdsong that to Pam sounded like a robin or maybe a summer tanager but that Jesse and her father both said was a rose-breasted grosbeak. Pam and Shelby had gone out with the field glasses to see if they could spot the grosbeak, and had quickly sighted the singer high in the canopy. When it was Pam's turn to look through the glasses, the grosbeak leapt to fill them, brilliant black and white, with a triangular patch the color of raspberry sherbet across its breast like a pointed bib, and a powerful pale seed-cracker of a bill.

It was the first rose-breasted grosbeak Pam had ever seen, and amazingly pretty. As it moved actively through the foliage of a large beech, feeding on the flowers and pausing occasionally to proclaim its territory, Pam managed to keep the bird centered in the field glasses. This one, she knew, was a male; only the male songbird sings. She asked, ''Is the female this pretty?''

''No,'' said her father, considering. ''The female's duller, like most of the other female finches. Looks kind of like a great big song sparrow, but a duller brown.''

Like her own parents, Pam remembered thinking: Frances dumpy and ordinary except for her big brown eyes and thick dark hair, Shelby tall and strong, with a blue-eyed, boyishly roundcheeked handsomeness.

141

At that moment the grosbeak had thrown back its head, opened its beak, and poured forth a long string of swooping, trilling musical notes; and in the middle of the song Shelby had chuckled suddenly and said, "You know something, you and that bird up there are a whole lot alike—he's got a big strong beak, and he's got a pretty pink breast!" He had laughed again, pleased with the conceit, inviting Pam to enjoy it with him. "Never thought of that, did you! I expect he likes both of his better'n you like either of yours, too."

The bird flew out of the glasses' field. Pam's arms were tired. Without looking round at him, without another word, she had handed the binoculars over and quickly climbed the steps back up to the house, where Jesse was making supper.

It was funny how neither of Pam's parents could pronounce *breasts* or *desks*. The problem was some consequence of their Louisville accents, apparently, though other people brought up in Louisville seemed able to manage the *-sts* and *-sks*. Frances would say the words leaving out their terminal consonants, making them rhyme: *bresss*, *desss*. Shelby pronounced the plurals exactly like the singular forms, only bearing down a little harder on the T and the K. Thinking of his complacent voice saying *breasT*—meaning both of her mother's, or her own enormous two—made Pam's skin positively crawl. She hunched forward in the canoe and shoved her paddle into the river.

The extra effort was needed. The wind had picked up as soon as they were well away from shore; and as they approached the red and green buoys marking the channel, the deepest part of the river with the strongest currents, the water grew choppy with wind waves, some of which even had little whitecaps. The stiff breeze blowing across the water was wonderfully cool, but it kept trying to push the canoe broadside to the current, and Liam had to fight hard to keep it headed downstream. It crossed Pam's mind that putting on the life jackets before starting across might have been prudent. Doing it now, out in the middle of the river, was impossible; neither of them could stop paddling long enough without losing control of the canoe.

For half an hour they bumped into and were splashed by waves encountered at the wrong angle, and shipped some water that soaked the towels in the bottom. At one moment, when for fifteen or twenty minutes she had been driving her paddle rapidly over and over into the brown water with all her strength, the first line of Stephen Crane's story "The Open Boat" popped into Pam's mind: "None of them knew the color of the sky."

142

She was a little scared; they seemed to be making such poor headway against the wind, and both of them were already working as hard as they could.

Because of the wind, the crossing was rougher and slower than usual, and the towboat and its barges came a little bit too close for comfort; but they got out of its way, finally, and out of the middle of the river, and worked the canoe at length into the relatively calm water near the Kentucky shore.

"Whew!" said Liam from the stern, "Now I know why there aren't any other canoes around. Let's pull out and rest for a few minutes, okay? My arms are like lead."

"Mine too. This is a private beach, but maybe we could stop here anyway for a little while. Nobody's around."

During the crossing the current had carried them downstream a quarter of a mile or so. Over in Indiana at this point the bluffs came straight down to the water; here the wooded hills were the better part of a mile away. They beached the canoe at the edge of a long narrow strip of muddy shore, beyond which cows and a few horses were grazing the fenced pasturage of the bottom land that stretched from the river to the road, half a mile inland.

The place where they had landed was actually a bare mud flat covered with drift, not a beach. There was nowhere to sit. They walked around for a little while, catching their breath and shaking out the kinks, but it wasn't comfortable and before very long they were ready to shove off again.

Now the paddling was fairly easy, and Pam began to sing in time with her strokes, a stirring, extremely appropriate gospel song, in six/eight time, two measures to a line:

Peace! Be Still!

Mary A. Baker

H. R. Palmer

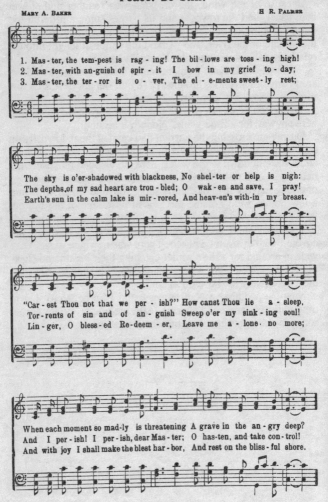

1. Mas - ter, the tem-pest is rag - ing! The bil - lows are toss - ing high!
2. Mas - ter, with an-guish of spir - it I bow in my grief to - day;
3. Mas - ter, the ter - ror is o - ver, The el - e-ments sweet - ly rest;

The sky is o'er-shadowed with blackness, No shel - ter or help is nigh:
The depths of my sad heart are trou - bled; O wak - en and save, I pray!
Earth's sun in the calm lake is mir - rored, And heav-en's with - in my breast.

"Car - est Thou not that we per - ish?" How canst Thou lie a - sleep,
Tor - rents of sin and of an - guish Sweep o'er my sink - ing soul!
Lin - ger, O bless - ed Re-deem - er, Leave me a - lone no more;

When each moment so mad-ly is threatening A grave in the an - gry deep?
And I per - ish! I per - ish, dear Mas - ter; O has-ten, and take con - trol!
And with joy I shall make the blest har - bor, And rest on the bliss - ful shore.

144

Peace! Be Still!

145

"Master, the tempest is ra-ging,
The billows are toss!-sing high,
The sky is o'ershadowed with black-ness,
No shelter or help! is nigh!
Carest Thou not that we per-ish?
How canst Thou lie! a-sleep,
When each moment so madly is threat-'ning
A grave in the ang-gry deep?"

"The winds and the waves shall o-
Bey! my will:
Peace! be still! Peace! be still!
Whether the wrath of the
Storm!-tossed sea,
Or demons or men or what-
E-ver it be,
No water shall swallow the
Ship! where lies
The Master of ocean and
Earth! and skies . . .

"They all! shall sweetly o-
Bey, my will:
Peace! be still! Peace! be still!
They all! shall sweetly o-
Bey, my will:
Peace . . . peace . . . be still!"

"What are you singing up there?" Liam called. "Sing louder, I can't hear." So Pam sang the song again, louder, with lots of dramatic emphasis; it was another of her favorites; she liked all the ones with the heavy drumbeat effects. *"Wheth-ther-the-wrath-of-the-/STORM! -TOSSED SEA! Or /de-mons-or-men-or-what-/EV-ER-IT-BE! . . . "* sang Pam. The chorus ascended the diatonic scale, starting low, one note per measure: Mi-mi-mi-mi-mi-mi/FA! -FA FA! Fa/Sol-sol-sol-sol-sol-sol-/LA-LA-LA-LA . . . —all the way up to "Mi," in the octave above, before breaking back into tunefulness.

Liam liked the song. When Pam sang the third stanza, which described how things aboard the ship had calmed down, he joined in on the boom-boom-boom of "The winds and the waves. . . ." After they'd sung it all the way through three times

146

he asked, "What's going on there? Who's talking? What's the situation?"

Pam half-turned to give him a look. "Wow, don't you know anything? Jesus and his disciples were out in a boat on the Sea of Galilee and Jesus fell asleep. While he was sleeping a storm blew up and the boat filled up with water. The disciples thought they were done for. They woke him up, very resentful, and Jesus told them they should have more faith. Then he said 'Peace, be still,' and the sea went calm." She laughed. "My parents and some friends of theirs were going out in a rowboat one time at a church picnic and Mr. Barnhill stepped in wrong or something and the gunwale almost went under, and Mrs. Barnhill screeched and said, 'Barney, carest thou not that we perish?'"

Liam laughed, but then he inquired dubiously, "So . . . you think that really happened? Jesus really said 'Peace, be still,' and the storm just fizzled out?"

Pam took a few paddle strokes, thinking about it. "Maybe the eye of a hurricane passed over . . . no, no, I'm joking. I never really know what to think about certain of the miracles. I don't *really* think that one happened . . . and yet, I can see it, I really can, I can see it just as plain as anything. A lot better than I can see Moses leading the Israelites through the middle of the Red Sea on dry land." She paddled more. "I *don't* really believe it, and yet . . . ."

"What about the other people in your church?"

"They'd give you different answers. Mom believes it. Dad probably doesn't. Mom believes every word of the Bible, literally."

"That's really . . ." Liam seemed to be searching for a polite enough word. He settled for "incredible."

"In a way, you know, it almost doesn't matter whether it really happened. It's a story about the power of faith to change things . . . and also, kind of, a story about how lonely Jesus was. Like, none of them understood him. There he was asleep, exhausted. There the disciples were, wide awake and petrified. Like all huddled together in the stern, muttering to each other, 'What manner of man is this, that even the winds and the sea obey him?' And there's Jesus, making the waves be still, knowing that was something he could do, but all by himself. There was nobody else like him. He was the only one."

They took five more synchronized strokes. "Well," said Liam, "I get your point. But I don't agree that it doesn't matter whether it really happened or not. I think there's a *huge* differ-

147

ence between thinking of all that as a story about faith, or about Jesus being lonely, and thinking of it as something that actually, literally happened in real placetime. I don't think *anybody*, in all of history, *ever* just told a weather phenomenon like a storm to stop dead and hey presto, no more storm.''

''You don't believe in miracles, you mean.''

''Right, I don't believe in miracles. I don't believe in events in which the laws of science are broken.''

Pam considered this. ''So, you don't think we create our own reality through the way we describe it.''

''Heck no!''

''That's what a lot of philosophers say.''

Liam shifted his weight, making the canoe lurch. ''Hoo boy, Carrie would kill me, she *hates* all that kind of talk! I mean, obviously, there's something to it—but do you know the story about Boswell and Samuel Johnson going to hear Bishop Berkeley preach on the unreality of the material universe? Well, when they came out of the church Boswell said he thought it was an unappealing philosophy but he didn't see any way of refuting it. And Samuel Johnson just kicked a big rock they happened to be passing and said, '*I* refute it *thus*.' ''

Pam laughed. ''I do too,'' she said. ''What a great story.''

Conversation is awkward in a canoe; the person in the bow, facing always away from the one behind, has to speak loudly to be heard, and Pam began to find the effort of loud speech a strain. It would have been easier to hear Liam, but it made sense for the stronger paddler to be in the stern, where he could steer. Deciding not to change places, they settled back to paddling and thought their separate thoughts.

The shore on their left was still grassy bottomland, the bluff on the Indiana side a dark green mass with a dark reflection. The distant bluffs ahead, where the river made a bend, formed a blue-green band between the blue sky and the blue water. They passed the mouth of a creek, and then another. Pam and Liam paddled as smoothly together as if they had been practicing for years: stretch-thrust-pull, glide; stretch-thrust-pull, glide. Liam kept them on a straight course. The breeze was light, not hard to make headway against. Though sweat stood in droplets on the skin of Pam's sunblock-sticky arms, though there was a place on her left thumb where the paddle would soon rub a blister, for minutes together life was just about perfect.

The 566.5 mile marker went by on their left, then a cluster of houses. Beyond the houses the bottomland butted up against trees and stopped; here the river switched sides again, hugging the Kentucky bluff, creating a two-mile-long stretch of cornfields over in Indiana. Pam's heart began to thump. She called back to Liam, "We're almost there."

The trees cloaking the bluff came right down to the waterline—tall, massed, and at the peak of bloom. The showy white flower clusters held high above the water released a powerful fragrance, and the treetops hummed with bees. Even before the advancing canoe had entered and disturbed the trees' reflections in the water, it had entered the zone of scented air, and Liam called, "What smells so good?"

Pam pointed up. "Dad says this year's bloom is"—dropping her voice an octave—" 'exceptionally fine.' They're black locusts. Some people call them lilac trees."

"I can see why."

Now on the left the bank gradually curved away; and as they cleared the bend Pam, in the bow, peering forward, could just make out where the chain-link fence which marked the property line of Hurt Hollow began. Beyond that was the dock of shiny metal, with Jesse's johnboat moored to it, and his green canoe overturned farther up the bank. In a couple more minutes they would be able to see the goat stable, and then the house, its large window in the gable flashing in the westering sun.

#About the title of this chapter, I see *us* as the two young roes that are twins. Right? Roe, roe, roe your boat . . . (Just kidding.)

#I think being short, for me, was/is something like being buxom was for you—but I won't pretend it puts me in the same league with you, anguish-wise.

#Could I possibly really have gone around saying "Wow!" all the time?? I don't believe it. Your memory's still busted, no pun intended.

#Where you talk about your arms not being able to pull you up a pole anymore, that whole paragraph—that reads like a description of somebody helplessly *turning* from a boy into a girl. A shape-shifter, and she's not going to shift back when the sun comes up.

#Funny you describe the dissociative effect as being like a lens—almost like the lens of the transceivers, dilating between one reality and another.

#Doesn't it strike you as weird that talking about biblical miracles etc. should have made me so twitchy, but I could chat about your period and your father's jerky behavior without turning a hair? It sure does me. (I dimly remember this.) Those topics should "by rights" have made me *at least* as uncomfortable as the miracle-talk. "There would be nobody but Liam to see her, and he wouldn't care." Too, too true. I worried constantly about being so switched off in general, but never once about being switched off where you were concerned, as if the two things had nothing to do with each other; and that was *weird*.

9

AND THE SERPENT

—Genesis 3:4

"Hunh, that's weird. The gate's still locked." Pam squinted uphill at the gate, whose huge padlock could be seen at quite a distance, like a burl on an oak tree. "Isn't it after two o'clock? Visiting hours start at two."

"It's three-twenty. Has Jesse got a doorbell?" Liam's paddle made a long smooth movement in the water and the canoe drew up smartly, parallel to the dock.

"Not over here. There's a dinner bell on the landing across the river, but the bell on this side is up by the house, inside the fence. *We're* okay though," said Pam, and power surged through her as she said this, "I've got a key."

When she had snubbed the canoe up to the dock, Pam shipped her paddle and felt in the pocket of her bookbag for this, her proudest possession in the world, the key that would admit her to Hurt Hollow at any time of her own choosing, any day in the year. (She also fished out a Tampax and stuck it in the pocket of her shirt.) Key clutched in her fist, she stepped out onto the dock, then turned and crouched to hold the stern against it so Liam could get out. "Jesse never opens late. I wonder if something's going on."

In single file they climbed the steep path—at one place so steep that Orrin had installed a staircase with a handrail—and peered up through the fence, eight feet high, at the house set into the hillside. "I don't see anybody, do you?" The gate had been padlocked from the inside; Pam stuck her hand between gate and gatepost, grabbed the lock and twisted it toward herself. She pushed the key in through the meshes and turned it. The hasp snapped open. She swung the gate outward just far enough to sidle through. "Come on."

151

Liam followed Pam and pulled the gate shut behind him. "Should I lock it?"

Pam hesitated. "Yeah, better lock it. Jesse might have some reason not to open up today."

Hurt Hollow was eerily still. Pam could hear things happening elsewhere—a tow passing on the river behind them, the regular chop, chop, chop of an axe a long way away, a dog barking, children shouting from the invisible houses along the ridge to the south, beyond the boundary fence in that direction, even the light clapping of the bell that told Jesse where the goats were and when they were coming home—but the Hollow itself was quiet except for the birds and the slapping of small waves from the passing tow. Pam had never been here on such a beautiful, mild afternoon in spring, between two and four o'clock, when at least one tour guide hadn't been leading a busload of noisy sightseers along the paths between house and studio, studio and goat stable, goat stable and guest house, guest house and gardens. She wondered—jabbed by a pang of alarm—if something might be not just unusual, but wrong.

From where Pam and Liam stood, inside the fence with their backs to the river, the bluff sloped sharply up to the house. Faced vertically with weathered planks, roofed with sheet metal, the house was fitted into the hillside at an angle to the shoreline, its gable end nearly filled with eight casement windows set side by side in two rows of four each, to make one big picture window on the view. Below the windows was a wooden deck, and below the deck the doors to the cellar stood open.

To the left of the deck wall, Orrin had terraced a level space into the hillside and flagged it with flat stones set in concrete. On the terrace stood a spool table and several of the low wooden chairs Orrin had made, a barbecue grill built into the retaining wall, a rough wooden workbench, and, beside the door, a dinner bell hung on a post.

The path up to the terrace was a series of switchbacks that ran past patches of garden, several cold frames covered with window sashes (empty now), and a blackened metal drum that Jesse used for smoking fish and goatmeat; Pam had helped him smoke a mess of catfish in it more than once.

"Come on," she said again. They climbed up to the terrace, and while Liam hung back, looking about him in wonderment, Pam went to the door, which stood ajar, and called, "Jesse?"

No answer.

She opened the screen door and stepped inside. "Jesse?" The

152

door, weighted to swing shut behind her, bumped her in the back. She frowned, unsure what to do; she possessed a key to Hurt Hollow but this was Jesse's house, not hers or anyone's to enter uninvited. Hesitating between reluctance and worry, she wavered in the doorway; but worry drew her forward, up three polished wooden steps into the second room, the smaller, upper, original cabin built quickly by Orrin in the fall of 1951, in a rush to get some living space enclosed before the cold weather set in. "Jesse?"

He was not in the house at all. Pam came back outside. "He's probably still up at the top of the hill, waiting to lock up. He probably went up early for some reason, or stayed up. He works with the bees this time of year, they're up there. We can just wait here on the terrace till he gets back."

"He climbs up there every day *twice* to lock and unlock the gate himself? How come he can't do it from down here?"

"Everybody asks that. Jesse hates the fence—being forced to fence the place, and the ugliness of it—but he hates anything automatic even worse. He'd rather walk up the hill in a snow-storm than throw a switch." Pam grinned possessively. "He's consistent, anyway. What would somebody who believed in electronic locks and alarm systems be doing living like this? Jesse won't have a power tool on the place, not even a chainsaw; he wouldn't even before the Directive. That's why the Hefn . . ." Pam trailed off and looked down, feeling her face get warm; she had been about to say, "That's why the Hefn are interested in Hurt Hollow." But they were interested in it only in the made-up world of *Pinny's Hefn*; here in the real world it was Liam who thought Humphrey should come and see what life in the Hollow was like, and Pam who kept trying to nix the idea. She had been about to argue against her own position.

They sat in two of the chairs and absorbed the view: the dense forest of mingled maple, tulip poplar, oak, buckeye, hackberry, elm, sycamore, cottonwood, and sweet gum trees, with here and there a white spray of dogwood or a pink one of redbud; the river, glinting through foliage that pretty well concealed both it and the metal fence; the goat stable peeking through the trees to their right, empty now, since the goats browsed up the bluff-side during the day and came back at evening to be milked. Pam named for Liam the birds whose continuous antiphony perfected the afternoon: wood thrush, peewee, towhee, robin, cardinal, titmouse, wren. She pointed across the creek to where the in-visible guest house was, and promised to take Liam over there,

153

and also to see Orrin's studio where copies of some of his pictures hung now, as soon as Jesse got back.

But half an hour went by, and then an hour. Pam's discomfort intensified. Before she could give herself up properly to being back at the Hollow, she needed to know that everything was all right; and the longer she had to remain in uncertainty the more her anxiety increased.

"I know!" she exclaimed suddenly with relief. "I bet he went to town. He's got a solarcycle up at the top of the hill. I bet he left a notice at the upper gate that the Hollow would close early today and rode into town for some reason." She got up. "Let's go up there and see if there's a notice posted. Maybe he says what time he'll be back."

"Would he leave the house open if he was going away for part of the day?"

This sensible question stopped her. "Well . . . not ordinarily. Hunh. You've got a point there. But—well—let's go up and check, anyway. What else can we do? I don't feel right wandering around when Jesse's not here."

"Okay, but I've got another question: would he post a notice at the top gate and not at the one we came through?"

Liam was right, it wasn't logical. Still . . . "I guess he might. There's a ferry Saturdays and Sundays this time of year, from the steamboat landing over there, but not that many people come in off the river on weekdays till June . . . but he always opens both gates, so . . . I dunno. But I still think we should go up there, find out if the bike's gone."

"Okay." Liam levered himself out of the low chair and followed Pam back down the terrace steps. As they passed the cellar's open door, Pam peered in and noted that the shelves were nearly bare, except for some mason jars of goat meat and what looked like blackberries in juice like blue-black ink. They went up another short flight of steps to the back door, from which a level path led to a smaller building with a steeply pitched roof, fifty yards away. "This is the studio . . . and this is the outhouse, and I guess I might as well use it while I'm here. I'll only be a minute."

It was Jesse's private outhouse, not meant for visitors; for them there were public conveniences next to the upper gate and behind the goat stable. Orrin had fitted the privy cunningly behind the studio and weighted its door, like the house doors, so it would close and keep out flies.

Inside, Pam took the paper-wrapper cylinder out of the pocket of her T-shirt, hung the shirt on a nail, and pulled her bathing suit all the way down to her knees. She lifted the lid and sat down on the smooth plank of the seat. Gingerly then she groped for the Tampax, pulled it out of herself by its string and held it up like a dead mouse, considering whether she ought to drop it into the drum below. The question, by some freak of timing, had never come up before. Was a Tampax biodegradable? Would it rot away along with the other stuff people left down there? She didn't want Jesse to have to find it next year, still intact, while spading the finished compost into the garden.

Still dangling the wet object from two fingers of her right hand, Pam held the new tampon against her thigh with her left and awkwardly peeled back the paper. What was it made of? Cotton fibers, surely? And cotton string, and a cardboard applicator? They *should* all rot down to nothing, given a year, but . . . ah. She managed to smooth the wrapper straight over the cardboard tube and read the tiny print: *Used tampons and packaging may be deposited in any solid waste composting system.*

That description definitely covered Jesse's privy. Pam let go of the dead Tampax, spread thighs, and pushed the fresh one in. She dropped the wadded up paper and the tube, peed, stood, hauled her damp suit back up over her sweaty, sticky body, and the shirt over her head, then lifted the seat—a hinged section cut out of the wider plank, one of Orrin's customized refinements on the usual outhouse arrangement—and dumped five or six scoops of wood ashes from the bucket by the door into the hole, burying the offending items. Finally she brushed the spilled ashes off the seat and closed both it and the lid.

What had Marion done with *her* Tampaxes? And Hannah before her? Most likely they had sewn their own sanitary pads from cotton rags, as Pam's grandmother had told her her own mother, Pam's great-grandmother, had done, and washed them out after each month's use. That would fit the style of life at Hurt Hollow, but the thought made Pam shudder. Better, as always a million times better, to be a boy—even here in this, the most wonderful place in the world.

Outside, Liam had wandered along the trail as far as the little wooden gate and was staring intently out across the lush green creek valley. "What kind of a bird is that?" he said when Pam came up behind him. "That one there, see—it just flew. There."

A streak of black and white, a flash of rosy pink. Pam said excitedly, "A rose-breasted grosbeak! Hey! I didn't get a very

155

good look but that's the only bird with those colors. Did you see where it landed? Maybe we can get closer.''

As she spoke the bird flew out of the tree, veered sharply above their heads and landed in a redbud halfway between them and the studio. It had chosen a bare branch; they could see it clearly. It threw back its head and sang. "They don't sing much this time of day except when they're pairing off," Pam said. "That's a grosbeak, all right. The first one I ever saw in my life was just last summer, back there in front of the house. You were lucky."

Liam was pleased. "I don't think we've got those back home. I sure never saw one at the feeder, just those little brownish-red birds that squabble and spill seed around."

"Those are house finches . . . I don't think grosbeaks winter over, but I think they might be around in the summer back there. Or maybe in winter too. Dad thinks the greenhouse effect is changing migration patterns."

The bird flew away toward the house. Pam said, "Come on, we better get going," and pushed past Liam to open the gate and lead the way down toward the creek. The Hollow was bursting with spring smells and sounds and colors, extravagant skunk cabbages in the swampy low places, foliage of a dozen different shades of green. The odor of wet mud, essence of springtime, volatile in the heat, suffused Pam's senses; again her heart leapt with explosive joy.

She started to quote, " 'For, lo, the winter is past, the rain is over and gone—' " when it happened again: a slight mental slippage, then the world changed, snapped back, brightened and was artificial, unreal.

Terror pierced Pam like a sword. She stumbled and looked down; Liam almost tripped over her. "Sorry. What were you saying? I couldn't hear."

"Doesn't matter." She tried to go faster through this place where Liam was himself part of the unreality, impossible to connect with. When she looked up again and quickly down, it was still the same. She could feel her heart pounding and a buzzing in her head—those were real—but the world outside her own body had gone away, into another dimension, leaving her utterly isolated, out of contact, out of control.

"What?" Liam's voice reached her through a plastic glaze.

"I said, 'It doesn't matter.' I'm, I'm kind of dizzy, I want to stop for a second." They had crossed the creek and the level floor of the meadow, passing the spot near the ruins of the old stone chimney where Pam had camped with Betsy several times last summer, and had reached the foot of the short-cut trail up the bluff, that would connect to the gravel road which would lead, soon after, to the fence, with the mailbox and the paved county road beyond. Jesse had chosen not to improve the trail, in hopes of controlling the numbers or at least the sort of persons who would use it. Most tourists walked down the road, which the Army Corps of Engineers had graded and spread with gravel when the Hollow had first been put on the National Register of Historic Sites.

Pam sat down on the ground in a patch of shade, wrapped her arms around her knees, and put her head down between them. With her eyes closed the world seemed normal. The thudding and buzzing inside her didn't go away, but they diminished. Her hands were clammy.

For one minute, and then another, Pam sat. She had spoken to no one about this fear when it had struck repeatedly a year before, because something about it felt shameful and wrong, as if the fear were her own fault. For the same reason it never entered her head to tell Liam about it now. She could hear him walking around uneasily, kicking stones and breaking sticks against a background of rustling foliage and birdsong and the pouring noises of the creek and, behind that, the inexorable drumbeat of her heart.

What must he be thinking? She made a tremendous effort to clear her head, return to normal.

But she couldn't. Opening her eyes once, she saw Liam in the act of hooking an empty cicada shell he'd found to the bark of a little tree a foot away from her nose. Cicadas in May? It must be last year's shell. When she looked again a little later he'd added three or four more of them, facing the shells toward one another as if in conference. At such close range they looked alien and monstrous—the Gafr, perhaps, deciding the fate of the world.

When more time dragged by and Pam still hadn't thrown off the fit, Liam finally said, "What's the matter, are you sick? Something to do with your, uh, your period?"

A little hope flowed cautiously into Pam at the suggestion. She looked up. "I don't know—maybe. I guess it could be. I just feel dizzy and weird." *And scared out of my wits.*

"Anything I can do?"

"Well . . . I guess you could go on up the trail to the gate by yourself, and see if Jesse put up a notice." Funny how her mind

157

went on working despite the panicky feeling of lost control. "Here, take the key; you might have to unlock it to read it. I'll stay here. I'll probably be fine by the time you get back." This at least was actually true; the fits had never lasted long. The one that very morning had been over almost as soon as it started. "If I snap out of it I'll come on up and meet you coming down, okay? Just go up the trail to the top and turn right when you get to the gravel road, and follow that on up to the fence."

"Well, okay." He sounded relieved. "Will you be all right down here by yourself?"

"I'll probably be fine in a couple of minutes, but you might as well go on ahead as hang around waiting."

When Liam had gone, Pam sat embracing her knees with her eyes squeezed shut, listening to the bumping beat of her own heart. The closest she had ever come to telling her mother about the fits was one time when she had stood in the kitchen door while Frances was cooking dinner and asked her, "Do you feel your heart beating? Right this minute?" "Well no," Frances had answered, distracted and a little aggravated. *What now?* her look plainly said. "I do," Pam had told her, and Frances had glanced at her and replied, predictably enough, "Oh, you do not!"

A bit later she had taken Pam to the doctor about the dizzy spells. When he jabbed her icy finger to take a blood sample, nothing happened: he squeezed, but no ruby droplet formed at the tip. He'd had to jab again. And after all that there was nothing in Pam's blood that shed any light on her condition.

The dizzy spells had stopped when she went to Washington, and everyone, Pam included, had been happy to forget about them.

Maybe it *was* her period. She'd never noticed whether the fits occurred around that time of the month. If they were starting up again she could keep track; the explanation might be that simple. Pam clung desperately to the thought. Maybe lots of girls her age were periodically assailed by inexplicable, shameful terror and heard choirs of angels singing, and never told anybody else. Maybe Betsy . . . or even Carole Cosby, that noodlebrain, maybe every girl in eighth-grade history class had been sitting there frozen with terror but keeping it all to themselves.

Very cautiously, Pam lifted her head and opened her eyes. There was the world, sunny, green, bright—too bright; hastily she closed them again.

But what about Mom, then?

Heck, she could have forgotten. *I'd never have thought of it again either if it hadn't ever happened again.* It wasn't the sort of thing you wanted to think about if you didn't have to. Although Mom remembered having cramps . . . but she'd had cramps her whole life, she still got them. Maybe the dizzy spells just happened when you were new at having periods. Your hormones probably weren't very stable, that could be it. Unbalanced hormones were capable of tremendously powerful physical effects, they'd learned that in health. . . .

But here came Liam, she could hear him crashing recklessly down the trail, shouting something incomprehensible. Pam's eyes snapped open; she was already on her feet when Liam appeared a few yards above her, grabbing at a sapling to stop his downward plunge. "Jesse's up on the trail—he's snakebit!"

Pam bolted up toward Liam, who turned and charged back up the trail ahead of her. "Snakebit? Are you sure?"

"That's what he told me. 'Am I glad to see you. I'm snakebit.' "

"Where'd you find him?"

"Right at the top of the hill. He's conscious but he's sick and his leg's swollen up so bad he can't walk on it."

Pam's brain clicked into high gear. "Hold on a second. Wait, stop. Let me think." She panted for enough breath to talk. "He'll have to be taken to Madison, to the hospital. If he can't walk—and he's at the top of the hill—it would be quicker if I run back to the house and call an ambulance from there. You go on back and stay with him. No—first, go on up to the gate and unlock it. They'll have to bring the ambulance down the road. How long ago did it happen?"

Liam shook his head. "I dunno. His leg looks like a tree."

"Did he say what kind of snake?"

"I think he said copperhead."

"I'm going," Pam said, and flew back down the trail she had descended so many times (at a fraction of this speed) that she knew every root, every sudden drop, every slippery spot and protruding rock. Even so she staggered and fell at the bottom—but was up in an instant and pounding, breasts going *ba-WHOOM, ba-WHOOM,* across the meadow to the bridge—up and over, through the gate, on to the house, in the back door and out the front in a second—and a last, scrambling plunge down to the fence, where the phone lived in a box on a post, because Jesse wouldn't have it in the house.

159

Hands shaking, gasping so badly she could hardly talk, Pam wrenched open the box and punched in her own number. Her mother answered on the third ring, listened to Pam's breathless message, and said she would call the hospital at once. "Tell them it was a copperhead," Pam said and hung up the receiver to break the connection so her mother could make the call.

She stood by the gate long enough to get her breath back before starting the long climb back to the place where Jesse lay. Her lungs burned. Through the meshes of the fence she could see Jesse's johnboat, and the canoe looking just the way she and Liam had left it, unaffected by the crisis. Scratches from the fall burned on her palms and thighs. She leaned forward, gripping the metal like a prisoner, staring through at the chimney swifts darting, flicking, swooping over the surface of the river.

Early evening was their time for this dazzling display; it must be getting late. The sun was behind the bluff above the house now; the water gleamed with reflected light from the sky and a cool breeze blew into Pam's face. Ripples from a passing tow rocked the two moored boats gently and pushed little waves against the shore. Behind her in the trees the rose-breasted grosbeak sang.

When her chest had stopped heaving, Pam turned and started back toward the house. Her legs shook so badly she had trouble getting up the hill, and she stopped in the house for a minute to get a drink; her bathing suit and T-shirt were sweated through and her hair plastered to her scalp. If Jesse had been lying up there long, he might want some water too. She regretted not bringing up one of the canteens from the canoe, but felt unable to go back for it. In a cupboard she found an empty glass jar with a screw-on lid, and this she filled with water.

Holding the full jar against her body, Pam went shakily back the way she had come. Halfway up the hill she heard the siren. She climbed all the way to the road without seeing anybody, and continued on toward the gate until she met Liam, coming back down. "They got him," he said. "I rode with them as far as the gate and locked it behind them."

"Great. That was good thinking. How was he?"

"He'd passed out by the time I got back up there. Like he'd just been holding on till somebody came. I got to the gate just as the ambulance arrived. Is that water? I'm dying of thirst."

Pam passed him the jar; Liam unscrewed the lid and gulped, tilting back his head, spilling the water all down his shirt.

Pam watched him. "Did they say whether he'd be okay?"

160

Liam came up for air and started walking again. "They said not to worry, that's about all. They lifted him onto a stretcher and shoved the stretcher in the ambulance and took off. The whole thing only took about a minute. One of the guys rode in back with him and stuck an IV in his hand." Liam stopped for another drink, almost emptying the jar. "How serious is a copperhead bite, anyway, do you know?"

"Not as serious as a timber rattler. That's why I asked you. They'd probably have brought anitvenin with them and used it right away if it'd been a rattlesnake. I know several people who got bitten by copperheads around here and none of them died, but they got pretty sick. And it's harder on kids and old people, and Jesse's pretty old."

They reached the top of the trail and started down in single file, Pam going first, very slowly on her wobbly legs. "When we get back to the house I'm going to call Mom again. She might've gone to Madison, to the hospital . . . maybe I should just call the hospital direct." The thought struck her that calling the hospital direct was what she should have done in the first place; but Jesse didn't have a directory program, naturally, and Pam hadn't known the number of the hospital . . . let it go. She'd done pretty well; they both had.

Suddenly Pam felt happy. Maybe they hadn't rescued Jeffrey from those louts on the *Delta Queen*, but they had rescued Jesse from a miserable night at best, and possibly even saved his life.

"What if we hadn't come along when we did?" Liam said, his thoughts obviously running along the same lines as Pam's. "What if he'd had to spend the night up there? Isn't it still supposed to rain? That could have been pretty serious."

Pam shivered at the thought of just how serious it might have been. Snakebite, exposure, shock, pneumonia . . . Liam was right, it was an extremely lucky thing they'd happened to come today. If they'd come on Saturday, and gone home Sunday, who would have come by that happened to have a key and could let themselves in, so's to find Jesse in time to get him rescued?

Maybe nobody.

So sometimes even cramps have a purpose. *Father,* she thought automatically, *I do thank Thee for bringing us here at the right time, and for letting us maybe save Jesse's life. And for the chance to do something important for him, something that really matters, because I really, really love him. And for letting it be Thy will that Liam be with me, because I sure couldn't have done it all by myself.*

161

At the gate Pam took the line of least resistance and called home again. When nobody answered she punched directory assistance, got the hospital's number, and called there. The tape said Jesse was resting comfortably and out of danger. Asked when he would be able to come home, the tape replied that it had no information about that.

An impulse to go down and bring up all the gear from the canoe made Pam realize that she had forgotten to get the key back from Liam, whom she had left sitting on the terrace. "Hey!" she called several times, until he had roused himself and come to the edge, a tiny shirtless figure in cutoffs. "Key!" Pam yelled. "I need the *key*!" Lifting an arm to show he understood, Liam started down.

They had mounted halfway back to the house, arms loaded, when Liam, who was leading, said, "Hey, look who's here!" The goats had come in; it was milking time. A big black-and-white ram, balanced on a gangplank leading from the hillside to the upper level of the stable, glowered at Pam and Liam. Behind him, a group of three brown-and-white does and a black-and-white kid stared more placidly at the humans.

Pam sighed. "Ever milk a goat?"

They left their belongings on the terrace. Pam got a sterilized milking pail with a half-moon cover, and the bigger milk can, from their cupboard in the shed behind the house, then drew a pail of water and led the way to the stable. The goats looked at them accusingly and didn't want to go in. "C'mon, you guys," said Liam. "Jesse's not here. You want to get this over with or not?"

"You don't browbeat them, you bribe them." When Pam had measured some iodine into the water bucket and swirled it around with a long-handled metal spoon, she pried the lid off the grain tub and poured a coffee canful into the plastic wash basin at one end of the milking stand. A nanny wearing a brass bell on a leather collar around her neck hopped up onto the stand and began to munch.

Though Pam hadn't done any milking in a while, she had as good as taken over the job from Jesse that last summer. Normally she would have enjoyed this, but she was so tired! She perched on Jesse's stool and tried to concentrate: wash the udder with a clean rag dipped in the iodine solution, dry it with another rag, clamp the milking pail between her calves, trap the milk in the teat as close to the top as possible in the circle of her thumb and first finger, and squeeze the teats from the top to the bottom, tightening one finger at a time.

It worked. Milk squirted out in a thin stream and rattled into the pail.

"Wow!" said Liam. "Show me what you're doing." He pushed close and the nanny stopped crunching her grain and nervously turned partway around. "Whoops! Sorry!"

"Just move more slowly. They don't like sudden movements, and we aren't Jesse so they're a little spooked anyway. Goats are creatures of habit." She began to milk with two hands. The milk streamed into the can. Pam's exhaustion vanished; showing off for Liam, she felt like a million dollars.

But she was slow. Belle had to be given more corn to keep her patient. Finally she got down, her udder more or less stripped. Another goat *baa'ed* and promptly jumped into her place. Pam looked at the swollen bag and groaned; her forearms ached from lack of practice. "Want to try it? The hardest part is squeezing from the top down—it's unnatural for me, somehow, I want to tighten my fingers from the bottom *up*. Then if I try to think about it it's like the centipede trying to figure out which leg comes after which—I can't do it at all."

Liam poured grain into the basin for Alice and slid onto the stool—and in five minutes, to Pam's mortification, was better at milking than she was. If she hadn't been so tired it would have been hard not to resent that Liam, graceful in all his physical actions, was better even at this totally unfamiliar homesteading art than Pam, who despite her experience was clumsy in so many of her own.

But she *was* tired. So tired she could scarcely pick up her feet as they trudged back up to the house in the fading light, Liam carrying the full can of strained milk and Pam the empty water bucket and pail. "Are we sleeping in the guest house?" Liam was asking, when Pam said, "Somebody's here. There's a light."

As they approached the terrace, a man stood up to greet them; the light was a kerosene lamp in the window of the house behind him. "When did you get here?" Pam asked her father. "How's Jesse? I tried to call but nobody answered."

"I got here, oh, about half an hour ago. I've just been sitting here enjoying the evening. A taxi brought me down to the landing and I came across the river in your little canoe, Pam."

Pam set down her pails and rubbed her arms. "How's Jesse?"

"He'll be all right. He's pretty sick right now, but he'll be

163

feeling better in a day or so. He'll have to stay in the hospital for a while, though—maybe a week, maybe more, depending on how things go.''

"Did they give him antivenin?"

"No, the doctor said they don't treat copperhead bites with antivenin, except in the case of children. Small body size, I expect. They'll watch his breathing and his liver and kidney function, but they don't expect any complications. Jesse's a tough old bird. It's a mighty good thing you and Liam found him when you did, though. A tour group leader brought a bunch of people over, and she apparently reported to the police that the gate was locked and they couldn't get in, but she didn't call till her bus got back to Louisville. If Jesse'd had to spend the night up there, why, it might've been another story.''

Pam and Liam smiled at each other. Liam said, "How long had he been up there when we found him?"

"He was on his way up to open the gate, so I guess it must've been three or four hours anyway. He started trying to walk out, but his leg swelled up and hurt too bad to stand on, and then he commenced to vomit.''

"Vomit" was one of Shelby's words. Pam said hurriedly, "Can we go see him in a couple of days?"

"I expect so . . . but Jesse wanted me to ask you if you'd mind staying here till he gets back. He says don't bother about the bees, he'll take care of them when he gets home, but somebody needs to be here who knows about the milking and seeing to the garden." Shelby grinned at her, pleased. "He said, 'Pam knows what to do. Let her take care of the place, I don't need anybody else there.' I told him I was sure it would be a pleasure for you to do that for him. I said Liam can keep you company, and I'd come over as much as I could, and spend nights here till he gets back.''

Delight that Jesse trusted *her* to take care of Hurt Hollow in his absence jostled everything else out of Pam's mind. Liam said, "Hey, that's great!"

"You'll need to stay closed to visitors while he's away; there'll be enough to do without having tourists all over the place, and most of the time I won't be able to be here during the day. Several people said they'd be glad to look in and lend a hand, people from the college and some from Madison. But you're the one with the know-how, so you're in charge.''

Again he smiled at her proudly. Pam said, "I'd really *rather* do it myself. It's a bother, letting people in if they don't have keys.'' She looked at Shelby suddenly. ''How did *you* get in— did Jesse give you *his* key?''

''Mm-hm. I'll keep it while I'm coming and going, but I know Jesse doesn't want a lot of people carrying keys and losing them so I won't make any duplicates. You give us a call if you want help, and somebody'll come over. But I expect you'll be able to handle things well enough. You're a pretty mature little girl.''

''Actually,'' said Pam, ''you wouldn't have to come over every night. We can manage okay.''

''Oh, your mother would have a fit if she thought you and Liam were staying over here together without a chaperon! No,'' grinning, shaking his head, ''I'll come over at night. You all can hold the fort during the day.''

Neither Apprentice mentioned that they had shared a stateroom aboard the *Delta Queen*. Pam opened her mouth to protest, closed it again, then opened it to say, ''The milk! We have to get it into the springhouse, it'll spoil! Come on, Liam, one more river to cross.''

Liam picked up the can and followed Pam down toward the creek. Behind them Shelby called, ''Your mother sent you-all some supper, so you wouldn't have to cook anything tonight. I'll have it on the table by the time you get back up here.'' He paused. ''Liam, would you care for the loan of a flashlight? Pam can find her way in the dark, but you don't want to trip and drop that can.''

''Okay.'' He backed up, took it from Shelby's hand, and went after Pam.

When they had eaten all of Frances's chicken salad and applesauce cake, the three of them sat on the terrace while the night came down. Eventually Liam said, ''Would it be okay to use the phone? I want to call home. I'll reverse the charges.''

He wandered off with the flashlight; they could follow his zigzag progress down the hill. Shelby said consideringly, ''Your friend Liam seems like a nice young man.''

''He is.''

''My kinda guy.''

The heck he is, Pam thought fiercely. She was aware of Shelby's appraising gaze upon her. ''It's cooling down,'' said his voice in the near-darkness. ''You might want to put on some long pants and long sleeves. A mosquito bit me a minute ago.''

''Dad,'' Pam blurted, ''why did you say that about my bathing suit being too small in front of Liam? I was embarrassed, and so was he.''

"You were?" said Shelby, genuinely surprised. "Why, your mother told me that you were talking in front of him about your having commenced to menstruate. I just figured you all talk about things like that nowadays."

"It's not the *same*," Pam said desperately, but why wasn't it the same? She couldn't think of how to explain the difference.

Sure enough, after a short silence her father said, "Well why isn't it the same?" and she had to say she couldn't explain. They sat together in mutual discomfort in the dark—or at least Pam was uncomfortable; it was hard to tell about Shelby.

After a minute or two he said, "While I was sitting out here a while ago, I heard a rose-breasted grosbeak down by the river. You remember the one we saw out here last summer?"

Trapped, she admitted, "I remember."

"Could be the same one . . . I said to your mother the other day, you know, we ought to see if something can't be done about Pam's nose. Nobody in my family, or hers either, ever had a nose like that. So she called around and got the name of a good plastic surgeon in Louisville, and when you go down to see your grandmother, before you go back to school, you and your mother are going to see him too—find out what he says. Did she mention anything about it to you?"

"No," said Pam, and bingo, there it was again—the slippage, the buzzing, the world gone away. Not into brightness, for it was dark, but infinitely gone. In all the excitement she hadn't even noticed when the earlier fit had ended at the instant of Liam's pell-mell arrival with the news of Jesse's plight, but for the past couple of hours Pam and the world had been existing in the same continuum of reality. Now Pam was one place again and the world another, and that made three times in one day.

Out of the plastic dark, Liam appeared. "I can't keep my eyes open. Where am I supposed to sleep?"

Shelby stood. "Did you get your call through all right?"

"Yes, thanks."

"Well," he said, "there's two ways we can arrange it. We can have the guest house be the boys' bunkhouse and let Pam sleep in Jesse's bed . . . or Pam and I can bunk over there and you can stay here in the house. Either way."

In the ensuing silence a corner of Pam's mind, separated absolutely from the world, nevertheless went watchful and clear.

166

She said, "I always wanted to sleep in Jesse's bed. You can take the guest house, okay?"

"Well," said Shelby, "if that's the way you want to do it."

Pam got up. "I'm absolutely bushed. See you in the morning, Liam. 'Night, everybody." She walked into the house without looking back, letting the screen door bang gently behind her.

#I looked it up about this world-becoming-plastic thing of yours. It's called *derealization*, and is a major symptom of psychic distress and trauma.

#Your dad wasn't actually all that far off the mark, you know. It *was* odd for us to be talking like that about your period, just like our bunking together on the *Delta Queen* was odd. We were both working at it too hard, like each of us was shouting to the other, THIS DOESN'T MATTER, DOES IT! NO, THIS DOESN'T MATTER! But it did matter.

I see it like a circle. He talks inappropriately (Julie's favorite word) to you. This makes you incredibly anxious, but you shove the anxiety under where you can't feel it too much. (The derealization is an attempt to get away from it too.) Since you can't really feel the anxiety that much, and also maybe want to deny it exists, you talk inappropriately to me. He hears about it and this expands *his* sense of what's okay to say and when it's okay to say it. At the same time I'm pushing stuff under as hard as you, so I pick up on the weirdness between you and him but not on the weirdness between you and me.

The problems clustering around that, what I guess we can call incest-related problems, you see all that pretty clear. Okay, but when you start imagining Hannah and Marion coping with their periods, you *also* get very upset and start up again on wanting to be a boy. Even though you don't mind things like cleaning catfish, and other fairly grotty homesteading stuff. See what I mean?

So here's my partial hypothesis, based on conclusions so far: There are *two* things going on here. It's easy to mix them up, because both have to do with being female, having big breasts, etc. But one is about your father's creepy behavior and the other one isn't. I can't tell yet what the second one *is* about, but I'll keep working on it.

#News: we think we've got a Hot Spot! A place in the north of Scotland, called Findhorn. Raghu's calculations plotted an intersection of beelines right there on the coast, and when Christa looked the place up it turned out to be a big New Age center where they used to grow enormous cabbages in pure sand with the help of nature spirits, etc., fifty-plus years ago! Pretty well documented for that kind of thing. So a couple of us and Humphrey are going over in about ten days, when the calculations are finished and the ground around there is completely mapped.

There's still a community of people living at Findhorn, descendants of the original movement. No information available about antiquities but I have a good feeling about this one. I'll try to finish the book and mail it back with my comments before we take off.

Shelby Pruitt gave Liam the creeps. He was like some kind of robot, all pleasant laid-back manner on the outside, and inside a lot of quietly whirring machinery. The way he *spoke* was weird—not just the southern accent (obviously he couldn't help that) but the artificial, robotic quality of his conversation. Liam had never known anybody who talked like Mr. Pruitt, the mild pleasantness combined with the formal vocabulary and sprinkling of correct but noncolloquial words and expressions. "Good morning, Liam," he had said when Liam came down to breakfast on the first day of his visit. "I trust you slept well? May I offer you a section of the paper?" To a fifteen-year-old boy? It was *weird*. Even without taking Pam's disturbing revelations into account, the way Shelby talked was very, very weird. It was like he didn't know *who* he was talking to—as if the machinery behind the pleasant manner couldn't distinguish between types of people.

You didn't talk like that to a guy Liam's age. You didn't talk to a daughter of any age like Shelby talked to Pam.

Liam lay on the floor of the guest house in his sleeping bag, listening to Shelby's phenomenal snores, like one of those gargantuan semitrailers he'd seen in old movies gearing up from a standing start, and remembering his mild voice stating, in that creepily casual way, "I don't expect old Jesse's up to the sight of you in that bathing suit." Just thinking about it made Liam squirm with embarrassment, not so much on his own account but on poor Pam's. He saw her shoulders hunched with humiliation, up ahead of him in the canoe, and made a pained face.

Imagine having a father with no better sense than to say a thing like that in front of *any* other person, let alone in front of a teen-aged male! Maybe Shelby was right, maybe Pam was trying to pretend something wasn't true that was, but the way to handle it . . . how would his own father have handled it, if one of his sisters was going out in public dressed inappropriately? Liam tried to imagine the scene. His dad would have probably taken Brett or Margy aside—let's say Margy; it was hard to imagine Brett making such a maneuver necessary—and told her quietly to keep her shirt on, the bathing suit was too small.

So it wasn't *what* Shelby had said, really. It was, one, his having said it in front of Liam, and two—even more—the way he'd *enjoyed* saying it. That was what felt so creepy. Liam remembered how Shelby had smiled as he was delivering the bombshell; he'd been amused and pleased. Liam's father would not have been amused, he would have been concerned about protecting Margy; but Pam's father was just using the situation as an excuse to say something about Pam's tits, not that different from what the guys at the BTP might have done. He'd just been pretending to care about Jesse's feelings, and hadn't even pretended to think about Pam's.

Being so altogether on the outside of the business himself gave Liam perspective. Understanding this much, he also understood that Shelby would have been genuinely surprised and distressed to know what Pam's real feelings were. It wasn't that he meant to be cruel. It was like Pam said: he didn't seem to realize he wasn't supposed to talk that way—for whatever reason, he really didn't know any better.

Liam had been relieved when she brought the subject out in the open. Trying to tiptoe around it was miserable, also very difficult. But what he'd seen, and the things she'd told him, made Liam feel awkward being in Shelby's company at all.

His feelings about Pam were becoming complicated. Though he now pitied her intensely, she wasn't merely pitiable. She was an enormously gifted, highly intuitive mathematician, better than Liam if less well trained, fundamentally better at the qualities needed to operate the Hefn time transceivers than all but two or three of the other Apprentices and as good as the very best. Pam was shy around Humphrey because she wanted so badly to please him; which was dumb, because—though Humphrey hadn't said so—Liam could tell he regarded Pam with particular respect.

It hadn't occurred to Liam to assure Pam of this particular regard. For the first time he wondered if that mightn't be a good idea. Although he valued his special relationship with the Hefn, he was not possessive about it; he had simply—also perhaps a bit callously, since it was kind of fun to tease her, she was such

171

an easy mark—failed to understand Pam's need. Now, sobered by recent developments, he resolved to mend his ways—be more thoughtful, make it up to her.

Actually, it was important to do that now for more reasons than one.

Back in Washington, two considerations in roughly equal parts had formed Liam's view of Pam: respect for her talent, and, after his long isolation, finding her company—well—not disagreeable. He had known instinctively, even if she hadn't made it plain as a pikestaff that night he invited her out to College Park for the first time, that Pam would not interpret any overtures from him as romantic interest, that her aversion to any such development between them was as active as his own.

This being so, he liked it that she was a girl. Getting to be good friends with only one other guy just wasn't something he was up to yet; and though he could have fallen in with a gang well enough, neither Apprentice gang appealed to him that much. Then too, a girl was good protective coloration. Pam might be nobody's idea of a real "catch," but there was no denying she was stacked, which made up for a lot of shortcomings with some people—the other Apprentices, for instance.

Actually, viewed strictly and crassly as a body (setting aside things like face and stylishness and personality), Pam wasn't that bad. It was true that Liam had no interest in Pam's body himself, but other people could think what they liked and he could reap the benefit.

As a matter of fact, he knew exactly what they did think. Older and more socially savvy than Pam, Liam was well aware that by mid-April the two of them had given every appearance of being a couple. Pam had the girls' lavatory to herself; Liam shared a lavatory and shower with seven other boys, none inclined to be particularly tender of his feelings, and they ragged him tirelessly, with a mixture of envy and disdain, about "Pruitt's big tits." None of them really wanted Pamela Pruitt for a girlfriend, but all of them thought constantly about getting laid and were frustrated by lack of opportunity. Where and how were BTP Apprentices, as rigorously trained and closely supervised around the clock as cadets at a military academy, supposed to meet any girls? At the National Gallery? John Chalmers had had a girl back home, but she never came to see him anymore; and their out-of-the-mainstream differences had isolated the rest. So they'd given Liam a hard time.

He didn't much mind the ragging. Having his own reasons

for drifting into the sexually neutral alliance with Pam, he sensed that the others envied him not only this imagined relationship, but also the real one—with Humphrey—that made him special, set him apart, in their eyes and Pam's and in his own as well, and that behind the envy was respect.

And really he got along with them well enough, not getting mad or defensive, joking back, keeping his thoughts to himself.

All in all, he felt things had worked out well—that he and Pam made good partners, stronger and safer together against the fantasies of mothers and the world's assumptions and expectations than either could have been alone.

Shelby halted in mid-snore and turned over in his sleeping bag a few feet away. Was he going to wake up now? The sky was beginning to lighten and the birds had started up. But his even breathing resumed, more quietly now, and Liam snuggled in deeper and went on turning things over in his mind.

The Fundamentalism puzzled him and made him nervous, once it was clear that Pam really believed some personal version of what Liam—raised without religious instruction, apart from that acquired by osmosis at his two Quaker schools, and whose deepest beliefs were grounded in numbers—couldn't help viewing as a lot of primitive horseshit. On the other hand, surprisingly enough, it didn't actually seem to get in the way. Otie Bemis's performance had infuriated him, but Pam's family and their friends had acted as if they found the sermon as offensive as he had. What she'd explained about her conversion experience was actually quite interesting. And he'd enjoyed singing the rousing hymns, so much jollier and less *finicky* than the pieces by Mozart and Schubert that Jeff always used to be practicing.

There were other complications. Liam's Washington-based view of Pam had not prepared him for the peacefulness he had felt himself relax into as they chanted Kipling's poem together aboard the *Delta Queen.* Nor had he at all expected to find himself talking to her about Jeff, a subject he had not yet discussed openly with anyone other than Humphrey and Julie, his counselor. The amount of satisfaction he took in their *team-work*—unsuccessful, true, but well-coordinated on board the steamboat; successful in the canoe, and in rescuing Jesse—had taken him equally by surprise.

Also, Pam's insider's knowledge of the way things worked here in Hurt Hollow had impressed him a lot. He'd been less struck than she by the contrast between her physical awkwardness and his own relative grace; without her to instruct him Liam knew he would never have figured out how to milk a goat, or what to do with the milk once he had it in the pail.

It was because Hurt Hollow itself impressed him so much that Pam's knowledge of how to live here did. No question that this was a special place, one he would never have known about in his life if it hadn't been for Pam.

Pity, admiration, pleasure, contempt, interest, puzzlement, gratitude, all these resolved into simple liking . . . Liam's life had been an emotional desert for nearly three years after Jeff died, and a kind of savannah since a year ago last March; having so many strong and contradictory feelings all at once, about the same peculiar person, made him uneasy. He needed to put some space between himself and Pam for a while. Get off on his own. Hike up the hill, bushwhack around in the woods—get his balance back, if he could manage this without making Pam feel snubbed, and—Liam glanced at the lumpy shape that was Shelby, visible now in the strengthening light—without leaving her alone with her father. He didn't understand what was going on there, but he didn't doubt Pam would be grateful if he stuck around till Shelby had left for the day.

He woke abruptly in full daylight. Shelby was gone, his sleeping bag rolled neatly and stowed in the bedding cupboard. There was no sign another person had ever even been there. Liam looked at his watch: nearly nine! Cursing, he scooted out of the bag and squatted in his underwear to roll it up and stow it next to Shelby's. Yesterday's cutoffs were dry but stiff; he pulled another pair of shorts and a T-shirt out of his duffle and put them on, and sat on the floor to tie his shoes.

Outside the cloudy-bright day already felt stifling. Liam stepped several feet off the trail to pee, then headed down to cross the creek and climb to the house. As he came out of the trees the humid heat descended like a tarp; it was going to be another bake-oven of a day. He hurried; no telling how long Shelby had been up there with Pam.

The little bridge over the creek afforded a clear view through and beyond the fence to the river, slate-colored and vast under the open, cloudy-bright sky. The gate stood open. Out in the water Liam saw the dark head of a swimmer, stroking lazily toward shore: Shelby. At the landing over in Indiana was a brightly painted steamboat. The whistle announcing its arrival, he realized now, was what had woken him up. No smoke billowed from the two tall stacks, since unlike the *Delta Queen* the stacks of the new steamboats were fitted with catalytic burners, but a massive distortion of the air above them told Liam the boilers were still fired up, that this was one quick stop on a regular run. He saw tiny figures moving on the decks, and the whole gaudy spectacle reflected, Chinese red and dazzling white, in the slate-gray water. The sight of it made him feel happy.

And now, sure enough, the bell clanged, the whistle blew, and the red paddle wheel began to turn, backing the boat into deeper water. Soon the pilot had straightened out and reversed the wheel, and the boat was passing merrily out of Liam's view from the bridge. As it vanished beyond the trees, the lively notes of ''The Boatman Song'' carried clearly across the water.

He glanced back at the beach below. Pam's father had arrived in waist-deep water and was wading ashore, head down. As Liam watched, Shelby strolled up out of the water. He was naked, completely naked. Liam glanced involuntarily up at the house, nearly invisible from the bridge if you didn't know just where to look, but Pam was nowhere in sight and he glanced back again uneasily at her father where he stood on the sand, drying himself unhurriedly with a towel. In another moment Shelby was climbing toward the gate wearing shoes and the towel, tied rather insecurely—it was considerably smaller than an ordinary bath towel—around his waist.

He closed the gate behind him and paused to snap the lock shut and remove the key, then continued on up the path, lifting his head now to scan the trees, probably for birds, which were making a clamorous, unintelligible racket in the woods surrounding them both. Unintelligible that was to Liam, not to Shelby—not at all to Shelby. The face raised toward Liam, unaware of being observed, was relaxed and strikingly good-looking beneath its crown of towel-tousled wet hair. Its smile was guileless and young.

Even to Liam's eye, Shelby looked like a nice person engaged in some harmless and pleasurable form of recreation. He frowned, uncomfortable with this complicating vision.

Would Shelby take the fork that led to the guest house, or the other fork to Jesse's house? On the bridge Liam waited to see which it would be. As soon as he turned left, toward Jesse's, Liam sprang into action—bounding to the far side of the creek and sprinting around the slope to the intersection, and beyond to where the trail ascended to the house.

He arrived on the terrace out of breath. Pam was sitting there, a pad of paper and a pen in her lap, and on the spool table two plates of crumbs, two empty cups, and a plastic pitcher; her father sat on the bench in his skimpy towel, talking to her. His shoulders, chest, and legs were very pale and blistered with drops of river water. Both turned their heads at Liam's appearance. "Well, good morning, Liam," said Shelby. "Did you sleep well?"

The reappearance of the robot made it easier for Liam to know how to feel. Clank. Whirr. "Yes I did, thanks." *What's the next line? Can't offer me a section of the paper, nyaa nyaa nyaa.* "Hi," he added to Pam, trying not to pant too hard. "Sorry I overslept."

"No problem." Pam smiled as if she were merely pleased, rather than overjoyed, to see him. "Want some breakfast? I can cook you up some cereal—that's what Jesse would do—or you can just have bread and honey like we did. There's half a loaf of bread left." She seemed perfectly all right, not upset or tense like yesterday—or no more than usual, Liam reflected; she wasn't a very calm-seeming person any more than he was himself, most of the time. Probably he'd got there before Shelby had had time to do much more than ask Pam how she'd slept. Or no—they could have had breakfast together.

Her father braced his arms, tan to just above the elbow, white above that, on the bench to either side of him and leaned forward. "What will you all eat for lunch?"

"I dunno. More bread and soy butter, I guess, and maybe some greens from the garden—I'm not sure how Liam will like those—and I noticed a few jars of blackberries in the cellar. I can make a batch of yogurt. We'll manage."

"The yogurt won't be ready by lunchtime, even if you start it now," Shelby said consideringly. "I'll bring more supplies when I come back this evening. We don't want to use up all of Jesse's food. Well, Liam," he said, standing, "I'm going to have to get going here. Got to get to work. Somebody'll be along to pick me up before long. I'll go in and get some clothes on, if you two will excuse me."

"Wait a second, Dad, I want to get the bread and stuff for Liam." Pam got up and ran up the stone steps to the door.

"Well, I can just change in the upper room. You come ahead and get whatever you want."

He followed her in. Liam heard her say, "I'll only be a second, and you can change down here," and Shelby reply vigorously, "Take your time! Take your time! It's no trouble to carry this stuff upstairs."

Disobeying this instruction, Pam banged back out the door in

176

thirty seconds flat, the elements of Liam's breakfast jumbled together on a small tray of metal-covered wood. She set the tray down and put a plate, knife, and spoon, the end of a loaf of coarse dark bread, a glass jar of dark amber honey, a worn metal cup, and a lump of butter on a little glass plate, down in front of Liam, who had pulled another of the low chairs up to the table and sat down. "Drat, I forgot the bread knife." She turned, took a step, paused. "Listen, could you get it? It's on the counter by the sink. I'll run down to the springhouse and dip you some milk."

She had grabbed the pitcher and bolted down the hill before Liam could offer to go himself, so he got up and went into the house for the knife. Crossing to the counter he had a clear view, through the opening in the partition between the upper and lower rooms, of Shelby pulling on his pants. He looked through at Liam and smiled that pleasant trademark smile, different from the half-smile Liam had seen from the bridge that morning in some important but puzzling way. "I take it Pam forgot something?" He planted his legs apart, tucked in the long tail of his shirt, fastened and zipped his pants.

"The bread knife." It was lying in plain sight next to the sink; Pam had been in a big hurry not to have seen it. He took it and went out again. God, the guy gave him the *creeps*! Liam appreciated his own father in a whole new way. He was very glad Shelby was leaving.

But when he had actually gone, after hanging the yellow towel on the line to dry and promising to come back by dusk with food and candles—and saying with obvious sincerity that he'd love to be able to stay all day—Pam and Liam sat on the terrace and listened to the tiny, diminishing putt-putt of the canoe's electric motor without saying anything about him. Liam chewed on the tough bread, which he didn't much like, smothered in butter and honey, which he did, and poured himself a cup of milk and drank that (strong, he thought, but not bad). Finally, mostly just to say something, he remarked, "This is goat butter, right?"

"Yep. Want to make some today? There isn't much left. It's kind of fun, in a boring way."

"How do you make it? Does Jesse churn it? Has he got a churn?"

"Not the kind you're thinking of, that tall wooden kind with a dasher; Jesse doesn't get enough milk, and anyway butter doesn't keep that well in hot weather. But he's got this cute little two-quart jar with a crank that somebody gave him—it's supposed to be a toy for Amish kids, but it really works! It takes forever but it's like magic the first time you see the butter come—like the first time you realized that the water can really hold you up, when you're learning to swim. I think it would be a good idea to make some. Maybe tonight.''

Your dad will be here tonight, Liam thought, but he decided not to mention Shelby unless Pam did. ''What about milking?''

''We already did it.''

''Oh,'' he said, disappointed. ''I didn't mean to sleep so late. I was awake for a while in the middle of the night.''

Pam sent him a funny, sidelong smirk. ''Aha. So you didn't *really* sleep all that well, eh?'' She gave a bark of laughter at his expression, then said in a low, intense voice, not looking at Liam, ''I told you, he always talks like that. It makes me feel like screaming.''

Unable to think how to respond to this, Liam was uncomfortably silent.

''Mom says he's just not at ease with kids,'' Pam went on, still looking at her plate. ''Like, he means well, but when I was younger, where Betsy's father would come in when we were playing and say, you know, like 'Hi, kids,' Dad would say, 'Good afternoon, young ladies.' ''

''Hmm,'' said Liam after a pause.

''It's like he's tone-deaf to English. Which he's not at all to music, by the way; he plays the clarinet and the recorder, really well. But it's like he never learned anything his whole life from listening to other people *talk*.''

To his relief, Liam finally thought of something to say. ''Well, heck, no wonder *that's* hard for you to take, you're so hypersensitive to English yourself. It would probably bother anybody, but it would be bound to bother you.''

Pam looked up directly at him, startled, slowly smiling. ''Hey, you know, that's a good point! That's a really good point! I never thought of that. Thanks a lot, Liam, I bet you're right. *That's* why it drives me nuts—the main reason anyway.''

''You're welcome. Anyway, as I was saying, I was really looking forward to helping with the milking and I'm sorry I left it all for you to do.'' *You and your father the robot. Shelby Pruitt, Human Milking Machine, clank clank whirr whirr.*

''Oh, that's okay,'' said Pam, partly reading his mind. ''Dad was up. He gets up early. He lived on a farm when he was a kid, he's a good milker. Anyway, you'll get your chance tonight. Are

178

you done eating? Let's get the dishes from last night and this morning washed, and take a quick look at the garden, and then we should check the trot line before we do anything else.''

Liam scraped back his chair and started stacking dishes on the tray. ''What's a trot line?''

''A length of underwater fishing line fastened at the ends, with short pieces of line tied to it. The short ones have hooks and sinkers. You bait the hooks, then you go out once a day or so in the johnboat to see whether you've caught anything.''

''It doesn't sound very sporting.''

''Hurt Hollow isn't about sport fishing, it's about surviving and self-sufficiency,'' said Pam, a little severely. ''So do you want to come along?''

He did, but the suggestion put Liam in mind of his resolve to get away by himself. ''Okay, but—would you care if I went off for a walk by myself later? I want to see if I can hike around up there on the hill without getting lost—and besides,'' he added honestly, ''I feel like I kind of need to get adjusted to being here, and a little solitude would be just the ticket.''

Rather to his surprise, Pam looked distinctly pleased at the suggestion; she must have been craving a little solitude herself. ''Sure, that's a good idea. You could go up and get the mail, or I could tell you where to look for wild strawberries. They might be getting ripe by now.''

''Great.''

''Want to go this morning or this afternoon?''

''I don't care. This afternoon, I guess.''

Afternoon found Liam climbing like one of Jesse's goats up the steep slope directly above the stable. Bushwhacking had won out over wild strawberries. He was wearing jeans out of respect for the brambleberry tangles Pam had said he would run into everywhere (she was right; he immediately did) and had begun sweating profusely almost at once. He thought with pleasure of a pre-supper dip in the river, also in passing of whatever Pam's mother would send over for supper itself. He definitely wasn't that crazy about Jesse's bread with Jesse's unsalted soy butter—made just like peanut butter from soybeans roasted and ground to a grainy paste—spread on it. The salad of dandelion greens, endive, and wild onion also left a great deal to be desired in his opinion.

Pam hadn't wanted to bother with a fire, so some lunch possibilities had had to be ruled out—like cream of smoked goat-

179

meat soup. Pam had made some Biblical joke about not eating a kid seethed in its mother's milk anyway, and laughed like anything. Or like fried catfish. There had been a couple of fish on the trot line when they rowed out to check, pulling the johnboat along from sinker to sinker, rebaiting, with minnows, any hooks that came up bare, transferring the two whiskery fish on the line to the live box, where they would be all right for a couple of days. The thought of fried fish made his stomach grumble, hot as it was. He burped a disagreeable memento of soy butter as he climbed, and made a sour face.

Lack of a fire also ruled out the yogurt gambit, even for supper. Since there was therefore no point in saving the jar of blackberries, Pam and Liam had eaten them with milk. The bowls of berries in pools of empurpled goat milk had definitely been the high point of Liam's lunch.

He now had a cheering thought: Jesse probably made that heavy kind of bread because he liked it, not because it was the only kind you *could* make of homegrown ingredients in a woodfired oven. If Mrs. Pruitt didn't send over any bread tonight, maybe he and Pam could bake a better kind. Liam's mother baked all their bread using whole-grain flour, and Liam had often helped her. He decided to suggest to Pam when he got back that they do a baking this evening when things cooled down. He could regrind the flour a couple more times on the old hand grinder Pam had showed him and get a much lighter, finer-textured flour.

At the thought of his mother's bread, warm from the oven, with butter and honey on it, his mouth filled with water. Time to stop thinking about food. Where was he, anyway? He had been climbing blindly, moving always higher, letting the slope of the hill guide him; the trees cut off the view, but he must be getting close to the top of the ridge.

Liam stopped to catch his breath, take a drink from the canteen on his belt, and wipe his face on the front of his shirt. Between the heat and sweat, and the steepness of the climb, his physical discomfort was considerable; yet, hunger aside, he was surprised to realize that he was having the time of his life.

He said it to himself: *I'm having the time of my life!*

Why was that? The mountainous country around Lake Wallenpaupack in the Poconos was more spectacular; Jeff had been better company than Pam; there had never been any of the kind of uncomfortableness created by the presence of Pam's father up there. What was it about Hurt Hollow that felt so right?

180

He mulled this over as he climbed on. Something about the grandeur of the Ohio River, so different from the lake or the young, shallow Delaware. Something about Jesse's house, and the fact that Orrin Hubbell had constructed it himself, with love and skill, as the basis of a way of life and not as a vacation retreat *from* ordinary life. Probably something about the goats; he liked that, getting milk for drinking, and for butter and other things—Pam was making cottage cheese this afternoon—right from an animal kept for the purpose. He really liked having learned how to milk a goat.

Maybe Pam was right—maybe homesteading à la Hurt Hollow was no answer to any of the world's problems now, because there wasn't nearly enough land left even if people wanted to live like Jesse was living here, which most of them didn't. That's why the Hollow was a museum and people traveled long distances to see it: a nice place to visit that you wouldn't want to live in.

All the same, something about the Hollow tugged at Liam, filled him with suppressed excitement. Though he couldn't pinpoint the source, it felt to him as if *some* kind of answer to *some* important question about humanity's future, an answer not implicit in the Carpenters' cabin in the Poconos, might be found here. But finding it would take thought and calculation. Liam was more certain than ever that Humphrey needed to know about this place.

He wondered idly, not for the first time, whether there could have been any way to *predict* that the Hollow would prove to be a special place.

At last the slope grew more gradual, then leveled out, and Liam could no longer count on keeping his bearings by always heading as steeply uphill as possible. He looked for the sun, but above the trees the solid cloud cover seemed to radiate diffuse sunlight from all directions at once. He was still in deep woods. Ten years before, this time of year, the sounds of motorized traffic and suburban landscape maintenance, and those of farming, would have guided him toward the road. But the modern (i.e. post-Directive) equivalents of tractors and lawn mowers and leaf blowers were just too quiet for the purpose, unless somebody decided to chop down a tree or roof a building. He heard a dog bark a couple of times a long way off, but dogs might be anywhere.

He missed the cars; he had loved cars and trucks and buses as a small child. Liam pictured the police car waiting to collect the four men from the *Delta Queen*, and remembered how Pam had interrupted his study of it with some Biblical joke he didn't get about the lock. He recalled a day, before the Hefn came back, when Carrie had picked up him and Jeff after school in her brand-new solar car, and driven them to the zoo in it to see the baby rhino, while Jeff sang a choral piece by Mozart in the back seat. He felt a pang to think that the baby rhino had certainly died too in the meltdown, along with all the elephants and lions and chimps. With all his preparation and care, Terry hadn't managed to evacuate the zoo.

Then, still deep in his reverie, Liam did hear something: the intermittent tinkling of a bell. Peering through the trees he saw nothing at first; then a movement caught his eye and a long brown-and-white face peered back at him from the undergrowth, placidly chewing. Beyond it he saw another head on a long neck reach up, rip a length of vine off a tree, and begin to work it in like a strand of spaghetti. He and the goats had found each other.

Captivated, he stood still and watched them browse. He had not been watching long before the kid came scampering up to one of the does and butted her udder hard, several times, before beginning to suckle. Then the ram appeared, and then the last doe, bag swinging. He had found them all.

Inevitably then he thought again of Jeff, in whose company he had climbed so many steep and wooded trails and come upon so many engaging sights: a wild turkey hen with her brood of chicks, a spotted fawn, even (once, in the Poconos) a bear. Jeff would have enjoyed bumping into the goats, would have thought of something funny to say about the kid butting its mother's udder before suckling like it had been starving for days. All his life Liam knew he would remember the precise feeling of what being in the woods or in a boat with Jeff was like; never in his life would anything be quite that good in quite that way, however well-adjusted to doing without Jeff he finally became. The feeling of Jeff's physical presence dragged at Liam's heart, the loss bearable but heavy and solid, permanent.

He swallowed, pulled air deep into his lungs. Okay, back to reality now. Back to the time of his life.

If he wanted to be led straight back to where he'd started from, he had only to wait till the goats got tired of foraging and follow them home. But Pam had asked him to pick up the mail; he needed to find the fence, and the country road beyond it. So after a while, given confidence by this chance encounter, Liam left the goats to their own affairs and tromped off in hopes of finding these human-made things. He tried to remember what his trajectory up the hill had been, and aim to the left of that; the gravel Hollow road was somewhere in that direction. He also tried not to go in a circle; but that was exactly what he did, or at least he had not yet crossed the road or hit the fence when, a few minutes later, the ground began to slope downward again. Exasperated, he backtracked to level ground and tried again.

An hour later Liam admitted defeat. He would have to go back without the mail, and give it another shot on a clear day or equipped with a compass. He wasn't *lost*, he knew how to get back: a straight line down to the river, then left along the shore to Jesse's house. Accordingly, he set off downhill; but instead of the broad Ohio his course led into the valley of a little creek, on the far side of which the land sloped uphill again.

Liam kept his head. Down was down; this little creek must be the upper end of the one he had crossed that morning by the bridge—either that one or a tributary. He would gamble that it was heading for the river and follow it down. What else could it do?

Sweating, he drank more water and dried his face again before pushing on. Soon his aching ankles drove him into the water; slipping around on the rocks and roots was easier than trying to walk along the steep, sandy grade of the bank.

He had only been wading a little while when he glimpsed, through the trees, a heap of rusty metal—some sort of rusted-out machinery. He stood in the creek and tried to see what it was. Some kind of farming implement, probably, the sort he and Jeff occasionally had found abandoned in the fields reverted to forest, up in the Poconos. He could barely make out a tumbledown shed of weathered boards beyond the rustbucket vat or milk tank or whatever it was. Liam knew—Pam had told him— that there had been a couple of farms in the Hollow before the Hubbells' time. He wondered whether there might still be anything in the shed worth carrying back with him—an old bottle with bubbles in the glass, say, or an Indian-head penny—and had an impulse to climb the sandy bank and explore the area, do a quick archeological sweep for more evidence of the abandoned farm. That was what Jeff would have done. Thirty seconds after his eyes had lit upon the machinery, Jeff would have been all over the place up there, snooping and prying, looking for treasure, casting about for the foundations of the house and barn and talking a mile a minute. Drawing Liam into the spirit of the adventure.

Sighing, he lifted his arms to haul himself up the bank by a couple of saplings, aware that he was doing this more out of respect for Jeff's memory than to satisfy his own low-ebb curiosity.

At that instant the muffled clanging of another bell floated up the Hollow—not like the tinkling bell on Belle the nanny goat but a deep-toned *bong bong* such as Liam imagined the bronze bell outside Jesse's front door would make if somebody rang it. He abandoned without regret the thought of exploring—*Maybe Pam could come back up here with me sometime*—and continued his descent of the creek, going faster now, slipping on underwater leaves and stones. Again the bell struck five or six tones. It crossed his mind that Pam might be signaling to *him*, thinking he ought to be back by now, giving him something to home on. If so, he was grateful—grateful also for the reassurance it provided, that he had succeeded in working out the problem for himself, without help. Though he was embarrassed to have failed in his errand.

Before much longer the high ground to his left seemed less and less high. A much taller ridge could be seen beyond it, through and above the trees; and soon another little creek flowed in from the far side to join the one he had been descending. So his little stream was a fork, and here was the other tine. Further encouraged by this sign that he was getting closer to the river, Liam slid and splashed along cheerfully, muddying the deeper water and soaking his pants to the knee. Ten minutes later he saw the upper bridge ahead of him, the one he and Pam had crossed the day before on their way up the trail in search of Jesse. Whew! He scrambled up the ladder-like plank and trotted the rest of the way back to the house.

If that *had* been Pam ringing the bell for him, she was nowhere in sight now. At the back door he called, then pried off his muddy shoes and padded across the wooden floor to the front door in his bare feet. There he dumped the canteen belt on the terrace next to the bell post and started to go on down the path toward the fence and the river. On impulse he turned back and yanked on the chain; the whole contraption swiveled in its mounting and the clapper gave the bell a few good whacks: BONG BONG BONG!

This was the bell he had heard in the woods, no doubt about that. Liam stifled the temptation to go on ringing—he didn't want to send some kind of message by mistake—and took himself on down the steep path, going carefully on his bare feet.

Before he had made it to the first switchback, Pam appeared, running up the path with a pair of binoculars in one hand. "Man, am I glad to see you! Somebody's been signaling to be picked up from the landing over there, and I signaled back before I remembered you had the key, and I couldn't get the gate open!"

"Oh!" He found the key in his pocket and gave it to Pam, who took it and ran ahead to unlock the gate. Liam followed more slowly. "Who's signaling? And how?"

"There's a bell over there, didn't I tell you? Somebody comes and rings it and Jesse rows the johnboat over and picks them up."

The gate swung open. Liam went through and Pam clicked the padlock shut again. "He rows all the way over there without knowing who's ringing? Criminy, he could spend all his time going back and forth for no good reason, answering false alarms." Pam jumped down the last three stair treads to the dock. Her steps made the metal buckle and boom as she hurried past the canoe to where the johnboat was tethered.

At the dock's edge Liam stopped short. "I can't walk out there, I'll fry the bottoms off my feet!"

Pam squatted to unfasten the combination lock on the chain. "Wade out a ways and I'll pick you up. Orrin always used to stop what he was doing and fetch people over if they rang. Even if he was painting, or in the middle of some project. It worked okay for a long time, but it got to be a major hassle when he got more famous. Now out of visiting hours Jesse just goes to get people if they ring a special signal in code. Drat this thing!" The lock wouldn't open. She spun the dial and started over.

"So whoever's over there now rang the right signal?"

"Yeah."

"Any idea who it is?"

"I tried to see with the binoculars but I couldn't make 'em out. It looks like a whole bunch of people. Probably from Scofield." The lock popped open; Pam stood, pulled the johnboat to the dock by the chain, and awkwardly stepped in. "Dad said a lot of people at the college offered to help out while Jesse's in the hospital. It's probably some of them, or people from Madison, or I guess it *could* be somebody off the afternoon steamboat from Louisville, it went by about an hour ago . . . they're more trouble than they're worth, whoever they are."

"Why not just ignore the signal, then? *They* won't know the difference." Liam, now knee-deep in the river, waited while Pam settled the heavy wooden oars in the locks and struggled to turn the boat. She looked like a three-year-old trying to ride a full-size bike.

"Naah. Jesse would want me to go get 'em—they can't walk in, with the upper gate locked, or they probably would have." The boat swung reluctantly in toward shore. Liam climbed in over the stern and crouched there dripping, unsure where to sit or what he was expected to do.

Pam shipped the oars now and looked up at him. "Are you as good at rowing as you are at paddling a canoe?"

"Well, I've *done* a lot of rowing. A regular rowboat, though, not a johnboat." The night before, Pam herself had done the little bit of rowing required; mostly they had pulled themselves along the trot line hand over hand. "I always have trouble getting this thing across the river," Pam admitted. "Orrin never used pins in his oars so naturally Jesse doesn't either, and these oars weigh a ton, and . . . anyway, if you want to row, go ahead. You're bound to be better than me."

Gratified, Liam sat down on the seat Pam had vacated and got set to justify this vote of confidence. The johnboat was a long, flat-bottomed boat with squared-off ends, about sixteen feet by five, making up in stability what it lacked in responsiveness and grace. Immediately Liam saw what Pam meant about no pins. The oars turned and slipped in the oarlocks; it was tricky to keep both oars balanced at the same fulcrum point, and even harder to make the blades stay perpendicular to the water; but Liam concentrated and before long was doing pretty well.

"Angle upstream," Pam told him. "If you don't the current will carry you past the landing." She sat in the stern, frowning at Indiana, lifting the binoculars to her eyes from time to time. Once she said, "We forgot sun block. Oh well, I guess it's late enough not to matter much." Another time she said, "More upstream, if you can." Liam, working hard, nodded and complied as best he could.

Luckily, traffic was light and the mild upstream breeze refreshing. About halfway across Liam panted, "I wish I had my shoes. It's hard to brace my feet; my heels are getting sore."

"How come you don't have 'em on?"

"They were too muddy to wear in the house. I took 'em off."

"How'd you get so muddy?" Pam raised the binoculars again as she spoke and stared hard at the shore. While Liam was still framing a reply with the little piece of his attention he could spare—Pam, after all, still hadn't heard about his misadventure—she had stiffened and blurted out a startled *"Oh!"*

"Can you see who it is?"

"It looks like—it is! It's a Hefn!" Pam lowered the binoculars and stared at Liam. "A Hefn! What would a Hefn be doing here? How the Sam Hill did he *get* here?" She raised the glasses and checked again. "I don't believe this. It really is a Hefn. Jeezle Pete."

Liam paused, half-turned toward shore, but they were still too far away. "Who are all those other people?"

"I dunno . . . people who live around the landing, probably. Or—could it be Jeffrey and the Water Bureau people? They got off the boat, though, didn't they, after that night?"

Liam didn't answer. He rowed; Pam watched the landing through the binoculars. Slowly they approached the shore. "More upstream," Pam barked one more time, and Liam pulled with all his strength against the current.

Finally they were above the landing, drifting down toward the dock, and he could look over his shoulder as he brought the boat in. Now Pam was glaring at him with outrage, and he felt a guilty pang, but in spite of this he could feel his own face split in a grin of welcome.

The Hefn stood at the edge of the dock to greet them: stumpy, hairy, gray, flat eyes doing their impression of twinkling, entire demeanor conveying pleasure. Most of all, familiar. Behind him on the dock, next to a small piece of soft luggage, Liam recognized the metal carrying case—black, with round corners—of a time transceiver. "Pam and Liam, hello," said the Hefn. "I rang the bell exactly the way these helpful people instructed me to, and here you are."

"Hi, Humphrey," Liam said, the grin almost cracking his face. "Here we are. What took you so long?"

Liam: We are now at the crucial juncture where the young genius first becomes intuitively aware of Holy Ground. I know I can't have gotten this 100% right, but how close did I come?

#No biblical title? Oh—because it's *my* chapter.

#I *did* see you as a better mathemetician than me. Humphrey *did* respect your talent. You got that much right anyway.

#I was not as sharp about (or as much bothered by) your father's creepiness as you give me credit for, not on that first trip. Like I didn't get it that he was totally unaware of his effect on you, or think of him at any point as looking "guileless and young." (Or "strikingly good-looking"—not my type, I guess.) On the other hand, you've made me out to be a lot more crass in my thinking about *you* than I was. Not all the other guys were the utter cads you imagine them to be, either. They did talk about getting laid and all that, but they didn't give *me* a bad time that I recall.

Really, where do you get these ideas? From your dimwit buddy Steve? We at the BTP were a finer class of male.

#I have to admit that my thoughts and feelings about you and your situation were just not as clear to me as you've described them here. The way I remember it, I went on that walk mostly to play explorer, not to get some distance from you. Loud emotional resonance between people was still very hard for me to relate to then. I just tuned it out. (And now, do I hear you saying? Could be, could be.)

You're right about the effect the Hollow had on me though. I was very, very curious and intrigued.

#You're *uncannily* right about one thing: Jeff, and how I thought about him. It was exactly like that. I do still remember and I always will, just the way you say. For all your wretchedness, you were much more acute about me than I was about you.

#How close did you come? Well, I don't recall wondering *on that walk* if Holy Ground could be predicted. (I do remember finding the "rusty machinery.") To be perfectly honest, I don't know when that idea started to form. All I'm sure of is that *when* it formed, whether then or later, Hurt Hollow was what it formed around.

11

A SWARM OF BEES AND HONEY IN THE CARCASE OF A LION

Judges 14:8

As soon as Liam left for his solo hike up the bluffside, Pam took a clean glass jar with a lid and went down to the gate to call the hospital; she was worried about Jesse. The tape told her his condition—stable—and that he was not receiving visitors, but that she should check back again tomorrow. That sounded fairly hopeful, as if the doctors expected another twenty-four hours would see him over the worst. Pam wanted to go visit as soon as they would let her in. She had looked forward for weeks to seeing Jesse and she missed him. Happy as it made her to be here, delighted as she was to be able to render Jesse this significant service, the place wasn't the same without his own (usually) good-tempered or (not infrequently) cantankerous presence, and she wondered for the first time, with a stab of alarm, what would become of Hurt Hollow when Jesse died.

But no need to think about that just yet. Pam took the path to the springhouse, where she lifted the can holding what remained of the previous evening's milking out of the cold water. She was going to use it up on cottage cheese—which she was pretty sure Liam wasn't going to like any better than he'd liked Jesse's bread, its flavor would be grainy and gamy compared to what he was used to. But her father liked it—better than Pam did herself—and she was determined not to let any of the milk go to waste. You had to keep using milk up; it didn't keep long, even immersed in the forty-degree spring water, and there was always more coming. Jesse made hard cheese when supply significantly exceeded demand, but Pam didn't feel up to that; cheese-making was a long, complicated process that she hadn't helped with often enough to manage without supervision. And Jesse's recipe wasn't written down anywhere as far as she knew.

Maybe when Jesse came home, he could give directions and

189

she could follow them. She pictured Jesse lying on his pull-down bed in the main room of the cabin, telling her when to pile the flatirons on, and smiled.

Cottage cheese was a lot easier; you just skimmed the milk, added rennet, hung the curds in a bag or whatever to drain, and there you were.

She unscrewed the lid of the jar and poured in the cream for the butter-making project later, then set the jar back in the water and hauled the can of milk up the hill by its bail.

When the pan of cottage cheese had been turned into a sieve set in a bowl to drain, Pam put it back in the springhouse on a shelf to keep cool till suppertime, covered it with a clean cloth, and looked about her. She intended to do some weeding, but not till it cooled off after supper. There were no other chores clamoring to be done. She poured herself a glass of water, stirred in some honey and a little leftover blueberry juice, got her yellow pad and a pen, and went out to the terrace.

She pulled a chair into the shade and sat down, kicking off her shoes. A breeze stirred the shadows on the flagstones under Pam's bare feet and stroked her face and arms with coolness. From the Ohio came a few short toots of an unseen towboat. Though effectively invisible, except for scattered glints in the moving foliage, the river's expansive presence dominated Jesse's house; and Pam as she sat on the terrace was intensely aware of it, steadily flowing, just out beyond her view.

"Strong Brown God," she thought. A wonderful strength and knowledge began to fill her. She, Pamela Pruitt, fourteen years old, was here in sole charge of Hurt Hollow, the most wonderful place in the world, for the very first time in her life. And *this is who I am,* she thought; *this is exactly where I'm supposed to be.*

It felt like joy, like ecstasy. It felt so good, in fact, that just sitting there seemed inadequate. She needed to do something to mark the day and the occasion.

A swim by herself in the river, à la Pinny and the secret plans to save the world? Perfect. Pam had already jumped up and started through the house to get her father's towel off the clothesline before she remembered that Liam had gone off up the hill with the only key. She was stuck behind the fence, caged in.

She made up her mind not to let disappointment spoil her mood. What could not be done in fact could be described instead. With an hour of solitude before her, buoyed on her wave of happiness, why not write down the story she'd been working on in church when Brother Otie "Bush-League Gus Griner" Bemis did his Hefn-hating act?

No! Back on the terrace a better idea occurred to her. This would be a super chance to try to apply what Liam had helped her see about her poetry, back on the *Delta Queen*.

See and say what's there, she reminded herself. Not just music, not just pretty language: what's *there*.

She wrote "Pinny's Swim" at the top of the page, then stared at the paper, intimidated. Ten minutes went by. I'll start with something easier, she finally thought—something boring, for a warm-up exercise. Spring in Washington, D.C., that should be bland enough.

Okay: *see what's there*.

Half an hour later she had an almost-illegible page full of crossed-out words and marginal scribblings, which she copied out clean:

> What do you see in the city in spring?
> A robin trailing a piece of string,
> Wild onion threads in the zoysia knit,
> Magnolia buds with their britches split,
> And wind, that breathes in the noonday heat
> Its searing breath, that scorches the street
> And blows black cinders across the sky—
> The cherry blossoms turn brown and dry—
> Nectar, pollen, and bees that sting;
> This is Washington, dead of spring.
> Honeyflow's here, but spring's too warm;
> The bees you trust are lost in a swarm—
> Gone from the buildings massive and dead,
> Over the fence to the forest ahead,
> And there in the place where two creeks meet
> A river is pouring, gold and sweet.

When she had finished the fair copy, Pam read the poem out loud, slowly. At the end she laid the page down again and stared at it. "Oh, brother. What the Sam Hill is *that* all about?"

Things had begun well enough; the series of sewing images was a little ho-hum but every single item in the list—nest-building robins, onion grass raveling from still-tan front lawns, magnolias coming into bloom—was something she had actually *seen*.

But then somewhere around the magnolia buds bursting out of their britches—an image she was particularly pleased with, the split bud cases like a kid's too-small clothing—the poem had taken that disturbing turn. It was hot in Washington, all right, but not hot enough—yet—to scorch pavement or shrivel flowers. A picture of blossoming cherry trees, each blossom cupping a clambering honeybee, each bee possessing a concealed stinger, had filled her mind: why? Like the fragrant black locusts, cherry trees did attract bees, of course, but Pam had watched Jesse working his bees enough not to be afraid of them. But the bees in the poem were frightening.

Then, presto, another provoking sudden turn and Pam found herself describing what sounded like her own escape from Washington back to Hurt Hollow: the honey pot—or, in this case, river—of gold at the end of her personal rainbow. Not that she and Liam constituted a swarm exactly . . . in fact she failed completely to see how "the bees you *trust*" could possibly refer to the two of them.

Actually, that phrase made no sense however you looked at it. Trust how? Not to swarm? Jesse worked hard every spring, feeding and adding supers and so on, to keep his own hives from swarming, which was what bees would always do if the hive got too crowded. You couldn't "trust" them not to, out of loyalty or something, it was a natural instinct! "What did I *mean* by that?" she complained. How extremely exasperating not to understand your own poem!

She picked up the pen, crossed out *trust*, and wrote *keep*. Then she crossed that out and wrote *kept*. But it still wasn't right; the feeling was, the bees were supposed to do one thing and they did something else *of their own volition*.

How about *need*? Better . . . but somehow also weaker.

You count on the bees to be there and they leave you, taking their hundreds of thousands of stingers along with them . . .

Write what you see, Pam thought, some help! I don't *see* a blessed thing in this poem after the first few lines, so what is it that's *there* that I *don't* see?

At that moment the bell across the river began to peal.

Pam's father had never met Humphrey. When he climbed up onto the terrace that evening he greeted the Hefn with considerable interest but without surprise. "The folks over across the way told me you'd arrived," he said, chuckling and shaking his head. "You certainly stirred them up! They've been watching the news commentary about what happened on the *Delta Queen* last week, and they've all got their views on that—and did the kids tell you? There's an evangelist who's been holding revival meetings at churches on both sides of the river these past few weeks, and he's had plenty to say about it too.'' He chuckled again. ''They're buzzing like a nest of hornets over there.''

Throughout his speech Shelby remained standing, legs spread and arms folded across his chest. It was hard to tell whether he had said all this to separate himself from the buzzing hornets and those influenced by Otie Bemis, or to remind Humphrey of his own local unpopularity (though that could have been simple tactlessness). The men on the *Delta Queen* who had assaulted Jeffrey weren't local people, but the event had been viewed in Madison as a local event; that was why Otie Bemis felt no hesitation about waving it around like the Confederate flag.

Pam, sitting with Liam on the bottom step below Humphrey, was aware of her father's discomfort in the presence of the Hefn's authority and felt his words as mildly placating: *I'm not one of those Yahoos.* She also sensed, as she knew he did, that the situation here had changed with Humphrey's arrival. Shelby was being edged out as the one in charge of herself and Liam, and by extension of Hurt Hollow. He objected to this but made no attempt to deny that it was so.

Humphrey stood on the top step, facing Shelby, with his back to the door. The Hefn's legs, pelted with coarse gray hair like the rest of his body, were also spread and planted, his hairy arms were also folded. When Shelby had finished speaking his piece, Humphrey said in his soft, rough voice, ''Ah, but the people of Indiana were extremely helpful to me this afternoon. The boat from Louisville let me off—I flew out from Washington, by the way—and there I was, in plain sight of Hurt Hollow with no idea in the world how to get across the river. I was at a loss, I believe is the expression? Yes? I waited, and then I walked up the bank to see whether I could hire someone to take me across in one of the small boats tied up at the dock. Almost immediately I encountered several women who told me, ring the bell a certain way and someone will come to fetch you. In fact they came down to the dock with me, and one of them rang the signal herself. And it worked! Your daughter signaled back! Here I am!''

''Well, the environment here certainly is fine. I trust you'll enjoy your visit,'' Shelby said. Then, perhaps becoming aware on some level that looking at Humphrey was a bit like looking at himself in a fun-house mirror, he dragged one of the chairs around and lowered himself into it. He looked bravely up at the

Hefn. "Humphrey, I'm curious to know how you found out that Hurt Hollow existed. Had Pam talked to you about the place?"

Pam's attention had been riveted upon the exchange between Humphrey and her father, the locutions of each as odd in their own ways as those of the other, and the inflections and facial expressions as alien by human standards. Now she gave Liam a dirty look. Liam said quietly, "I told him. I'd told him about it already, but I called him again last night, after I called my parents. I knew he would want to see the Hollow anyway, and I knew it was hard on you to have to come over here every night after working all day, and so I just . . ."

Humphrey said smoothly, "It's what I do for a living nowadays, you know, Mr. Pruitt—keep these two out of trouble, along with the other Apprentices. I hope Jesse will forgive my arriving and taking charge without having been invited."

All three humans understood that Humphrey was being politely insincere about Jesse. No Hefn needed an invitation to do what he wanted and go where he liked. Since Humphrey wanted to be at Hurt Hollow, that was the end of it. Jesse had no say.

Shelby nodded, calm in his acceptance of having been outfaced, pushing his resentment under.

It disturbed Pam to sense her father's discomfort and humiliation, and the effort it cost him to put a good face on both. She had tracked his feelings precisely from the minute he got here. In all that time the smiling mask had hardly slipped, but now for an instant her father's face lost its pleasant smoothness and she saw him flash an angry glance at Liam—who by inviting Humphrey here had wildly exceeded the bounds of good-guest behavior both toward the Pruitts and toward Jesse.

Pam was good and angry at Liam herself. She felt another queasy-making surge of sympathy for Shelby.

Yet it was strange. Even as she watched Humphrey smoothly but ruthlessly annihilate her father's will, Pam's own feeling of being railroaded into a situation not of her own choosing began to change. Humphrey had the power to push into Hurt Hollow with no regard for Jesse's feelings or her own or anyone's, but that meant he also had the power to make Shelby keep away from the Hollow. By allying herself with Humphrey's will, and against her father's, some of Humphrey's power rubbed off on Pam. And power—that sweet, heady, unfamiliar sensation—put the whole matter in a different light.

For instance, power made her generous. "What did you bring us, Dad? I'm starved," she said, and had the queasy-making

194

pleasure of watching Shelby turn back from a thwarted school-boy into a grown-up benefactor and start unpacking the full sack of provisions he'd set down on the flagstones.

For a second, as they were helping him set out bowls of potato salad and applesauce and a platter of cold chicken, a miniature flashed into Pam's mind: her father and Humphrey standing facing one another in postures of unconscious mutual mimicry, smiles which were not real smiles on both their faces. She stood still, clutching a fistful of Jesse's forks and spoons, understanding why she'd been unable to imagine Humphrey and Jesse together in the real Hurt Hollow. In *Pinny's Hefn* the question of power—of forcing people to do things they didn't want to do—had never come up. Joshua *wanted* Comfrey there, he loved and respected Comfrey, they were working together on a plan to save the world.

Then and there, right in the middle of setting the table, Pam understood once and for all that Joshua was not Jesse. Saving the world was not on Jesse's agenda. That kind of global thinking wasn't in his line at all. Jesse was interested in living a certain kind of personal life, and was resigned to letting people come, look, and take away whatever they could from his example; but he was fiercely individualistic, and had never in his life knowingly imposed his views on a living soul.

Jesse, the real person lying in Madison Hospital full of copperhead venom, was going to *hate* the idea of having Humphrey here, and Humphrey was going to stay here for a while regardless of how Jesse or Shelby or even Pam felt about it.

The truth was, Pam hardly knew how she did feel, except confused. She was angry about Liam's uncivil use of his own power, but had to admit she stood to benefit from it. She felt sorry for her father but tremendously relieved that he wouldn't be coming to the Hollow anymore. She felt very bad about Jesse but also a little critical of the narrowness of his perspective (a criticism which, she now recognized, had come out in her novel). And grateful as she was for Humphrey's protection, and much as she loved him (in Washington), his perfect willingness to ride roughshod over Jesse and Shelby made her anxious, as well as resentful.

Everybody seemed to fork like a Hubbard tree, some of whose branches had "good" end points and some not.

"What have we here?" Liam's voice broke into her reverie; he had found the yellow pad where Pam had dropped it when the bell rang. "Another poem? Can I see it?"

195

Pam snatched the pad out of his hand and bolted into the house with it, nearly bumping into her father, who was bringing out four tumblers of water on the tray. "Sorry," she blurted to his startled exclamation. In the upper room she flounced onto the bed—accidentally kicking the case of the time transceiver, where Humphrey had stashed it out of harm's way (and out of her father's sight) as soon as he'd arrived—and ran her eyes down the page. *Nectar, pollen and bees that sting;/ This is Washington, dead of spring./ Honeyflow's here, but spring's too warm;/ The bees you kept are lost in a swarm* . . .

Taking a pen from the small table beside the bed, Pam crossed out *spring's too warm* and wrote *stings do harm.* She put the pen down and read the poem through from start to finish. On the whole, she now saw, it did make a weird kind of sense.

Picking up the pen again, she hesitated—then crossed out *kept* and slowly wrote *trust* back where it had been in the first place.

"What's this for?" Liam had asked, puffing up the hill to the house with the black metal case on his back. "We're on vacation, you know—we're not supposed to have to do any work. That's what a vacation *is*, Humphrey!" His tone was joking but so genuinely curious that Pam decided the time transceiver was Humphrey's own embellishment on the plot for his invasion of Hurt Hollow.

Humphrey, climbing behind Liam with his personal effects, said in his Santa's-elf voice, "This is a place of present importance largely because of its historical importance, yes?"

"Well, yeah, to some extent, but I think it has a lot of potential importance right now. That's why I thought you ought to see it." Liam reached the terrace and swung the case off his back, setting it down carefully. He straightened up, soaked with sweat, and turned to Humphrey. "Wait a second—you mean you're thinking of *using* the transceiver? Here?"

Pam, last in line, stepped onto the terrace saying, "I don't think we should do that!"

Humphrey stood blank and still, observing her. "No? I should have thought that you particularly, Pam, would appreciate a chance to meet the people who built this place, since you are so particularly attached to it. Or so Liam tells me. What is the difficulty?"

Pam thought, *The difficulty is, how will they feel, being the kind of people they are? You haven't even thought about that!*

But what she actually said was, "The Hubbells never said a word about a time window."

"So? Perhaps they had good reason not to."

"I still don't think it's right."

"Or perhaps they did not remember."

This was worse. "*Mindwiped?* Hannah and Orrin?"

Humphrey came closer. Pam stuck out her jaw and clenched her fists. "I see you are upset about this," the Hefn said. "You must try to help me understand your feelings about it. But, Pam, let me remind you also of something you know very well, but which vacation may have driven out of your mind for the moment: Time Is One, and nothing we do or fail to do *now* can possibly change in any way what already happened *then*."

Under the Hefn's fixed regard Pam relaxed slowly. Finally smiling for the first time since recognizing Humphrey on the dock she said, "Okay. I'll *try* to explain what bothers me about just slamming a window open on Hannah and Orrin, but I'm not sure I can make you understand it."

In the flat eyes a gleam appeared and vanished. "But you'll try? Good."

"Only, you know what? Sometimes I think . . . I'm not sure 'Time is One' isn't just a rationalization for using the transceivers for *any reason at all*. You could always just say, what's done is done, this doesn't change anything, every action we cause has already had its effect on the past. There's something *dangerous* about that."

"I don't think it's dangerous so much," Liam put in, "as, well, immoral. I hate the idea of mindwiping people without their consent, but if you start using the transceivers all the time, you have to accept a lot of mindwiping."

"I just *hate* the idea of doing that to Orrin and Hannah! It's— disrespectful, it's undignified! In fact," Pam said, squaring up to Humphrey, "I don't want any part of contacting them unless you agree that they won't be mindwiped."

Humphrey seemed intrigued. "You need not be present, of course, if it would distress you."

"You don't get it, Humphrey! This is *important*! I know I can't stop you but I'm telling you, I *really care* about this."

The Hefn stood like a statue, processing the exchange. Pam also stood her ground, breathing fast. Presently the gleam reappeared. "Explain to me then this bond with two people who died before you were born. Why do you care what happened to them?"

"We're connected anyway. Jesse connects us, Hurt Hollow does—they made the place out of nothing, and here it still is. Those might be the main things, but I've read Orrin's books and looked at his paintings, and seen the film of what he and Hannah were like and how they lived here, and I admire them, and feel grateful to them." I love them, she meant; but this was not a thing she ever said aloud.

"Even though you never met them."

"Right."

"Liam, do you understand this?"

"Sure," said Liam. "I feel like that too—not as strongly, I only just found out about the Hubbells and Pam's been coming here all her life. But I agree it would be wrong to wipe their minds. It would be wrong to use the transceiver that way."

Pam had a sudden inspiration. "Anyway, we *know* they never said anything about a time window. If they remembered, they kept the secret, right?"

"But did they keep it because they did not remember?" Humphrey twirled on his short legs from Pam to Liam and back to Pam. "The decision must still be made correctly. We know the outcome, but never why or how."

"*I* think," said Liam, "that things between the three of us will be very bad if you insist on mindwiping the Hubbells, and in that case it would be much better not to contact them at all."

Humphrey gave off an air of suppressed excitement. "I begin to see it, I think. Remarkable. This is remarkable, and you are right, Liam, to point out that preserving our own harmony requires the decision to fall one way rather than the other. Very well, I agree. I do agree. Orrin and Hannah Hubbell may keep their memories of us."

Jesse wasn't exactly crazy about the idea of Humphrey being at Hurt Hollow, but he didn't hate it either. Pam perched on a straight chair; the old man lay in the oppressive whiteness of his hospital bed, arms behind his head, considering what she had told him—which, so far, only amounted to the bare fact that Humphrey had come to stay at the Hollow for a while.

"How much of a while?"

"I don't know. He hasn't said."

"Has he said what he came for?"

Pam squirmed on the hard chair. She had decided it would do no good to mention the time transceiver or Humphrey's wish—which meant his intention—to use it, but it put a serious crimp

198

in the conversation; Pam was a miserable liar, even by omission. "He *said*, to take charge of us, and because Liam convinced him that Hurt Hollow was worth seeing. Two birds with one stone. So he said."

"I see." Jesse thought that over. "Then if he came to take charge of you two, he'll leave when I'm back on my feet."

Pam thought Humphrey would leave when he was good and ready, but what she said was, "Well, the interviews for the new Apprentice class will be starting soon. He'll have to leave before that."

"When are they scheduled for?"

"I think later this month. School starts June fifth, so we have to be back by then, so it's probably at least a week before that."

Jesse would be out of the hospital in a week at the most. Pam watched him ponder the prospect of sharing the Hollow with an uninvited Hefn guest and cringed. "I'm really sorry this happened," she said miserably. "I had no idea Liam would ask Humphrey here without even telling me. That is, he told me he thought Humphrey should visit the Hollow, but I kept saying I didn't see the point."

Jesse gave Pam a sharp look and said kindly, "Never mind, Punkin, it wasn't your fault. This is a big favor you're doing for me, you know, taking care of the goats and the garden while I'm cooped up in here. Not to mention finding me in the first place. I might have died if you and Liam hadn't come along, did you realize that?"

Pam nodded, feeling her face grow warm.

"So," said Jesse, "I figure on balance it's worth it, don't you? So let's not worry about it anymore."

"Okay," said Pam with relief. "How are you feeling, anyway? You look fine. Maybe a little wiped out."

Jesse grinned. "Thanks. I feel pretty good *now*, but I had a miserable couple of days. Crank me up just a wee bit higher, would you?" And when Pam had made him comfortable, "Hefn invasions aside, how are things going? Any problems?"

"Not so far. The goats are fine. I taught Liam to milk. The cabbages and Brussels sprouts and onions and, let's see, there was something else . . . oh, right, the beets!—they're all weeded, and I transplanted tomatoes and peppers this morning, and tomorrow I'm going to plant beans and melons if it doesn't rain."

"How are the peas doing?"

"They're almost done. I picked some for supper and left the

rest for seed. There's hardly any more flowers. Humphrey loves peas."

"Does he? My, my." Jesse looked intrigued. "Have you put Humphrey to work?"

"Well, he just got here last night. I will if he's interested in that. So far he just watches and wants to know about everything."

Jesse moved restlessly in the bed and pushed the covers off his chest, revealing more of the silly-looking hospital gown. "This Humphrey. Do you know, Punkin, I've never even seen a Hefn on television, though I did see a picture in the paper a few years back, right after their ship turned up again. They told me what the Hefn did to those men on the *Delta Queen*, but I remember you wrote that you liked Humphrey."

"I do. A lot."

"So what are the Hefn like, then—are they like people?"

"No," said Pam. "Not like people. At least the one Hefn I know isn't anything at all like a person. Everybody always asks the Apprentices what they're like, but it's hard to describe them." She had a thought. "Maybe Humphrey could come and see you, and you could see for yourself. Would you like that?"

"I don't believe I would, to tell you the truth," said Jesse. "I'm at enough of a disadvantage as it is. Though it would have been courteous of him to offer, since he's settled into my house without so much as a by-your-leave." He grinned ruefully, remembering the agreement not to worry, and shook his head. "No, I'll tell you, if he's still hanging around when I'm released I suppose I'll meet him whether I want to or not; and if he's gone by then, that'll be all right too."

"Then I won't bring it up to him." Pam looked at her watch. "I guess I better get going soon, I'm catching the 5:40 boat back." She stood. "Anything else you want done?"

"No, not really . . . I'm fretting some about the bees," Jesse admitted, "but I don't want you trying to work them. If they swarm, they swarm. Tell you what, though; you could keep an eye peeled, and if you see a swarm I guess you might try hiving it." Jesse's voice got deeper and stronger, and went up and down more, as he began to see possibilities in this idea. "There's two or three books in the house about beekeeping and every one of them explains how to hive a swarm. Read up on it, and if you feel like trying it—why, go ahead."

"Okay!"

"You won't get stung, not this time of year, but wear at least

200

a veil and gloves anyhow, just in case. There's an empty hive body in the workshop, and a bottom board and covers—get your friend Liam to help you move it up the hill. Would you happen to know offhand whether Liam's allergic to bee venom?''

"I never heard him say he was. I don't think it ever came up.''

"Well . . .'' Jesse frowned, subsiding a bit. "Read up on it and see what you think, but I don't want you kids taking any chances, Pam. You've got plenty to do without worrying about hiving any swarms. And don't worry if you try to hive one and the bees won't go in, either, do you understand me?''

"Sure,'' said Pam, but she vowed to herself that Jesse wouldn't lose any bees if she could help it.

"Good.'' The old man lay back and smiled at Pam. After a moment he reached out, took her hand and squeezed it. "You're *my* apprentice too, aren't you, not just Humphrey's. Apprentice homesteader! When I get out of here we'll have us a good long talk about Washington, and you can tell me how you like it, and all about your training.''

Pam left Jesse and walked along the white corridor toward the hospital's main door in a state of mingled happiness and guilt. In all their hour together and all the talk of Humphrey she had been unable to bring herself to mention the time transceiver.

Liam was waiting with the johnboat when Pam got off the steamboat. He now maneuvered the unwieldy vessel like a pro, pulling out into the river with a flourish of oars as soon as Pam was seated. "How's Jesse?''

"Pretty good, I guess. Not really sick anymore, just weak. He'll be okay, though. He wants us to keep an eye on the bees, and if they swarm he wants us to hive the swarm.''

"Wow. Did you ever do that before?''

"Unh-unh. It might not work, but I'm going to try if any of them swarm before he gets back. How was your afternoon with Humphrey?''

"Fine,'' said Liam. "I started some bread. Listen, I know you're mad at me for getting him to come here. I'm sorry, I realize it was terrible manners not to ask permission, but you didn't want him to come and I was so sure it was important that I just went ahead.'' When Pam didn't reply he added, "Anyway, you'll probably say it's just a technicality but I honestly wouldn't have known who to ask permission *of*. Jesse was sick in the hospital. Your dad wasn't in charge of Hurt Hollow, not in the sense of deciding who could and couldn't come here. I had to make the decision and I'm glad I did. But I really don't like you going on and on being mad at me about it.''

"I don't know that you've got much choice," Pam said. "I think you went way out of bounds in about six different directions, but I'm not as mad now as I was at first. Jesse's not happy about Humphrey but he's not as upset as I thought he'd be. Give me a couple of days to get used to it, okay?''

"Okay, as long as you *do* get used to it.''

"What do you care if I don't?'' Pam said crossly. "You can't just do stuff to people and expect to get off scot-free.''

"Well,'' said Liam, "I know that, but I . . . don't *like* things being like this with us. I feel bad.''

She looked at him, surprised but not blandished. "Well, I guess you should have thought about that before you decided to be Mr. High-and-Mighty and take everything on yourself.''

Liam stopped talking and rowed, looking unhappy. Unhappy or not, his smooth, rhythmic strokes made the johnboat skim along; already they were a quarter of the way across. The chimney swifts were into their usual evening circus act, and Pam turned sideways on the seat to watch them skitter and flick above the surface.

The truth was, she too felt bad about being on the outs with Liam. Anywhere else the change in their relations would have made a chronic ache inside her, but anywhere else Pam would have been weaker and less resolute—anywhere! Just like with Humphrey: Pam had always been shy in his presence in Washington and knew she would have been just as shy with him anywhere else in the world; but here she was not. It almost seemed as if some essential nutrient, chronically missing, were available to Pam in just this one place, Hurt Hollow—or perhaps more as if some toxin, elsewhere ubiquitous, were neutralized only here in the land of prickerbushes, copperhead bites, and honeybee stings.

As they moved into midstream the river, luminous and pale, began to fill the world just as it always did; and gradually a kind of peace settled down over Pam as once again the knowledge flowed in and filled her the way the river filled the world: *This is where I belong.*

It was the day's most fundamental truth, wider and greater than the awkward facts of Humphrey's presence and Liam's perfidy (if that's what it was). *I belong somewhere, and this is where. Not Washington, not Scofield: here.* As it had the previous afternoon, happiness brimmed up in Pam. *Jesse squeezed my hand and called me his apprentice.*

Her eyes stung. Facing into the breeze, she blinked and watched the swifts.

They were out of the channel and approaching the cleft in the foliage where Hurt Hollow was when Liam stopped rowing for a second and said, "Would you look at that!"

Something like a dog or an otter was splashing about in the shallow water off the dock. The splashing stopped; they watched the sleek form glide beneath the surface to re-emerge much nearer to the johnboat. It dove again and surfaced, and this time it raised a hairy arm and waved.

Differences forgotten for the moment, Pam and Liam looked slack-jawed at one another. Here was a mystery the whole world wondered at, decisively solved. The Hefn could swim.

"What does a swarm look like? How do you know they're swarming, I mean? Did you ever see one?" Liam asked. Supper, fresh garden peas and grilled catfish—Pam had finally consented to fire up the cookstove—was over, and the heavenly smell Liam's bread was making filled the house and wafted through the screen door. Pam had a big pan of skim milk ready to go; it would sit all night on the cooling stove and be yogurt by breakfasttime. The three of them sat on the terrace, enjoying the breeze while Liam cranked the little Amish churn and Pam leafed through Jesse's three old beekeeping books one after the other, reading up on swarms.

"Unh-unh, I never saw one. Here's what it says: 'Before you see your first swarm, you'll hear it—a low-pitched murmur that grows and swells and builds to fill the air with a gentle but insistent roar. You look up to see this humming, whirling vortex of bees rising and swirling around in a mini-tornado that's twenty feet across and treetop high.' "

"Criminy, how're we supposed to hive *that*?"

"We're not, while they're flying, but they land." She turned the page. " 'They will form a fairly quiet cloud, mill about for a bit, then will land on any handy support within a stone's throw of the nest and stay there anywhere from a few hours to days. Scouts will look for new quarters, and the swarm will decide on the new location. Then the bees will rise in a tornado again and head off, tail trailing like a Texas twister, toward the new nest.' That's when we hive 'em, before they take off, while they're still close to home. We give 'em another hive with comb inside, that already smells like bees, and in they go. Or if they're on a bush or something we put the hive underneath and shake 'em in.''

''Without getting stung to smithereens?''

''So they say. The swarm makes a big clump of bees all holding on to each other, with the queen in the center, and they're supposed to be very gentle if you don't upset them. You're not allergic to beestings by any chance, are you?''

''Not that I know of. Doesn't it upset them to be shaken into the hive?''

''It says not.'' Pam turned more pages. ''Here's how you can tell if a hive is about to swarm: 'A colony will prepare for swarming by building elongated queen cells . . . the old queen ceases laying and her body shrinks for flight. Young house bees loaf at the bottom of frames while flying-age workers cease foraging and mill around nervously. Large numbers of bees may hang out on the front of the hive.' ''

''I'd mill around nervously too,'' said Liam. On the table before him the thickening cream went round and round to the faint whirring of the crank. In his own chair Humphrey sat still as stone, his gaze fixed on the dashers of the churn.

''Most of that's going on inside the hive, and Jesse said we were absolutely not to open up the hives. I guess about all we can do is check them every day to see if large numbers of bees are hanging around on the outside—that and move the hive body up there so we'll be ready to go if it happens. How's your bread doing?''

Liam glanced at his watch. ''Five more minutes. How's your fire doing?''

''I better check.''

Pam was still inside the house when Liam let out a yell: ''Hey, butter! Look! It worked! Look at that!'' Talk about perfect timing. Smiling, she peered critically into the oven at the four brown loaves in their pans, then grabbed a couple of pot holders and lifted them out, one after the other.

Liam burst through the door, brandishing the churn. When he saw what she was doing he let out another yell, of indignation. ''What are you doing? That's my job, I'm the one who says when they're done!''

Smugly Pam said, ''You were busy, and it seemed important, so I just made the decision myself.''

''Very funny.'' They glared at each other. Things hung in the balance; but then Liam took a deep breath and looked at the bread, crusty and fragrant and obviously done to a turn. ''Okay,

204

I get your point, you don't have to keep on making it. But it's not really the same thing. If you'd asked me, I'd have said yes.''

Pam considered this. ''True. But that's because I was right already, as you can see.''

Liam stuck out his jaw. ''The trouble with you is, you can't see *I* was right too!''

The heavy door creaked as Humphrey came inside. His pelt, still slightly damp from his swim, added a gamy, wet-animal smell to the odor of freshly baked bread. ''May I put in my two cents' worth? A loaf of bread is either properly baked or it is not. My coming to Hurt Hollow at this time is neither right nor wrong in the sense that a loaf either is or is not done. You and Liam, Pam, are trying to compare two things which are essentially incomparable. Does that help? Will you be friends again now? It distresses me to be the cause of your dissatisfaction with one another.''

One tended to forget what exceptionally keen hearing the Hefn had. Pam couldn't think how to reply. Liam, too, was silent, perhaps abashed. Humphrey waited expectantly. When no one spoke he said, ''While you're thinking, perhaps you could tell me something: where does that expression come from?''

''What expression?'' they said together.

'' 'My two cents' worth.' What are my two cents?''

Pam cleared her throat. ''Cents is another word for pennies, a little coin worth one one-hundredth of a dollar. We don't use them anymore. I have some in my jewelry drawer at home that Mom saved when they took them out of circulation.''

''Ah.''

Pam decided to take the plunge. ''Humphrey,'' she said, ''see—it's just really hard for me to fit things together. This place was the best part of my life before I went to Washington, and it still is now. The best part of my Washington life is, well, *you*. They're both 'best,' but they're so *different*!'' She looked at the stumpy, flat-eyed figure, gray as an elephant, hairy as a goat, standing in the middle of Jesse's house of wood and stone, and felt intensely the truth of what she was saying.

But Humphrey, waiting still with the same expectant air, obviously failed to appreciate the incongruity. ''Ah?'' he said again helpfully.

''I can't figure out why you came!'' Pam burst out. ''Jesse asked me why today and I couldn't really tell him.''

''Ah!'' Humphrey did his little pirouette on Orrin Hubbell's hand-laid floor of sycamore planks. "If I tell you my reasons quite plainly, will the two of you be friends again?"

"I don't *know*. Maybe. It depends."

"Ah. Well. In any case, here they are. I came here, it is true, to discover and ponder the meaning of Hurt Hollow, the unusual life being lived here, the place which you both, in your different ways, had intuitively recognized as important. But I might well have come at a more opportune time, had that been my only purpose. The more important reason I'm here now, and not some other time," said Humphrey, "is that Liam needs me."

Startled, Pam stared at the Hefn, then at Liam, who met her gaze uncomfortably but did not deny the allegation. "What do you mean, he *needs* you?" Pam said, almost wailing; but before Humphrey could reply, "Oh!" she cried, fed up with all three of them, herself included. "Never mind! Forget it! I'm not mad, all right?"

"Fine by me!" Liam sprang into action, deftly inverted one of the bread pans and set the hot loaf on the cutting board. In another instant three thick slices lay on three china plates of different patterns, smoking gently, and Liam was scraping lumps of butter off the dashers onto the bread with his finger. "Grab the honey pot, Pam. Let's go outside with these, it's boiling in here."

Grateful for this flurry of activity, Pam did as he directed. Humphrey trotted out behind them, smiling his winsome, enigmatic smile.

That night, lying in her underpants and T-shirt on top of the covers of Jesse's bed in the hot house, Pam dreamed that she and Liam were trying to hive a swarm of bees hanging in a football-size cluster from the bow end of the big canoe in her own garage in Scofield. The canoe rested in its usual place, upside-down on two sawhorses, and the bees were hanging from the tip like a big drop at the tip of a runny nose. She and Liam, with some difficulty, managed to spread a sheet on the ground below the swarm and set the wooden box of the hive body down on it, very close to the bees. Pam's mother kept complaining that Pam was getting her good sheet dirty, and Pam kept explaining over and over, "I have to do this for Jesse!"

Then the moment came for the bees to be dumped on the ground so they would go into the hive. Liam lifted the canoe a few inches and let it drop heavily onto the sawhorse, and sure enough, the swarm fell all in a clump onto the sheet, and the bees untangled themselves and began to walk toward the hive and into the entrance.

Following the example set by somebody in one of Jesse's bee books, Pam straddled the hive body and watched the bees walk in. She was trying to spot the shell bee, larger than the others—the central member of the colony. If the shell bee didn't enter the hive the others wouldn't stay, so she had to keep watching to be sure it had gone in.

Like peasants entering a castle to escape marauders, the river of bees flowed into the hive. Pam watched for a long time. Finally she saw the shell bee, stepping along with the rest, an armored knight among peasants. It was wearing a shed cicada shell split down the back; its long transparent wings stuck out through the split. The shell bee had almost reached the hive entrance when Pam suddenly realized that the sky visible through the open garage door had turned black with storm clouds, and that the roar she heard was an approaching tornado.

She woke in terror, heart pounding, to the sound of wind and hard rain, and lay a moment breathing fast before she had the presence of mind to get up and shut the doors. Back in bed she dragged a sheet over herself—the house was cooler now—and lay listening to the rain's loudness upon the tin roof and the windows. *That was one weird dream!* she thought. *I must be more worried about Jesse's bees than I realized.*

After a time the rain slackened and the sound of it grew soothing. Pam turned on her side and snuggled down into the bed. Not until the next morning, when she stepped on it with her bare foot while sleepily stumbling around getting dressed to go do the milking, did she remember the yellow pad and poem and take note of the funny coincidence that she'd had swarms of bees on the brain even before Jesse asked her to watch out for real ones at Hurt Hollow.

She found a pencil and wrote SYNCHRONICITY in a blank place at the top of the page, to think about later.

Liam: *"I don't see a blessed thing in this poem after the first few lines, so what is it that's there that I don't see?"* That's my basic question at the end of the poem-writing scene (which is pretty much made up, though I did draft that poem the day Humphrey arrived). I can now answer easily and fully, but again in this larger work the same question applies. Something's there, but I can't see it. Can you?

#I'm getting there, I'm getting there.

#That feeling you describe when I'm rowing you across the river, that Hurt Hollow is "where I belong," the one place in all the world where an essential nutrient is available to you or a toxin is neutralized? I'd love to know if you feel that *just* because you had already "lived into" the place enough to make it personal holy ground, or because you had intuitively identified it as a Hot Spot, or—the most exciting possibility—both. I really can't wait to get out there. Think I'll do the calculations myself, if Raghu doesn't get to it soon (he's still plotting Findhorn).

#I'm sure you *see* the substitution of Humphrey for your dad when they both go swimming from the same beach on the same river, as well as during the face-down on the terrace (that's when the lion turns into a carcass, right?). I get the idea you're in touch with all that level of symbolism.

#Why did I need Humphrey? I think in retrospect it was because he was the sole repository of my memories of Jeff. I still hadn't retrieved a lot of them. He had 'em all. And the relationship fascinated him, too. So in both those ways he was what was left of Jeff in my life. I'd never been away from him before and didn't know how hard it would be. Julie was important there too, but she only knew what I'd remembered up to a given time. Humphrey was like a bank vault full of treasure.

Funny. I valued Jeff in him. You obviously valued him mostly as an alternative father figure. Poor Humphrey, I'm beginning to wonder if anybody ever loved him for himself alone, and not his yellow hair (is that Yeats?).

#Wow, *what a dream!* Made up or real? If real, then unconsciously you understood exactly what the score was with your dad; but I'm guessing this dream is made up.

12

LITTLE CHILDREN, IT IS THE LAST TIME

—I John 2:18

Thursday brought them a wonderful morning, brilliant, dripping, and blissfully cool after the storm. They dried off the chairs with towels and had breakfast on the terrace. The first loaf of Liam's bread disappeared completely, as did half of the second and most of a jar of honey. The yogurt turned out well; they opened another precious jar of blackberries.

To Pam it felt inexpressibly good to sit in dappled sunshine that you wanted to luxuriate in rather than escape, stroked by a gentle current of air, "eating bread and honey" with Liam and Humphrey like three queens in a nursery rhyme, and being—or seeming to be—on almost as familiar a footing with the Hefn as Liam was. She inhaled the deep, stirring scents of the wet earth and the river, and the faint underscent of Humphrey's mist-dampened pelt, and thought: *This is as good as it gets* and *I wish Jesse was here, but I like it that Humphrey is.*

Looking at Humphrey now as he spooned up blackberries and yogurt, almost purring with pleasure, Pam tried to see him the way Jesse would, or the way Orrin and Hannah might view him as a guest at their own table. His head was large for his body and covered all over, even his face, with gray hair, short like animal hair except that by some quirk of parallel evolution he was bearded. His eyes were large, without visible pupils or irises, and flat—flat in structure, flat in expression, though to look into them was to have the sense of meeting someone's gaze. His mouth and nose and ears were like those of humans—in placement and, presumably, in function. This humanoid appearance explained why it had been possible for the stranded Hefn to be taken for hobs in Northern England, and for "tomtes" in Sweden.

"Do you clever children know, either of you, how to cook a

'cobbler'? No? Ah,'' he said wistfully, "but this too is very, very fine."

Humphrey's body was small and compact, his short legs the same length as his arms, all hair-covered, some of the hair falling out in patches now as a side-effect of the antihibernation drugs. There were no external structures humans were able to recognize as genitalia. Small though they were, the Hefn were unbelievably strong for their size, several times as strong as a strong man. The gravity of their home planet was stronger too, according to what the hob Elphi had told the humans in Yorkshire, and the Hefn ship simulated the gravitational effect of their home planet, even on the moon. Instead of ordinary one-way knees and elbows, Humphrey's were equipped with a sort of swivel joint more like a ball-and-socket, that let them bend and lock in any direction at any angle. His back, on the other hand, didn't bend at all.

The pelvic and shoulder arrangements had no analog in vertebrate anatomy; they were what enabled the Hefn to run swiftly and efficiently on all fours as well as walk upright on two legs, albeit with a somewhat inhuman gait. Each of Humphrey's hands, now occupied with holding his tumbler of milk and his yogurt spoon, had four short digits, two of which were opposable to the other two, and a very short palm. The arrangement was repeated on his feet, with shorter digits and a longer sole. The Hefn were without a dominant hand.

Humphrey's body fit into Orrin's low-slung slant-back chairs no better than it did into ordinary straight chairs or upholstered furniture, which asked more of Hefn hip joints than they could easily give (unless the Hefn were able to lie down). Yet, sitting there in one of these chairs with his plate in his lap and the hair all around his mouth sticky with honey and stained with berry juice, he looked as if he belonged at the Hollow after all.

Pam imagined Hannah, of the legendary graciousness toward the strangers who constantly wandered in to see Hurt Hollow for themselves, asking Humphrey what sorts of things they ate where he came from, and offering him more milk. She imagined the innocent delight on Orrin's face as he relished yet one more piece of evidence that the universe was an astonishing and wondrous place.

With sudden pleasure Pam realized that even though Jesse was not Joshua (and perhaps partly because Jesse was not *here*), before her eyes Humphrey was turning into Comfrey! She watched the tongs-like alien hand lift the aluminum tumbler of

210

milk—watched Humphrey drain it—then stood herself, in Hannah's stead, to fill the tumbler again from the pitcher.

Without actually thanking her, or so much as looking at her, Humphrey made it clear—however it was the Hefn did such things—that he was grateful.

With the regular supply line from Scofield shut down, keeping fed had now replaced doing chores as the major preoccupation of Hurt Hollow's temporary caretakers. While nearly all their chores ultimately were concerned with food production, the garden would not start pumping out produce in a big way until later in the summer, and by dinnertime the care package Frances had sent over with Shelby on Tuesday would be empty. Pam still agreed with her father that it would be best if they could manage to avoid eating up all Jesse's stores, but not to fall back on what remained of them was going to be difficult. In fact, even if they did use the stuff in the cellar, keeping the three of them fed looked like being a full-time job, one for which they weren't too well equipped. Even Pam, the one with the most experience, felt daunted. And if they truly tried to abstain from using Jesse's own home-grown supplies, it would be harder for them to keep eating than it would have been for Jesse himself.

Breakfast gradually evolved into a conference about food.

"We've got plenty of wheat and yeast—Jesse buys or trades for that so I don't feel bad about using it up. We can keep ourselves in bread. There's also a big tin of cereal for breakfast if we want to cook it up, which I don't particularly. Jesse buys that too. It's mostly cracked wheat, and then he puts in raisins and sunflower seeds and stuff. He does grow the sunflower seeds, I guess we could leave those out."

"Let me have a look at this breakfast cereal," Humphrey said. He peered into the tin, sampled a small handful of grain. "This will suit me very well, and no one will have to cook it."

Pam nodded. "Great. That's about it for staples. There's salt. No sugar. Lots of honey and a little maple syrup. I think we should leave the maple syrup for Jesse, it's a lot of work to make, but we can hit the honey as hard as we like without using *that* up. Now: the goats."

Humphrey listed, "Milk. Butter. Yogurt. Cottage cheese." (Liam made a face.) "Hard cheese?"

Pam shook her head. "Takes too long, and anyway, I don't know how. And that's about it in the way of dairy products."

"Okay, the garden," said Liam. "Lettuce."

"Bolting fast, it's been too hot. We should eat it all up as fast as we can."

"Right. Peas."

"What's still out there has to be left to mature for next year's seed. The batch we ate for supper last night was the last of 'em."

"Check. Spinach. I hate spinach."

"Raw or cooked?"

"Both. Sorry."

"Never mind," Pam said, "that'll just make more for us. Something else we'll need to eat before it bolts. Or we could try canning it . . . but I don't think I'm up to that on Jesse's stove, to tell you the truth, unless it was a matter of life and death." She thought. "What else out there is edible now—anything? I wish it was August, or even July, this would be a lot easier."

Unfortunately, it was early May. The beets and carrots were no more than slender red and yellow threads, and the other crops in a state of rapid vegetative growth; they would not flower for weeks, or head up or produce fruit for months. The bean, melon, and squash seeds weren't even in the ground yet; Pam had planned to plant them this morning but the night's rain had drenched the soil, making it much too wet for planting.

"Asparagus," said Humphrey surprisingly. "That at least is what it resembles. Tall, scaly, green?"

"Asparagus! I forgot about the asparagus! Let's go see." They jumped up and ran together down the hill to the lowest gardens. "Orrin put these perennial beds in over here, separate from the part of the garden that gets dug every year." The wet, weedy asparagus bed was thronged with slender spears and Pam was more delighted than she would have thought possible at discovering this unexpected abundance of a mere vegetable. Liam looked less happy; he really was not much of a vegetable man.

Back on the terrace they continued taking stock. Pam had already checked the cellar and counted the mason jars. "I think we can start eating the canned goatmeat. Jesse keeps that mostly for emergencies this time of year, when the trot line's pretty productive, and I guess this qualifies as an emergency. He doesn't do any hunting and doesn't keep a gun or any traps. He used to have a big dog, Captain, that would catch groundhogs for him, but he died a couple of years ago. Jesse probably ought to get another dog, just for a watchdog . . . Well, anyway, I feel okay about using up the goatmeat."

Liam looked gloomy. Pam felt a flash of irritation, though in

212

the spirit of reconciliation she tried not to show it; at the food level Liam wasn't exactly adapting well to the homesteading life. He was too picky. The thought of his bread-baking softened this response, but did not eradicate it. So far, all Liam had liked of the Hurt Hollow provender were his own bread with butter and honey, milk and yogurt, blackberries, and catfish.

Humphrey said, "I believe . . . I might try to discover whether I could become a predator again, after all these many cycles of offworld living. The Yorkshire Hefn managed it. Yes, why not? I believe I'll try."

This made Liam perk up. "A predator?"

"Yes. A predator. Perhaps a watchdog also. But first and foremost a hunter able to catch groundhogs and squirrels for the pot. It's a knack we all begin with, we Hefn, but it atrophies for lack of use or need. But now I recall that Belfrey spoke of grouse . . . Pam and Liam, I am going to try my luck. Perhaps I'll return with something for our dinner." He had darted out the back door almost before he'd finished speaking, moving faster on all fours than either of them had ever seen him move on two.

They shared an affectionate laugh at their teacher's expense before getting back to business. "You know," Pam said, "it might be nice to have some eggs. Spinach and hard-boiled egg salad, mmm. Jesse sometimes trades butter for eggs with the farm at the top of the hill. How about we take that single hive body up there, and I pack up some butter, and we pick up the mail and see if they've got any eggs to spare?"

Liam's grin spread clear across his face. "I would *love* to have some eggs!"

"We could ask about apples, too. They've got an orchard. If there's any apples left by now they'd probably be glad to give them to a good home, 'cause they won't keep much longer anyway and nobody wants to fool with pies or whatever in planting season."

They trudged up the hill together. Pam, in the lead, wore khaki shorts and one of her voluminous T-shirts, and carried her half-pound of butter in a plastic refrigerator box swaddled in several towels, to keep it cool. Liam followed with the single hive body, a wooden boxlike object, dark old wood within and painted white without, which they had brushed free of dust and cobwebs. The square hive sat on Liam's shoulder between a bottom board, an inner cover, and a "telescoping" cover clad in metal. The combination made an uncomfortable, awkwardly heavy burden and Liam perspired freely as he climbed the trail.

Jesse's apiary, sixteen beehives arranged four by four in a rough square, was located at the top of the hill in a clearing close to the fence, so the gardens and crops of the houses and the farm just beyond would be handy to the bees; in high summer, when the trees and bramble fruits had finished blooming, these would provide a more reliable source of nectar and pollen than the Hollow's woodland could. The hives were far enough off the road to avoid most problems with visitors, but near enough for easy access with a cart when it came time to take the honey off.

Liam stopped in sight of the apiary. "Where should I put this thing?"

"Anywhere, I guess. Not too close."

With a *Whuf!* of relief Liam slung the hive body off his shoulder onto a carpet of needles under a pine tree. Standing at a cautious distance, Liam rubbing his shoulder, they watched the bees, dark pellets whirling and zipping toward and away from each of the sixteen hives. The combined activity of so many of them made a steady, droning hum. The landing boards at the hive entrances, as well as the cracks where Jesse had offset the covers and some of the supers for extra ventilation, were crammed with bees, but Pam remembered noticing and asking about this the summer before. During periods of exceptional heat (Jesse had told her) some bees spend time on the front porch. It wasn't swarming behavior.

"I wouldn't call that milling around nervously, would you?" Liam asked.

"Nope. Everything's normal here. So far so good."

They backtracked and went on to the gate, then on down the road for about a quarter of a mile. "Seems funny to be out in the world," Liam remarked as they walked easily along on smooth pavement still dampish from the previous night's downpour.

"I know what you mean."

Still, it was not a very worldly stretch of road. Despite the rows of modest houses on half-acre lots, not a single wagon or other vehicle passed them in the ten minutes it took to arrive at a white farmhouse and turn into the drive. Behind the house a thin woman in a housedress was hanging out the wash. Pam knew her slightly from having come on similar errands for Jesse the summer before, and greeted her with confidence. "Hi, Mrs. Kovach. Remember me? Pam Pruitt, from Scofield?"

Mrs. Kovach finished pinning a sheet to the line and squinted at Pam. "Yes indeed, I remember you. How's Jesse doing?"

"He's better. I went over to see him yesterday. He'll be home in a week or so, he thinks. This is Liam O'Hara, he goes to school with me. He's helping out with the goats and everything while Jesse's in the hospital."

Mrs. Kovach nodded and shook Liam's proffered hand without much enthusiasm. "I seen you on the television. Seen both of you." Her expression was an odd mixture of curiosity and distrust.

Pam, who remembered this woman as friendly and talkative, began to falter. She dropped the pleasantries and came to the point: "We've got some butter to trade for eggs, if you have any to spare. Or eggs and apples."

"Butter?" The woman's eyes shifted to Pam's bundle.

"We made it just last night."

"Oh, I reckon we could spare half a dozen eggs. Don't know about apples, you'll have to look for yourself. You're welcome to 'em if you find any that ain't gone soft." She began to move toward the house, then turned suddenly with a hard expression. "That Humphrey ain't going to be eatin' none of them eggs, now, is he? I ain't looking to give *him* nothin' of mine, I tell you that right now!"

Pam gulped. Liam said, "Excuse me, but how'd you know Humphrey was even here?"

"Everbidy knows it," the woman replied scornfully. "He come Tuesday, on the afternoon packet from Louisville. A lot of people over at the landin' saw him, and people talk. I ain't feedin' no eggs to no Hefn, now."

Liam said flatly, "Why not?"

"I'll tell you why not!" Mrs. Kovach squared up to him, hands on hips; she was not more than thirty, probably less, but her stance and shrillness gave her the menacing air of an older woman. "Because it's worse'n murder, what they done to them men! *He* don't have no right to come around Hurt Hollow, no more'n all them Hefn have to be here on the Earth atall! Sneakin' in here, with Jesse in the hospital! I call it a shame!"

The exponentially increasing intensity of Mrs. Kovach's feelings made Pam feel faint. She backed up a step, then another; but Liam stood his ground. "He didn't sneak in," Liam said. "I asked him to come."

Mrs. Kovach reared back in outrage. She paused for dramatic emphasis, then said fiercely, "*You* asked him to come? Without

Jesse's say-so? A snotty-nosed brat that don't have no business bein' here in the first place?'' She shook her head disgustedly. ''Brother Bemis's just as right as he can be, you kids oughtn't to have nothin' to do with them Hefn.''

''Why not?'' said Liam again.

''I'll tell you why not! Because the Hefn are the Antichrist, that's why not!'' Behind her, lifted on a gust of wind, the sheets flapped emphatically.

Pam almost dropped the butter. ''Who the Sam Hill says the Hefn are the Antichrist—Otie Bemis? Is *he* going around saying that?''

''He's sayin' it, all right, cause it's the truth!'' Mrs. Kovach leaned forward from the hips again to shout this right in Pam's face, with a spray of spittle for good measure. She took another step forward. Her eyes looked a little crazy.

A cold warning sounded in Pam's brain. Stepping back again, she grabbed Liam's arm just in time to stop him from making some retort. ''We've got to get back. Can we just get the eggs now? We won't give any of them to Humphrey if you feel like that.'' Liam gave her an outraged look but she quelled him with a quick headshake and a jerk on the arm.

''You kids git on outa here. You don't git no eggs from me. You git off my property. Git on back there and tell that Humphrey he better look out. God is not mocked, do you hear me? If them Hefn are going to start doin' human bein's like they done them men on the boat, they're gonna pay!''

She kept on yelling things like that while Pam and Liam beat an undignified retreat across her yard and back along the road, carrying the rejected butter. Liam, fizzing with fury, looked back over his shoulder and drew in his breath. ''Don't say anything—don't answer her back!'' Pam told him sharply. ''Jesse has to live with these people. She'll probably be mortified when she calms down.''

''Jesus, she's a total nut case! She ought to be locked up!'' He jammed his hands in his pockets and kicked a stone off the road as they hurried along. ''Who or what the fuck is the Antichrist?''

''He's, like, the opposite of Jesus. Anti-Christ. The enemy of Christ. When he turns up, the end of the world is just about here. He's supposed to be a kind of monster. Lots of people thought Hitler was the Antichrist.''

Liam stopped walking—forcing Pam to turn around to face him—and stared at her as if she'd lost her wits. ''You're not

216

serious! You *can't* be! That's—absurd, it's loony! Nobody but a cretin could take stuff like that seriously!''

''Take my word for it,'' said Pam tightly, ''she does take it seriously, whatever *you* happen to think about it.''

Breathing hard through his nose, a series of small expressive snorts, Liam started walking again. Without looking at Pam he said ''So, what's all this Antichrist horseshit got to do with Humphrey, tell me that.''

She chose not to take offense; they had enough problems as it was. ''I don't know,'' she told him, ''but my best guess is, Otie Bemis must have decided—maybe just since last Sunday, maybe when he realized people at Scofield really didn't like what he said—that the Hefn are the Antichrist, collectively. So now he's going around saying that at all the places where he preaches. Steve Harper said he was going around to different churches preaching against the Hefn, remember.'' Pam stopped in the road herself, struck by a thought. ''That's how come they know about Humphrey on this side of the river—Brother Otie told them! Last night was Prayer Meeting night, he probably got a good turnout, wherever he was—over here in Kentucky now, I bet.''

Liam looked appalled. ''I got the impression that the other people in *your* church thought Brother Otie was an idiot, a joke!''

''Yeah, but that was Scofield. Outside the college community people are more likely to take him seriously.''

Liam sent another large rock into the roadside bushes with a vicious kick. ''Hell, I guess Humphrey was right. This *isn't* a good time for one Hefn to be traveling around alone—especially not right here where Jeffrey got jumped by those guys.''

''If he knew that, how come he changed his mind?'' When Liam didn't answer right away, Pam plunged ahead: ''Because you need him, he said. *Do* you need him?''

''Yeah, I do,'' said Liam gruffly, ''but now I wonder if maybe we better both go home.''

Pam had been on the verge of asking, ''What for?'', but the idea of their leaving dropped into her stomach like a stone. Instead she said angrily, ''How come you agreed to come in the first place then, if you couldn't manage without Humphrey for a couple of weeks?''

Liam looked away. ''Lay off, okay? I didn't know what being away from him would be like. Or what being here would be like,'' he added. ''It's both together, really. The combination.''

The rage she had managed to short-circuit on the *Delta Queen*

217

now surged through Pam, escaping her control. "What's so un-
bearable about being at Hurt Hollow?" she said savagely. "The
food?"

"Don't get *mad* again, goddammit!" Liam shouted. "Hurt
Hollow's wonderful, I've been having a great time—mostly—
but there's a lot more emotional static than I bargained for and
I just . . . need Humphrey. Or Julie, but Julie couldn't come if
she wanted to and Humphrey can, and I wanted him to see the
place anyway, and that's why I asked him."

"Emotional static?" Pam had stopped in the middle of the
road. A wretched suspicion washed through her like ice water,
dousing the flames of wrath. "You mean—Dad?"

"Partly him," he added. "Partly *you*. And partly other stuff,
but the point is, I brought Humphrey here and I can get him
away from here to someplace safer, and then Jesse's neighbors
will calm down, and everything will get back to normal. Relatively normal."

They had arrived at the mailboxes. Pam handed her bundle
to Liam and emptied Jesse's large box of its accumulated letters
and catalogs—no bills, interestingly—including several items
that looked like get-well cards. On top of the bundle was a large
sheet of cheap gray paper folded over twice. Printed on the
outside in elegant capitals was FOR THE HEFN.

"Uh-oh." Hastily Pam set the stack of mail on the ground
and unfolded the piece of paper. On it someone had written out
some Bible verses in longhand. The handwriting was beautiful,
almost calligraphic. Pam held the sheet so Liam could read over
her shoulder:

And then shall that Wicked be revealed, whom the Lord shall
consume with the spirit of his mouth, and shall destroy with the
brightness of his coming; Even him, whose coming is after the
working of Satan with all power and signs and lying wonders.

II Thes. 2:8–9

Now the Spirit speaketh expressly, that in the latter times some
shall depart from the faith, giving heed to seducing spirits, and
doctrines of devils; Speaking lies in hypocrisy; having their conscience seared with a hot iron; *Forbidding to marry*—

I Tim. 4:1–3

Little children, it is the last time: and as ye have heard that

218

antichrist shall come, even now are there many antichrists; whereby we know that is the last time.

I John 2:18

And lastly, in large block capitals:

AND I STOOD UPON THE SAND OF THE SEA, AND SAW A BEAST RISE UP OUT OF THE SEA, HAVING SEVEN HEADS AND TEN HORNS, AND UPON HIS HORNS TEN CROWNS, AND UPON HIS HEADS THE NAME OF BLAS-PHEMY!

Rev. 13:1

All around the wide margins, like a doily decoration, the same scribe had written: working of Satan—HEFN—all power—GAFR—doctrines of devils—HEFN—forbidden to marry—GAFR—little children—BTP APPRENTICES—many antichrists—HEFN—beast—GAFR—sand of the sea—EARTH—the sea—SPACE—

And at the very bottom of the page in red ink: *Humphrey we know thee who thou art!*

Pam turned the paper completely around. Liam looked at her when they were finished reading, personal rancor forgotten. "Am I paranoid, or is this really scary?"

"It scares *me*. Let's get out of here." Scooping up the pile of mail they hurried back along the road to the gate.

On the gate below the sign saying "Hurt Hollow Is Closed To Visitors Until Further Notice," and fastened by a twig skewered brutally through the paper and meshes of the fence and out again, was another sign, this one scrawled in pencil on cheap white paper. HUMFRIE ANTICHRIST MERDERER it said.

The sign had not been there when they came through the gate half an hour earlier. They looked around in alarm, but the woods on both sides of the road were quiet and no one was in sight. Pam unlocked the padlock, hands shaking, and clicked it shut behind her with a sense of having had a narrow escape.

Humphrey was standing on the terrace with an expectant air when they came through the house and out the front door. He started talking as soon as he saw them. "I am not a very good predator, Pam and Liam, but I show promise. I caught a squirrel! Only one, however, only for me. I therefore made canned goatmeat sandwiches, and now I will bring you some milk." Sure enough, there were two sandwiches, carefully sliced in half, on two plates.

Humphrey seemed quite excited, for him. The hair around his mouth was wet—recently washed, Pam thought, and shuddered, imagining the blood—and there were several tufts of reddish-brown fur in the longer hair on his head, which gave him a rakish look.

Liam prevented him from scuttling down the path to the springhouse and Pam handed him his mail, the carefully penned gray paper and the scrawled white one.

"Ah," Humphrey said, and "Ah" again when he had finished reading them. He looked up, unperturbed but alert as a fox. "Now then. First I will fetch the milk, and then we will have a discussion."

While he was gone, Liam unwrapped the towels, peeled the top slice of bread off his sandwich, and buttered it with the butter they had carried all the way up the hill and back again. Pam watched him but declined to butter her own.

"Might as well."

"It's too depressing."

They told Humphrey about Mrs. Kovach while they were eating. "Liam thinks you and he should leave," Pam said. She tried to sound neutral. "He thinks it's too dangerous for you to stay here right now."

"The sentence carried out on those guys aboard the *Delta Queen* was supposed to be a deterrent," said Liam. "It didn't work like that at all, did it? People aren't scared, they're wild with rage. It didn't work."

"That would appear to be correct. Let us say rather, some people. Obviously, there's a great deal left for us to learn about human beings." Humphrey munched a handful of raw cereal grain and sipped some water. He glanced at Liam. "Had you meant to leave Pam here alone? Surely that would not be allowed. She would have to go home."

Liam protested. "Why? Heck, she wouldn't be *alone*. Somebody could come stay with her, she had lots of offers from people who want to help Jesse. She wouldn't have to go home."

Humphrey turned to Pam. "*Would* you have to leave Hurt Hollow if we went back to Washington? What other arrangements might be made?"

"Oh, he's right," Pam said in the same neutral voice. "Somebody would come—people from the college, or from Madison. Don't worry about it."

"Your father, perhaps?"

Liam's head came up. Pam stared at the table, feeling tears

press against the backs of her eyes. "Perhaps . . . or, well, I guess I *might* go home, if somebody else could take over."

Liam said, "Listen, Pam—"

Humphrey interrupted, something he almost never did. "Has anyone ever broken through the fence—vandals, art thieves, anyone?" Pam shook her head. "Then I think we should be sensible. If there are further incidents we may wish to reconsider, but there seems insufficient cause at present to panic and run. Frankly, I would be very reluctant to go. Liam was correct: there is a great deal to ponder in this place. I have not yet had time to assess it thoroughly, and I wish to stay until I have done so." He paused to sip more water. "However, I do have one more question." His hairy gray hand darted out suddenly and closed around Pam's hand where it lay on the table.

His touch was cool. Startled, she looked up and met the strange, flat eyes. "Are you still unhappy that I came?"

Pam shook her head. "No. I was thinking at breakfast how nice it is to have you here. When Liam started to talk about leaving I realized I really want you to stay."

"And why did you change your mind?"

Pam tried to think. She didn't want to come right out and say, "Because if I look at you the right way you turn into Comfrey," or "Because Jesse doesn't actually *hate* it that you're here." Finally she settled on "I guess it just seems like you've kind of started to fit in."

"Ahhh."

Liam said, "I take back my suggestion. I've changed my mind too, I think we ought to stay. Pending further developments, as you said."

Humphrey let go of Pam's hand. "Very well! For the time being, we shall stay."

"I *was* thinking," said Liam, "that maybe we should notify the police."

Wonderingly, Pam flexed her fingers. "I don't think that would do much good. The police are all from around here, and I would guess they probably all pretty much agree with Mrs. Kovach."

"Well . . . okay, how's this. We have to go up tomorrow to check on the bees. We can check the mailbox too, and the fence, see if any more poison pen letters get delivered. If they do, we can reconsider the whole situation. Okay?" Pam nodded. Humphrey, whose head was not joined to his body in a way that allowed it to nod, indicated his agreement. Liam added, "I wish I knew what Brother Bemis is gonna get up to tonight."

221

"He'll be preaching someplace, no doubt." Pam looked at her watch. "I think I'll call Mom in a while. Maybe she knows what's going on."

"*I* think," said Humphrey, "that might be wise. And now, if the matter is settled, I propose that we attempt to establish contact with Orrin and Hannah Hubbell."

They had argued, not about whether the Hubbells should be contacted, but about whether the contact should end in mindwipe. Framing it that way, Pam realized belatedly, *assumed* that contact would take place. She had expended her best effort on the wrong argument. She still didn't approve—of the intrusion, the perfect indifference to their feelings, the imposition of power—but she recognized that Humphrey had made his mind up. Contact would be attempted. Time would be One.

"Maybe they never talked about it because it wasn't successful," Liam suggested to Pam while Humphrey was assembling the transceiver.

"Not much chance of that. They hardly ever went anywhere."

Though the Hubbells were nearly always to be found at home, there was another problem. In the years following 1974, when Orrin's book *Hurt Hollow* had been published—the same years during which he had become more widely recognized as an artist—uninvited visitors turned up at the Hollow almost daily. Humphrey had therefore determined upon an earlier date, well before the period of heavy visitor impact, and before advancing age had caused Orrin and Hannah to pull in their horns—give up the goats and bees, reduce the size of the garden.

A facsimile of the guest book the Hubbells had kept through all that time was on display in the house; this Humphrey consulted, and chose a week in August, 1964, when no visitors' names at all had been recorded (in case he landed wide of the target—the transceivers could not be aimed with pinpoint accuracy). He set up the terminal near the back door, in the flat place where the path widened to become a little clearing.

Now that the attempt was inevitable, Pam gave in to her excitement. Moral scruples aside, the idea of actually talking to the Hubbells thrilled her to death. She whirled in place like a Hefn, hugging herself to keep her breasts from bouncing, trying not to get in Humphrey's way.

Liam was nearly as excited as Pam. All the Apprentices' training had taken place in a lab mock-up; neither Pam nor Liam had ever seen a time window used in the field. It wasn't always easy to keep in mind what the exercises in controlling and focusing brainwaves were *for*; but this—precisely this—was the practical application of what they had spent the past eight months learning to do.

When Humphrey was finished, the contents of the black metal box had been unpacked and assembled into a delicate tripod-based structure of molded metal surfaces and meshwork, spread out like a cobra's hood and facing the back door, ready to generate the temporal field.

Pam and Liam and the rest had been taught how to activate and direct the transceivers, but not how to put them together, and nothing about how the terminal box and its contents worked at the level of mechanics and engineering. Nor had they learned how it was powered. There was no intention of ever teaching the BTP Apprentices these things. The Gafr did intend to create a second class of specialists, an engineering class, which would be selected and trained at such time as the machinery began to require maintenance and repairs, or replacements were needed; but this would not be soon. For all their apparent delicacy the transceivers had been built to last.

Nothing had been said about giving humanity the technology that would enable them to build their own working transceivers, contact the past without Hefn supervision. The presumption was that this would not be permitted.

The Gafr had observed enough about humans to know that if they understood how something worked, one clever person might eventually figure out how to build a working model; perhaps with this in mind, the Apprentices had been told—and so had everyone else—that the transceiver components could not have been manufactured on Earth even at the peak of humanity's former technological prowess. They had to be made in space. It was going to be a long, long time before men and women went into space again, if they ever did.

John Chalmers had said once, in a fit of after-lunch grousing in the cafeteria, that they were all like a bunch of worshipful chimpanzees. The Apprentice chimps were being taught how to drive a car, the Engineer chimps would be taught to service it and fix it when it broke, but—for reasons so multiple and obvious as to be beyond argument—nobody would ever even try to teach a bunch of chimps how to *make* a car.

Free speech was the one civil right the Gafr were known to tolerate well. People could complain and criticize to their hearts' content, in private and in public, without rubbing any Hefn fur the wrong way, so long as they *did* as they were told. Humphrey, who had been present at this outburst, had twinkled and said cheerfully, "Would *you*, John, wish to try teaching chimpanzees how to make a car?"

"Yeah, but what if people aren't chimpanzees?" Marshall put in.

"What if the time transceiver is not a car? What if it is a device of power for destruction greater than any of you can imagine?"

"How can it be that," said Marshall wickedly, "if Time is One?"

"Marshall, that is very good," said Humphrey. "You have put your fingers on a paradox you will be in a better position to understand after you have had another year of training. Or perhaps another two years. For the moment I will say only this: It does matter how and why the decisions to use the transceivers come to be made."

How and why Humphrey had made the decision to contact the Hubbells Pam didn't know, but she had watched him go through the process of arriving at the secondary decision not to mindwipe them, and felt she now had a better intuitive understanding of what they all called Marshall's Paradox.

They were ready. Humphrey slipped his hands into dimples in the cobra fan and the air in front of it began to shimmer. Pam and Liam watched attentively as the shimmer resolved into a swirling pattern. This part they had observed many times, and both understood in a rough way how to read the shimmer patterns. Pam recognized what was happening as the swirls reduced under Humphrey's control: three thousand years in the past, one thousand, several hundred, one hundred. Presently Humphrey removed his hands and turned to his students: "Here we are I believe you would say in the right ballpark. Which of you is prepared to do the fine-tuning?"

Liam said, "How come you can't get it through your furry head that we're on vacation?"

"I'll try," Pam surprised herself by saying. "It should help that I'm so tuned in to *them*, wouldn't you think?"

"It's quite possible. Good." Humphrey stepped back while she gripped the metal dimples and then did one thing Humphrey had not needed to do: leaned forward so that her head was above the fan and within its forward-facing curve. She closed her eyes and, for the first time in over a week, went rapidly through the steps that would invoke the necessary light trance state in herself. Though her eyes were closed, the shimmering in the air gradually intensified almost visually in her mind, until she was aware of being accurately attuned to the power source of the machine.

"That's very good," she heard Humphrey say. "You're doing well." He was monitoring the shimmer pattern visually, and was also partially tuned in both to the transceiver and to Pam.

Pam, concentrating, now deepened her trance state and entered upon the most pleasant part of the procedure, the strong alpha-wave part when she felt powerful, relaxed, exhilarated, as if she were standing at the prow of a ship that was driving forward through a beatific sea. At precisely the right instant she brought up the Hubbell-feeling which was her personal contribution to this attempt at contact. As the pattern responded, she heard Liam murmur something admiring and Humphrey say, "Beautiful. Very good indeed."

It took a teetery few moments for a smooth relation between the elements of personal feeling, alpha-waves, and transceiver-generated power to be achieved. Pam was not able to detach enough from Orrin and Hannah to be in firm control of her conceptualization of them, and there was an instant when the whole complex threatened to overbalance; but she righted herself and steadied and smoothed the revolving pattern, and when she was ready said, "Okay. Feed me the numbers."

Humphrey began to reel off a slow sequence of numbers; she could hear the clicking beads of the little abacus-like affair that was the Hefn "pocket" calculator. As he spoke each one, Pam caught it mentally with a maneuver not unlike catching a lacrosse ball with a twist of the stick to keep it in the net, then slung it with force and great accuracy into the right place in the shimmer pattern, number after number, knowing for once exactly where to put them, one by one. The effort was all-absorbing, but as she caught each number, shining white on a black field, and hurled it into its place, the sense of mastery, of being really equal for the first time to the challenge of this work, filled her with an almost athletic confidence.

The transcendental moment was upon her before she knew, the moment they all waited for but only rarely attained, when total conscious concentration was subordinated to the trance and the placing of the numbers was controlled from the unconscious alone.

Once, in a Ping-Pong game with Betsy's brother Ralph, Pam

had lapsed into an automatic state in which it became impossible for her to miss a volley no matter where it was placed, as long as she didn't think at all about what she was doing. When she finally missed, it was because her ability to trust herself "on automatic" had given out. Now her courage did not fail her. She placed the last number, the equivalent to the final position of the tumblers on a combination lock, and knew with perfect certainty that by her efforts a window into August Something, 1964 hung unlocked before her face. All that remained to do was to push it open.

But there she stuck. Opening that window took mental muscle, not finesse—more muscle than she possessed. After a short spell of futile trying she felt Humphrey's forked hand on her shoulder. "A beautiful piece of work, I could not have done the job myself with greater precision. But what's needed now is power, and that you must let one of us supply."

Sweating, Pam opened her eyes and arched back out of the field. She saw with a shock of pride and pleasure, as she lost attunement, that the pattern she had made *was* perfect, like a perfect dive. Liam was grinning at her, obviously impressed. She grinned back. "Whoo! I'm a wimp."

"Hey, you're the cox in the racing shell. Anybody can be musclebound."

Humphrey said, "Liam? Are you still on vacation, or would you care to push this casement open?"

As Pam stepped back, Liam placed his hands properly, leaned carefully into the field, and closed his eyes. Mopping her forehead with her sleeve, Pam watched as the pattern she had made swirled into a vortex and began to clarify from the center outward, until even the rim of the lens had vanished and there was a round dark place in the air directly before them, about two meters across, where it was pouring cats and dogs.

They stood gazing through the time window, listening to the rain—which was falling so heavily it was hard to see the house not twenty feet away, or tell the time of day with any certainty—and to the sound of hammering coming from inside. Liam murmured, "Now we know why nobody came to visit."

As they watched, the rain slackened. Soon two very wet medium-sized dogs came trotting up to the door. One had longish hair and the other's coat was short, but both were so lean and ugly and brindle-colored, it was obvious they were littermates. The short-haired dog barked once, a sudden sharp sound.

They waited, heads up and noses quivering, then began to undulate expectantly, wagging their long tails.

Presently the door opened inward and Hannah Hubbell stepped outside onto the wet bare ground under the eaves of the house.

She was dressed in black pants and a white cotton blouse with a spread collar under a gray V-neck sweater that had seen a lot of use. Over this she wore a stained apron. She had on white cotton socks and blue canvas shoes with thick rubber soles, and her beautiful white hair was loosely pinned up on top of her head. In her hands were two white enamel pans—presumably filled with scraps—which she leaned over and set down on the ground. Straightening up, she spoke to the eager dogs as they shoved their noses into the pans, something mock-admonishing, inaudible above the rain, and wiped her hands on her apron.

As she turned to go back into the house, she saw them.

#Did I say I needed Humphrey at the Hollow because of the "emotional static"?? I don't remember saying *or* thinking that. I'm wondering if you made it up, or if I was more bothered than I remember.

#About the mindwiping not working like a deterrent—Humphrey told me not long ago that when he read those two pieces of hate mail was when he started to understand, really understand for the first time, that people could not all be frightened into doing what the Gafr wanted, any more than they could all be educated into doing what they wanted. That was a big shock. He didn't let on, but for the first time he felt some serious pangs of doubt that even if we had the right behavior modeled for us—i.e., if we found the placetime where humans were still in balance with the rest of nature, which is what the BTP had been established for, though *we* didn't know that yet—it might not work any better. And if it didn't, that might be curtains for people on Earth, because he knew the Gafr weren't going to stand for very much more from us. It was when he faced up for the first time to the possibility of failure.

Your title could've been righter than you thought.

13

"ALMOST THOU PERSUADEST ME TO BE A CHRISTIAN"

—Acts 26:28

Hannah started, put her hand to her mouth, peered through the curtain of light rain at what must have appeared from where she stood as an anomalously sunny, brightly colored sphere, containing three figures and unaccountably suspended at the center of her own dull gray day. Instinctively Humphrey and Liam moved back, leaving Pam at the apex of a triangle. "Hello, Hannah," she said. Her voice came out scratchy with excitement and nervousness; she had to clear her throat. "Hello," she tried again. "Hannah, my name is Pam Pruitt, I live over at Scofield College, my father is head of the college library, and I'm talking to you from the future. I know that sounds crazy but I really am. Over here where we are, this is the year 2014—it's the twenty-first of May, 2014."

Now Hannah moved, pulled open the screen door behind her—the same door Pam came and went through every day—and called into the house: "Orrin? Could you come out here, please? There's something strange going on."

There was no reply from Orrin. Hannah let the door close behind her, stepped to the edge of the shelter afforded by the overhanging eave, and peered hard into the rain. She said nothing, everything about her demeanor conveying the impression that she was waiting for Orrin to appear. She waited outside where she could keep an eye on the three of them, however, instead of running fearfully into the house, or screaming, or losing one shred of her natural dignity. Pam loved her for that, though it did not surprise her. More than ever, she was anxious that the intrusion not disturb the Hubbells' peace of mind.

Presently the hammering stopped, the door opened, and Orrin came out. Hannah offered no explanation, obviously trusting Orrin to see for himself what she had seen and draw his own

229

conclusions, but again her demeanor changed; Orrin was now the one in charge, she his first line of support. Orrin was the Alpha Male here, the person Pam most needed to communicate with.

Clearing her throat once more, she said again, "I'm Pam Pruitt. I already explained to Hannah that I'm talking to you from the future, by way of something like a cross-time videophone called a time transceiver."

Orrin peered intently into the rain just as Hannah had done, taking in the circle of sunshine and dry ground in the middle of the downpour, and gave Pam a look in which there was no trust at all. At that moment the dogs stopped licking their dishes and noticed the lens of light and odorless people where nothing of the kind should be. They set up a clamorous barking. Orrin had to speak to them several times to make them stop and lie down.

With the dogs settled, the old man came again to the edge of the sheltering eave and stood there, lean, bony, barefoot and bare-chested, his only garment a pair of rolled-up baggy jeans held up by a thin worn belt. From her long study of the film and the hundreds of published pictures, Pam knew intimately the entire look of Orrin Hubbell in all its detail: his beautiful feet and large, lumpy-knuckled hands, his closely cropped gray hair. To be able to see so plainly that she had displeased this mythic figure was awful.

Orrin decided to respond. In his strangely high voice he said, "Is this some kind of a prank?"

Pam shook her head very hard. "No. Honest. We really are talking to you from the future."

For proof Orrin stepped deliberately into the rain and walked toward the lens. From Pam's point of view, of course, he disappeared; from his own he knew he had walked straight through what seemed a holograph of three figures and a weird mechanical device, all of which had vanished when he turned around. "Are they gone?" he called to Hannah through what was now—for him—an unobstructed view of the house.

"No, they're still there. Can't you see them?"

"Not from here." Orrin reappeared, stood a few feet away from Pam, bare feet on the slick muddy ground, rain trickling steadily down his face and chest and soaking his pants. Pam bravely met his gaze, which presently shifted to Liam and Humphrey behind her. When it lit on Humphrey, Orrin glanced quickly back at Pam. "Not a prank, eh? How do you explain your friend there?"

"He's a Hefn. He comes from another planet. The time transceiver—this machine—is Hefn technology." It was Gafr technology, but things were complicated enough already.

All at once Orrin must have made up his mind to believe his eyes; he was, after all, an artist, with a different relationship to *seeing* than other people had. He was also someone who had lived his whole life on the edge of things most people took for granted. Orrin Hubbell had been endowed both with a wonderful nose for nonsense and with a wonderful ability to accept and appreciate the unexpected. His rain-streaked face lost its irritated skepticism and became lively with interest. "What year are you talking from, did you say?"

"Twenty-fourteen."

"Well, what for?"

"What for?"

"That's right, what *for*? Why come here and talk to *us*? What do you *want*? You must want something, most people do!"

Helplessly Pam glanced back at Humphrey, who, seeing that she was in trouble, stepped forward to stand beside her. "This communication is my doing, I'm afraid, Orrin and Hannah Hubbell. The responsibility for intruding upon you in this way is entirely mine. Pam is not to blame. In fact, she tried her best to dissuade me, but my curiosity and concern were not to be denied. My name is Humphrey. As Pam has told you, I am not a native of Earth."

"I can see that!"

At the appearance of the Hefn in the focused foreground of the field, Hannah gasped and shrank back against the house. Orrin went at once to stand beside her, and incidentally out of the rain, but amusement brightened his face still more and he grinned the boyish, open grin Pam knew so well. "I can see that!" he said again. "And you're talking with Hannah and me, you said, because of your curiosity and concern? What about?"

Humphrey made a small, restrained pirouette; he was excited. "You come to the point in a most refreshing way, Orrin Hubbell. I meant that I am concerned about the future of Earth, which my own people are attempting to reestablish as a viable and sustainable ecosystem, and I am curious as to whether there is a lesson to be learned from the example of your 'experiment in living' carried on here in Hurt Hollow."

Orrin, listening alertly, made no response. Hannah, too, was silent. Her apprehension showed in the stroking movements her hands made down the front of her apron, and in how momentarily pinched and old she looked, but she too was listening.

"More precisely, I hoped that you yourself might be able to suggest part of the answer to the tremendous problems which face us, and which we are trying to solve. Now this place, as you undoubtedly know, possesses a *specialness*. You found Hurt Hollow and built a life here, you sustained this specialness for many years, and it has not failed in the many years since both of you departed. Thousands upon thousands of people have come here since you began it all. They still come in great numbers. Nearly all have claimed to feel that this place, this way of living, the people who have carried on this life, have showed them or made them aware of something important, yet all but a very few have found it difficult to sustain the something, the feeling, after returning to their own lives, except as a kind of memory of unattainable happiness and peace."

Orrin nodded soberly. "Yes, people seem to need to come here, they seem to get something out of being here, and so we have to let them come." He gave the three a wry smile. "Even you, I suppose. You're just one more group of seekers, aren't you? Come further than anybody, though."

Hannah smiled suddenly too, a smile that transformed her from a strained, uncertain-looking old woman into a beautiful, ageless one. "People still come to Hurt Hollow—in 2014? The house and everything will all still be here, fifty years from now?"

"Yes indeed," said Humphrey. "Everything."

"Who lives here? Who takes care of things?"

Humphrey again deferred to Pam, who said, "A wonderful man called Jesse Kellum. Hurt Hollow is—like a museum people can come to. Like Lincoln's birthplace. It's very famous. Jesse kept the land together—sixty-one acres. To me it's the most wonderful place in the world."

Orrin and Hannah beamed at Pam, identical expressions of delighted gratification making them look for that moment like a pair of twins. "Jesse Kellum, you say? We don't know anyone by that name," Orrin mused.

"You will. I don't think I ought to tell you any more than that."

"No, don't tell us any more," Orrin said quickly, almost aggressively. "Isn't that the way you feel, Hannah? Don't tell us. I'd rather find out about life as I go along, wouldn't you?"

Hannah, still smiling, tilted her head a bit and said, "Well, I'm a little uneasy with that word 'museum.' I'd love to know if

232

this Jesse Kellum just keeps the buildings up, or if he tries to make the place yield him a living. Is that all right with you, Orrin—if I ask Pam just about that?''

"Oh, I'd rather not know about it." Orrin frowned a bit, and the illusion of twinship was broken.

Pam knew instinctively what Orrin didn't want to know if it should be true: that the present tenant of Hurt Hollow was nothing but a ticket-collecting, hammer-wielding caretaker. She said boldly, "He keeps goats, and bees, and he has a trot line, and a big garden—and I help him!''

Orrin's evident pleasure at hearing this canceled out his equally evident annoyance at having his express wishes ignored, but now he brought his arm down in a sharp gesture. "All right now! No more! Ask your questions, I'll answer if I can, but don't tell me anything else. No, wait a minute, I want to get a towel and dry myself off.''

Hannah went into the house with him, giving the three visitors a chance for a quick consultation. Liam, in the background throughout the whole encounter, now pushed himself forward. "What are you going to ask them?''

Humphrey said, "You shall hear. Do you have a question of your own? Liam? Pam?''

Now that the once-in-a-lifetime opportunity had come, Pam's mind was blank. Liam said, "I have to think.''

"Think efficiently, then. There will not be much time.''

Orrin reappeared, having changed his wet jeans for a dry pair and put on an old gray sweatshirt. His hair, toweled but uncombed, bristled like a small white strawstack. Hannah came out too, and again the couple stood regarding the strangers through the curtain of falling rain.

Humphrey said, "This is my question. There is a quality about this place, such that people come from far and near to be in contact with it. Where does the quality reside? In you, Orrin, and you, Hannah, and your life together here? In the Hollow itself, or in your bond with the Hollow, separately or together? What is the answer? What do these visitors come here hoping to find?''

Orrin said, with a sharp shake of his head, "I can't tell you that, I've never known why they come, I just know I can't stop 'em. Hardly a one of 'em really wants to live the way we do. They know that, yet they keep coming back.''

Hannah said, "They want what we've got, you know, but without putting in what we've put in. When they see what it

233

takes to live our way, all the work, and the isolation and so on, they throw up their hands: 'Oh, I could never do without this, or give that up.' Then, the next year, back they come again, sniffing around as if they were looking for something and don't quite know what it is.'' She gave a small snort, but her look was forbearing.

"One thing you've got that nobody else could ever have,'' said Liam, moving up now to stand beside Humphrey, ''is each other. That's probably part of what draws people back. They might not realize it, maybe they think what they want is to live on the river and keep goats, but it makes them feel good to be with you, and then they go away and can't figure out how to get that same feeling into their own lives.''

But this was too personal for the Hubbells, whose expressions showed their discomfort. Instead of replying, Hannah asked Liam what his name was; he told her, adding, ''I'm at school with Pam and I'm visiting her right now. And I play the piano.''

This won a warm smile from Hannah. ''Well, I wish you could come over here and play ours! We have a Steinway grand piano in the house. Is *it* still there in 2014?''

Orrin moved uneasily, but Liam answered. ''No. I wish it was, but Jesse's not musical. I heard you play on a film, though. You were really good.''

"Jesse lives here by himself,'' Pam said now, wanting to get back to Humphrey's question. ''Ever since Marion died, that's like eight years or something, and people *still* come from everywhere to see Hurt Hollow, I mean *everywhere*—China, Russia, Germany—and they all still talk about it like Humphrey said, so it's got to be more than just the relationship. I mean, from what I've read, I'm sure that was a big part of the magic when you and Orrin were here, Hannah, but *I* think there's also something about the *place*.''

Hannah nodded. Orrin said thoughtfully. ''Maybe we're too close to see it.'' His gaze wandered out toward the studio and the slope beyond, out past the lens where Pam and Liam stood with Humphrey. ''We've found our end of the rainbow here, but what other people come looking for, and think they've found, and go away without having figured out how to hold on to—I don't think Hannah or I can tell you what that is.'' He gave them another of his wonderful smiles. ''But I'll give you some advice. If they're still coming here by the thousands, why not just ask *them*?''

Hannah laughed. ''Yes, that's the thing to do! Ask *them*! You

234

might as well ask one of Orrin's pictures to explain why it's so beautiful as ask us why our life here is important to other people.''

"Perhaps you're right," Humphrey said thoughtfully. "Yes, I believe you are right, Hannah Hubbell, and I thank you for your advice. I shall take it.''

Hannah smiled and nodded at Humphrey, then said, "Pam, tell us a bit more about yourself. You're from Scofield, you said. How old are you?''

"Fourteen. And a half.''

"And have you been coming to Hurt Hollow for a long time?''

"All my life, really," Pam said, "but last summer I was here a *lot*. I live right on the campus, so I didn't have far to come.''

"And didn't you say your father is head librarian at the college? I used to be a librarian, you know. In Cincinnati. I met Orrin in the Cincinnati Public Library; he'd come over from Fort Thomas to borrow art books.''

"I know," said Pam. "I even know about your first date." I already knew everything anybody my age could possibly have known about you, Hannah, she thought, except how *much* I wish I'd really known you in person.

"And you say you came here a lot last summer? Why was that?''

Flattered by Hannah's interest, but cautious, Pam said, "Well, I used to tell myself I was coming over to help Jesse. But really it was because I loved being here so much, and it was the first year I could get here all by myself, 'cause I had my own canoe—it's a solar-powered canoe—and because I was writing something. A novel, actually. And this was a good place to write it.'' *And because Steve and Charlie had turned into brain-damaged strangers, and because I wasn't comfortable at home.*

Orrin smiled directly at Pam, as if really seeing her for the first time. "Hurt Hollow is a fine place for doing any kind of creative work. Were you interrupted by visitors all the time, the way I am when I'm painting?''

"Well, only during visiting hours—two hours a day.''

"Visiting hours?''

"Mm-hm. Jesse has visiting hours. From two to four.''

Orrin chuckled. "Now, why haven't we thought of that? We could put up a sign . . .'' He glanced at Hannah, who shook her head. "No, I suppose not. It wouldn't do, would it?'' Pam let the subject go by, knowing the hours would be unenforceable without the fence, intuitively sure that the pleasure of knowing

Hurt Hollow had survived intact for fifty years into their future would be seriously undercut for Orrin if he also knew that a tall metal fence had been thrown around the whole place, including right across his majestic, open view of the river. "I do just love being here," she added earnestly. "I always wish I could stay forever. Whenever I'm here I can hardly stand to leave. I really do think this is the best place in the world."

"Yet leave you must—at least, you must leave the Hurt Hollow of 1964. We must close the window," Humphrey said. "Now, at once. This contact must end. Orrin and Hannah, thank you again for your time and your advice. And for making this home of yours; I am enjoying my visit very much. Goodbye."

"Goodbye," they called. "Goodbye, Pam," Hannah added, and hers were the last words that made it through before the lens, spiraling out from its circumference, opaqued and then vanished, leaving the three staring at the back of the house—abruptly older, emptier, drier, dappled in sunshine, part of its spirit lost irretrievably.

"Whew!" Liam sat down right on the ground. "What a boggler!" He wrapped his arms around his knees and watched, looking dazed, as the Hefn's hands flew about, rapidly and neatly disassembling the terminal supports. "Why'd you pull us out so fast? You never even told them not to talk about us."

"Yet they said nothing, ever—and therefore we can rest assured that despite our abrupt departure there was no need to caution them to silence. Now do you understand why I say *what we never know is how*? Had we closed the window in a more decorous fashion, we and they might perhaps have discussed the matter and arrived at an agreement, and *that* would have been 'how' silence was assured. But circumstances have arranged otherwise. I broke contact because someone is coming up the path from the river. Someone with a gate key, perhaps your father, Pam, or another person sent by him to bring supplies or check to see that all is well—in any event, a visitor who will be here in less than a minute, and I wish no one apart from ourselves to have knowledge of what we have been doing here."

Parts of the cobra hood and tripod were being collapsed and folded or fitted into the metal case throughout this rapid-fire speech, and now Humphrey lifted the whole contraption, loosely boxed, and scooted back along the path. They watched him open the door to the studio—and then Frances Pruitt's voice was calling from the terrace, out of breath, "Pam! Liam! Anybody home?"

Collecting her wits as best she could, Pam went to the back door she had just seen Orrin and Hannah pass through, opened it—resting her own hands on latch and frame where theirs had rested—and walked on through the house to greet (and waylay) her mother. Liam scrambled up off the ground, dusted off the seat of his cotton shorts, and followed.

Frances stayed for supper, which was only fair, since she had brought most of it with her. Her friend Dorothy Barnhill had come along; or rather Dorothy's husband Barney, who had business downriver at Wise's Landing, had given the two of them a lift in his boat, a launch equipped with an electric motor much like the one built into Pam's canoe, though more powerful. They had come well supplied. Liam and Pam made several trips down to the landing to bring up the sacks of provender, which at a stroke made their efforts toward self-sufficiency seem meaningless. But even Pam could not help feeling this was as much a good thing as a bad one, and Liam was plainly delighted and wolfed his way through so many ham sandwiches and helpings of potato salad and pickles that Frances said with mock severity, "My gracious, Pam, aren't you feeding this boy right?"

Pam and her mother were glad to see each other, and Pam hugged her with real pleasure, but every other sentence Frances spoke made her daughter cringe or fume. Predictably, her reaction to Humphrey fell more toward the "cringe" end of the spectrum. Uneasy and nervous in the presence of the Hefn, only a few feet across the terrace from his hairiness and peculiar hands and slight animal smell, Frances fell into a manner Pam had been discomfited by more than once, that of girlish flirtatiousness. Whenever Humphrey spoke, almost no matter what he said, Frances would shriek with laughter and make some coquettish remark in response. Humphrey's reaction when this occurred was to gaze at Frances quizzically, obviously trying to work out the cause-and-effect relationship between his statement and Pam's mother's hilarity. Once he said, "Have I made a joke perhaps? I do not as yet understand humor as well as I might."

Frances laughed again, a little scream, and said, "Oh, Humphrey, I just don't know what to make of you!"

"Nor I of you," he replied soberly, provoking another series of small screams, in which she was joined by Dorothy.

Pam gritted her teeth till her jaw muscles ached, but she got through supper somehow. "Mom," she remembered to ask over dessert, a really delicious dried-apple pie, "what's Otie Bemis been doing with himself since last Sunday? We had kind of a run-in with that Mrs. Kovach, up at the first farm? *She* says he's telling people the Hefn are the Antichrist! Did you hear anything about that?''

"Lordy, yes," said Frances, turning serious. "Somebody ought to ship Otie Bemis on back where he came from and keep him there. Honestly, what an ass!" Saying "ass," she dropped her voice and blushed; that she used the word at all showed how strong her feelings were. "You're not going to believe what he's been insinuating. I'd thought I wouldn't say anything about it to you, it's too disgusting." But she continued without a pause. "Mildred Adams told me that night before last, right after Humphrey got here, Otie Bemis announced right from the pulpit that you and Humphrey were down here together, and he said something, I don't know just what, implying that Humphrey was up to no good with that little bitty ol' girl down at Hurt Hollow!"

"He *did*?" Pam glanced involuntarily at Humphrey, who gazed back at her benevolently.

"Quoting some passage from Exodus about whosoever lieth with a beast—pardon me, Humphrey. It makes me so mad I could just die! Tonight he'll be somewhere in Kentucky—Carrollton, I think—and tomorrow night at the First Baptist Church in Bethlehem, and then Saturday afternoon at that little church above Milton, by the road to Moffett Cemetery. And Saturday evening he'll be someplace else, and he's winding up the week on Sunday at First Congregational in Madison—that's his grand finale. I suppose he'll be spreading that kind of dirt every time he preaches." Her tone was a funny mix of genuine anger, which is what she wanted them to hear, plus a dash of covert excitement at having her daughter (and, by extension, herself) at the center of all this commotion. "Everybody at the college is up in arms about him but the people hereabouts think he's God's gift to human dignity or some such thing. Well, they're always in such a big hurry to mind other people's business. I said to Dorothy the other day, I wouldn't be surprised if I looked out the window one of these nights and saw a cross burning, right in our front yard! I'll be glad when Otie Bemis goes on back where he came from and things get back to normal." Despite her indignation her color was high and she looked animated and quite pretty.

"Do you think he really believes there's anything *going on* between Humphrey and me? That's crazy! Doesn't he know anything?''

238

"I don't know what-all he knows. I think he's just seizing an opportunity to get people all riled up and emotional. It makes for a successful revival anyway—lots of people are coming forward." Her tone was scornful; this was religious Fundamentalism of a considerably more primitive sort than her own.

Liam perked up. "Coming forward?"

Frances smiled her approval of his interest. "At the altar call, to profess they want to be saved."

Before they could wander off the subject, Pam jumped in again. "So *does* he really think the Hefn are the Antichrist, or is he just saying that too?"

"Well, he's saying it, that's for sure. I've heard it from quite a few people. Dorothy went to one of the services earlier this week, didn't you? and he said it there. And Mildred Adams told me several people had mentioned it to her. You know, I don't think it's a bit scriptural. The Antichrist is supposed to rise up from among the people, like Hitler did—there's no way to read the Bible to make it sound like he comes from outer space. Everybody's just mad at the Hefn on account of the *Delta Queen* incident—excuse me, Humphrey, but they are, and I can't really blame them—and spoiling for a way to get even, and here comes Otie Bemis, getting everybody's bowels in an uproar. Tell you the honest truth, I don't believe he or they either one *gives* a durn whether it's true or not."

Pam sprang desperately from her chair as she saw Liam open his mouth to say something about the letter they had found, full of quotations meant to prove that the Hefn *were* what the Bible meant by the Antichrist. "The milking! We've got to get the milking done! Come on, Liam, we're late! Humphrey can talk to Mom and Dorothy. Hurry up, you get the pails and I'll go on over and get started brushing Belle off, I think she's been rolling in something, she'll dirty the milk if I don't clean her up."

"Good heavens, Pam, do you have to create such a ruckus?" Frances protested, but Liam had gotten the message and that was all Pam cared about.

"If Mom finds out about the poison pen letters she might decide it's too dangerous here and make me leave," she explained as she and Liam walked down to the stable.

"Yeah, I figured that was it. I should have thought of that."

"No harm done. I wanted to get out of that conversation anyway, and you know Humphrey's not about to say anything he shouldn't." She laughed, a little edgily. "Poor Humphrey, he was trying so hard to figure out why Mom was acting like she was, you could practically hear his circuits humming.''

Liam tactfully kept his eyes on the path and didn't answer.

A little later Pam, leaning her forehead against Belle's warm side, stripped her nearly empty bag with a few quick, efficient pulls down each teat. Her milking skills had speedily returned, as had the strength to her forearms and hands; she could easily keep up with Liam now. Belle's ample udder, covered with a short coat of hair like the hair on Humphrey's face, was warm and yielding and smooth, its naked, rubbery teats pleasant to grip and squeeze.

Pam stroked the smooth bag pityingly. Would it be easier to carry your mammary glands slung underneath you in this great sack of flesh, that you kicked every time you took a step, than where she was forced to carry her own? It looked awfully uncomfortable, but the does never seemed to be bothered. Though how could you tell? Dairy cows had it even worse; some of those were so overbred that their udders when distended with milk were truly enormous, and dragged so low the cows stepped on their own teats and tore them.

The Directive had put a stop to that kind of thing. Holsteins particularly were being back-crossed to reduce udder size in cows and overall size in bulls, which would eliminate the need for artificial insemination. Milk production would drop, but that was okay by the Hefn if it meant the whole business of breeding livestock could proceed in a less unnatural way.

Belle moved restively, her grain long since gone. Pam released her, stood and poured the milk through the cloth-lined strainer into the storage can. "Finished?" she asked Liam.

"Yep."

The light was fading as they climbed the path from the spring-house to the terrace, an empty pail with a half-moon cover swinging from each of Liam's hands. Frances and Dorothy, descending toward the dock, met them halfway down. "Barney said he'd pick us up around eight," Pam's mother explained. "Honey, I called the hospital before I left and spoke to Jesse. I told him we were coming over and asked if I could take you a message, if there was anything he wanted you to know, or do, or whatever. He said you'd been in to see him yesterday so there wasn't much to tell, but the doctors told him last night they think he'll be able to leave Monday or Tuesday if there's somebody that can take care of him for a few days, while he builds up his strength.''

"Does he want us to stay? I don't mind, do you, Liam?"

Frances nodded. "I think he'd like you to stay, but your father and I want to see a little more of you ourselves before your vacation's all used up, so we don't want you to be away too long."

"Just till he's up and about and feeling better," Pam promised, hugging her pleasure to herself.

Later still, while she and Liam were inside washing up the supper dishes to the tune of round after round of "Peace, Be Still," Humphrey—immune to mosquitoes avid for terrestrial blood—sat on the terrace, thoughtfully gazing into the deepening dark. Thinking what? Pam wondered, glancing over her shoulder at his indistinct form, small as a child's in the low chair, though much more still. About what Hannah and Orrin had said (and hadn't said)? *That* at least had worked out for the best. About her mother's unfathomable behavior, and the generally puzzling but fascinating nature of human relationships? If she asked him, she knew, he would tell her, simply and directly. A wave of love for Humphrey poured over Pam, warming and calming her. Why was it she had so resented his coming to Hurt Hollow at first? She couldn't remember, couldn't even imagine; the feeling seemed to belong to somebody else.

That night, Pam was too excited to sleep. Long after Liam had gone off to bed in the guest house, and Humphrey—who slept scarcely at all in warm weather—had departed for some nocturnal prowling, she lay awake in Jesse's bed, the same bed once shared by Orrin and Hannah, and thought about the contact. Urgently though she needed to, there had been almost no chance to discuss it with Liam and Humphrey. The mood following the departure of their guests had been wrong for the sort of reflectiveness appropriate to the subject, and all three were tired. Liam had yawned himself away almost as soon as the dishes were done, and shortly thereafter Humphrey had followed him down the path, leaving Pam with nothing to do but go to bed herself.

Being in bed made no difference. Her mind spun like the opening time window, throwing out images and feelings from the crammed day: Mrs. Kovach ranting, Liam furiously kicking a rock into the roadside bushes, her own sense of perfect mastery as she had hurled the numbers precisely where they needed to go, Hannah turning from the dogs to see the lens and through it the three beings from the future, Orrin's cheerful acceptance

241

of the fact, once it was obvious, that Humphrey was no earthly creature.

Which explained her own change of heart, she realized now: if *Orrin* accepted Humphrey's presence at Hurt Hollow, then unquestionably he did belong here.

Thinking about the day's happenings made her toss and thrash. After an hour she gave up expecting to fall asleep anytime soon. She got up and quietly let herself out onto the terrace in her underpants and T-shirt and bare feet.

In an open patch of sky between clumps of foliage a moon like a bent bow was riding, its points sharp as a sickle blade. Seized by a sudden desire to see the river magicked by even this lesser moonlight, Pam went back inside for her shoes and the key. At the last minute she snatched a towel out of the linen cupboard. With this wrapped about her shoulders like a shawl, she stepped off the terrace.

Day by day, as her period drained toward its conclusion, her breasts had deflated and grown less tender; but now, unsupported, they swung from side to side like udders with each slightly jarring step, as she moved on through the shadows and down the path. Partway down, she clamped her left arm across them and muttered, "Peace! Be still!"

In the moist night air, the intoxicating sweetness of the black locust blossoms made Pam feel a little dizzy. Leaving the gate open and the key in the lock, she went on down to the riverbank, into the zone where the fragrance was most intense.

About a year before, her awareness of the passage of time had undergone a change. As a young child the days had seemed endless to Pam, as an older child they had seemed nearly so; but after passing through the needle's eye of puberty she'd noticed that something was different. Time had speeded up. Not with the gradual acceleration of her earlier life, but dramatically; so that the previous summer a day at Hurt Hollow, once an endless joy, could rush by from late morning to early evening so fast it gave her motion sickness.

The last time Pam had stood on the bank of a river luminous with moonlight, time had not yet accelerated but still had moved with a syrupy slowness. This was two summers back, almost two years ago. She and her father had taken the big canoe—the same one now tied up at the dock right in front of her—and gone canoe camping on the Kentucky River, which flowed into the Ohio at Carrollton, eleven miles above Madison. The Kentucky was a much smaller river—very user-friendly, very suitable, as she had explained to Liam, for unpowered canoes.

One of the other librarians in a college car had dropped them off twenty miles or so upstream, with all their camping equipment and the canoe. They had paddled all the way down to Carrollton, camping along the way.

The trip downstream lasted three days, and took them through several locks. By the end of those three days Pam had worked her way into and out of a complete set of very sore arm and shoulder muscles, and the bases of both her thumbs had acquired bandaged blisters whose burning she could still remember—and her father, not a patient teacher, had hollered at her more than once—but she had learned to paddle a canoe, bow or stern, and that was more important than blisters or muscle aches, maybe even than wounded feelings.

The second night of the trip there had been a clear sky and an enormous moon, not like this one but perfectly full, romantic, stunningly beautiful, making a silver pathway on the smooth surface of the water. After supper, drawn by the beauty of the night, they had paddled out into the middle of the river. Pam remembered repeating to herself the lines of a poem she had read in school: *Slowly, silently, now the moon / Walks the night in her silver shoon./ This way and that she peers and sees / Silver fruit upon silver trees . . .*

"Want to go for a swim?" Shelby suggested. "Nobody's around, and even if they were they couldn't see anything."

The idea was irresistible. Shelby looked the other way while Pam wriggled out of her clothes and slipped over the side of the canoe. She was a good swimmer, and though any river has its treacherous currents Shelby was right there with the canoe and the life jackets; she was perfectly safe. Thrilled and transported by the touch of the chill dark water against her naked body, between her legs, on the skin of her sensitive breasts that bobbed and floated independently when she turned on her back, Pam swam deliberately up the path of moonlight, making it shatter and dance. Her father in the canoe was quiet, a shadow, paddling just enough to hold his position in the current. No moment in her life up until that time had felt so magical.

The magic stopped when it was time to get back into the canoe. Her arms weren't strong enough, and anyway were very sore; she couldn't pull herself in. In the end Shelby had to help; she remembered his hands on her slippery cold skin, gripping, somehow keeping the wobbling canoe from overturning while hauling her over the side.

Now with this other, far vaster if less splendidly moon-burnished river filling the whole world before her, creating again an ephemeral road to the Neverland where answers to all her impossible yearnings seemed to beckon, the memory of cold water enfolding bare skin swept over Pam again, delicious, unbearably exciting, so different somehow from the near-nakedness of a bathing suit. Hurrying, she turned aside and walked a short way along the shore to where a flat, sandy stretch of beach sloped into the water, downstream from the dock and the moored boats. She skinned her shirt over her head as she walked, folded it and laid it on Jesse's overturned canoe, along with the towel. Her underwear went next, and then her shoes.

Shivering with excitement, she waded in. At once a tape began to play in her head, from the passage Pastor Seidler always quoted at the beginning of a baptismal service: *See, here is water, what doth hinder me to be baptized? And they went down both into the water, both Philip and the eunuch . . .* Sand underfoot was packed and firm while the river rose lapping to her knees, then began to slip as it climbed her thighs toward the cold shock at crotch level. People used to be baptized in *this* river in bygone times, before churches had baptistries filled with heated water and ministers wore hip boots under their baptismal gowns. As the river crept upward toward her waist she plunged forward, kicking out—and in an instant skin against water had become the whole of her contact with the world.

Even thus carried away, Pam knew better than to go out too far. Nor was that necessary. What she wanted, the focus of the adventure, was to swim again up the track of the moon toward the reflection of the moon itself. And the moon's track spread across the whole face of the river like a comet's tail, dancing light upon blackest black. With easy breast strokes, head out, face toward the slender moon's reflection, she began to swim.

And now, rhythmically moving once again toward the unattainable goal—stirring the ungraspable silver—indescribable feelings surged through Pam. Foremost among them was a sense that both in what it was, and in what it seemed to promise, this instant of time contained the best of what life had to offer. Under that perception lay the bittersweet knowledge that all such moments arouse longings they cannot fulfill, that there's no way to get to the end of a road made of moonlight; and yet, for now, the longings seemed their own fulfillment.

As long as these powerful emotions upheld her and bore her forward, Pam went on swimming. When, abruptly, she felt let down and a little scared, she turned at once in the water and headed back toward the relative darkness of the shore, satisfied, eager to be out.

This time there was no ignominious end to the glorious immersion; Pam simply side-stroked back till one scissors-kicking foot struck bottom, stood, and walked up out of the river, pouring water, breathing hard, thoroughly chilled, stirred to the absolute depths. *And when they were come up out of the water, the spirit of the Lord caught away Philip, and the eunuch went on his way rejoicing.* She dried herself with the towel and, shaking still with cold and with unnamable feelings, pulled her skimpy clothes back on.

Pamela Pruitt, Girl Adventurer, towel over her shoulder, walked out to the end of Jesse's dock to take a last look at the black-and-silver-scene. A tow was passing now, disturbing the reflection. She looked higher, deep into the huge sky sprinkled with stars, at the real moon where the Gafr ship was, that no human being had ever glimpsed.

Like a puff of wind, a lingering whiff of magic blew through her as she stood there, making her eyes prickle and her breathing deepen. "Father, I thank Thee for this night," she said quietly. "Let me never forget what it was like, my whole life through. I don't think I could very well be happier than I am right this minute. And thanks for letting us contact the Hubbells. Please bring Jesse back here safe and sound, and please help the people around here to stop hating the Hefn. And let the Hefn get so they care about people too, and not just the Earth. And I ask that Thou be with me and help me do a good job taking care of things here. And I guess that's everything. In Jesus' name. Amen."

Then as she lingered still, gazing out over the rippling blackness, for it was hard to go in, lines of a poem began to speak in Pam's head—perhaps unwittingly invoked by her state of prayerfulness and the excitement of the swim:

> Stars above and stars below,
> Floating on the river,
> Till an arrow cleaves the flow,
> Setting all a-shiver.
> Then I take the two apart—
> Face impassive, beating heart—

> When I feel the secret dart
> Burning in my quiver.

The words of the poem gleamed in her mind like automatic writing, white letters on black, finished, complete. Pam was all a-shiver herself. Her mood shattered, she started up the path to bed.

Once started she climbed in a rush. The lock snapped on the gate with a reassuring click; she tucked away the key. "*Archery* metaphor!" she muttered between gasps, half-running. "Write about what's *there*, oh sure. I never shot an arrow in my whole life!" Although that was not strictly true if you counted the bent green sticks strung with twine, and the unfeathered thin ones sharpened to a point by a jackknife, that everybody makes, playing Indian. But Pam had never shot one of those arrows into a river spangled with stars.

"Pretty sounds again!" she puffed; but they *were* pretty. It was a neat little form, one she couldn't remember having come across before—a nonce form, then. "Did *I* make it up?" Evidently, and without intending to. "But I don't understand it! It's still not *about* anything! I don't know what it means!"

—A piercing punctuation mark, then, set at the end of the night's adventure—all but unendurably rich already, made richer still thereby . . . a tart dessert after a big heavy dinner . . . " 'Secret dart'—criminy! Too much snakebite! Too darn many mosquitoes and *bees*!"

She could hardly wait to burrow into Jesse's bed.

Liam: FYI when I remembered the details of that canoe trip with Dad, and connected that swim with the one described here, that was what tipped the scales from repressing the anxiety evoked by Dad's behavior to making contact with it, feeling it. I put in a couple of unspeakably horrible months, dissociating like mad every single day. If I hadn't had this writing task to anchor me to the world I don't know what I'd have done.

#Godamighty, as your sainted granny used to say.

Humphrey blocked my agonizing memories, you pushed yours under. But in the end, as Julie never got tired of telling me, the only cure is to feel the feelings. Easier said than done, no?

#Otie Bemis insinuates that Humphrey was humping you (neat trick). You rush back to burrow into Jesse's bed. It's all fathers and it's all a little sinister, a little bit tainted, like there's no getting away from that where fathers are concerned. At least that's how I read this, with all my alarms going off: DANGER. DANGER. DANGER. And then *you* become the third swimmer! It's excruciatingly obvious, isn't it, why those buried sexual feelings found this one megacreepy conduit to express themselves through. A way-out baptismal experience, no lie (you even call *God* "Father").

But this is still the problem (anxiety, danger) you do see, and I'm still trying to spot clues leading to the other, the unseen problem. And I don't think I've spotted any here.

#Your title seemed cryptic till I hit the contact scene. Reference is to the Hollow visitors, right? Who revere and envy what they find there, but aren't moved to choose that kind of life for themselves, not on the terms offered. The sacrifices involved are too great.

Orrin and Hannah didn't ever try to persuade anybody to do anything. They were *modeling* Gaian-type behavior, not preaching it. And modeling wasn't enough, that's what Humphrey would have derived from this conversation. He'd already had his crisis of doubt, that the idea behind the BTP was mistaken. It must have made him even more worried than he already was. So when he accepted Hannah's advice to ask the visitors why they came, I'm sure what he really meant to do was pump them about why the example of the Hubbells' lives *wasn't enough* to make them imitate it. And actually, I think you're wrong; he wouldn't have told you the truth that night if you'd asked what he was thinking about. Not if it was really about that.

#When I said to Orrin and Hannah that their relationship was what attracted people to the Hollow . . . I wasn't talking about them, or the Hollow, was I? I was talking about Jeff and me.

Your memories of all this, what everybody said and did, how we all looked—they coincide perfectly with mine, except for mine being generally less complete.

14

HOLY GROUND
—Exodus 3:5

The next morning the sparkling weather had again grown sullen and sultry. After breakfast Pam and Liam slathered sun block on themselves and got to work spading up the raised beds where Jesse wanted the beans to go. They took turns, one digging, the other coming behind, using a rake to smooth the surface of the freshly turned soil. It was beautiful soil, river bottomland, dark and full of worms. When the bed was ready, Pam walked along backward broadcasting the light brown beans so they fell at the right spacing, and Liam followed and covered them with an inch or so of loose soil which he lifted from the edges of the beds with the rake.

They had nearly finished planting the first bed when a lowing cry arose from somewhere up the Hollow.

"That's Humphrey." Liam dropped the rake and started up the path at a run. Pam set down the sack of beans and tore after him, heart in her throat. *HUMFRIE ANTICHRIST MERDERER* read the scrawl in her mind.

The cries continued, but when they came upon Humphrey—at the bottom of the hill, in almost the same spot where Pam had had her incident of dissociation—there were no assailants to be seen. The Hefn was rolling on the ground in a circle of crushed weeds, clutching his ankle and bellowing. His leg had virtually doubled in size, the bristling gray hairs making it look even more swollen than it was. Pam's first fear was jostled aside by another: had Humphrey stepped on a copperhead, like Jesse, or even a rattler? Did she and Liam have *another* snakebite emergency on their hands?

But it hadn't been a snake. "A bee stung me," the Hefn told them in a strained voice. "A very big bee, not a honeybee. Ai! It is exceedingly disagreeable. But don't be alarmed, Pam and

249

Liam, I will be all right." He let out another deep-toned howl, making them both flinch. "I am isolating and containing the venom, but it took effect at once and has made me inconveniently sick. I'm unable to proceed efficiently. I'd best go back to Orrin's and Hannah's house and lie down; I will concentrate better in an enclosed space. But bring the sack."

Casting about, Liam found a burlap bag containing something lumpy, flung into the weeds. Clutching this by the neck in one hand, he returned and (with a little help from Pam) lifted Humphrey onto his feet—or foot; the swollen leg could bear no weight at all.

An arm around the shoulders of each Apprentice, Humphrey slowly hopped and hobbled—not without an occasional weird outcry of distress—back across the ladder bridge and along the hillside to the house. Once there, he leaned on Liam while Pam pulled down the bed—which always spent the day standing on its bottom end looking like part of the wall—and the Hefn lay down.

The sack proved to contain potatoes and onions—both somewhat sprouted—as well as some enormous, dirty beets. "I found them in a hole in the ground, lined with stones and covered by a wooden lid," Humphrey explained from his supine position on Jesse's (Pam's) bed. "I was hurrying back to show you my find when I encountered the misbegotten bee."

"Back on one of the abandoned farms? That's Jesse's root cellar, I should have remembered about that. Look, Humphrey, shouldn't we call and notify one of the other Hefn or something? I don't know if a human doctor can doctor you. I was worried about Liam being allergic to bee stings but I never even *thought* about *you* being allergic."

"Boy, there's bees all over the place, those trees with the perfumy flowers are *full* of bees!" Liam said anxiously.

"I require no doctoring," Humphrey assured them. "What I need are solitude and silence; I must concentrate."

"Shouldn't we make arrangements to get you back to Washington, though?" Pam's earlier distress at the thought of being abandoned here because of a theoretical danger had vanished; this danger was real. Nobody who reacted to a bee sting with this kind of swelling and pain should be living at Hurt Hollow.

But Humphrey was definite. "No, no, no. Now that I know this can happen, I know also how to prevent it from happening again. But leave me alone now. In one day I will no longer be sick, in two days I will be do you say right as rain?—but I need *solitude* in order to arrange all this and I need it quickly!''

"Okay! We're going!'' Liam headed for the door.

"We'll check on you at suppertime, all right?''

Humphrey grunted. They left him and wandered uncertainly down to the garden again.

"Whoo, that scared me!'' Pam said unhappily. "Do you think he'll be okay, I mean can he reverse an allergic reaction just by concentrating?''

"If he says he can, I guess he can. Anyway, what's 'allergic' mean when you're talking about a Hefn? But there's gotta be *something* about Hefn physiology that has a toxic reaction to bee venom.''

"Bumblebee venom. It must've been a bumblebee he bumped into, or stepped on or whatever. Boy, a bumblebee stung me once when I was a kid and it swelled up in a big red lump and hurt like the very dickens—and then it *itched* like blazes for a week or so—but it was nowhere near as bad as this.''

They finished planting the beans, first one bed and then the other, then walked down both, tamping down the soil with the backs of two hoes. "Why are we doing this?'' Liam complained. "I feel stupid.''

"To get good soil contact.'' Pam's apprentice gardener, though willing, was completely without experience. However, nothing about learning to plant beans was as challenging or complicated as learning to milk a goat. "You're doing fine. Remember when you get back to College Park, I taught you everything you know.''

They started on the melons and squash. The part of the garden destined to be this year's melon patch had to be dug out from a vigorous jungle of weeds, pokeweed and some smaller weeds with weak, water-filled stalks—jewelweed was the only one Pam knew by name, though she recognized them all by shape and habit of growth. Since Jesse had only one spade, Pam went first, pulling up the huge pokeweeds by the roots. Big as young trees, they were this year's weeds, sprouted from seed and lacking the tough taproots of older plants. They slipped from the moist soil without a struggle. Liam came after, digging the lesser weeds under.

With several huge armfuls of pokeweeds disposed of in the compost pile, Pam regarded the melon-patch-to-be, where Liam was nearly finished digging, and said, "This all ought to sit a couple of days so the green stuff can break down some before we put the seed in, but I'd really like to get this planting over with.'' She mopped her forehead with her sleeve. ''I'm going to stick a couple of extra seeds in every hill, and then if they rot I'll just replant. Or Jesse will. There's lots of seed here.''

They worked more and more doggedly as the morning wore on. The air grew hotter and muggier by the hour; the humidity was terrible. Liam pulled off his shirt. They were working without gloves, and had to keep stopping to reapply sun block, which their grubby hands made an especially unpleasant business. When the horseflies found them Pam threw down the spade— she was taking a turn digging while Liam raked—and said, ''I've got to cool off or I'll die. I'm going in the river. You coming?''

''I thought you'd never ask.''

Pam waited by the gate while Liam climbed up and crept into the house to get the key off its nail. ''How's he doing?'' she called as he came down the path toward her.

''I don't think he even noticed I was there. He's lying with his eyes open—concentrating, I guess. Dammit, I wish this hadn't happened.''

''Yeah.''

They went swimming in their clothes. Along with the food supplies Frances had brought Pam some clean laundry, so she didn't mind getting what she was wearing wet, even the bra. It no longer concerned her in the least that once dunked in the river her shirt would cling revealingly, so utterly uninterested was Liam in all that side of things.

''I'm hungry, now that I'm not so hot,'' Pam said later. They stood dripping and trickling on the path and looked up at the house, not sure what to do. ''Should we try sneaking in to get some food?''

''I guess we could live on milk, but I'd just as soon not.''

''You don't have to live on *milk*. What's left of the ham's in the springhouse.''

''So it is!''

''Some bread would be nice, though.''

Liam grinned. ''Your turn.''

''My turn, I guess. Got to feed that boy right.''

They climbed the hill together, Pam steeling herself to tiptoe around a glassy-eyed, oblivious Humphrey; but when they reached the terrace, there were the milking pails and cans grouped tidily on the flagstones, and on the table two plates and two tumblers, and a basket with the end of a loaf of bread and the remaining third of the dried-apple pie, covered with a dish towel. Pinned to the towel was a note: *I am making progress. This is for your lunch. Please do not come in again till after the evening milking. H.*

"I guess he noticed me," Liam said ruefully. "Oh well, if he could write this I guess he really is making progress. I'll go get the ham, and some milk."

"Okay. Don't get more milk than we need, it turns in no time when it's this hot. Hey—and how about some yogurt for the pie?"

They sat in their wet clothes on the shady terrace, finishing off the ham and bread, talking in hospital-visitor voices.

"Have you been thinking about yesterday?" Liam asked Pam.

"I almost haven't had any time to, and then all that with Humphrey scared it out of me. You?"

"Well, some. It was fantastic, wasn't it?" Pam nodded, chewing. "I've been trying to think, what *is* it about this place? Why *do* people come so far to see it, and then come back? I mean, sure, it's a great place, but there are lots of great places in the world. And then I thought, well, so, what *are* some of them?"

"Some of the other great places?"

"Yeah, that people travel long distances to visit, because of something they read or see on TV."

"I take it you don't mean, like, Walt Disney World?"

"What do you take me for, an Ellis De Marco clone? Of course not!" He lowered his voice guiltily. "Not vacation spots, or natural wonders like, you know, Victoria Falls or the Grand Canyon. There's nothing that *spectacular* about Hurt Hollow. I mean, it's not a place that would interest serious sightseers."

"No, I see what you mean." Pam considered while she ate. "I'm trying to think about the people who *do* come here—I sure saw enough of 'em last summer."

"Do they say what they're looking for?"

Pam swallowed and drank some milk. "Most of them've read one of Orrin's books, or Hannah's journal, or somebody else's book about the Hubbells and Hurt Hollow—there's like seven or eight of them now—or they went to an exhibit of Orrin's paintings . . . They say things like, 'I just had to see the place for myself.' " She thought; Liam waited, sneaking a glance at the pie. "You can hear this note in their voices. You know, 'I read Hannah's journal and I realized I'd finally stumbled onto something I've been looking for my whole life.' "

"So they come here. Do they act disappointed?"

"No, not usually. Sometimes. Mostly they act—kind of be-wildered, like *Where is it? Where is it?* Like, they know it's here, but they can't quite put their finger on *what* it is."

"So they go home and then after a while, back they come."

"Mm-hm. It's like they're seekers, like Orrin said—kind of a religious thing. Seekers after truth, or salvation . . . though the Hubbells weren't religious, not in the sense *I* am, or most of the people at Scofield are, and they sure never tried to make con-verts."

"Were they, like, *spiritual*, though? Ready for some pie, by the way?"

"Sure." Liam cut her a piece and set it on a plate, then cut one for himself. "I honestly don't know if they were spiritual or not." A picture from the video of Hannah canning tomatoes, putting red spheres through a funnel into mason jars with a big slotted spoon, flashed into Pam's mind. "They were *reverent*, I'll say that much. The way they lived—I think you could call it prayerful, not that they went in much for praying in the prayer-meeting sense. Or even in the private sense, far as I know. And the only time they ever came to church was once a year, for the Christmas concert . . . but all their actions, everything about the way they lived, was . . . I'm having trouble figuring out how to say this." She spooned some yogurt from the pan onto her piece of pie, picked up her fork, and cut off the point.

Liam's pie had disappeared. He pushed back his chair and slid down on the end of his spine, hands behind his head. "Okay, try this on for size: maybe Hurt Hollow is a kind of Lourdes."

"What's a loords?" When, a second too late, the correctly spelled word flashed into her mind, her bite of pie went down the wrong way and she coughed till her face turned red and her nose ran. "You mean that place in France, where sick people go to get cured?" she croaked when the coughing finally stopped. "Where the Virgin Mary was supposed to have done a miracle or something, about a hundred years ago? Ha, that's a good one. Boy, good thing you didn't ask Orrin if people came here so *he* could say hocus-pocus and fix what ails them, I can just see the look on his face." She wiped her nose on her sleeve.

"But that *is* what they did!" Liam braced his feet, in their tattered, still-damp sneakers, against the rim of the table. "Think about it! Why do you have to be so literal? They *did* come here hoping he and Hannah could cure them—I don't mean physi-cally, but fix whatever was wrong in their lives, give them what-

254

ever they needed that they didn't have. Fix their *lives*," he said again.

Pam shook her head stubbornly. "It wasn't *just* them, it's not *just* Jesse—it's the *place*, I keep telling you. The Hollow itself."

"Why couldn't it be both?" Liam sat forward suddenly in his chair. "The perfect combination of place and people? The whole equal to more than the sum of its parts? Maybe that's the explanation."

"It could be, except that even after you subtract the Hubbells from the Hollow, what you have left is *still* equal to more than the sum of its parts, if you follow me."

"Yeah, I do. You're right, and that's the fascinating thing." Liam thought, frowning. In a minute he said in a different voice, "Well *anyway*, maybe I'm dumb, but I frankly don't see the difference between the Virgin Mary curing somebody's cancer, and Jesus standing up in a boat and making a storm stop."

Pam said stiffly, "We don't believe the Virgin Mary stayed a virgin," aware as she said this how irrelevant it was.

Liam, with an impatient wave of both arms plainly agreed. "All this is beside the point. Okay, Lourdes might be a lousy example, but what I meant in the *first* place was, couldn't there be some anomaly that makes certain places, for lack of a better word, *holy*—magnetic resonance, or something we can't measure yet?"

"*Holy?*"

"Well, yeah." Liam squirmed a little self-consciously. "Maybe Hurt Hollow's a 'holy' place in some sense. Holy ground."

At the familiar phrase Pam's prickliness and irony dissolved. "Oh," she said, "as in when God told Moses out of the burning bush, 'Put off thy shoes from off thy feet, for the place whereon thou standest is holy ground.' I see what you're saying. Sorry."

"No problem. What was that, something from the Bible?"

"Need you ask?"

"Well, okay, just for the record, how come *that* ground was holy?"

"Do you seriously want to know?" He nodded. Pleased to be asked, Pam said, "Well, let's see." She scrolled the passage about the burning bush backwards and forwards in her memory. "I guess maybe because God was promising to deliver the Israelites out of bondage, but—no, actually, I think it was holy ground just because God was *there*. You know, present in the bush that burned and was not consumed."

255

"Run that by me again." When Pam had repeated the passage, Liam leaned forward to pull his laces loose and kick off his shoes. "Just in case!" He settled back, grinning, wiggling his toes.

"Very funny," said Pam, but she grinned too.

"Now, 'was not consumed,' meaning the bush didn't burn up?"

"Right. Like a gas log, if you know what that is."

"Unh-hunh. So that was a kind of mini-miracle right there? So that would be why that ground was holy—because something miraculous occurred there?"

Pam frowned and slowly shook her head. "I guess it was technically a miracle, if by miracle you mean something that defies the laws of nature. But that's not why it was holy ground. It was holy ground because that's where God *was*."

Liam considered this. "Hmm. So, in the Bible, did it *stay* holy? After God went out of the bush?"

Pam wasn't sure, but she was the only Bible expert they had. "I wouldn't think so. Wherever God was for the time being would be holy ground. Permanently holy ground would be what we call the Holy Land—Galilee, where Jesus lived, and the countries all around there. Jerusalem's called the Holy City, because the Temple was there, and the Ark of the Covenent was in the Temple, and God was in the Ark of the Covenent."

"Permanently?"

"Permanently. And I think Mecca's a holy city too, for Muslims. Aren't they all supposed to make a pilgrimage to Mecca?"

"I think so. They face Mecca when they pray, too." Liam watched the last bite of Pam's slice of pie go down. "Something else I just remembered is that Native Americans used to believe certain places were sacred. We learned about it in school. Now, why were they sacred? Because their ancestors were buried there, or something more?"

"We can look it up in the library next week, when we get back. I remember something like that too. The Indians believed the land they lived on was holy, they had a sort of religious attitude toward it . . ."

"Yeah, and so the way they lived on the land was like the way you said Orrin and Hannah lived here. Reverent. They had, like—a relationship with the land that was part of their religion."

In a minute Pam said, "So you're saying—what?"

Liam looked at her. "I guess I'm saying, one, that the idea

256

of certain places being holy places has been around for a long time, and two, maybe *that*—that feel of holiness, produced by some force we don't understand yet—could be what people are reacting to without knowing it when they come here."

Pam sat back in her chair. "Does that mean you think Hurt Hollow really is a holy place? I thought *you* weren't religious. What do you think 'holy' means, then?"

Instead of answering this directly, Liam looked out toward the river and said, "There was this place in the park near Carrie's house, Ridley Creek State Park, where Carrie used to take Jeff and me when we were little. She'd bring tea in a thermos and a sack of Dunkin' Donuts, and we'd walk up one of the trails to a big rocky outcrop, and climb up on top of that and pass out the doughnuts and drink the tea . . . We did that for years, almost clear up to the meltdown . . . We called it the Ragged Rock. And so last year—" He broke off, glanced at Pam, glanced away. "Remember I told you on the *Delta Queen* that Humphrey saved my life last year?"

"Yeah, you said that's why everybody in your family is so fond of him."

"Right." Liam frowned down into his lap. He gripped the arms of his chair and flexed the muscles of his forearms. "Well, if I tell you something, promise you won't tell anybody else?"

"Sure."

He looked up, locked eyes with Pam. "What happened was, last year I tried to kill myself by going into the contaminated zone around Peach Bottom."

"You *did*?" Shocked, Pam tried to imagine being so desperate that you would deliberately choose to die. The memory of the angel choir in eighth-grade history class, and her terror at her own impending death, flashed through her mind. "Weren't you scared?"

"I was scared, but not of being dead. Someday maybe I'll tell you more about it. The point I'm making now is, I wasn't just trying to get as far into the zone as I could, I was heading for a specific *place*."

"The Ragged Rock."

Liam smiled briefly. "You can put two and two together like nobody's business, I can see why they let you into the BTP. Right, the Ragged Rock. I wore a radiation suit so I'd have at least a chance of making it all the way. That's where I wanted to die. Because—" his voice wobbled a little and he got up, clearing his throat, and went and stood at the edge of the terrace, hands in his pockets, his back to Pam "—the Ragged Rock is a holy place as far as *I'm* concerned, even if I don't know exactly what it is I mean by 'holy.' But, see, my point is—" he turned back to face Pam "—it's holy for me and Carrie and I guess Terry, but not for anybody else, not as far as I know. It's personal to us. But Hurt Hollow, people treat it like holy ground even if they've never been here before in their lives. Like they *recognize* something here, that was here before they came. Maybe not everybody, but too many people to ignore. That's what we need to figure out: what it is they recognize."

Pam's reaction, when she thought Liam might be going to cry, was panic. Now he seemed all right again. She said, not expecting him to agree, "That this is a place where God is?"

"Well," dropping back into his chair and bracing his bare feet against the table, "not that I know what I mean by God exactly either, but maybe something like: this is a place where God *still* is. Or used to be. Or something like that." He laced his fingers behind his head and raised his eyebrows at Pam. High in the foliage, invisible, a cardinal sang the same liquid song, over and over: Sweet-*er*, sweet-*er*, sweet-*er*, sweet-*er*.

"Well," said Pam with relish, "that's real interesting, but doesn't it raise a lot of other questions? Like, if this is holy ground, what does that make Orrin and Hannah, and Jesse? Holy *people*? Or here's another one: are the people that live in a holy place, holy because they live there, or is the place holy *because* that's where the holy people live? Or do both have to be present for holiness to happen, like you said before? Or how about this: is a place only holy if supernatural things have happened there, like bushes burning without burning up, or cripples throwing their crutches away?"

"Christ Almighty, *I* don't know! I don't know the answers to any of that!" Liam bounced out of the low chair and stretched, then abruptly sat down on the flagstones to jam his shoes back on his feet. "Let's go check out the bees, what do you say? I've had enough of this topic for one day."

By the time they arrived at the apiary their shirts, which had almost dried during lunch, were damp again, glued to their backs with sweat, and Pam's bra was again a tight elastic tourniquet around her ribs. But what she saw next put mere physical discomfort out of her mind.

The entrances to all the hives were dark and active with bees, some coming and going, some apparently just hanging out, some

258

doing a funny backward-and-forward two-step on the projecting white bottom boards. But it was apparent at once that something more serious was going on at the hive at one corner of the square. There, bees were not only crowded but actually clustered around the entrance and clinging in clumps to the front of the hive, and none at all seemed to be flying—in the middle of the day, when most of them should have been out foraging. The kids stood wilting in the heat and watched. Pam groaned.

"Are they going to swarm?" Liam asked.

"I don't know, but I'm pretty sure that's not normal behavior. I guess I better take another look at the bee books." What was it they had said about large numbers of bees milling around nervously in front of the hive? And then what? Here indeed were the bees, acting unusual, behavior perhaps preliminary to swarming; here in the weeds was the empty hive body Liam had carried up the day before; but how did you induce the bees to go in?

"Well," said Liam, "I hope it's not too urgent, because we can't get back into the house till this evening."

Pam slapped her head. "Yikes, that's right. Oh great. Maybe I could call Jesse and ask *him* if this means they're about to swarm, and what do we do now."

"Too bad we're on bad terms with Mrs. Kovach. Her phone's a lot closer than Jesse's."

They debated about asking to use the phone at one of the other houses, but Liam dreaded a recurrence of yesterday's unpleasantness and Pam found that Otie Bemis, or the poison pen letters his preaching had provoked, made her reluctant to go outside the fence at all.

They unlocked the gate just long enough, and Pam went just far enough, to retrieve the mail before heading back down the hill.

The hospital recording said Jesse was doing well and would be released soon. It repeated the visiting hours. Pam hung on impatiently until a live person, a woman, came on the line. "Could I please speak to Jesse Kellum? This is Pam Pruitt. I'm staying at Hurt Hollow, taking care of the place for him while he's away."

"Mr. Kellum's sleeping. You'll have to call back later."

Pam said, "It's really important. It's about something he wants me to do for him and I need to ask him some questions."

"I'm afraid they'll have to wait," said the voice rather sternly. "We don't wake up our patients here just to take routine calls."

Pam's own voice squeaked in frustration. "This *isn't* routine—Jesse would *want* you to wake him up! He's going to be upset if he finds out I couldn't get through, no kidding!"

The woman hesitated, then said in a low, intense voice, "Why don't you ask your hairy little pal what to do? Doesn't he think he's God Almighty?" and broke the connection. Pam snatched the receiver away from her ear.

"What's the matter? What'd they say?" Liam had been leaning braced against the taut mesh of the gate with both hands, watching a passing tow; now he pushed off and came toward Pam. "You're staring at that phone like it was a snake."

Pam hung up the receiver and looked at him, heart racing with anger. And with something else: fear. "They wouldn't let me talk to Jesse, and this woman said why didn't I ask Humphrey—doesn't he think he's God?"

They stared at each other. "Wow," Liam breathed. "Mrs. Kovach's doing, d'you think?"

Pam shrugged, baffled, and made a face. She had been born and raised in this community. Often feeling like a misfit, misunderstood, unsupported and unhappy, she had never before been an object of general hostility. It was an awful feeling. "It might have been her, but it seems like everybody's just taking the opportunity to jump on the bandwagon." She looked uneasily at Liam. "I'm beginning to think you were right. Humphrey should get away from here. Something creepy's going on. I don't think he's really in danger, but his being here right now at the same time Otie Bemis is around is having a bad effect on people. I'm starting to get worried."

Liam looked worried too. "Yeah, that *Delta Queen* thing just had to happen when Otie Bemis was up here doing the revival." He glanced sideways at Pam. "I guess you were right too. I shouldn't have worked on him to come."

"Naaah. Well—yeah, but if I was, it was for the wrong reasons. Now I think it's great having him here, it's great we got to talk with Orrin and Hannah, but this is just a real bad time for *any* Hefn to be around. Especially with Jesse laid up." Impulsively—she still had the key—Pam unlocked the gate. "Let's go down and sit on the dock."

"Too hot."

"We can splash water on it. It'll be okay. I want to watch the river."

"Sun block?"

"In my pocket."

The metal dock buckled and boomed as they walked out past the johnboat and their own canoe and sat on the end, dangling their feet above the water, smearing the smelly sun block on their arms and legs and faces, passing the bottle back and forth. "I wonder," Pam said, "what it was like not to have to do this, or put on a hat, every single time you went out in the sun."

"I wonder what it was like to be able to just drop down flat and drink right out of a stream when you got thirsty." He glanced left, to where the creek from the Hollow emptied into the Ohio. "Could you drink out of that one, back up the hill?"

Pam considered. "I wouldn't. I never do, and I'm sure Jesse doesn't. Septic tank seepage from the houses on the ridge, runoff from the fields . . . The spring's tested every year and so far it's always been pure, but Jesse hasn't ever used the cistern Orrin and Hannah had, up on the hill above the house. Rainwater was getting too polluted to drink untreated right about the time he took over here."

The river, with its flotsam of boats and branches, swept by, its far shore faded and grainy viewed through the heavy air. A faint offshore breeze stirred the locust trees, enlarging their invisible cloud of heavy fragrance, which momentarily overwhelmed the odor of sun block. The whole expanse of the sky was dirty white. Squinting across at Indiana, Liam said, "God, that smells so good. Where did your mother say Brother Otie was gonna be preaching tonight?"

"I don't remember, but you know what I think? I think we should try to get Humphrey to go. As soon as he's well enough, and that should be Sunday, right? Or," she corrected, realizing that her father would be back at Hurt Hollow the minute he knew the post of chaperon had been vacated, "maybe Monday morning. Jesse's supposed to be released Monday." If Jesse were here, even bedridden, he would be back in charge. Surely Frances could not reasonably insist that anyone else be here too.

Liam appeared to have followed her train of thought precisely. "Do you think if Jesse was here, it'd calm people down about Humphrey?"

"You mean, maybe if Jesse were here too, Humphrey might not have to leave?"

"Yeah."

"Hmm." Pam mulled this over. "Well . . . people around here think the world of Jesse, more than they think of Otie Bemis by a mile. If *he* wanted Humphrey here . . . thing is, I haven't talked to Jesse for a couple of days and I don't know exactly

261

how he's thinking about all this by now. He hates a fuss. And I don't know if he'd approve of using the time window to talk to Orrin and Hannah, and we'd have to tell him about that right away. And even if he hasn't got any personal objections, he might want to get Humphrey out of here just to quiet things down.''

"If he'll go," Liam said, expressing the thus-far-unspoken thought in both their minds. If Humphrey wouldn't go, none of them could make him. Whatever the rest of them decided would be best, the final decision would be his and nobody could do anything about it if he chose to stay and pursue his investigation.

A whistle from upstream and a sudden burst of calliope music announced the arrival of the afternoon steamboat, out of Cincinnati, bound for Louisville. They watched as the boat came in sight: one of the rare new double side-wheelers, heading for the Indiana landing at a languid speed, the orange-red paddle wheel on the larboard side churning a broad wake, the whole pleasant spectacle a little dimmed by haze. As "Camptown Races" came faintly across the water, first Pam and then both of them sang along with the calliope. Then they sang "The Glendy Burk," and then "My Old Kentucky Home," Liam humming where he didn't know the words. The boat drew up to shore and delicately probed at the landing with its stage, like a large white bee tasting a flower. Its red wings, the paddle wheels, had stopped turning; the calliope player finished his number and desisted.

Liam said, "Hey, I meant to ask. What was that you told Hannah and Orrin about writing a *novel* here last summer? Did you really do that?" Pam nodded. "What's it about? Could I read it?"

"It's not for anybody to *read*!" she said, alarmed at the idea. "It's about—uh—it's sort of about what we're doing right now, come to think of it. There's this girl . . . and she lives in Hurt Hollow with a person like Jesse, and there's a Hefn Observer assigned to the Hollow who lives there too. They're trying to figure out how to—uh—" She balked at saying "save the world," but didn't know how else to put it. "—to make things better," she ended lamely. "Kind of like what Humphrey's doing, if I even *know* what he's doing. They have a lot of conversations like the one we had at lunch." Leaving out Pinny's many instances of heroism, and the intense mutual attachments among her three characters, this was a fair summary. "I didn't ever think to have my Hefn character use a time transceiver to contact

Orrin and Hannah; we—they—the three of them—worked on the problems without any help from the Hubbells. Of course, in the novel, the Jesse-character isn't in the hospital, he's right here.''

"And the Liam-character isn't.''

"Well, no, there isn't any Liam-character obviously, it's just the three of them.''

Liam reflected. "What's Jesse's name in the story?''

"Joshua.''

"What's the Hefn's name?''

"Comfrey.''

Liam laughed. "There's no actual Comfrey, is there? Not in the landside delegation at least. Pretty good! And how about you—what do you call yourself?''

Pam blushed. "That's a secret. Hey, we left the melons about half-planted, I forgot all about them. Let's go finish up that job, okay? By the time we get done the goats'll be back, and then we can go in and see how Humphrey's doing, and read up on the bees.''

Liam rolled his eyes at Pam as he scooted back to put his heels on the edge of the dock. "No point asking again if I can read this novel, right?''

Pam shook her head. "I told you, it's not for people to read. I just wanted to write it.''

"Will you at least tell me how it comes out?''

"I'm not actually sure if it's finished coming out yet.'' Liam made a sound of mock-exasperation. "I might tell you sometime, after I'm sure. But don't bug me about it, okay?'' She started back along the dock.

As they stepped up on the bank there came another ripple of music. The side-wheeler had hoisted its stage and backed into the river; they turned in time to see its wheels reverse and start to churn the boat on downstream. "Cruising Down the River'' drifted across to the Kentucky side, but Pam, who didn't much like "Cruising Down the River,'' declined this time to sing, and Liam too was silent.

When they arrived at the house lugging the full milk cans, Humphrey was still in bed, but alert and waiting for them, his leg shrunk down nearly to normal size. "I am very much improved, Pam and Liam. Thank you for respecting my wishes; I have not lost my ability to isolate an invading toxin, but the concentration required is not as easy to achieve as it once was. I'm rusty. Too

263

much easy, offworld living, as I said. Well! What have you two been doing today?''

Both Humphrey's Apprentices beamed at him, delighted to find him looking so well. Liam said, "Not much. Planting beans and melons and squash, checking on the bees, talking. Wait till we get this milk down to the springhouse, then we'll make you some supper.''

"Nothing for me, thank you just the same, until tomorrow," said the Hefn cheerily. "But tomorrow I would be very pleased if there were some of that delightful cottage cheese to eat.''

Liam screwed up his nose. Pam said, "I was going to make some this evening with yesterday's milk, and some more yogurt. We'll be right back. By the way, some of the bees are acting funny—I need to check the bee books again, I think it might mean they're getting set to swarm.''

Humphrey got the books and took them back to bed with him. By the time the kids returned he had looked up the relevant passage. "What are the bees doing? If they are *clustering* on the front of the hive, that appears to presage a swarm. You must look inside for what the book calls 'capped queen cells' to be sure. What is a capped queen cell?''

"I don't know, and it doesn't matter. Jesse told me not to open the hives.''

"Do you always do exactly as you're told?" Liam said impatiently.

"I do when it's Jesse doing the telling," said Pam. And then to Humphrey, "Does it say what to do if you think a swarm is coming but you can't look in to be sure?'' She itched to get her own hands on the book and look the answers up herself.

Humphrey turned pages. "The book says that even if you could look inside and ascertain that there are capped queen cells and the bees are definitely preparing to swarm, there's nothing you can do to stop them at that stage. Nor must you bait an empty hive with honeycomb, which will attract ants, wax moths, and/or robber bees. You must wait until the swarm has occurred before doing anything at all. The swarm will usually hang on a nearby bush or tree for one or several days. You can then put honeycomb into an empty hive and try to entice them in.''

In possession of the book at last, Pam flipped through it, skimming, glancing at illustrations. Hiving a swarm looked complicated. "Good grief. Why couldn't they have waited another week? I'm going to try getting a call through to Jesse after supper . . . or maybe not," she amended, thinking of her attempt that afternoon, and the woman who had obstructed her. "I think I'd better go see Jesse myself tomorrow. The stupid bees can hang on for one more day if they try."

After she and Liam had dined on cold chicken (and she on fresh asparagus, steamed over a tiny fire), they spent the evening making cottage cheese and yogurt. They were low on bread, but it was far too hot for baking, even after dark. The night was close and cloudy, the moon obscured.

When bedtime came, Humphrey insisted on giving Jesse's bed back to Pam and retiring to the narrow cot in the upper room. "I'll be wide awake all night in this heat, consolidating my gains and gathering my strength. I will be perfectly comfortable and I won't make a sound."

As she went along the path to the outhouse before turning in, Pam saw heat lightning flickering against the cloudy sky. She came back from the brief excursion with five new mosquito bites, to stretch out atop her sticky sheets and fall asleep in spite of everything, safe in the house of Humphrey's watchful presence.

But the bees refused to wait. When Pam and Liam hiked up to check on them, through a morning even more oppressive than the one before, they found the corner hive, which had been hung with clusters just the day before, looking much like all the others—a few bees coming and going—and, at the edge of the cleared space, a pendulous bronze-colored mass dragging a low branch of a small pine tree nearly to the ground.

They halted a few feet away, regarding this mass with a mixture of curiosity and trepidation. "Well," said Liam finally, "the good news is, they didn't all fly away somewhere never to be seen again."

"Yeah, and the bad news is . . . I don't think I'm going to have time to go over and see Jesse. I'm gonna have to try calling him again, because I don't know where he keeps the comb foundation, or if he's even got any, or if that's what he would have used to get them to go in."

"Comb foundation?"

"Sheets of wax. The beekeeper hangs them in the hive, and the bees build the comb on the foundation. Didn't you look at the pictures in the books?" Pam turned and started back down the hill, hurrying through the breathless heat. "They say you're supposed to put a thing called a feeder full of sugar water in too. I don't know if Jesse's got one of those. Boy, I hope they let me talk to him! If they don't I'll have to try to get Mom or Dad to keep calling the hospital.''

Pam grimly punched in the number, stomach tensed against another run-in with the nasty nurse from the day before. But the person who came on the line when the tape had run out was male, and he put Pam through immediately.

''Which hive is it?'' asked Jesse. Pam told him. ''That's number twelve. Yep, I was worried about that one. Okay, here's what you do. There's some capped honeycomb on that high shelf in the springhouse, saved from last year. It's wrapped up in cloth in a black plastic box. You'll find a sealed-up plastic bag of frames full of empty drawn comb in there too—that's comb I extracted the honey from last fall. Take out two frames of capped comb and eight of empty comb. You want ten altogether. Put them in that single hive body—you'll see how they fit, suspended from strips along the top edges, just like hanging files. They'll automatically be the right distance apart. Put 'em in, put on the covers, and you're in business.''

''Do I put the two with honey in them in any particular place?''

''Well, not side by side, but it doesn't really matter. Now, did you read about spreading the sheet under the swarm and shaking them off the branch? Think you can do that?'' Pam said she did. ''All right. Be careful, Punkin. I know it's awful hot, but I think you'd better suit up—my coveralls, and hat and veil, and gloves, are in the workshop under the studio. You can roll up the sleeves and cuffs. Don't bother with the smoker, you shouldn't need to smoke them. Now—'' belatedly Jesse mastered his excitement—''I don't want you doing this if you don't feel good about it. I'm not worried about losing a swarm every so often, it's nature's way and it happens sometimes no matter how careful I am.''

''No, honest, I want to,'' Pam assured him.

''Liam and Humphrey can help carry the frames, can't they?''

''Liam can. Humphrey got stung by a bumblebee yesterday and had a reaction, and he's still recuperating, so we don't want him getting anywhere near any more bees.''

''Well, Liam, then. Good luck. It's usually not hard to hive a swarm, but bees are mighty unpredictable critters, Pam. Don't you worry if it doesn't work. Promise me, now.''

''Okay, I promise.''

''And give me a call tonight if you can, to let me know how it went.''

''I will.'' She hung up, squared her shoulders, and once again set off with Liam on the long trek from the very bottom of the bluff up to the very top, making stops at the springhouse and the studio.

Liam: Writing this chapter, I got a shock. I realized for the first time why the angel choir I heard singing in history class, what they call a "brief psychotic episode," had flashed into my mind as you were talking about trying to kill yourself. It was because I wanted to die too then. I was producing signs of the Rapture because I wanted the world to end—the end of the world was actually less frightening than having things go on the way they'd been.

That was a real shock. Granted that the stuff Dad was doing was bad, you wouldn't think it was bad enough to make me want to die! It doesn't stand to reason, considering how much worse some people's fathers behave.

#It doesn't work to compare yourself with other people. It might have been bad enough. But *I* think it was what he was doing *plus something else* that made you want to die. Stay tuned, and don't expect the answer to necessarily "stand to reason."

We were more alike than we knew, no?

#I'm starting to see double here. We've got the Hollow visitors saying, "Where is it, where is it, I know it's here but I can't put my finger on it," and you saying essentially the same thing about this novel and yourself.

#Would you believe that till I read this I didn't remember *one thing* about that lunchtime conversation of ours the day Humphrey got stung? But *that* was *definitely* when the Holy Ground wheels started to turn (or grind). I do remember now, talking about Lourdes and Moses and the Ragged Rock, using the term *holy ground* for the first time, but I needed your memories to jog mine. Amazing, how we came so close and then kind of veered off the track there at the end, assuming "God" as separable from place in time.

My own unassisted memory for the details of all these crucial events is so bad that I'm starting to wonder if the mindwipe a year before that mightn't have done some damage. Temporary damage—my memory's okay now. But a lot of what you describe here so vividly I retain only as vague impressions and dim visual blips.

Hypothesis: till all the memories of Jeff had been restored, my memory function itself was impaired.

I've wondered before if the mindwipe could have had anything to do with my several years of repressed sexuality. Probably post-trauma denial and depression are enough to explain it, but this makes me wonder again if the mindwipe mightn't have been a factor too. As you know by now, pain can't be repressed without causing side effects.

#Know what? I just saw something else. I was starting to confide in you a little bit on the trip (between skirmishes), but was still quite well defended against anything you could call real intimacy with you, sexual or otherwise. But I was *consumed* with curiosity about that novel. It must have looked to me like a way of getting closer while still keeping a safe distance, don't you think? If I hadn't wanted on some level to get closer, why would I have been so curious? *That's* what doesn't stand to reason.

15

PERFECT LOVE CASTETH OUT FEAR

—I John 4:18

At the edge of the apiary clearing, partially concealed by the long needles of the little pine, the golden-brown swarm still hung. It had the asymmetrical shape of a scrotum, only more stretched-out along the branch, and was about the size of a lopsided basketball. Liam carefully set his bundle down on the other side of the clearing. He fetched the empty hive body, removed the outer and inner covers, and began to unwrap the honeycomb and fit the frames into the wooden box. As Jesse had said, it was obvious how they were supposed to go in.

While he was busy with this, Pam had laid her own burden of protective clothing down and set about puzzling out how to put the various pieces of it on. Jesse's white coverall, comfortably loose on Jesse, was enormous on Pam. "I shall wear the bottoms of my trousers rolled," she muttered, holding the coverall upside-down to fold each leg into a thick cuff.

"What?"

" 'Prufrock.' T. S. Eliot."

"Oh. Carrie's not that crazy about *him.*" He had finished fitting the frames into the hive, and had set the hive back on its bottom board and replaced both covers. "What now, O beekeeper?"

"Nothing, till I get all this gear figured out." She held the coverall against herself, decided the legs were short enough, and started rolling up the sleeves. Finally she climbed in and zipped the long zipper shut. "Wow, this thing is *hot.* How'm I supposed to put those cuffs inside my socks? And I don't think the gauntlets will go over the sleeves, either. Great. Bees love to fly up your pants leg." Awkwardly she put the scratchy bee veil, tied to the brim of a pith helmet, over her head, holding the brim with both hands. Like the coverall, the helmet was far too big. Its crown rested directly on her head, so that the hat almost covered her eyes. She pulled off hat and trailing veil again. "Maybe this thing can be adjusted inside to make it smaller . . ." But Liam was sitting on the ground, head in his hands. Pam stood with the hat and veil in hers and asked, "What's the matter?"

"It's just . . . you just . . ." Liam stopped and tried again. "The beekeeper outfit. It looks so much like my radiation suit. The one I bought last year, when I . . . so I could . . ."

"Oh!" She looked down at herself. "I see what you mean."

"*That* suit was much too big for *me*," he explained apologetically. "It just reminds me."

Pam nodded, but there was no space for this, not now. She said matter-of-factly, "Well, this hat's got to be made a lot less big for *me* or I won't be able to see what I'm doing. Could you see if there's a way to adjust it? I can hardly move in this thing, I feel like Darth Vader."

Liam accepted the hat, folded back the veil, and did something quick and neat to the band inside. "Try that," he said, standing up again in one smooth motion.

Pam struggled back inside the veil, and this time the band of the hat settled around her head. "Thanks." She fought clumsily with the veil, trying to straighten it and tuck it into the collar of the coverall. "I think this thing is supposed to go inside." Sweat streamed down her face, soaked her sides and back. The netting of the veil, almost as stiff and tightly woven as window screening, was as bulky and aggravating to work with as bird netting. Liam had to help stuff it down in back, and cram the rolled-up sleeves of the coverall into the canvas gauntlet sleeves. Whereas everything else was oversize, the only gloves Pam had been able to find must have once belonged to Marion, whose hands had obviously been a lot more delicate and ladylike than Pam's; the gloves were a tight fit. For years Jesse himself had worked his bees bare-handed.

When Pam was finally ready to tackle the swarm she was drenched and stifled, but if no bees flew up her pants legs she was also proof against being stung.

Luckily, getting dressed for it turned out to be the hardest part of the job. When Pam, robot-stiff and partially blind, shuffled over and spread the sheet she had brought on the ground right under the bees, they paid her no attention at all, not even the few strays flying around unattached to the ball around the queen. Their weight had dragged the pine branch so low it was almost

271

touching the ground; clumsy as the awkward clothing made her, Pam had to use great care to avoid bumping the bottom of the ball of bees while spreading the sheet beneath them.

When the sheet was down she went back for the hive. Puffing hard—the box with its bottom board and covers was heavy—she struggled across the clearing and set it down on the edge of the sheet, with the entrance toward the center. Again, the bees ignored her totally.

Then—this was the part that took the most nerve—she grabbed hold of the pine branch on either side of the swarm—standing on the sheet and putting her gauntleted hands right in among the bees—settled her feet, readied her mind to do this right the first time, and gave the branch a hard, firm shake.

Bees dropped in a mass onto the sheet—and also onto Pam's shoes, in plain view of the inviting dark retreats of her coverall legs. More quickly than the books advised (they all said not to make any jerky, sudden movements) she squealed and leapt backwards, away from the moving mass on the ground. At a safe distance she bent arthritically to reassure herself that none of them had actually gone up inside.

Liam, seeing that the bees were paying no attention whatsoever to Pam despite her massive intervention in their affairs, came closer to watch.

Then an amazing thing happened. The instant they hit the sheet and smelled the smells of honey and wax wafting out of the hive, the whole swarm began to *flow*, in an orderly stream exactly the width of the entrance, over the lip of the bottom board and through this opening into the hive body—flowing in a small current one bee deep and yet so densely packed that Pam could glimpse no speck of the white sheet beneath them. She was struck by a strange resemblance: the packed bees looked like a heap of bronze-colored, animated coffee beans, a commodity she had once seen in Liam's mother's kitchen but not for many years in her own.

It was like magic. *The bees you trust are lost in a swarm,* said Pam's mind again and again, automatic and regular as a metronome. *Honeyflow's here, but stings do harm. The bees you trust*—Quite a few bees were flying. Those on the ground, on the side nearest the hive, kept on walking in that brisk and orderly way into their new home; the rest were milling a bit, waiting their turn—but all of them, the whole swarm, tightly packed and moving as one, the separate cells of a single gold-brown animal. Massed together like that, you couldn't see the black and yellow stripes of the individual bees; each bee looked to be the same uniform cinnamon or bronze color.

It was the most fascinating natural phenomenon Pam had ever seen. And I did it! she thought triumphantly, I did what Jesse said and it worked! I made it happen! She forgot that she was uncomfortable, that she was sweltering—everything, except this wonder of nature and culture and her own triumph.

Liam's voice penetrated this self-congratulatory reverie. "How many bees in the whole swarm, would you say?"

"No idea. Swarms are all different sizes." Pam kept her eyes on the procession. "I think it said around twenty or thirty thousand. On that order."

Liam said in a triumph of his own, "This is a pretty big one then—thirty-one thousand, eight hundred and eighty-five bees, plus the ones that went in before I got over here."

At this Pam did take her eyes off the bees for a second. "Hey! I didn't know you could do that!"

He was grinning smugly. "I can do beans in a jar and quarters in a bowl, too, but I never did bees before. Moving objects are more of a challenge."

She dropped her gaze again to the marching swarm. "How come you never did it on *The Talk Show*? People love that stuff."

"I can only count, I can't calculate. It's not as showy and it's too easy to fake."

Pam said, "Well, did you spot the the queen when you were counting? I can't see that well in this dratted veil. We're supposed to watch to be sure the queen goes in, otherwise the hive doesn't take off and you have to get another queen from somewhere."

"I saw her, I guess—at least there was one bee a lot bigger than the others—but I don't think I actually saw her go in."

"Well, look again. Once we know the queen's in, we can leave. Then we come back after dark and block up the entrance, and move the hive to wherever it's supposed to go, which I guess Jesse will have to tell me when I call him back."

"Okay, I'll look." Liam sat cross-legged on the ground and fixed his attention on the little tide of bees.

The beekeeping outfit could safely be dispensed with now. The instant Pam understood this she felt desperately suffocated and claustrophobic, and clawed almost frantically at the scratchy veil to drag it out of her collar. Head blessedly free in the air, she tossed the veil and hat on the ground and pulled at the leather gloves; but they were glued to her skin with sweat and stuck tight. Tugging was futile. Finally she appealed to Liam: "Can you help me get these off and watch for the queen at the same time?"

He reached a blind hand up and Pam stuck the fingers of one glove into it, but then instead of taking a grip he let the hand drop and looked up from the swarm, in the direction of the gate. "What's that noise? What's going on?"

Pam realized she had been hearing it for some time: a grinding roar, increasing moment by moment, from the direction of the road. "Some kind of powered vehicle, a really heavy one. A fire engine? Maybe there's a fire."

"Wouldn't there be a siren?" said Liam. "Listen, it turned off the main road. I think it's coming this way." He jumped to his feet.

"Probably a plastic miner heading for the Mount Pleasant landfill, or a cement mixer or something. Somebody's building a house. Come on, help me out get these gauntlets off, I'm melting—and you're supposed to be keeping an eye out for the queen, remember."

"Building a house? On Saturday afternoon?" Liam objected; but he grabbed Pam's hand again and pulled. Jerk by determined jerk, the glove began to come free. With one terrific final jerk Liam and Pam fell apart as glove and gauntlet released their grip; and at precisely that moment came a tremendous crash of metal on metal, as whatever had been making the roaring noise collided with Jesse's gate.

Liam was as quick as Pam to understand what had happened. "Christ, they hit the gate! What kind of moron's driving that thing?" He sprinted off toward the sound of the still-roaring motor.

Pam tried to follow, still pulling desperately at the fingers of the second glove with her swollen free hand; but her sense of responsibility to Jesse was like a leash that yanked her to a somersaulting stop when she hit the end. She was supposed to see if the queen went into the hive. Fighting the infuriating gauntlet, looking from the swarm to the path down which Liam had disappeared, she tried to think what Jesse would say.

Well, really, there was little doubt about what he would say: Leave the bees, deal with the crisis.

But she had to get Marion's glove off first, and then the coverall. A wave of fury at Liam for abandoning her in this hampered state made her scream his name; but Liam couldn't possibly have heard her above the racket at the gate, for now the sound of the motor had changed from a roar to a deep growling. Had it been damaged in the crash? As she stood tugging and yanking there was another change, and then a second crash and a horrible screeching of metal, loud as the first. What the dickens was going on?

The glove came free at last; Pam flung it away and tried to make her swollen, sweaty fingers grip the little tab of the zipper—which opened a few inches and jammed. While she was working to loosen it there came a third crash, and a fourth—and then what sounded like people yelling.

Stop. Pam stood still, forced her arms to hang loosely at her sides, closed her eyes, drew several deep breaths. Calm. Be calm. *Father in Heaven, I don't know what's going on and I'm scared. Please help me unstick this zipper so I can get out of this coverall and go find Liam. And if it's trouble, be with me, and let me keep my head. In Jesus' name.*

The zipper wasn't so badly jammed; Pam was able to strain back the cloth, work the slide back on track, and pull it all the way open without getting caught again. She shook the sleeves off her arms and sat down on the ground to pull her legs out—carefully, so her sneakers wouldn't get stuck. Wholly free of the hateful thing at last, she kicked it aside and was struggling to stand up when the motor suddenly shut off. In the relative quiet the yelling sounded much louder.

Then Liam was back, running like a rabbit. He grabbed her arm, yanked her into the woods; off-balance already, she fell into the brambly undergrowth. Liam's hand was over her mouth, the weight of his whole body was on top of her, she couldn't breathe. There was a dim impression of a mass of hoarsely shouting people pouring down the road beyond the clearing full of hives. Then Liam's hand was gone, she sucked in air, and his weight was gone, and she could move.

"I think they all went down, but better not make any noise," he whispered, breathing hard himself. "They broke through the gate *on purpose*. They had a fire engine, with a big front bumper sticking out like a battering ram, and they drove it full speed into the gate, and backed up and rammed it again and again, until they broke through."

Pam sat up, her bare legs covered with bleeding scratches. She looked detachedly at the red blood. Her fear was miraculously gone; she was floating like a tethered astronaut in free fall, detached and sedated, though her mind still appeared to function. It told her that Liam expected a response. She could respond. She whispered, "Who did?"

"Otie Bemis and a bunch of other men."

Pam looked straight at Liam, directly into his eyes, physically closer than she'd ever been to him before; she saw his chest rise and fall rapidly with his frightened breathing, and the pulse beating in his neck. Otie Bemis, he had said. "Otie Bemis? Are you sure it was him?"

Liam nodded hard. "I saw him, sitting in the cab next to the guy driving. I got a real good look at him. The rest of them were hanging on to the sides or riding on top." In his white face the pupils of his eyes were huge, with narrow brown irises; some part of Pam's brain coolly recorded this, the one time she had actually seen someone's eyes "dilated with terror." "The front of the fire engine got busted up some—they broke the headlights, scratched off a lot of paint—"

"How many of them were there?"

"Twenty-four, counting Brother Otie," said Liam. "Pam, they're going after Humphrey. They're going to try it again. What are we gonna do—how are we gonna stop them?"

They stared at each other. The hoarse shouting had stopped, either so the men could sneak up on Humphrey, or because they were too far down the Hollow by now for the voices to carry through the dense foliage. Probably the former. "Humphrey's sick," said Pam out of her flotation tank of detachment. "Can he handle those goons when he's sick?"

Liam's breath hissed in through his teeth. "I don't know— he's better, but . . . twenty-four of them! And those guys mean to kill him if they can, they looked—crazed, you should have seen their faces. Bared teeth, like wolves! God—" Liam scrambled to his feet, "God, we've got to get down there and *do* something!"

A powerful drowsiness weighted Pam's limbs and eyelids. It was hard to think of moving at all, and the idea of decisive action seemed altogether unreal and implausible, like the time she and Betsy ate the marijuana brownies. She struggled against this lethargy while Liam tore himself out of the brambles, paying no attention to the long scratches on his arms and legs; in a second he was in the clear and bleeding worse than Pam—who, making a tremendous effort, managed to say, "What good is it gonna do Humphrey for us to go barging down there, just the two of us? I haven't even got a Swiss Army knife on me. I think we should go for help."

"What good will it do him if we bring the whole Swiss Army down there, if he's dead when it gets there?" Liam shouted. And when she still sat stupidly in the nest of briars, "Stay here if you like, but I'm going."

"We can't *do* anything by ourselves!" Pam wailed, but at the thought of Liam dashing to the rescue without her she discovered she could move after all. "All right, I'm coming. Wait up." As they rushed from the apiary she glanced back once at the abandoned swarm. Oblivious to all these human doings the bees—with their queen or without her—still continued to march over the spread sheet into the hive body; from across the clearing the dwindled mass appeared like a brown stain, perhaps of dried blood, splashed across the white wood of the bottom board and the white cloth of the sheet.

Up the road, the bright blood-red of the fire engine flashed through trees, from where Otie Bemis's Christian soldiers had abandoned it. They could have scraped between the gateposts, barely, but there was no way a vehicle that heavy could make it down to the river, let alone back up again.

Within her slug of a body, Pam's mind stirred alertly. Somebody must have known that, because—though at the top the road looked passable enough—they hadn't even tried, but had left the fire engine thrust through the broken gate and proceeded on foot.

Local people then, maybe. Maybe even people who knew Jesse.

Stunned and stupid with sleepiness, Pam forced herself down the road after Liam. It was like an expression her mother often used: wading in molasses. She could barely make her body obey her. When they came to the place where the trail broke away from the road, Liam plunged straight down. Pam followed, moaning, wondering whether the men would have opted for this short cut or let Brother Otie—who wouldn't know of it—lead them down by the longer, easier, plainer route. In the absence of sound there was no way to tell. Twenty-four large, heavy humans had just passed this way, but Pam was no tracker in dry gravel and packed dry dirt, and neither, obviously, was Liam. Also, they were not exactly proceeding in silence themselves. Any small sounds made by the men would have been covered by the noise of their own precipitous descent.

Liam was getting too far ahead; she called to him to slow down. "If they came down the trail you'll run right into them!" she heard herself say. And Liam went more cautiously.

When they reached the floor of the valley it was empty, but bootprints had churned the mud at the creek's edge and the ladder bridge with its toe cleats was fouled and slippery with wet mud. The sight made Liam cry out and go scrambling and sprinting recklessly up and over the bridge and the last stretch of path toward the house.

Pam labored after, miles above her bulging, unreal body, miles away from all this pure unlikeliness. It was impossible to believe that Otie Bemis and his mob might hurt Humphrey, equally impossible to imagine how she and Liam and one sick, incompetent Hefn could prevail against two dozen furious grown men if they *did* mean to hurt him. The whole situation, in all its aspects and alternative versions, felt literally incredible to Pam. It couldn't be happening. She was not part of it. None of this—nothing since the hiving of the swarm—could be real. The bees were real, the hive was, the sheet, the suffocating beekeeper outfit, all that was real. This couldn't be. As the studio lurched into view, without warning Pam's whole being was wrenched by a wish for time to turn back to the moment when the swarm began to flow into the hive, so that starting from that moment a different future could spin itself out.

The awful wrenching snapped her out of the still more awful lassitude; her body lightened, taking back its normal weight, and she was back inside of it. Color and vitality poured into the monochromatic world, things snapped up into focus. Anguish and terror filled her at last. And here was Liam, hurtling back along the path, tears squirting out of his eyes: "They got him! He's gone! There's nobody here!"

In the house—Jesse's real house, from which, Pam was now able to feel intensely, a real Humphrey had just been abducted—the floor was scuffed with mud and the sheets dragged off the bed, but other signs of violence were absent. "These *are* local people, they respect Jesse. They wouldn't wreck his house. They probably think they're doing Jesse a favor," said Pam bitterly.

"How'd they get away so fast? Where could they have gone? How come we didn't run into them going back up?" Beside himself, Liam rushed like a trapped fox from the back door to the front and back again.

The flash of a mental picture, of a tied-up Humphrey being thrown with a quiet splash from the johnboat into the middle of the river, sent Pam dashing to see if the gate key was gone from its nail below the cupboard, but there it still hung. "They didn't take the key, they're not on the river—unless somebody brought the key back after opening the gate, which I can't imagine they would. So they're someplace here in the Hollow *unless they went back up the road!*" Pam grabbed Liam: "What if they went back up the *road*, instead of going up the same way they came down? We would have missed 'em—they wouldn't have needed more than a few minutes' lead. They could be taking him away somewhere, outside the Hollow—they could be anywhere!"

Liam stared, white as the sheet on which they had hived the swarm. More tears squeezed unnervingly out of his eyes. "If they took him away from here, we'll never find him in time. We'll never see him again."

He's thinking about Jeff, said Pam's cool brain. And if they really took Humphrey away, he's probably right—neither of us will ever see him again. But if they didn't . . . "There's sixty-one acres of woods inside the fence. Lots of room to hide. There's a good chance they're still somewhere here, right in the Hollow . . . Hang on, I'll go see if the phone still works."

She tore down to the gate, hoping against hope, but the line had been cut. She shook the cut end of the cable at Liam as he caught up. "They didn't have time to *look* for a phone line—they *knew*. At least one of those guys was here before this. I bet a lot of them were." It was Jesse's neighbors, people he liked and had made welcome, who had done this to Humphrey. The thought made Pam feel sick and dizzy. She flung the cut cord away and started back up the hill. "I keep wondering who these guys *are*. What did they look like, anyway?"

"Like wolves," said Liam. "I told you."

"I mean, how were they dressed? For rough work?"

"No—slacks and sport shirts. Loafers."

"So they weren't planning to do this. They'd been to the revival," said Pam. "They must have all come straight from the church. Something must have happened to stir them up."

"Otie Bemis happened," Liam said savagely. "Pam, if we don't find him soon, I know they're going to kill him! We're wasting time! We have to figure out where to look!"

On the terrace they reviewed options. Splitting up seemed pointless; whatever chances they had to help Humphrey, weak as these might prove, would be weaker still if only one of them found his abductors. They would have to stick together. Should they row over and call for help, or try to find a phone they could use at the top of the bluff, assuming nobody was guarding the gate up there? The racket must have attracted considerable at-

279

tention, help might already be on the way—but neither of them, Pam any more than Liam, really believed there was any help to be had from the community above. The gang of men *was* the community above. Mrs. Kovach was the community; the nurse at Madison Hospital was; and the people directly across the river were no different. They would have to get all the way to the Scofield campus itself to get help, nearly half a mile across the river and six miles by road. It was too far and too long; whatever the men had in mind to do to Humphrey would have been done, long before they could get back with reinforcements.

Both Pam and Liam understood that the Hefn might already be dead.

As they went on dithering—still without a means of choosing between going for help and staying to search the sixty-one-acre haystack for human needles—Liam grew visibly more paralyzed with worry and fear and less able minute by minute to reason or plan. He had stopped crying, but inaction was doing him in. Before long it seemed he would slump into hopeless apathy. Pam's own paralysis, by contrast, was gone completely; while Liam's expression went blank, her own mind clearly, calmly, sought for the factor that would tip the balance, and presently she had it. "Listen. I'm going to try to activate the time transceiver."

Without waiting for a reply Pam flew toward the studio, thoughts tumbling over themselves, shaping a strategy. When Liam caught up, yelling "How? What for?" she had already heaved up the trapdoor and slid down into the workshop.

"Humphrey dismantled the transceiver in a big hurry when Mom turned up, remember? I'm pretty sure he just stuck it down here to take apart later—and then the very next morning he got stung. If only it's still set to the right coordinates—"

"—we can call up the Hubbells and ask *them* where those guys might have taken him!" Liam exclaimed, finally getting it. "Good, Pam, good! It's worth a try!"

The device was there on the earthen floor, loosely folded into its black metal traveling case, looking exactly as it had looked when Humphrey scuttled away with it two days before. The outer cellar door was locked, but between them the Apprentices managed to boost the transceiver up the ladder and rush it back to the site where the first sending had been made. Neither Pam nor Liam had ever set up a portable unit or seen it done, except for that one time, but the design was elegantly simple, easy to puzzle out. In a few minutes of teamwork, perfect in spite of their frantic haste, the cobra's hood on its tripod base had been re-created.

Those of the controls they knew how to read had not been cleared. Liam's face grew desperate with hope. "It *should* still be set for August 1964, but what if we're just the slightest bit off and we hit the middle of the other transmission? Or some other, totally different time—maybe an earlier time?"

"Time is One," said Pam. "Do you want to do it or shall I?"

"I will." Liam put his hands into the dimples on the transceiver's molded surface, took a deep breath, activated the field, and held the breath during the few seconds it took for the shimmer to resolve into its pattern of swirls. Then both cheered with relief. On the other side of the still-closed window, it was still fifty years ago. Humphrey had not altered or cleared the settings. The transceiver would not need to be fine-tuned—a procedure almost certainly beyond the powers of either Apprentice to accomplish intuitively, and neither Pam nor Liam had been gifted with the sort of memory, eidetic or auditory, that would have enabled them to retain the full set of coordinate numbers they had heard Humphrey measure out to Pam on Thursday.

Liam thrust his head into the field and closed his eyes; to Pam his lifted face looked like the face of somebody wrestling in prayer. In a moment the swirling formed a vortex whose center cleared and widened, and widened further, until the rim was gone—and there before them hung the same round window, open upon the same dark, wet, rainy weather they had left so abruptly.

Liam pulled his hands free and his head back, out of the field. "Orrin!" he shouted. "Orrin! Hannah!"

The door opened and Hannah's face peered out, surprised. "Back so soon? Did you forget something?"

"It's two days later for us," said Liam, "and Humphrey's in trouble. We came back to ask you if there's anyplace here in Hurt Hollow where a person could be taken and nobody would ever find him. Some secret spot—a cave, something like that."

Hannah came out while he was speaking and stood under the protection of the dripping eaves, still in her same gray sweater and black slacks; for her it was only a little later on the day of the previous visit. Orrin stepped out behind her. "Has somebody taken Humphrey away?"

Liam nodded, talking fast. "We have to find him and we don't know where to look."

Pam said, "It was twenty-four men from a revival service—there's an evangelist from Arkansas doing a revival on both sides of the river, stirring people up against the Hefn. A bunch of them came and kidnapped Humphrey, and we thought—we hoped you might know of someplace right in the Hollow—if they've taken him anywhere else we'll never find him—"

"They're going to kill him!" Liam's voice shook.

"Kill him! Oh, surely not!"

Orrin said loudly, "Any chance the Ku Klux Klan could be involved?"

Aha, said Pam's cool brain. Into her memory flashed an image from a TV documentary, made before the Hefn came: vaguely humanoid figures in white sheets and tall pointed white hoods that came down over their faces, standing around a tall flaming cross and singing "Onward Christian Soldiers." The hoods had eyeholes cut out and the sheets had crosses sewn on. A youthful Brother Gus Griner was there, in sheet and hood, singing lustily. Then the screen image had dissolved into an old newspaper photo of a black man hanging from a tree by a rope around his neck, hands tied behind him, neck stretched, head bent at an unnatural angle. Pam heard her father's voice saying, "Plenty of Klansmen around this neck of the woods, don't think there's not." Shocked, she had asked him, "*We* don't know any, do we?" Shelby had replied mildly, "Oh, I imagine we do. I couldn't tell you just who, but they were still pretty thick hereabouts not too many years ago. I recall somebody in the Sociology Department doing a research project—worked with an informer and got a lot of information, though I don't believe he ever did publish."

"Yes," she said now to Orrin, "I'd say there's a real good possibility."

"I might not have thought of it, but we had a visit from a friend the other day, who told us about some terrible things that have been happening, down in Mississippi. It took me back, put me in mind of this. The Ku Klux Klan used to have a Klavern—a meeting place, you know—here in the Hollow, back during Prohibition. A lot of people knew about it. They haven't been around at all since we've been here, but back then there used to be a still back up in the woods, right by the creek, the branch on the left as you walk up the Hollow. They used the branch water to make moonshine. They say the Klan would meet up there, and drink and carouse. They were supposed to support Prohibition and be against drinking, but a lot of them drank, and some made and sold whiskey, too. They kept their sheets and hoods and I-don't-know-what-all up there in the woods, and every so often they'd dress up and have themselves a big party. The law knew all about it, some of 'em—policemen, sheriffs, justices of the peace too—they were Klansmen themselves, and none of the rest wanted to go up against that crowd. Don't guess you could blame them, either, not if they had families."

Liam broke in: "But this guy leading them is a preacher! He's a jerk, but he *is* a preacher."

"So's Brother Gus," Pam reminded him.

Orrin snorted. "Yes, and so was Billy Sunday a preacher. Heard him preach myself once. *He* thought pretty well of the Klan, I can tell you—took their money quick enough, too. Plenty of preachers were in it themselves when I was a young man. Indiana was pretty much run by the Klan in those days, between the Fundamentalist preachers and the politicians." He looked from Liam to Pam. "They've not been much heard from around here in recent times, but that kind of thing never dies away completely. If the Klan's involved, I believe I'd start by trying to find out if they took Humphrey up there where they used to have the still."

"Oh!" Liam shouted, "I know—I think I know where it *is*! I found it!" To Pam he said, "When I went on that walk by myself, the day Humphrey arrived—I thought it was old farm machinery or something but it must have been the still!" He gripped the dimples and poked his head back into the field. "We got to get up there right now. So long again, and thanks a million. You might have saved Humphrey's life!"

"But you and Pam aren't going after those men by yourselves, surely?" Hannah put in anxiously. "Two unarmed kids? You'll have to get help!"

Liam said rapidly, "There isn't any help. We don't have time. I'm sorry, I have to kill the field now—we'll try to get back in touch and let you know how it comes out."

The Hubbells surged toward them, Orrin calling "Be careful!" and Hannah crying "Wait—"; but the rim of the lens was already spinning and thickening and an instant later the field had vanished, and Liam was heading back up the path toward the creek at a dead run. A distant rolling grumble of thunder made Pam pause long enough to collapse the transceiver before tearing after him. She hated to leave the shiny alien object there, keeled on its tripod in the packed dirt of the path, to be rained on and for anyone who came along to see; but really—again—there seemed to be no choice.

Liam had gone rushing up the bed of the creek, right in the water, so wild to find Humphrey that he wasn't going to slow down for anything until he knew for sure whether the Hefn was or wasn't up there in the woods, was or wasn't still alive. Pam could not keep up with him and didn't want to waste breath or risk discovery by yelling for him to wait. Soon a twist in the course of the creek took him right out of view.

All alone, and very scared, Pam fought her way up over the slippery footing, through water opaqued by Liam's passage, not at all sure how far a climb it was to the place he thought might be—had to be—the place Orrin had described, the one-time Klavern. Even in deep shade here the air was absolutely stifling, motionless, and the mosquitoes were terrible. Pam was getting very tired. They had completely forgotten about lunch. Twigs poked into her eyes; sweat stood in droplets on her forearms. The grumble of thunder came again, somewhat louder this time. She wanted this adventure to be over, and she wanted it to end happily. She wanted to write that happy ending herself, tapping it out on her NotePad in the screened porch at home, with a plate of oatmeal cookies and a glass of cold milk on the table next to the swing. All this exhausting, terrifying, famished part would be fine to remember but it was horrible to live through, not knowing if the story was going to come out right.

A low call sounded from up ahead. When Pam had waded another hundred yards up the creek, Liam was still out of sight but she saw what he meant for her to see: a cigarette butt, not yet swelled up or dissolved, floating in a pool. So they were here, and not somewhere in central Kentucky by now. So she and Liam still had a chance to keep Humphrey from being killed, if they could figure out how to get the advantage of twenty-four strong men.

She stopped for a minute to catch her breath and try to get her bearings. Where was the road? Somewhere over to the right, Pam had no idea how far. It might be really close, right on the other side of the screen of trees. If it was, the gang of men could have come up the road and through the woods to pick up the creek at this point or somewhere lower down; Pam had been concentrating too single-mindedly on struggling after Liam to observe the condition of the ground, and Liam himself had stirred up the fine silt of the creek bottom.

She started up again—and almost at once overtook Liam at

284

the point where the west and east forks of the creek flowed together. "It's not much farther," he muttered. "Did you see where they came down the bank?" Pam shook her head. "A little bit before the cigarette. The creek's all churned up, see?"

Sighting ahead, Pam saw he was right; the water looked like black coffee, and sticks and rocks on both banks were wet with splashes. You didn't have to be any sort of tracker to know how to read a sign that plain. "Why were they walking in the water? Why are *we*?"

"The bank's too steep and soft, and there's no trail. Maybe there used to be one, back when people used this place all the time, but not anymore."

She tried to see farther ahead. "They're right up there?"

"I think so, yeah."

"How come we haven't heard them? Twenty-four guys—how can they go that quietly?"

"How do I know? Maybe they practice! Anyway, that place Orrin was talking about *is* right up there, so—" As he said this, above the bright tinkling of the water, a low chant like a drumbeat began: Dum duh-dum. Dum duh-dum. Dum duh-dum. It was a sound so primitive, and so chilling on that suffocating day, that Pam stifled a terrified cry and grabbed Liam's arm.

Shaking her off, Liam was away—scrambling and slipping through the coffee-colored water toward the chanting, plainly oblivious to everything but Humphrey's nearness and fear for Humphrey's life. It took all Pam's will to follow now—force herself forward, when what she wanted to do was run as fast as she could *away* from the terrible sound. Her mind, detaching again, made yet another cool assessment: Liam goes to pieces when he can't see how to act. Put him in a situation where the right action's obvious and he turns into a hero.

Even then, quaking with terror, Liam's single-minded drive to get to Humphrey made Pam feel angry and ashamed. *Perfect love casteth out fear!* As the sound grew rapidly louder—DUM DUH-DUM! DUM DUH-DUM!—she felt to the depths of her soul how imperfect was her own love for the Hefn, how far short of Liam's selflessness she fell. BEES YOU-TRUST! BEES YOU-TRUST! clicked the maddening metronome in her brain. The rhythm was obscured momentarily by a loud peal of thunder; when that had rolled by the words of the chant suddenly stood forth clearly: DUMP THE HUMP! DUMP THE HUMP! DUMP THE HUMP! At almost the same instant, too quick to be frightening, something like a sack was thrown over Pam's

285

head, powerful arms pinned her own arms painfully to her sides, and a man's voice snarled in her ear, "You snoopy little Hefn-lovin' brats gon' be sorry you was ever *born*, time we get thew with *you*."

#The swarm was the shape of a *scrotum*?? Mercy. Looks like you lost your grip on the view from age 14 for a minute there.

#Bemis's thugs poured out of the square, white, wooden church like angry bees pouring out of their square, white, wooden hive. (Seeing double again.)

#I noticed this before, in the part about finding Jesse. You're dissociated but your head still works, you analyze, plan, reach sound decisions. And, as you say, I get paralyzed. It makes me ashamed to think of you beating up on yourself and seeing me as so selfless, when I'm sure it was nothing more or less than my terror of being left without Humphrey *or* Jeff that made me act in that reckless way.

#Humphrey was very impressed, you know, by this example of how basically nice people could be got to act against their usual natures by the right sort of emotional manipulation. But he'd already decided that this demagogue type of rabble-rousing wears off too fast to be useful unless constantly reinforced.

Next day
Pam: I read this chapter right before bedtime last night, then fell asleep and had a truly horrific dream. You and I were on a stretch of bare sand—desert, beach, something. Maybe Australian Outback. You were all bundled up in a bulky white beekeeper suit. You kept begging me to help you get out of it, and I kept refusing, feeling powerless and perfectly awful.

The chapter did upset me a lot. A reminder of getting totally unmanned, etc. Those radiation/beekeeper-suit associations obviously still carry quite a charge. Also, I didn't see any new clues here, and there's not too far to go now so I must be getting worried that I might let you down (you ask for help, I "refuse"). That may be why some of my comments on this chapter seem so sort of frivolous, now that I look back at them.

I think I'm going to just push on to the end now and write something longer when I'm done and can think over the whole book.

16

AND THEY SET HIM BETWEEN THE PILLARS

Judges 16:25

The cloth over Pam's head turned out to be the shirt of the man who had nabbed her; it reeked of sweated-out deodorant. The man dumped Pam on the ground and stood over her, buttoning the shirt back on and showing all his teeth in a terrifying grin. He was not a very big man, but he was strong; her attempts to struggle and kick had had no effect at all. Before putting her down he had stuck one of his hands up under her shirt, and squeezed and handled her breasts; and now, his own shirt all buttoned again over his hairy chest, he squatted down and shoved his hand between her legs. "Got chu some mighty big titties for such a little Hefn-lovin' girl. What else you got here, little Hefn-lover? Hunh? What chu and him been gittin' up to down here? Hunh?"

He squeezed and shoved roughly between her legs, and Pam left her body. Not by floating above it in a stupor of detachment, as she had done earlier that day, but by the abrupt, acute dissociation of her first day at Hurt Hollow, the day they had found Jesse. Her hands were untied, she might have tried to avoid the man's gropings—a different girl certainly might have tried to squirm away—but the thought of escape never entered Pam's mind. Her entire response—automatic, not chosen—was to hope he would stop, or be stopped, and to go somewhere else altogether until he did. The world became plastic, bright, other-dimensional. She felt the customary ghastliness of isolation and loss of control. Physically, she felt nothing.

"Here, now, let's not have none of that," she heard somebody say. "Keep your pants on, Euall." Another man walked up and hauled the first man upright. "The Reverend don't hold with no rough stuff for girls, even Hefn-lovin' ones. Let's us just do what we come fer."

288

Euall yanked his arm out of the other man's grasp. "Well just what *does* the Reverend intend to do with this here girl, then? He gon' just let her go on home and tell everbidy at the college what she seen? How he gon' let her do that, Mister Know-It-All Callaway?"

"Well why don't you ask him? He'll figure somethin' out. We come here to teach them Hefn a lesson they won't fergit. *Period.* You let Brother Otie do the figurin', he's a durn sight better at it than you are, Euall. Now come on. Come back where you belong. He'll be back out here in a coupla minutes."

"What about the other kid? Somebody orter go after *him.*"

"He's halfway to Milton by now. Come on now, Euall. Have yourself another nip and just sit tight till Brother Bemis gets back and tells us—"

A long roll of thunder drowned out the rest of what he was saying. "He best hurry up," Euall grumbled. "We in for a soakin'."

"That's all right, Euall," another voice called, "you kin skip yore bath this year!"

Euall made an irritated noise. Callaway looked down at Pam and said mildly, "You move one foot from where you settin' right now, Miss Big Tits, and we gon' hogtie you, you understand?"

She nodded. The men withdrew; and presently, trying not to move more than an inch at a time, Pam sat up and made an effort to assess her situation.

She was on level ground, under a tall pine tree whose shade and shed needles had kept the area around it relatively free of undergrowth. Seven men were squatting in a group nearby, sharing a bottle—only seven; somehow the mob of twenty-four had lost seventeen—no, sixteen—of its members. Their faces were stern and determined, but Euall's was the only one savage enough to make Pam think of a wolf.

Beyond the group she saw what had to be the still, a squat brick furnace with a metal door sagging open on one hinge and showing the blackened interior. There was a big round tub or something on top of the furnace, the metal entirely oxidized and crumbling to lace. Beyond that was a listing shed of weathered boards, some broken out.

Beneath the artificial shine which her dissociated state imparted to the world, everything was very dark; over what she could see of the sky through and above the trees, black clouds

289

were roiling, fast and low. It looked as if they were certain to be caught in a thunderstorm.

Maybe if a storm broke, with a lot of heavy rain—and if they didn't tie her up—she could give them the slip.

Liam had been spotted but not caught. With all her might Pam willed him to have gone for help, but in her bones she knew he was still out there somewhere, probably able to see her and frantically trying to think of something to do. He would not have been able to drag himself away from Humphrey, or from the slim hope of being able to rescue him, on the very long chance that help could be fetched from elsewhere in time.

Otie Bemis was not part of the group passing the bottle around, nor was Humphrey himself anywhere in sight. Maybe Brother Otie was questioning him or talking to him or something. Callaway had said "the Reverend" would be back any minute. He had also said some things that made Pam think Humphrey might still be alive and uninjured, but mightn't be for much longer if Brother Otie went ahead with his plans.

Thunder had been rumbling almost continuously while they waited, and now the men looked up uneasily as it banged loud and close. A stiff breeze sprang up; the sugar maples and pin oaks showed the pale undersides of their leaves and the boughs of the pine rustled and sighed. Then someone said, "Here they come now." The men got up, and Pam turned her head in time to see the door of the ramshackle shed be pushed open with a screech and the evangelist come out and stride toward the others.

Behind him came Humphrey. When she saw him, Pam bit down hard on her lower lip and clenched her elbows in her hands. The Hefn's arms were bound to his body with layer upon layer of rope. More rope had been used to hobble him, so that he shuffled and stumbled after Brother Otie at the end of a short rope leash. He had been blindfolded and his mouth stuffed with what looked like rags of some kind. The lesson of Jeffrey and the *Delta Queen* had not been lost on someone, Otie Bemis or one of the original mob. Someone had worked it out that a very well trussed-up Hefn, deprived of both eye contact and the power to make spoken suggestions, would be as helpless to take control of the minds of human beings as any human would.

When the evangelist and the Hefn emerged from the shack, the other men sent up the ugly chant again: "DUMP THE HUMP! DUMP THE HUMP! DUMP THE HUMP! DUMP THE HUMP!" There was a bright flash of lightning and a crash

290

of thunder less than a second later, so loud Pam hunched her shoulders and gritted her teeth. When it was over the men were still chanting.

Brother Otie held up his free hand for silence. "Put that bottle away," he said, and Callaway screwed on the cap at once and set it down. "Now, which rock did you fellas find that little girl underneath?"

"She was climbin' up the creek," said Euall importantly. "I thowed my shirt over her head and hauled her on up here. She had the other'n with her, but he taken off—headin' for the police at Milton, I reckon."

"If he is, the boys down't the station'll fix his wagon," said Otie Bemis calmly. "Well, we knew they was around some-wheres. Now, little lady, we didn't ask you to butt into our business here, but you let yourself get caught, so you're stuck with the consequences. Now, we don't mean you no harm. You're just a child, there's still time for you to be led out of your wicked ways."

"I never seen tits like that on no *child*," said a man with a bushy beard. The others snickered.

Otie Bemis turned on him sharply. "None of that, now, I don't want to hear no filthy talk. We got us a job to do here and it's fixing to blow up a storm, so we best get on with it. Now then." He hauled on Humphrey's leash. "I been in that shed wrestling with this here creature of darkness. I want him to *know* why he's gonna be dealt with like he is. I want him to *know* the Antichrist cain't do human beings like they done them men on the *Delta Queen*. Oh, they can *do* 'em like that. They can take away their memories and make 'em helpless as a passel of little children, but they cain't do it and get away scot-free! Human beings gon' fight *back*! Human beings ain't so helpless, and human beings ain't so stupid, that they cain't knock out a Hefn or two in *retribution* for their wickedness! And the rest of the Hefn Antichrist gon' know, and every human being on this Earth gon' know, that the Hefn can wreak their wrath upon us, but no Hefn ever gon' feel safe, or *be* safe, on this Earth again, after today!"

He turned to Pam. "Little girl, I believe the Lord sent you here this day to bear witness. You go back and tell them oth-er Hefn: You are not safe here! Human beings will resist you to their dying breath! God-fearing human beings will shield and protect God's people in their struggle against the wickedness of the Antichrist! You cannot prevail against us. There ain't a thing for you to do but give us back our babies, and then pack up and go back where you come from.''

A vivid flash and another terrific thunderclap made an impressive backdrop to this speech, but still the rain held off. Pam's brain observed how Brother Otie was working himself up with rhetoric and the rhythms of preaching, and kept track of his lapses in logic—how were ''God-fearing'' human beings going to shield him and his fellow fanatics from a race of mind-readers? Why would the Hefn restore fertility to humanity before leaving, even if they could be induced to leave?—but she knew better than to try to argue. To the shiny plastic figure of Otie Bemis she whispered, ''What are you going to do to Humphrey?''

''We'd cut him and hang him if we could,'' said Otie Bemis, ''but ain't a one of us knows what to cut and where to hang. Nobody ever got their hands on a Hefn before. Ain't nobody on Earth knows how to kill one. Do their necks break? Where's the vital organs? We could shoot him full of holes or chop off his head, we could burn him or we could blow him up. But the Lord has given us a better plan. Little lady, we're going to tie this Antichrist Hefn up, and then we're going to skin him alive.''

Pam screamed. ''Oh no, oh *please* no!''

''Oh please yes,'' Otie said, arms folded, eyes flashing. ''We literally gon' nail his moth-eaten hide to the barn door.''

Pam's dissociation response intensified, blackness crowding at the edges of the unreal brightness till she could barely see at all. ''Oh please, oh please don't hurt him!'' she begged, and then into the shrinking lens, into what little remained of the visible, spoke the one thing she had never breathed to a living soul, the thing that felt so dangerous even at that instant, even compared with Humphrey's real and immediate peril, that she could hardly force out the words: ''Please don't kill him, I love him.''

''Why shame on you then,'' Brother Otie said severely, ''but I reckon you don't know no better.'' He turned his back on Pam. ''Let's get this show on the road, boys. Who here's got the best knife for the job?''

The bearded man produced a hunting knife with a bone handle. Otie Bemis jerked suddenly on Humphrey's leash, and the Hefn fell heavily to the ground, close to Pam's pine tree. ''Okay, now, you fellas hold him down while I cut him loose. Cain't skin him tied up thisaway. You, Tully: you pick us out a coupla trees to tie him to.''

It couldn't be happening, but it was. Pam twisted, clutching her stomach, teeth chattering, mind lurching crazily. Shiny as the outside world, two pictures stretched from side to side across the whole field of her inner vision: hairy Humphrey, gagged and blindfolded, arms stretched between two trees; Samson, "Eyeless in Gaza," his own hair grown out again, wrapping his arms about the pillars of the temple and pulling them down, thereby destroying both his enemies and himself.

What did Humphrey have that was the equivalent of Samson's hair? The two pictures weren't about *hair*, but about what hair stood for: the unsuspected source of power. What, what? *Father, help me, I can't think!* she pleaded. But nothing came.

While Pam agonized and prayed and cudgeled her wits, jerking every time lightning and thunder crackle-*boomed* through the woods, the men were re-tying Humphrey between two medium-sized sugar maples with the same rope that had bound him before. A spatter of rain struck down through the foliage, but stopped as suddenly as it had started. When they were finished, the Hefn stood in his hobbles, his wet, patchy pelt flattened, arms stretched to the limits of their length. No one present could have failed to recognize the resemblance to Jesus on the cross; but Otie Bemis said, "Step back and give me some breathing space, boys," and flourishing the knife in his right hand moved in front of Humphrey and lifted the blade to press it just below the Hefn's beard.

As he did this, four or five stones flew flat and straight, one after the other, at Otie Bemis. One of them struck him in the side of the face, another knocked the knife out of his hand. It happened so quickly the seven henchmen were still staring open-mouthed at Brother Otie sprawled on the ground when Liam ran out of the trees carrying a whole armful of rocks, which he started to fling with the force and accuracy of a very good baseball pitcher. The men shouted with surprise and then, several of them, with pain. They scooted for cover—all except Euall's friend, who ran to where they had all been waiting for Otie, snatched a shotgun up from the ground, whirled and fired. At the first, point-blank shot, Liam went down.

Pam screamed, scrambled to her hands and feet to go to him. "You take one step and I'll shoot you too," Euall's friend snarled at her. "Sit down and shut up."

He meant it. Pam sat, straining to see how badly Liam had been hurt. He lay sprawled on his back, bleeding everywhere, not moving. Pam crouched under the pine with her forehead on her drawn-up knees and watched blackness, plain blackness, fill the world entirely. She drifted, willing the nightmare to be over. Just let it be over. Nobody was coming to the rescue. There was nothing at all she could do to save Humphrey or Liam or herself.

At the same time in the far distance she was aware of Brother Otie, sitting up holding a handkerchief to his face with his left hand; he was bleeding too, and he was mad. One of Liam's rocks had struck his elbow hard enough that he couldn't stand to bend it. Some of the other men were also nursing injuries, but none was as badly hurt as Brother Otie. Or as Liam.

"Looks like one of you boys will have to do the honors," she heard Otie Bemis say. "That little peckerwood there, that little David, looks like he done put Goliath out of business. Which one of you boys knows how to skin a groundhog?"

The men looked at each other. "I kin sure skin me a *dead* groundhog," said the bearded one, Tully. "Ain't never skinned me one that was still kickin' before. Reckon it ain't too late to learn."

"You start to skinnin'," said Otie Bemis, "and if it ain't to your liking we'll see kin we kill him first. Maybe strangle him, he must have somethin' like a windpipe in there. Don't like to shoot him if we don't have to, though, don't like to spoil the skin. I want that Hefn hide."

Pam looked up. The blackness receded, and through a world turned a sickly yellow-green she saw Otie Bemis, grunting with pain, lean over, pick up the knife and hold it out hilt first toward the bearded man. At the same moment one of the others said, "Sweet lovin' Jesus, what's that I hear?"

For a slow moment they formed a tableau: the loose group of men in their sport shirts and good slacks, wet and muddy at the bottoms, and their ruined good shoes, one holding a shotgun in the crook of his arm; the small still figure of the Hefn crucified between two trees; beside him the evangelist and Tully, the latter a little tipsy, with *their* arms stretched out and extended toward one another, hands joined by the knife; and every head in the group twisted the same way—toward the invisible river, and the unbelievable roaring that second by second increased in volume.

"Tornado!" screamed the bearded man, dropping the knife. "It's a tornado!"

Somebody else shouted hoarsely, "Make for the creek!" The other men were already running, all but Otie Bemis, who stood staring upward as if unable to accept this second interference with his purpose; and now in a patch of open sky they could all see it, the long, black, tapering, ropelike thing dangling from

294

the clouds, crossing the river, heading directly toward them up the hill.

The knife had landed right in front of Pam, its point stuck into the soil. With intolerable slowness—it was hard to move— she reached to pull it out, to struggle to her knees and then her feet, and fight her way through the suddenly terrific wind toward Humphrey. Her ears were popping. Dead branches started crashing down around her. She managed somehow to reach the nearest tree to which Humphrey was tied, braced herself on the leeward side and sawed at the ropes, four or five strands of them. The knife was very sharp but it seemed to take innumerable slow-motion cuts before the last strand parted and Humphrey fell down, dragged sideways by the rope tied to his other arm.

On her hands and knees, Pam crawled around to the opposite side of him, reached up and sawed again at the ropes. The force of the wind was almost enough to pick her up bodily, the noise beyond anything she had ever heard or imagined in her life: a hundred freight trains, a million bees, exactly the way her teacher, Mrs. Hopkins, had described it. More branches were falling and flying, and the maple trees were whipping and groaning in the wind. Holding on to the ropes to keep from being swept away in the blast, Pam fought to sever them. Several times she and Humphrey were struck by falling or blowing tree limbs.

When his second arm fell free at last Pam dropped the knife. Pulling herself on top of the Hefn and using their combined weight to hold them both down, she dragged the blindfold away. Humphrey's eyes were open—flat and expressionless the way Hefn eyes always were but alive and looking at her, not blank, not dead. Humphrey could see her. Then his gaze went beyond her and she too threw a quick glance over her shoulder at the tornado dangling from the clouds: nearer now and still coming directly toward them. Holding on to Humphrey with desperate strength, one arm under him and one leg flung over him in a scissor grip, she struggled to work the gag out of his mouth. The rags had been rammed in cruelly tight and Pam's strength was almost gone; nevertheless she managed to pry out one, and the rest came out fairly easily.

The din had now reached a mind-numbing pitch. When Pam looked up again she saw that the long snake of the tornado writhing out of the sky was now much larger, much nearer, and coming fast. Too late to try getting down into the creek bed; it was no longer possible to move at all. She lay on her side, gripping Humphrey's pelt and the end of one of the ropes still tied to a tree, and watched the tornado sweep toward them.

It was nearly here. She saw what appeared to be thousands of birds whirling around inside the funnel, and had time for one irrelevant thought—*Oh, the poor birds!*—before realizing that what looked like sparrows and starlings were complete roofs and pieces of buildings and chunks of nameless debris. Around her, whole trees began to fall as if a giant hand were pushing them over. A million pins and needles seemed to be stinging her skin. Her ears hurt and she had to struggle to breathe. Another second, and another, and the vortex of the funnel dangled directly above them, wide as half a city block, shedding water and debris out of its sides and shrieking like ten billion souls in torment.

The pine tree snapped like a pencil. Pam looked straight up into the heart of the tornado.

She saw a hollow cylinder of black cloud spinning perhaps a hundred feet above her—it was hard to judge—lit continually by brilliant zigzags of lightning that darted back and forth inside the hollow center. The end of the funnel wagged about, an elephant's trunk bluntly and blindly seeking its prey; but another second passed, and another, and the funnel was no longer approaching but passing, and then past. The hail of boards and bricks, and of water sucked up in its passage over the river, ceased. The roar died gradually away. Behind the wall of clouds that had spawned the tornado the sky was perfectly blue and clear.

In the stunned silence, Pam felt Humphrey move and heard a strained squeaking. He was trying to speak. She struggled to sit up, but had to pry her own fingers loose from the hair of Humphrey's back before she could manage it, and put her ear next to his mouth in order to understand him.

"Can you cut the ropes? They are very tight. My arms and legs . . ."

"I'll try," Pam said, but the knife was gone. The whole hilltop was gone, unrecognizable; she and Humphrey lay in a littered island surrounded by a sea of utter devastation. The still and wooden shed, which had survived ninety years of history and weather, were gone without a trace. Wherever Pam looked, every tree, even the largest, lay flattened, all pointing uphill; the top of the bluff had been clearcut by the tornado. She had an unobstructed view all the way to the river. Branches lay all about them, bricks, plastic toys, window glass, a still-flopping catfish, part of a boat . . . it was too much. "I can't . . . I can't find the knife," she told Humphrey. "I'm sorry."

"Help me!" came a weak voice from somewhere nearby. Pam shook her head, tried to clear it, tried to locate the voice. "Is somebody there? Help! There's a tree on me!" The top of the pine tree lay where it had been struck off and a pair of legs stuck out from underneath. As quickly as she could Pam crawled through the rubble, cutting her knees on glass, and pushed feebly at the branches. Otie Bemis lay there with the treetop right across his chest. "Help me," he pleaded when he saw Pam. "Help get this off me. I cain't move, I cain't breathe."

At the sight of him the motor of Pam's brain turned over and began to hum, showing her in a sequence of clear pictures exactly what to do.

She let go of the branches without answering and worked her way painfully back across the clearing to where the wounded Hefn was now trying to push himself upright. "It's Otie Bemis over there under that tree. He's conscious. Can you talk at all?"

"A little," he creaked.

"Have you got enough voice to control somebody's mind with?"

"It should be adequate. Since I can now also see."

"Okay," said Pam. "Now, I know you're in a lot of pain, but we need to get you over to where Brother Otie can see and hear you."

"I am going to kill Otie Bemis," said Humphrey, the words incongruous in the squeaky-hinge voice.

"No," Pam shot back, sharp and firm. "I've got a better idea."

"I shall kill him. The prey becomes the predator."

"No! No! Listen to me, I said I've got a better idea!"

Humphrey looked at her then, the familiar friendly hairiness of his countenance wholly Other, alien beyond the power of human bonds to restrain; and in that instant Pam's conviction quailed, and she thought, *He means it, he's going to kill him— help me, Father!*

In his inflectionless squeak Humphrey said, "What is the idea."

At once the thought-pictures, blurred by panic, leapt back into focus. "We get you over to where he can see you and hear you," she said, "and then, when you've established control, here's what you say."

She told him what to say to Otie Bemis. Then she fell silent and waited.

Everything hung in the balance then—more by a great deal than either of them knew. But finally Humphrey's expression changed, became less Other and more humanlike again. Perhaps he felt that Pam had earned the right to intervene, or perhaps her idea did seem better to him than his own. At any rate, "Very well," he presently agreed. "Very well. You will have to help me over there."

While he lay speaking in creaky phrases to the evangelist, Pam wrapped a long sliver of broken glass in part of Humphrey's gag and carefully, gripping her right hand in her left to keep it from shaking, shaved through the ropes around Humphrey's wrists. Then, while Otie Bemis—still pinned down and using his only good hand—worked awkwardly to free Humphrey's ankles, Pam got up onto her wobbly, bleeding legs and began to search methodically through the wreckage of fallen branches for Liam's body.

17

AND THE LORD GOD ANSWERED JOB OUT OF THE WHIRLWIND

Job 37:1

On Sunday afternoon Pam and Jesse were shown into Liam's room in Madison Hospital by the surgeon who had operated on Liam the night before. By coincidence the room was next to the one that had formerly been Jesse's. But Jesse had been released a day early, along with a number of other patients, to make room for the emergency admission of tornado victims. Liam's roommate was one of these, a man trapped in a collapsed house. He had been to surgery that morning and was still sleeping off the anesthetic. Dr. Clemens pulled the curtain between his bed and Liam's while Pam was introducing Liam and Jesse to one another.

The doctor had been operating all night. His white coat was dirty and bloody, and his eyes had dark circles underneath. He was carrying a steel bowl that made a scraping noise as he handed it to Liam. "I thought I'd drop these off on my way home. Thought you might like to keep them for a souvenir." To the other two he said, "It's the pieces of lead I dug out of this young man last night."

Liam, liberally bandaged and white though he was, squinted briefly into the bowl and said, "Oh. Only forty-nine? It seems more like two thousand four hundred and one."

Pam laughed. "Twenty-four-oh-one is forty-nine squared," she explained to Jesse and the doctor.

"As it is you're going to have a lot of interesting scars to tell your wife about," Dr. Clemens said. "But you were mighty lucky, even if it doesn't feel that way right now. Nothing vital damaged, no significant disfigurements—the fellow that shot you wasn't much of a marksman. I've seen hunters just cut to pieces with buckshot. But who told you there were forty-nine

299

shots in the bowl? I only just counted them myself, while I was washing off the blood.''

"So did he," Pam said loyally, knowing—for the first time, but with perfect clarity—that the day Liam would be explaining his forty-nine scars to any wife would never come. She pulled a straight chair close to the bed and sat down. "He can do beans in a jar, too, and quarters in a bowl. And bees—oh!" She swiveled toward Jesse. "I forgot to tell you—we hived the swarm! It's a good big one too, thirty-one thousand, eight hundred and eighty-five-plus bees."

"I take it that's according to the human calculator here?" Jesse exchanged a grown-up look with Dr. Clemens. "Would that figure be exact or approximate?"

"He doesn't calculate, he only counts. But he's accurate. I just hope we got the queen—and I wish we'd had a chance to move the hive."

The night before, after she and Humphrey and Otie Bemis had dragged Liam out from under the pile of branches and trees, Pam had gone alone for help. Almost at once she had blundered into a nightmare tangle of more broken branches, crushed bodies, and blood. Her tormentors had run and lain down flat in the creek bed, which is what you were always supposed to do if a twister caught you in the open; but the funnel had apparently dropped or dragged a huge tree right on top of them—some or all, Pam didn't try to find out how many bodies there were. Numbed beyond shock, her only response to the sight had been to back off and work her way around the carnage.

Within the path of the tornado the landscape had been destroyed beyond recognition, as if a bomb had exploded. But the path of destruction was not very wide, and Pam had climbed and forced her way out of it before too long—long enough, though, given the vulnerability and slow-motion responses of her bare, leaden limbs—and shortly thereafter had struck the Hollow road that led past the apiary and out into the world. Limping by the apiary, she had looked in. All sixteen of Jesse's hives stood undisturbed, and the single hive body sat on the now-sodden sheet exactly as they had left it, except that now, in the deepening dusk, there was not a bee to be seen.

Pam had crossed the clearing, ignoring the discarded coverall and veil, with some vague thought of carrying the new hive to a site within the group of established hives. The annoyed humming that resulted from her attempt to lift it proved the bees were still inside, but the wooden box might as well have been made of iron; Pam could no more move it by herself than she could spread her wings and fly to Milton. Nor did she have the prescribed piece of hardware cloth to plug the entrance and prevent the bees from coming out until they *could* be moved. By now, a sunny Sunday afternoon, the bees would have been flying all day, orienting themselves to their new location. As far as they were concerned, this was home now. If Jesse moved the hive, they would stubbornly return to the spot where it presently stood.

Jesse said, "You did a fine job, you two. For the time being I think I'll stick some cement blocks underneath and make the best of it. To tell you the truth, a hive of bees in the wrong place just doesn't seem worth worrying about right now, somehow." He had fetched a chair from the tornado victim's side of the curtain for himself and sat forward, forearms on thighs, hands clasped together.

Dr. Clemens, who had been on his way out the door, stopped and leaned on the jamb to ask, "How did Hurt Hollow come through the tornado, Jesse? Is the house all right?"

"Yes it's all right. Pam's seen it," Jesse told him. "She got a bird's-eye view of the whole area—she rode in the helicopter that picked Liam up."

Pam had had more than a bird's-eye view of Jesse's house. Humphrey had ordered the chopper pilot to land on the beach, and sent the pilot to pick up the time transceiver; but she said nothing of this now. "It was getting dark, but I could still see where the tornado went through, from where the trees were down. It was unbelievable—like if you made a little model town out of sand, and somebody dragged a stick right through the middle. The funnel must've touched down first on the other side of Hurtsville and stayed on the ground all the way to the river and partway across. Then it must have lifted up, because the lower part of the Kentucky bluff is still wooded all along the shore in both directions. So the house and stable and gardens and everything are okay."

"Well, thank God for that," said the doctor, and Jesse nodded soberly.

"Then I guess it touched down again about halfway up the hill on this side, the—what is it, Jesse? The northeastern side of the Hollow?"

"Yes, that's right. The northeastern side, where the old still used to be."

"That's it. The whole top of the bluff around there looks

blasted. It pulled all the water out of the creek, it took out the fence—Otie Bemis could lead an army down there today if he wanted to, though they'd have to climb over a lot of jumbled-up fallen trees."

Liam spoke from his bed. "Is the house being watched?"

"Watched? You mean by the police?" In his relief that the tornado had overleapt his home, Jesse had plainly put other dangers out of mind; but now he looked concerned. "I doubt the police can spare anybody today. I need to get back over there myself."

"You can stay with us another night anyway. There *is* a guard," said Pam. "Humphrey ordered one, before he left. Two state troopers from Louisville, that came up in the helicopter. They spent the night there and they're down there right now." If Jesse hadn't thought of looters and vandals, or worse, Humphrey had. While the army medics were transferring Liam's stretcher from the chopper to the ambulance at Madison Landing, in the near-dark and bewildering dazzle of flashing red and blue lights, Humphrey on his own child-size stretcher had been issuing orders to the unenthusiastic troopers.

He could order the troopers around, but orders of his own had come through that could not be disobeyed. The same helicopter that had brought him—and Liam and Otie Bemis, and Pam herself—out of the tangle of devastation, had afterward flown him and the evangelist from Madison to Louisville, where a plane to Washington was waiting. By now he was back on the moon.

There on the hill after the storm, Humphrey had braced himself on his peculiar knees and hooked his peculiar elbows around the branches piled on Liam, and lifted and heaved, and the brush-heap melted away like a pile of snow. But he could neither stand on his feet nor use his hands, and had to be hauled up into the chopper on a stretcher just like Otie Bemis and the bloody, barely conscious Liam.

"It's just as well," he had squeaked when the helicopter pilot passed the radio message along to him. "I'll recover more quickly in my proper gravity, and I have some hard persuading to do—best done in person, I believe." But he obviously wasn't looking forward to confronting the Gafr.

Eleven hours of sleep in her own bed, a hot bath, and a huge breakfast had done wonders for Pam. Not even her mother had expected her to put on a dress and high heels and go to Sunday school or church today. Apart from the bandaged cuts on her knees and the crisscross of long scratches on her arms and legs, and a kind of generalized soreness, she felt like her old self. Better than her old self: she felt like a person entirely in contact with the world she lives in, one who has helped give a happy ending to a story. In a clean pair of loose khaki shorts and a brand-new white T-shirt with the sleeves rolled up, she sat in her chair at Liam's bedside and glowed gently with fulfillment.

"I'll leave you folks alone now," Dr. Clemens said. "Don't you two wear this boy out, he needs his rest. Don't you wear yourself out either, Jesse." As he spoke the doctor tried and failed to cover a yawn.

"Look who's talking," said Jesse. "Get along on home, Dan. We'll be fine."

As soon as the doctor was gone, Pam got up and closed the door. "Okay," said Liam, "let's have it. What happened? I want to know *everything*."

Equipped with information provided by Humphrey while they were taking Liam aboard the chopper, and more information absorbed from her mother and amplified by the morning paper, Pam had pieced the story together. She started at the beginning:

The previous afternoon, while Pam and Liam were occupied in the apiary, Humphrey was lying on Jesse's bed "resting and concentrating" when the back door burst open and the room filled up with angry men. The attack came very suddenly and the Hefn was still somewhat enfeebled by the bee sting; if his attackers had known enough to inject him with more bumblebee venom, nothing could have saved him. As it was, unable to redirect his attention quickly enough, Humphrey could not prevent some of them from pinning him to the bed while others covered his eyes and stuffed rags in his mouth. When he was gagged and blindfolded they tied him hand and foot with a great deal of rope, and then one of them slung him over his shoulder "like a sack of oats" and carried him out of the house. All this took only a few minutes.

The picture created by Pam's narrative—intruders violently invading his home—was deeply disturbing to Jesse, who interrupted at this point to ask, "How did they get through the fence? And who were they, anyway?"

Pam knew the answer; by now it was general knowledge in the community. On Saturday afternoon Otie Bemis had held a revival service at the Milton Church. A lot of local Hefn-haters were there, people who'd been hearing all week what Brother Otie had been saying about the Hefn being the Antichrist, and about Humphrey committing abominations with his only female Apprentice down in Hurt Hollow, while Jesse was in the hospital. Apparently Otie really outdid himself at the Saturday service, raved and carried on and cranked everybody up, including himself, and they all just decided then and there to go on down to the Hollow and teach Humphrey a lesson.

"Were they talking about killing him right from the start?" Liam asked.

"The best I can figure it, most of them probably weren't—some of them just wanted to come down and rescue *me*—but a few of 'em were in the Klan, like Orrin said, and I think maybe *they* had it in mind to kill him right from the start."

"What clan?" Jesse wanted to know, and then immediately, "You mean Klan with a K?"

"Yep."

"Well, what did you mean, 'like Orrin said,' then? I don't recall Orrin ever going on record about the Klan."

Pam put her hand on Jesse's knee. "I'll explain that part later. It gets complicated."

She went on. According to the rumor mill, and confirmed by what Humphrey had overheard during the climb up the creek, several of the most vocal and virulent Hefn-haters at the revival service were indeed members of the Klan. Two or three in the congregation were also volunteer firemen in Madison. These men drove a buggy over the bridge and borrowed a fire engine, and used that to break in; then the whole mob of them poured down the Hollow and made their surprise attack on Humphrey.

"Something I don't know," said Liam, "is where did they all go to then? Twenty-four guys came through the gate, but there were only eight, counting Otie Bemis, when we caught up with them."

"Brother Otie sent them back." Humphrey had explained that part to Pam. Once the Hefn had been trussed up and was in no danger of breaking free, and the men had seen that Pam wasn't around, and therefore not available to be rescued, Otie Bemis told most of the men to go on back and return the fire engine to the station, and wait for further instructions. A lot of them were cooling off by then and glad to do as he said. One suggested it would be a good idea to disable the phone in case the Apprentices turned up, and Otie agreed. "We missed them because we were coming down the trail while they were going up the road, just like I figured."

The seven Klansmen stayed with Otie and Humphrey. Strange

that Pam had lived at Scofield all her life without ever hearing anybody mention the Klan, except her father that one time, and what the media reported off and on about the notorious Brother Gus Griner way off in Louisiana, and now everybody seemed to be talking about it. The appearance of the Hefn on the scene had given the Ku Klux Klan in Indiana and Kentucky, never really moribund, a whole new lease on life. But it took the *Delta Queen* incident to bring the Klan mentality seething to the surface. Nobody seemed to know whether Otie Bemis himself was in the Arkansas Klan, but he had not been slow to take advantage of the situation, certain that the Hefn would not attempt to prevent him from *saying*—even from the pulpit—anything he liked.

"How could they ever have thought they'd get away with it?" Liam said wonderingly. "They must have known they'd be identified. Did they *want* to be martyrs?"

"Martyrs to the cause of avenging the guys on the *Delta Queen*, and proving the Hefn can't control us completely . . . maybe, but I think they were probably just so wrought up they weren't *thinking* at all. You don't know how emotional and wild some of these revival services can get. There are preachers that can sweep you right into the stratosphere."

"They were a mob," said Jesse. "A small mob, but a real one."

"Like the tornado, small but very, very destructive," said Pam. "Did you know that as tornadoes go, this was actually a pretty small one? Hard to believe."

Liam said musingly, "They started as individual people in the church, and Otie Bemis got them to start whirling together till they turned into one thing, a mob. Then after a while they turned back into individuals again. Does a tornado do that?"

Jesse said, "Not exactly. But I'll tell you what does: a swarm of bees."

When they had all pondered that thought a moment, Pam went on with her tale:

Apparently the old meeting-place in Hurt Hollow, the Klavern, was part of local Klan folklore. Humphrey heard them talking about it—that one of the men remembered hearing his grandfather tell about being brought there as a very small child. It was the grandfather's earliest memory. He recalled the burning cross, and the white robes and hoods, and the singing. They'd stopped using that site after the repeal of Prohibition, a good while before the Hubbels arrived in the 1950s, but dozens of local people knew where it was and would take their kids in to see it, with Orrin and Hannah none the wiser. The fence put an end to that, but some of the lynchers had been taken there as kids and still knew exactly where to find the place, and Otie Bemis said it was the hand of Providence that had arranged for that spot to be so convenient to the place where they caught the Hefn Antichrist, proving that even corn likker had a part to play in the working of God's will.

When they got there, Otie put a leash of rope on Humphrey and dragged him into the shed.

"Where he tried to get Humphrey to tell him how the Hefn do mind control," said Liam.

"Nope. A vermin Otie Bemis may be, but he's not a hypocrite. He told Humphrey how Jesus had wrestled with the devil in the wilderness for forty days, and the devil had offered him worldly power and glory if Jesus would bow down and worship him, and Jesus said, 'Get thee behind me, Satan: for it is written, Thou shalt worship the Lord thy God, and him only shalt thou serve.' He was comparing himself to Jesus, see, and Humphrey—all the Hefn, really—to the devil, alias the Antichrist. Otie said humanity would never bow down to the Hefn. He said the Lord God would bring the Children of Israel out of bondage, and a lot of other things. He prayed for about ten minutes, and it was while he was praying that he got the idea of skinning Humphrey alive, and keeping the skin as a sign and a token of humanity's power over the Hefn."

"The guy's a nut case! Doesn't he realize the Hefn can get fed up with us any day and make us commit mass suicide, or leave *without* 'giving us back our babies' or whatever the hell it was he said?"

Jesse stirred. "You don't have to be a nut case to feel that life lived according to somebody else's dictates isn't worth living."

"But—"

"No, listen to me a minute. With the Hefn around, you two are better off than you were, but you're in the minority—the kind of people who kidnapped Humphrey feel truly oppressed by the Hefn presence. It's changed their lives for the worse, and they weren't real well off to start with. I've been thinking a lot about this, lying next door with nothing much else to do."

"But in the long run *everybody's* better off because they're here!" Liam protested.

"In the long run," Jesse reminded him, "everybody's dead. In the short run too, some of them—or as good as dead, like those four guys on the *Delta Queen*. That's what these Klansmen know. Don't expect people like Otie Bemis to consider all the facts and arrive at a rational conclusion about this or anything else; that's not the way most people live, or ever did."

"Which is why the world was dying when the Hefn came," Pam broke in; she had heard this argument done to death for years, and tension between Liam and Jesse was the very last thing she wanted, especially today. "The kind of people who join the Klan aren't as lucky as we are, and we need to remember that. But even if they're not, we still have to fight them. Listen, it's almost time. The rest of the story's gonna have to wait till after the telecast."

Liam took the hint and clicked on the viewscreen, using the remote on his bedside table. "Crank me up a little higher, would you?" Pam got up and rotated the crank at the foot of his bed; Jesse turned his chair around to face the screen. "The people those Klan types have always hated most are even less lucky than *them*," Liam couldn't resist adding.

Jesse nodded and smiled around at him. "You're sure-as-shootin' right about that. I've been living in this part of the world all my life, you know."

"Okay, everybody, it's starting," Pam said, shushing them both; Otie Bemis's ferret face and showily bandaged head had appeared on the screen. Liam clicked on the sound.

As they watched, the camera drew back to reveal Brother Otie in a wheelchair, dressed in a plain black gown like an academic robe. A bit of white collar showed at the neck. His skin was colorless, and the eye below the bandage purple and swollen nearly shut, but he still somehow managed to look exalted. "Behold," he said loudly, "a whirlwind of the Lord is gone forth in fury, even a grievous whirlwind: it shall fall grievously upon the head of the wicked." He paused dramatically, face tilted upward. "Then the Lord answered Job out of the whirlwind," he intoned. "Then the Lord answered Job . . . out of the whirlwind."

"Job 37:1," Pam muttered, "but he looked that other one up himself." Jesse glanced at her.

"My brothers and sisters in Christ," said Otie Bemis, "I want to tell you about something that happened to me yesterday afternoon. I want to tell you a story that will astonish you just as much as it still astonishes me. I want to tell you a story that has changed my life in a moment, in the twinkling of an eye.

"I want to say to you that like Saul of Tarsus before his conversion I have been a religious man, and I have been a godly

307

man. I have preached the Word of God up and down this land. I have preached against the Hefn just as Saul preached against the followers of Jesus Christ, and just as he persecuted the followers of Jesus Christ. Yesterday afternoon, I stood by while another man raised a knife against the Hefn Humphrey, the Instructor of the Apprentices at the Bureau of Temporal Physics, and I was consenting unto his death, my brothers and sisters in Christ. I was consenting unto his death, just as Saul was consenting unto the death of the martyr Stephen.

"Now you all remember how when Saul of Tarsus was traveling to Damascus one day, when he was 'breathing out threatenings and slaughter against the disciples of the Lord,' he was struck down by the Lord on the road, struck blind, and he heard a voice saying unto him 'Saul, Saul, why persecutest thou me?' And I have to tell you, my friends, that like Saul I was struck down yesterday by the hand of the Lord. I was struck down—I was struck to the ground—by a tornado that passed through a part of southern Indiana and northern Kentucky yesterday afternoon. There was a number of tornados in that part of the world yesterday, and one of them sought me out and it struck me *down*.

"When the tornado came, I and some other men had the Hefn Humphrey in our power! We were going to kill him, and I tell you in all sincerity, my friends, I had a clear conscience about it, because I sincerely believed what I'd been preaching, that the Hefn were the Antichrist—the enemies of our Lord and Savior Jesus Christ on Earth.

"But before we could raise the knife to strike the Hefn Humphrey dead, that tornado came and stopped us. It stopped us cold! We were standing right in its path. And my friends, I'm here to tell you today, that like Job I heard a voice speaking out of that whirlwind, and that voice said just as plain as I'm talking to you right now, that voice said: *'The Hefn are my beloved children: hear them.'* "

Otie Bemis paused again. His voice shook; his whole body shook quite visibly. No one watching could doubt the man in the wheelchair was sincere. " 'The Hefn . . . are my beloved children . . . *hear them*,' " he repeated.

"Wow," said Liam quietly. Pam glanced around at him and blushed to see how impressed he looked. She turned back to the viewscreen.

"Now, you all know the Hefn can control the human mind, and some of you might be thinking, just like I would probably be thinking in your place, Brother Otie, that Hefn, Humphrey, he took control of your mind somehow, and he made you *believe* you heard the Lord's voice answering you out of the whirlwind like he answered Job.

"But let me assure you, my good brothers and sisters, let me say to you with all my heart and soul, that that tornado was no *imaginary* tornado. That was no *make-believe* tornado. That tornado registered on the weather maps of two states, it destroyed millions of dollars' worth of property, it injured hundreds of people, and the seven men who were with me—those men were *killed*. Now, you ask the folks who lost homes, and you ask the folks who lost loved ones, and the folks laying in the hospitals right this minute in pain from their wounds and their lacerations, if that was a make-believe tornado we had yesterday over there in Kentucky!

"Yes, the Hefn can control the human mind. But can the Hefn create a tornado? Can they make the clouds whirl together in a funnel, and come straight across open country for the very spot, and at the very moment, that we were standing yesterday with a knife raised to kill the Hefn Humphrey?

"There may be those of you that believe they can. There may be those that believe the Hefn can do just about anything, and I cain't prove to you that you're wrong. But I know one thing for certain. Seven men are dead, and their families are grieving for them this afternoon, because they were with me at the moment when that tornado ripped through the trees above the Ohio River, and dropped a pine tree on me that cracked my ribs, and cracked my head, and drug another big ol' sweet gum tree up the creek bed where those seven men were taking shelter, and killed ever' last one of 'em, except for me. And I know—I *know*—I heard the Lord's voice in that whirlwind, and nobody ever gon' persuade me I didn't.

"And I only am escaped alone to tell *thee*. I only . . . am escaped alone . . . to bear this witness to the Lord's word."

Liam murmured, "What about you?" Pam shook her head, not looking around.

"And so my message to you this day, my brothers and sisters in Christ, is the same as the Lord's message yesterday to me, and it is this: *The Hefn are the children of the Lord. Hear them.*"

Otie Bemis's pale face was shiny with sweat. "Let us pray," he said.

"O Heavenly Father, I come before Thee this day a man chastised and broken in body, but resurrected in spirit. Let me say with the boy Samuel, 'Speak, Lord, thy servant heareth.'

Thy servant heareth, O Lord! Thy servant Otie Bemis will spend the rest of his days, and wear out his strength, telling the story of what happened to him on the banks of the Ohio River on May 24, in the Year of Our Lord two thousand and fourteen. He will spend the rest of his *days* lamenting the deaths of those seven men, that he led to their destruction, but he will give thanks as long as he lives that the whirlwind came to prevent him from harming Thy beloved servant, the Hefn Humphrey.

"And now bless I beseech Thee the families of those men I led all unwittingly to their deaths. Strengthen them, strengthen and support the wives and little children of those men. And help and support all those who suffered in the whirlwind. May their wounds be healed, we pray, and may their homes be built again.

"And now in closing, bless Thy children the Hefn on Earth, and teach us all, Hefn and humans both, to work together, that by doing their will, we may do Thine.

"All this we ask in Jesus' name. Amen."

Otie Bemis's head remained bowed; he must have been exhausted. The TV camera switched to a robed multiracial choir, which had begun to sing "O God, Our Help in Ages Past." Stanza by stanza the words scrolled by on the screen as the choir worked its way through the hymn. Soon Pam was singing too, switching back and forth between the alto and soprano parts. By the third stanza Liam had learned the tune and was patching in the tenor part, and finally Jesse joined in too with the bass:

> A thousand ages in Thy sight
> Are like an evening gone,
> Short as the watch that ends the night
> Before the rising sun.
>
> Time, like an ever-rolling stream,
> Bears all its sons away;
> They fly, forgotten, as a dream
> Flies from the opening day . . .

The words of the hymn rolled over the image of Otie Bemis detaching his microphone and being wheeled away by a uniformed nurse. Then he was gone and the choir was back, and finally the hymn ended, and with it the broadcast.

When a sitcom started to run, Liam clicked off the set and the three sat in silence. "*Can* the Hefn make a tornado?" Liam finally wondered aloud. "Or the Gafr?"

"I don't know," said Pam, "but I bet you anything you like the Hefn had nothing at all to do with this, except for putting Otie on the air so quick. None of them even knew what was happening to Humphrey."

"Unless they had some way of intercepting our transmission."

Pam frowned. Jesse said, "Transmission?"

Arguing voices outside the door made their three heads turn. There was a loud, rapid knocking. Before Pam could get up and open the door it opened by itself, and there, backlighted by the hallway lamps and looking as if he had slept in his clothes, stood the junior senator from Pennsylvania, saying in a tone both relieved and aggravated, "*There* you are, you infernal scalawag! How many more years are you planning to whittle off my life before you're done?"

18

HOW SHALL WE SING THE LORD'S SONG IN A STRANGE LAND?

Psalm 137:4

Two weeks later Pam stood at the railing of a stern-wheeler called the *Sandy* and waved goodbye to her parents on shore as the boat backed out into the river, bell clanging, "Camptown Races" sounding smartly from the calliope. Frances and Shelby stood together, waving and smiling on the sand at the very edge of the water. Only one other passenger had boarded at Scofield Beach; Pam's parents were the only people seeing anybody off.

"Call us when you get there!" Frances called.

"I will."

"Enjoy your trip back!" This was Shelby.

"I will. Thanks for everything."

"See you at Thanksgiving!"

Pam nodded, a big nod so they could see. Last Monday she and her mother had been to Louisville, to the plastic surgeon, who had poked a pronged metal instrument up each of Pam's nostrils and said "This nose has been broken at some time in the past." A bike accident, falling out of a tree—several memorable nosebleeds came to mind, any one of which could have been the fateful one. So that explained the excess cartilage in the tip.

The operation was scheduled for Thanksgiving vacation (but anything might happen before then).

"Don't work too hard!" her mother called. "Give our best to Liam and tell him we hope he's well soon!"

"Okay." He was well now, as Frances knew—she had talked with him herself a couple of days ago—but it was just something to say. Frances wasn't going to be deflected from her "boyfriend" notion if she could help it.

Shelby looked to Pam as if he would have liked to add something else, but he just kept smiling and waving. As the water

312

widened between her father and herself, Pam was struck lightly, as if by a trailing wing, by an obscure, unnamable pain. Yesterday she had been swinging on the screened-in porch, waiting for Betsy—they were taking a picnic to the woods below the Point on Pam's last day at home—when her mother's voice had floated through the house. "Shelby!" she called. "Shel-by! Shee-e-l—beee!" And into Pam's mind had flashed an image from a completely forgotten dream: the swarm of bees hanging from the bow of the big canoe, herself straddling the hive—watching and watching for the shell bee, in its suit of cast-off cicada husk, to enter.

Now the merest whiff of dissociation threatened, a puff of smoke. *Oh no you don't*, Pam thought, and shut her eyes and shook her head. *That's enough of that*.

The *Sandy*, well out in the river now, had begun to straighten out for the upstream run. A breeze caught them, billowing the flag, blowing Pam's straight, fine hair sideways and molding her shirt against her body; but the figures on shore had grown small and harmless and she leaned comfortably against the railing. Again the obscure pain—part longing, part loathing—brushed over her. She breathed deeply, turned and sighed as far as possible down the river, away from her shrinking parents, toward where (if you knew where to look) you could pinpoint Hurt Hollow, a fold in the dense summer foliage below the bald crown of the bluff.

Three days after the tornado had torn through all their lives, two days after Terry Carpenter had appeared and whisked Liam back to Washington, all the fallen trees had been cleared along the Hollow fenceline and the fence itself rebuilt and wired. As soon as the work was finished and the troopers dismissed, Pam had gone home with Jesse, to stay for the week it took him to make a full recovery, both from the snakebite and from the enfeebling effects of so many days in bed.

It had been a good week, but different from what she would have expected a month earlier. The outside work was Pam's to do, but Jesse's sister had come up from Louisville to see to the housekeeping (and, incidentally, to relieve Frances's concern about Pam staying at the Hollow alone with even a convalescent Jesse).

Also, before leaving for the moon, Humphrey had given orders. The first, of course, was about Otie Bemis's television appearance, which both he and Brother Otie were anxious to have go forward without delay. But then he had issued a whole set of orders about Hurt Hollow. Repairing the fence was to take precedence over all other clearing and reconstruction in the district. Furthermore, for the time being at least, the Hollow was to remain closed to the public.

"Humphrey's pretty high-handed but I think I know what's in his mind," Pam told Jesse when the word came through. "He thinks Hurt Hollow might have a solution to an important problem for the human future on Earth, and he wants it protected till he has a chance to explore the question in more depth."

"I wish he could protect it from tornadoes," Jesse grumbled. Much as he disliked the summer floods of visitors, Hurt Hollow was after all, his home, and Humphrey had not consulted him. And Jesse was further aggravated by another of Humphrey's orders: that, pending further investigations, the fence be electrified and operable from the house, and that a modern videophone be put in. "The Hefn treat us like parents treat their children—like children sometimes treat their elderly parents, too!—and damned if they don't make all the same mistakes. I don't want *Humphrey* telling me I've got to put up with one of those goddam videophones in my own house *for my own good*!"

Pam had kept quiet while Jesse griped, but she privately thought that, however tactless his style of operating, Humphrey was probably right. Whatever it was that made Hurt Hollow important—would you call it Project Holy Ground?—remained a mystery. Till the mystery was solved, it seemed a good idea to shield the place from, well, desecration.

Of course, it was the presence of Humphrey himself in Hurt Hollow that had roused people to desecrate it in the first place. Members of the local Klan, and other Hefn-haters given to violence, might believe Otie Bemis's testimony about the tornado and they might not. Terry Carpenter doubted they had heard the last from the Klan. Still, it seemed unlikely they would try to break in again with Humphrey gone and Jesse reinstalled in his proper place.

And of course, it was also quite possible that isolating the Hollow from its pilgrims amounted to a desecration too.

They would all have to wait and see how things went. Meanwhile, as far as Pam was concerned, keeping the Hollow under Humphrey's temporary protection seemed a great idea.

In his present frame of mind Pam hadn't found it easy to tell Jesse about contacting the Hubbells. He listened in grumpy silence to the story of the two contacts with the Hurt Hollow of 1964, many years before he and Marion had met Orrin; but, as before, his reaction was milder than she had feared. "We didn't get a chance to go back and tell them how it all turned out," she wound up. "Humphrey took the transceiver back to Washington with him, but maybe he'll bring one back another time. I wonder if . . ." Pam was thinking, if Jesse should be present during some future transmission, then the Hubbells would know who he was before they met him—which would mean that they had kept that fact a secret from him when they *did* meet him. (Along with the facts that the previous two contacts had taken place—which they had apparently kept a secret from everybody.)

But Jesse's thoughts had been running in the same vein, and he was shaking his head. "No, I don't like that idea. Much as I'd love to talk to them both—I never met Hannah, you know . . . but Orrin never said a thing to me—not that I'd have had any notion what he was talking about in 1985, but I don't like the idea of his keeping that kind of secret, all the time we knew each other."

It was on the tip of Pam's tongue to say, We told them your name, but she bit it back and hung her head guiltily. This whole business was too complicated. It just wasn't possible to work it out so that everybody concerned would be happy.

"Why not just call them up from Washington?" Jesse was saying.

"We can't. The transceiver has to be at the place you want to contact. That's how it works—even though the place is literally enormously far away, in space as well as time. *We* don't know why. I'm not even sure the Hefn do."

Jesse looked at his watch, got up and started assembling milking equipment. "Nice to think there's something the Hefn don't know." He stopped and stared at his hands holding the pail and several clean rags. Slowly he set them down and looked over at Pam, a sad, troubled, look. "I forgot again."

The stable had survived the tornado. The goats themselves, still browsing high on the bluff in the late afternoon, had not. One of the does and the kid had been found crushed beneath fallen trees; the rest of the flock had vanished. The one good thing was that the doe whose body had been found was Belle, the bellwether. Her brass bell and collar would grace another goat's neck one day soon, when Jesse had been able to rebuild the flock—a small note of continuity, but important to Jesse.

The *Sandy* was in midstream now, forging against the current, heading toward Madison. Despite the overcast morning, visibility was excellent, the hills cut against the gray sky so sharply it almost seemed as if every individual leaf could be distinguished from every other. The leaves on each stalk of corn in the bottomland shone with knifelike crispness. The broad gray water stretched out ahead, full of glancing light. Pam stood at the forward railing and let the breeze blow her bangs straight up. She looked back as the first bend cut off her view of where she knew Hurt Hollow to be. "Bye again for now, Jesse," she said aloud, "but I'll be back soon. Hold the fort."

The tan strip of Scofield Beach was empty; by now her mother and father would have driven the college taxi back up the hill. "Bye, Mom," she said, and then scarcely audibly, "Believe it or not, I love you. I do."

The stacks of the Clifty Power Plant were coming into view on the larboard side of the boat, and after them Madison Landing. From this vantage there was no visible sign, upstream or down, that a tornado had passed through the area only two weeks before. The legendary twister that devastated the Scofield College campus and three sizable towns in 1974 had traced a path exactly parallel to this recent one, but several miles to the north and many miles longer. By crossing the river at Hurt Hollow, the recent tornado had missed all population centers in the area except the little town of Hurtsville, Indiana, and the houses clustered at the landing across from the Hollow; the injured people crowding the Madison Hospital Emergency Room had mostly been brought there from the outlying suburbs of Milton, where the tornado had done most of its damage. It was considered a miracle that the only deaths had been those of the seven Klansmen, crushed while cowering in the creek bed, and Jesse's flock of goats.

"Holy ground," Pam murmured. She faced back into the wind.

Getting Humphrey to make Otie Bemis believe the Lord had spoken to him out of the whirlwind was an idea born under conditions so harrowing and extreme that it was hard for Pam to feel it had been her own. She had prayed for help, meaning that somebody would come and stop Brother Otie and make the horror end. Instead she got a tornado—and, right after that, this wild idea, clear and complete in her mind. "Maybe that's what's meant by inspiration . . ." Whatever it was, she couldn't understand, even now, how she had managed to think it up herself.

But the tornado, that was the element of the plan *entirely* out of any mere creature's power or cleverness to produce. It was

316

the tornado that actually *rescued* Humphrey, and Liam, and Pam herself. If the tornado hadn't come when it did—"Funny," Pam had said to Humphrey that evening, "I've been so scared of tornadoes my whole life, and now . . ."

"And now, except for the tornado, *I* at least would be, not temporarily crippled as you see me, but unpleasantly and permanently dead. And so might both of you, yes, yes . . . This tornado that might so easily have saved us all from Otie Bemis only to kill us itself . . . a violent and terrifying agent of fortune. I hope never to see another."

Liam thought—assumed—that Otie Bemis was a simple dupe. "Good thing Brother Otie's such an egomaniac," he had said when Pam was cranking his bed down flat again after Terry had whirled away to collect his things from the Pruitts. "Imagine thinking the Lord of the Universe went to all the trouble to make a whole tornado, just to teach *him* a lesson!"

"Well, and to save Humphrey's life, not to mention yours and maybe mine."

"Yeah, but still! An actual tornado!"

"So you're dead sure he's wrong."

"Sure I'm sure! Aren't you?"

"No," said Pam.

How could anyone be *sure*? The consequences of her brainstorm—if it *was* hers—were so far-reaching that trying to think them through overwhelmed her every time she tried, made her anxious and confused, like trying to think about agency and effect in the time transmissions. Once again she decided *not* to try, not now.

Think about something else. There were plenty of other, better topics to pick from.

For instance, there was Liam's saying, while waiting for Terry to come back with his luggage, "How about printing me up a copy of that river poem? I could write a musical setting for it while I'm convalescing—give me something to do."

Pleased as she was, Pam felt herself hesitate. "Would you mind if I gave you a different one? If you don't like it I could always modem you the other one." And she had borrowed a NotePad from a nurse, and typed the poem up.

"Oh, sure, this'll be fine," Liam said when he read it. "It's an old one, right?"

"Not really. Just in the old style."

"The one you wouldn't let me read before?"

"Nope, I still won't let you read that one! This is even newer."

Pam pictured Liam lying in his room in the big house in College Park, working with a keyboard and a MusicWriter program and her page of text, and felt happy. Her mother would go on thinking of Liam as her boyfriend so long as they had any relationship at all. "But that's not it," Pam said aloud. Frances might never be able to see the real situation: that her peculiar daughter and the (less visibly) peculiar boy she had brought home were linked not at all by the things Frances could understand, and yet were linked.

What by? Paddling. Singing. Gardening. Hiving. Thinking and doing. *We're a team*, Pam thought with deep satisfaction, *we collaborate. And argue and disagree too, but so what? That's not the main thing. We're—I know!—we're a* song! *Music by him, lyrics by me. But it's not a romantic song. That's what Mom doesn't get.*

A number of pleasure boats from Madison were on the river now, some with interchangeable young couples in bathing suits aboard, laughing, teasing, smooching. Any one of them might be Steve Harper and Carole Cosby. Barbie and Ken. Pam sniffed and moved to the starboard railing, where she could watch the Kentucky bottomland and its cornfields taper now to meet the bluff.

There was one other thing—equally unfathomable to her mother, had Frances known of it—linking herself and Liam. Maybe the most important thing.

At Madison Landing, waiting for Liam to be offloaded and Otie Bemis's ribs to be taped so the helicopter could leave for Louisville, Humphrey had said, "Pam, I am curious about something."

He kept trying to talk, despite his damaged, rusty-hinge voice. Beside his stretcher Pam sat gobbling a cheese sandwich that one of the medics had given her. She swallowed and said, "What?"

"Once in Hurt Hollow you told me that *I* was the most important part of your life in Washington. Yes?"

"Yes." She took another bite.

"Was it true?"

"Mm-hmm."

"And then today . . . today you told Otie Bemis that you love me. 'Please don't hurt him. I love him.' I believe those were your exact words."

Pam felt her face begin to glow in the dark. Every inch of her went stiff.

318

"Do you remember?" Humphrey nodded helpfully.

"Ye-e-e-e-s." A deprecatory, sliding agreement, starting low, ending high.

"What does it *mean*?"

Rigid with self-consciousness, Pam said "What does *what* mean?"

"Why am I important to you? Why do you 'love' me?"

All Pam's new ease and confidence with Humphrey drained away. She sat, eyes unfocused, the bread and cheese turned to sawdust in her mouth.

Humphrey peered, trying to see through the stringy curtain of her hair. "I am, as you know, Pam, deeply interested in bonding as a phenomenon. Between Gafr and Hefn, yes, and also very much between Hefn and human. Yes, very much that as well."

Pam was silent as a stone. "Today," Humphrey continued, "you cut me free, at some cost to yourself. And afterward you were able to thwart my intention. You were able to prevent me from killing Otie Bemis by invoking our bond, the bond between us. That was unexpected. The power of the bond is unexpectedly great."

He waited hopefully. When Pam still made no response he added, "So you see why I am so extremely curious to know how it has come about that *you*, Pamela Pruitt, a human female, feel love for *me*, Humphrey, a Hefn."

How could he keep going on about it, after all he'd been through? "I don't *know*," she wailed. "Why does *Liam* love you? Why not ask *him*?"

In the dark interior of the helicopter a gleam came and went in Humphrey's flat eyes. "Does Liam love me?" There was a pause, filled with luridly flashing lights, crackling radios, and medics rushing around and between them. "He *needs* me," the Hefn said thoughtfully. His helpless, cloven hands twitched at his sides. "Might it be that Liam loves me—if he does love me—*because* he needs me? And does it follow, Pam, that you also feel some need of me?"

"Well . . ." Pam croaked miserably.

"I understand Liam's need, I think, but what is yours? What could it be?" And then belatedly, "But discussing this subject is perhaps distressing to you?"

"You said it." She stuffed the rest of the sandwich into her mouth.

Humphrey sighed. "Then I must apologize for pressing you.

319

I'm afraid I got a little carried away. These questions of bonding are so *very* fascinating . . . Do you think we might reopen the topic another time, in Washington perhaps, with all this unpleasantness behind us?''

"We might. But ask Liam, it's probably much easier for him to talk about it. You have to remember, Humphrey,'' said Pam, "that I'm not a typical adolescent female of my species.''

"A typical adolescent female could tell me what I wish to know?''

Pam pictured Carole Cosby explaining to Humphrey why she loved him, and didn't know whether to laugh or cry; but Humphrey said, "It was as well for us all that you were not so typical today. I thank you, Pam, for your atypical efforts to help me, and especially for your most excellent idea.''

Eyes prickling, throat aching stupidly, Pam leaned on the railing and watched the approaching shoreline. The whistle tooted and the calliope struck up "Beautiful Ohio'' as the *Sandy* began to swing her stage toward Madison Landing. On shore the waiting men, talking and joshing, shouldered their bundles of firewood. Two weeks and two days before, on the exact spot where the woodmen were standing now, Pam had said goodbye to Humphrey and watched the chopper whir off into the darkness above the inky river. A hundred years ago.

She waited restlessly, muttering some Kipling and hitting the railing gently with her fist in time to the meter, while the *Sandy* took on fuel, supplies, passengers; but soon enough a strip of brown water was widening again between the steamboat and the landing. Pam's heart gave a leap; she waved her whole arm, both arms. "Bye, Madison High School. Bye, Charlie. Bye, Steve. So long, Miss Carole 2013 Southern Indiana Middle School Cosby, you major-league cabbagehead! From now on— *from this day to the ending of the world!*—I'm not having a thing to do with any of you, not one single thing! You'll never get your claws in me again!''

The steamboat straightened out, the paddle wheel reversed itself with a dramatic swirling and churning of the waters. Bell clanging joyfully, the *Sandy* sailed beneath the Ohio River bridge and headed upstream, toward the shapely, humping, sharp-cut bluffscape beyond, that ran unbroken clear to Pittsburgh.

The calliope played "Dixie.''

Stars

Stars a-bove and stars be-low, float-ing on the ri - ver,

Till my ar-row cleaves the flow, Set-ting all a - shi - ver.

Then I take the two a-part, Face im-pas-sive, drum-ming heart,

When I feel the se-cret dart Burn-ing in my qui - ver.

WORDS: Pamela Pruitt
MUSIC: Mark William O'Hara

Liam:

Well, that's it. Did you solve the mystery?

Before we leave this placetime Hot Spot, I want to know if my understanding jibes with yours of how events developed from then to now. It's easy to feel cut off from the rest of the world, here in the Hollow.

This is how I see it. The Hefn had tried mindwipe threats, fear of quick annihilation, fear of slow extinction, education, and passive "good examples" as means of controlling human behavior. (Speculation: those are what the Gafr use to control the Hefn.) On people, all had failed to work as expected; but now Humphrey had learned of a couple of others he thought might work better. We'd had a very close call—much closer than we knew—after the Bemis incident, but he managed to get the Gafr to agree to let him try these other means out. They were:

1. Bonding. My bright idea of how to handle Otie Bemis had worked; killing Bemis would not have worked; I had stopped Humphrey from killing him by "invoking our bond." The powers (and benefits) of bonding to affect behavior had thus been powerfully confirmed in Humphrey's mind.

2. Religious-Style Persuasion. Bemis's goals were vile, but his techniques were extremely effective. Like Hitler, he'd been preaching against something; why shouldn't it be just as possible to preach in favor of something, using those same techniques? Humphrey could see that by lowering the volume, and buttressing the appeal to emotionalism with rational arguments, the approach had real potential.

That summer after school started again, Humphrey and I had several long talks about conversion experiences. He even went to church with me in Washington for a while, remember? And shortly after that, they started recruiting the Missionaries.

For eight years each Missionary class worked with teams of environmentalists, psychologists, evangelists, and (via time transceiver) unwitting Neolithic villagers, studying how to put a message over so people will want to change the way they live.

Unlike the Apprentices, the Missionaries were powerfully bonded among themselves. Powerfully but non-exclusively; each year's new Seminary class was warmly welcomed. (Nice work if you can get it.)

Five high-tech Seminary Homesteads were set up in different parts of the country so the kids could all practice, under different conditions of climate and soil, what they were learning to preach. After eight years the first class went out and the tide began to turn. The results of making the practical need for humanity to change life-styles into a religious movement were dramatic. Instead of people doing what the Hefn said because they had no choice, the Gaians began to convince them that if the Hefn had been wrong in their means, they were right in their goals.

Having changed deliberately and voluntarily, converts tend to stay changed; backsliding, so far, is almost nonexistent. Gaian converts go through a standard training program on a cooperative farm in their locality until ready to choose a personally meaningful bit of Ground to be their own. By then they know from experience what the Missionaries found out in Seminary: that the Gaian message is true.

The movement's spreading. People are Coming Down to Earth in impressive numbers. Missions, local communities of bonded converts, are springing up everywhere.

The discovery of Holy Ground (if your equations work in the field, which I'm sure they will) can only strengthen the tendency of all this. Not to count my chickens, as some illiterate cliché-monger said in *Time*, but I wouldn't be surprised if the days of the Baby Ban were numbered now.

Fair summary?

I'll wind up with a revealing bit of marginalia. In chapter 17, when I wrote down the words to "O God Our Help," I did it from memory. Then I checked a hymnal and found I'd changed

> They fly, forgotten, as a dream
> Dies at the opening day.

to

> They fly, forgotten, as a dream
> Flies from *the* opening day.

Not "dies." Recoils. Hides its face. Goes underground. Can't endure the light. I muse about my recent repeated dream of being Jeff, and cringe from understanding it; I don't want to know, however "therapeutic" knowing might be. This box of turmoil is sent in the same spirit: I ask you to tell me what you see, what I'm afraid to let myself see, hoping against hope that what you see is nothing!

Anyway, here it is.

Oh, it's not nothing, no no no.

Yes, I solved the mystery, I think. Yes, it's a fair summary, though I'd have put in something about continuing trouble from the Klan between 2014 when the first Missionaries were recruited as ten-year-olds to 2022 when they first started preaching.

You are the kingpin person, do you realize that? What if you hadn't stopped Humphrey, what if you hadn't thought of using Otie Bemis to defuse that situation, what if you hadn't known first-hand from yourself and your family what being converted feels like—where would we all be now?

Not building greenhouses and wrapping hives in Gaian collectives.

Not plotting lines on maps of Scotland either. But still, I'm glad you gave the Baptists up, once all that was taken care of.

Okay, two things. One, the hospital scene. I'd nearly been killed. Even allowing for the effects of shock and pain pills, it's obvious from this that I was already scuttling away from the knowledge of my narrow escape as fast as I could—trying to act like everything was normal with me. I think that's a telling detail. Two, it wasn't easier for me to talk about loving Humphrey. That's why he didn't know. I did, but it was for Jeff-in-him, not for his own sake. In that sense I don't think I've been up to loving anybody, or getting really close to anybody, since Jeff died. What happened between us at the Hollow belonged to that place; it didn't work the same way in Washington, did it, when we got back.

Okay, I have to try to figure out how to say this.

The thing that startled me was when you said you *knew*, "for the first time, but with perfect clarity," that I would never be explaining my buckshot scars to any wife. How the devil did you know that? You wouldn't have tucked that observation in as something you knew *then* because you know it *now*, not in this book. You did know it then, but *how*? *I* didn't know, not for years! With both of us straining as far away from anything sexual as possible, what the devil were you picking up? Could you have just believed I would never have a sexual relationship with anybody? Somehow I don't think so. I got agitated, stewing about it.

That night I went to sleep and had the same dream I described before: the desert, you in the bulky beekeeper suit begging me

324

to help you get out of it, me adamantly refusing but feeling terrible.

Also the next night. Also the next.

We're working very hard here getting everything ready for the trip to Findhorn and I just did not have time to be losing sleep. I started to get pretty upset. Last night I picked up the manuscript to finish the last two chapters and send it off to you, with or without any final solution to the conundrum. I was angry, as if you were blaming me for not being able to help, and just wanted to get the book out of my room/life.

I did finish with no further insights into the invisible problem and thought, okay, I gave it a good try, maybe something will occur to me later on but for now I'm getting rid of this thing. So I scribbled a final note: "Sorry, no dice and no more time. More when we get back." I packaged the box back up to send off in tomorrow's (i.e., this morning's) mail. Then I took a sleeping pill as insurance. Then I went to bed.

Surprise, I had the dream again, only this time it had changed. And this time I knew *in the dream* that I had had this dream many, many, many times before, and always forgot it, till this week when it was zapping me every night.

You were trapped in the beekeeper suit as usual, but it was shaped like a thick white plaster-of-Paris woman, with a heavy torso and big white plaster breasts on the outside. There's some sculptor that did figures like that, I forget who. Your eyes were closed. You were wearing a pith helmet and bee veil, the veil tucked into the neck of this woman-shaped coverall. Bees were buzzing and flying everywhere. I stood watching.

You try to take off the suit, moving stiffly like a robot. It won't come off. You struggle awkwardly and weakly. Then you face me and say, "Help me out." I'm instantly paralyzed with terror and can't move.

Up to this point the dream's the same as always except for the naked female body molded on the outside of the suit. This is when I always wake up. But last night I didn't wake up and it went on.

You say again, "Help me out." I don't move; but there's a kind of voiceover, someone disembodied saying, "Time. It's time. *Time*." And it's like I've been waiting all those other times for permission, because though I'm still terrified, I'm now released from my statue-like state and able to move. I approach you and raise my arms—this takes all my strength—and fumble at the suit, which comes apart at once despite the feebleness of my efforts. It separates into chunky sections, like big blocks of hardened plaster cut by a saw. First the hat and veil come off, and your eyes open and you look at me. Then the top left half of the torso, the shoulder and breast, come off in one piece. Then the right half. They fall to the ground. Underneath is a slim bare boy's body—or maybe it has very small breasts (like Pinny's? I think to wonder only now as I write this).

In the dream I'm somehow not surprised at this development. I'm still afraid, but less abjectly terrified than before. Now the rest of the suit comes off in big blocky pieces. Bees are still flying all around us, but they aren't stinging and I realize in the dream that they're not going to, and am relieved.

When all the pieces of the suit have fallen away, you stand there naked on the sand. You have a body like a boy's, with those very small breasts and a small, soft penis like a child's. And no balls. You look at me and smile, and my terror resolves completely into immense relief and gladness. I say, "So *that's* the answer!" And you say, "It's about time." And I wake up.

—Long break. It's now afternoon. Writing that dream out I was shaking the whole time, I had to quit.

Now let me finish what I have to say and get this mailed.

Okay. As soon as it got decently late enough I called up Julie. I told her about the novel—hope you don't mind, but I had to; I was shaking like a leaf in an earthquake—and about the dreams. She asked a lot of questions. I tried to answer carefully but I was really in a state and probably garbled some of it.

Julie says that what I was describing from the novel about you, that you played with boys, wanted to be a boy, loathed the changes that made you into a woman—she says that sounds like something called *gender dysphoria*. It's when—I wrote it down—it's when a person is discontented with their biological sex and wants to have the body of the opposite sex and be regarded by others as a member of the opposite sex. Extreme gender dysphoria is transsexualism.

I told her about your father. She said that would be consistent with some of the body-loathing, but might not necessarily account for the early strong tomboyishness and identification with boys, even if your father had started on you earlier than you thought. She thinks, in view of the persisting anxiety, you ought to talk to a professional about all this (I know, they always say that).

She made *me* say what I thought my dream meant. I said: the sands of lost time. The desert bare of intimacy or commitment to another person. I said I didn't know what the shrinks would tell Pam about herself, but I *know* that my own mind has "recognized" or "designated" her as some kind of replacement for what I lost when Jeff died, and that I've known this for years and years at a deep level, which is why I've had that dream over and over again, but never until now let myself finish or even remember the dream, let alone understand it. And just then I remembered that you'd said in your letter—twice, as if to be sure I didn't miss it—that *you'd been dreaming you were Jeff!*

So—(gibber gibber gibber)—

So it looks like there was something *I* couldn't see for looking that was *in me*, and that I couldn't see it because I was afraid to, afraid of what admitting it to consciousness would mean. The fact that I've finally let myself see it must mean I'm more ready and less afraid now. In other words, "It's time."

But I'm only really talking about how *I* see *you*. I don't know at all if this changes how you see yourself or me, given how you already see and present yourself (age 14) in the book. Julie did say that all the gender dysphorias are always established by age five or six, that if something like that was already in place it might help explain why your father's relatively non-intrusive moves were experienced by you as so devastating. The fallout from all that could be why the drives and wishes typical of the syndrome are being kept under, out of consciousness.

Obviously, conclusions like those would have to be drawn on the basis of much, much more hard data, knowledge of generations of family history and so forth.

Pam—*I'm coming out there*. The minute we get back from Findhorn. Whatever all this means, whatever we've found out, we need to see each other. No: I need to see you. (I hope like hell that you won't feel you need *not* to see *me* after you read this!) The last time I *needed* to see somebody it was Humphrey, almost thirteen years ago, so this is a Very Big Deal and I'm scared perfectly shitless but I'm not going to wimp out. I promise not to rush things or pressure or scare you, but I'm dying to see you, talk, find out—whatever.

Okay? Please say it's okay. Leave a message for me here as soon as you decide. Get the damn phone reconnected! The plane's coming back via Washington; I can hop a train and get a boat at Cincinnati, and be there by the time of the first big honeyflow.

We're leaving tomorrow, be gone about ten days, coming

straight back—I am; Christa and Ellis and maybe Humphrey are talking about possibly going on to Stonehenge—so don't take too long to make your mind up. If it's yes, I swear—I'll bribe the calliopist and play "Stars" for you myself while the boat's coming in to the landing—what do you say?